Fat Chance, Charlie Vega

Fat Chance, Charlie Vega

CRYSTAL MALDONADO

HOLIDAY HOUSE • NEW YORK

Library of Congress Cataloging-in-Publication Data

Names: Maldonado, Crystal, author.
Title: Fat chance, Charlie Vega / Crystal Maldonado.
Description: First edition. | New York : Holiday House, [2021] | Audience:
Ages 14 and up. | Audience: Grades 10-12. | Summary: Overweight
sixteen-year-old Charlie yearned for her first kiss while her perfect
best friend, Amelia, fell in love, so when she finally starts dating and
learns the boy asked Amelia out first, she is devastated.
Identifiers: LCCN 2020015942 (print) | LCCN 2020015943 (ebook)
ISBN 9780823447176 (hardcover) | ISBN 9780823448906 (ebook)
Subjects: CYAC: Self-esteem—Fiction. | Best friends—Fiction.
Friendship—Fiction. | Overweight persons—Fiction. | Dating (Social
customs)—Fiction. | Mothers and daughters—Fiction.
Classification: LCC PZ7.1.M346954 Fat 2021 (print)
LCC PZ7.1.M346954 (ebook) | DDC [Fic]—dc23
LC record available at https://lccn.loc.gov/2020015942
LC ebook record available at https://lccn.loc.gov/2020015943

ISBN: 978-0-8234-4717-6 (hardcover)

To Bubby, Papaya, and Obi,

my three hearts that walk outside my body,

and to every Fat brown girl out there— I see you.

* * *

Chapter One

I imagine being kissed about a hundred times a day.

The tense moment just before the kiss, when they look right at me like there's no one else in the room. The way they caress my cheek, maybe put their hand on the small of my back. To be so close to someone I care about, someone I like or maybe even love, feeling the warmth of their skin near mine, would be magic. They smell good, and I can almost feel their lips on mine, even before they're there. And then they are—soft, gentle. And I forget who I am, just for a second. I forget *everything* else.

I forget that I don't always have the right thing to say. I forget about comparing myself to my best friend. I forget about the issues with my mom. I forget how badly I wish I were a size two.

I forget it all.

Except for that kiss.

And it's not so much the who. It's more about the what. The kiss. A kiss. To *be* kissed.

It's the stuff my dreams are made of.

But it hasn't happened yet, and I'm beginning to think it never will.

At least, not like this—not the way my best friend, Amelia, and her boyfriend, Sid, are kissing up against my car.

I should be mad at them, and normally, I would be. But for right now, I'm kind of okay with the show.

That's how pathetic I am.

Like, it should set me on fire that Amelia and Sid are kissing as if I don't even exist. And yeah, that part is kind of annoying. But also, it just sends me spiraling off into my own thoughts about kissing and boys and I'm feeling wistful and alone and find myself missing something I never even had.

I honk the horn.

Amelia finally pulls away from Sid, shooting me an apologetic glance but smiling and giggling. She and Sid whisper to each other, then kiss once more, and Amelia finally starts to get into the car.

"Sorry, sorry," she says as she slides into the passenger seat. "I'm a total jerk. I know."

"You're not a total jerk," I say, pulling onto the road and heading toward my house. "But you think you could say goodbye before I pick you up? It's kind of weird to have to watch."

I leave out the part where their kissing basically makes me have an existential crisis.

"Next time, I promise."

"Sid always leans right up against my car like it's his," I say. "I know my car is a piece of shit, but it's *my* piece of shit."

I'll admit that I get easily annoyed at Sid. He's a senior at another school, and I think he's a little too vain, too aloof. Amelia is kind and giving and warm, and Sid is just sort of *there*. He's nice enough to me, which is good, but he's just…underwhelming. Like, in a slacker-who-smokes-pot-all-day kind of way that doesn't seem to align well with Amelia's popular-and-pretty-with-a-million-extracurriculars vibe.

He is hot, though. Super hot. All muscles and a beard a teenager probably shouldn't be able to grow. I'll give him that. Amelia says he treats her well and that it's nice to have a boyfriend at another school because she doesn't feel suffocated and it gives her a break from everything, so fine. I deal.

"I'm sorry, Charlie, for real. I'm just lucky to have a friend who'll put up with that and still give me a ride home." She smiles and bats her long eyelashes at me. I grin. "So, how was work?" she asks.

"I spent the afternoon putting together a hundred marketing packets for some trade show next week," I say. I work part-time as an office assistant at a small, family-run business that sells medical products, mostly to hospitals. "So, totally riveting, as you can imagine. How was Sid's?"

"If I were lighter-skinned, you'd be able to tell that I'm blushing just thinking about it."

I wrinkle my nose. "Ugh. Let's leave it at that, all right?"

"Sorry. I didn't mean to make you feel weird or anything. *Lots* of people have never been kissed." She shoots me a sympathetic glance, and now it's me who's blushing. Acknowledging my virginal lips out loud makes it *so much worse*. I've mentioned this to her before, and yet...

"Yep."

We're quiet for a sec, but I relax a little when she pulls out her phone, eager for a subject change. "Did you look at the video I sent you earlier?"

"Which one?" I ask. Truthfully, Amelia and I send each other about a hundred things a day—some of it's just us talking back and forth, but a lot of it is trashy or hilarious things we find online. "Oh, wait! The one of the sleepy puppy who falls off the couch?"

"Yes!" She squeals and the sound of the little puppy snoring fills the empty space in the car. "It's sooo cute. I've watched it ten times already, I swear. Look, look—he's about to do it!"

At a perfectly timed red light, I lean over and watch as the dozy puppy droops right off the couch, and we both erupt into giggles.

"God, we should totally get a dog," I say.

"Right? We could share him—"

"Or her," I interrupt.

Amelia corrects herself, though I know she's probably playfully rolled her eyes at me from the passenger seat. "Or *her*. Some days that cutie could be with me, other days with you. It would be the most well-loved pup ever."

As we pull up to my house, a single-story white ranch with my dad's beloved Puerto Rican flag dangling from the porch, I point to my mom's Audi in the driveway. Then I sigh. "Puppy would have to live with her, too, though."

I had been not-so-secretly hoping that my mom's job as branch manager at the local credit union might keep her late so that she wouldn't be home yet, but now that I work, too, that's not always the case.

"We could go to my house instead, if you want."

"We're already here." I pull the keys out of the ignition. "Plus, she'll be pleased to see her favorite daughter."

I mean Amelia and she knows it, so she gives me the finger.

We head inside. I'm immediately hit with the sweet scents of apple and cinnamon, and without stepping into the kitchen, I know a candle is burning on the windowsill. It's Mom's favorite to light because it "goes with the theme," meaning the red accent wall and carefully placed apple knickknacks on most of the oak surfaces.

"Mom, I'm home!"

"Charlotte, I'm right here. There's no need for yelling!" my mom calls from the other room. She's yelling, too, though.

"*Amelia* is here," I say, tossing my keys onto the side table next to the door.

The tone of Mom's voice changes immediately. "Oh! Amelia!" she says, and she's suddenly in the living room to greet us. Her hair is pulled back into a sleek ponytail, and she's wearing yoga pants, a fitted athletic top, and sneakers, signaling she's likely on the way to the gym. She kisses my cheek, then Amelia's. To Amelia, she says, "So good to see you. Don't you look beautiful! Special day at school?"

I glance at Amelia, but I don't really need to to know that yes, she does. She *always* looks beautiful. She has flawless dark skin that never blemishes and curly black hair that never seems out of place. She's tall and thin and everything looks good on her and it's completely unfair but also, like, if anyone deserves to be that flawless, it's Amelia.

"No, nothing special today," Amelia says, glancing down at her retro-chic outfit—a fitted black turtleneck and tights under a curve-hugging spaghetti-strap dress—with a shrug.

"See, Charlie. You always say people don't dress up for school, but they do! Look how put together Amelia looks." My mom's eyes flit over my outfit—jeans, ballet flats, and what I thought was a pretty cute sweater—as if to say *compared to this*.

"Gee, thanks, Mom."

Mom waves her hand at me. "You know what I mean. Anyway, Amelia, you look great."

"Oh, thanks, Jeanne."

"You *know* you can call me Mom!"

She's offered this to Amelia about a hundred times now. I suppress an eye roll. "Mom, I think we're going to go hang out in my room and do some homework. Okay?"

"Okay. Let me know if you need anything."

"We will," I call over my shoulder as we walk to my room. Behind us, I close and lock the door as Amelia starts giggling and flops on my bed, tossing her bag on the floor. I laugh a little, too.

"She *really* wants you to call her Mom," I say.

"It just feels too weird to me! I've *never* called her Mom, not since we met in the second grade. Why does she keep saying that to me lately?"

"She just really likes you." I shrug, trying to keep my voice cool. "And you know how she is. Once she's made up her mind about something she wants, that's it. So if she hasn't stopped offering that to you yet, she never will."

My conspiracy theory is that my mom secretly wishes Amelia was her daughter and is doing this to subtly reveal it to me. My more realistic theory is that my mom doesn't realize how overtly she dotes on Amelia and that *maybe* it might make her daughter feel some type of way.

That said, it's true Amelia embodies a lot of the characteristics my mom wishes I possessed. I sometimes can't blame her. I wish I could be more like Amelia, too.

As far as best friends go, Amelia and I probably don't make much sense on paper. It feels like she's pretty close to perfect, and I'm more of the surviving-not-thriving type—the sidekick, the brown bestie. Aside from being beautiful, Amelia is the walking embodiment of Black excellence—her grace and warmth and wit are on another level, one which I aspire to someday come near. (But I know that's a long shot, so I find myself being fine just circling in her orbit.)

An athlete who does track and volleyball, Amelia's got a lot of friends. She's an infectious laugher, charismatic, and toes that line between tough and kind. She tells it like it is, but in such a genuine way that no one minds. And her love life is something I've envied for years. She's dated people of all genders—Amelia identifies as pan, and has since at least sixth grade—and I've always admired her unwavering confidence, which I think draws people to her.

I am not sure any of the adjectives I use to describe Amelia can also be used to describe me. I'm anxious and insecure, full of self-doubt, and probably annoying. There are good things about me, sure, but I'm mostly friendless (unless internet friends count?) and I'm certainly not athletic or popular. (I do have great hair, though.)

I've also never dated anyone. And I'm fat. Those things don't necessarily go hand in hand, but for me, I think they do.

I've *always* been fat, but I didn't know I was fat-with-a-capital-F until I was in fourth grade, having a great time on a field trip, and one of my classmates told me so. There I was, sitting with Amelia on a bench at the local science museum, when Mason Beckett suddenly *needed* to sit next to his BFF, Elijah McGrady, and he tried to squeeze in between me and him. When Mason struggled to fit—*he* had a chunky body, too—he turned and looked me square in the face and said, "Jeez, Charlie, why do you have to be so *fat?*"

That seemingly small moment made me acutely aware of my body and its bigness, and it was then that I realized that being fat is a thing: A Very Bad Thing, according to most.

The world around me has reiterated that fact over and over in hundreds of ways since: the way people eye my body and shift uncomfortably away when I'm getting on the bus; the way the gym teacher loudly *tsk*s me—and only me—every time I have to get weighed at school as part of the "physical fitness test"; the way my doctor doesn't even *hear* me when I'm complaining about sinus pain, and instead assures me that if I "try and lose weight" that'll fix my problems; the way most stores refuse to make clothes that even fit me and then if they do, they're *much* more expensive, as if my fat body comes with a fat wallet, too. So you can see why I envy Amelia so much.

Currently, Amelia is texting—probably with Sid—so I pull out my ancient math book and binder and settle in at my desk.

"I saw you talking to *Benny* outside of study hall today." Amelia is focused on her phone, but she doesn't hide the coy smile as she speaks. "What was that about?"

I roll my eyes. Benjamin (*not* Benny) is this boy that Amelia thinks is obsessed with me, but really we're just classmates. I'm nice to him because he's a generally nice guy and we're in the same biology class. "It was about him needing clarification on the homework."

"I think it was about him *liiiking* you," she says, looking up at me. I roll my eyes again. When Amelia is talking to me about boys, I'm usually rolling my eyes. "Think about it. Benjamin is basically a science genius. Did he *really* need homework clarification? Or was he just looking for an excuse to talk to you?"

"He *really* just needed homework clarification," I say. "You know he can't always see the board. He has really bad vision." I instinctively push my own glasses higher up on my face.

"He could check online, though," Amelia presses.

"It was easier for him to ask me."

Amelia makes a face like she's not convinced. "I'm just saying. You two are awfully cozy."

"I appreciate you being the biggest cheerleader for my love life, but Benjamin and I are just friends. And hardly that. He's really sweet, but a little weird. You know that," I say. "Besides, I like someone else. You know that, too."

Cal Carter. What is about people with alliterative names that makes them so much better? I don't know. But he's amazing.

Tall. Muscular. Piercing green eyes. Sandy blond hair that falls just so. A smile that's often a smirk, like he's in on some devilish secret.

Amelia groans. "Don't remind me."

For a while now, Amelia has been after me to give up on Cal, mostly because she thinks he's sleazy. That's what I love most about Amelia. She thinks I should give up on Cal not because I have no chance in hell with him, but because she genuinely thinks *he's* not good enough for *me*.

But she's right that I shouldn't be into Cal—mostly because he's actually into Amelia.

I know, I know. She's told Cal a million times it's not going to happen, but he still hangs around. I should have better sense than to like someone who persists even after they've been turned down, yet here I am. Fawning over him.

Because he's nice to me. Really, really nice to me. He tells me jokes. He makes me laugh. He has conversations with me. He even says hi to me when he's around his football friends, which is huge. Basically, he's one of the few guys who will give me the time of day. And have I mentioned he's the knees-weak, butterflies-in-your-stomach, stay-up-late-dreaming-about type of hot? His real smile—not the smirk, though that's great, too—could probably inspire world peace.

And I'd never tell Amelia this, but here's my secret and way-too-embarrassing-to-share hope: one day, he'll realize it was me all along.

Chapter Two

"*Psst.*"

The psst is not exactly soft. In fact, it's kind of loud. It's not at all an appropriate volume for the library, but whatever, I guess. It's Cal.

He smiles when I look over at him, revealing his dimples, and my heart catches in my throat. (It sometimes hurts my eyes how pretty he is.) For a minute, I think he's calling for Amelia. But then I remember Amelia's not here yet, which means that *psst* was for me.

"Hi," he whispers.

"Hi," I whisper back, unable to wipe what is definitely a goofy grin off my face.

"Whatcha up to?" He's sitting a table away.

I definitely didn't carefully choose my seat so I could steal glances at him. Nope.

"Nothing. Reading." I hold up my book. In class, we're reading *The Catcher in the Rye*. I hate it. Holden Caulfield is not a sympathetic character to me, and I'm over the way he calls everyone a phony. "What about you?"

"Trying to convince you to let me borrow your history notes."

For some reason, I giggle at that.

"So?" he pushes. "Can I?"

"Oh! Yeah, of course," I say, letting go of my book (and not bookmarking my page), digging through my bag (and dropping some pens on the floor in the process), and pulling out my notebook.

Cal, Amelia, and I are in the same history class, even though Cal is a year ahead of us. He almost never shows up to class... which is probably why he's repeating junior history. He always asks to borrow my notes, and I always say yes.

I turn to the correct page and hold the notebook out to him. He gets up from where he's sitting so smoothly it's like he's practiced it. Confidence just comes naturally to him. What's that like?

When he reaches me, he leans down and scoops up my pens and holds them out to me.

"You dropped these," he says.

"Thanks," I say softly, trying to hide how badly my hands are shaking when I take them from him. In exchange, he swipes my notebook and his eyes scan the page.

"So, all this, huh?" he asks.

I glance at the meticulously highlighted notes. "Oh. Yeah, I sometimes go a little overboard." I'm kind of embarrassed he noticed. "You don't have to copy all of that. The highlighted stuff is what's really important."

"It's *all* highlighted...." He chuckles and rubs his hand on the back of his neck, and I find myself wishing I *were* his hand. "So, like...let's just say you were only going to focus on the really, really super-important parts. You know, the stuff Mrs. Patel would probably put on a test. What might those be?" He leans over me, holding my notebook, glancing at the paper and then at me. "Think you could help me figure that out?"

And then he adds, "You're just really good at this, Charlie."

"Oh, um, s-sure," I stammer, feeling heat creep up my neck. He's so close to me now. "She spent most of class time talking about the Boston Tea Party. Here." I point to that section in the notes. "'No taxation without representation.' That was really what she lectured on, so...probably that."

"So focus on this," he says, pointing his finger where I'm

pointing so that our hands are touching. "And I can ignore all this other stuff?"

That's absolutely not what I'm saying, but his hand by my hand has me nearly breaking out in a full-on sweat. "Yes." I look at him. "More or less."

His gaze meets mine and he smiles at me, dimples and all, letting the look linger a beat longer than it needs to. "Great. Really great. You're the *best*, Charlie."

My neck and face get even hotter. "Oh, I don't know about that," I manage to say.

He rises to his feet, motioning toward the notebook. "I'll give these back to you in class, okay?"

"Okay. No problem," I say, and he takes the notebook and goes to sit back down at his table.

Did we just...have a moment?

Kind of felt like a moment.

See? This is why my insides get all jumbled like a bunch of weird emojis strung together whenever he's around. *Screaming face, lady in the tub, hospital, screaming face, heart.*

I keep finding myself glancing over at him and smiling as he copies down the notes. I need to do something to stop looking so goofy, and I decide I'll double-check my math homework—until I realize that my math homework, due next period, is in that notebook. Which Cal isn't going to give back to me until after lunch.

Well, shit.

Amelia interrupts my panic by plopping in the seat next to me.

"Mr. O'Donnell is an ass!" she says, not bothering to speak quietly. The librarian looks over and shushes us, but Amelia ignores her and shoves her biology test in my face. There's a 68 at the top of it.

"Oh, no," I say, frowning. "I'm so sorry, Amelia. What happened?"

"He's a terrible teacher, that's what happened. It's all

memorization, and I hate it!" She sighs, then shoves the test in her bag. "Whatever. I'll do some stupid extra credit and be fine. Anyway. Hi. How are you?"

"I'm *great*. Cal and I just kind of had a moment," I whisper. I try to be nonchalant, but I'm sure I sound super excited. True, I don't typically like for us to dwell on how pathetic my love life is, but could I really not share *this* with my best friend?!

"Oh, yeah?" Amelia is humoring me. "What'd he want?"

"To talk," I say casually. Well. Kinda casually.

"To talk, huh?" Amelia asks, and it bothers me a little that there's a hint of skepticism in her voice—likely directed at Cal's intentions, but still.

"Yeah, to talk," I repeat. Then I pause. "And to borrow my history notes."

She gives me a look. "Of *course*." And that stings a bit. As if Cal couldn't ever possibly talk to me unless he wants something. "Why do you even let him see your notes?"

"I let you see my notes all the time."

"I'm your best friend! Cal is just a slacker. He doesn't deserve your kindness."

I decide not to tell her about how our hands touched.

"Yeah, well. He's cute. And he seemed really appreciative this time." I shrug. "But I just realized my math homework is in that notebook. And he's not going to give it back to me until history class, so..."

"So? Go over there and get it back!"

I just blink at her. "I can't."

"Why not?" she asks.

"I'm not good with confrontation."

"Not sure this counts as that, but fine. I'll do it." Without a second thought, Amelia waltzes right over to Cal, who looks up and shoots her that dazzling smile of his.

"What can I do for you, boo?" Cal asks, eliciting an eye roll from Amelia.

Did he really just call her boo? My stomach drops.

"Not your boo. And I need Charlie's notebook back. Her homework is in there." She reaches for it. Cal uses the opportunity to slip his hand into hers.

"Moving a little fast, aren't we?" he asks with a grin.

She yanks her hand away from his. "Ugh. Give it."

"What's in it for me?"

"I'll consider not breaking your hand off and using your own middle finger to flip you the bird."

A smirk from Cal as he hands her the notebook. "You're coming around to me."

"Not even a little," Amelia says, walking back to our table. Cal watches her go.

She plops the notebook down in front of me. "Thanks," I say, a little more curtly than I intend. I try to push my irrational jealousy aside and focus on ripping my homework out. Amelia holds out a hand, a silent offer to return the rest of the notes to Cal.

I sniff. "I can do it." She shrugs, so I turn and walk over to him and smile. "Hey, Cal. Sorry about that," I say, making my voice soft. "Here you go."

"Finally. Someone who treats me right," Cal says flirtatiously.

It makes me feel good, until I notice that he's not actually looking at me; he's still looking over at Amelia. I sigh, walk back to my seat, and wish I were her.

Chapter Three

Sometimes being at work is a nice retreat from my life.

I don't do anything particularly exciting—mostly filing, sorting mail, scheduling meetings, that kind of thing—but I actually find the work oddly soothing. There's something rewarding about organizing, about anticipating others' needs. The group of people I work with are great, too. It's mostly women—even the big boss, Nancy—although many of the higher positions belong to men (of course).

Even though sixteen-year-old-me is the baby by a lot, almost everyone treats me with respect and appreciates what I do. It's nice. Here, I can just be good at my job, and not worry so much about whether I'm cute or pretty or thin or popular or any of those things I wish I didn't worry about but do.

Nancy—who launched this company on her own and made it a success—has even told me she sees potential in me, so she's always trying to give me jobs with more responsibility. Whenever Sheryl is out, Nancy asks me to sit at her desk and answer phones. Nancy also knows I like to write, so sometimes she tasks me with writing projects, too. I can't help but like her.

I *don't* like Sheryl, who's always really snotty and makes passive-aggressive comments about me sitting at her desk when she's not in, but it's like, if you weren't out so much, I wouldn't be in your space.

Then there's Tish and Dora and Tammy, and they're really,

really sweet. They ask me about school and my home life and they think I'm cool even though I'm absolutely not. That's nice, too.

"Any big plans for the weekend?" Dora asks as I'm doing some filing. She asks me this every week. And every week, I make something up so that I sound more interesting than I am. I feel a little bad about it, but less bad than I'd feel admitting I mostly do nothing with no one.

"Probably going to the movies with my friends," I say.

"Will that boy you like be there?" Dora thinks things with Cal have progressed into us hanging out. I may have implied that once, and now there's no going back.

"Yes! He'll probably be there. It should be fun," I lie. "What about you?"

"I'm taking the boys go-kart racing." Dora has seven-year-old twins who she says keep her on her toes.

"You're going go-kart racing?!"

Dora laughs. "No, no. Not me. I'll be watching from the sidelines. Just the boys. And my husband, of course. He'll be riding."

For some reason, the idea of her husband go-karting with the kids while Dora watches from the sidelines makes me sad. She's fat like me, and I can't help but think that's what makes her unwilling to ride. It sounds like something I'd do, hanging back because I'm too scared that the seat belt won't buckle or something.

"You should do it with them," I say. "I think the boys would like that."

"Oh, no." Dora laughs again. "I'm too old for that." But she's conveniently ignoring the fact that her husband is even older.

"Charlie?" Nancy calls from her office.

I hurry over. "Hi, Nance. What can I help you with?"

"Dave needs some help preparing packages for a big shipment to St. Francis. Think you're up for it?" she asks, with a look in her eye that shows she already knows I'll say yes. Nancy, all of five feet tall, with piercing brown eyes and cinnamon-colored hair that's been cut into a blunt bob, is as commanding and assured as she is kind and soft-spoken—a pretty badass combination, if you ask me.

I smile at her. "Yeah, I think I could do that." I've been asked to do this kind of thing before, so I walk back to the warehouse, where Dave is already waiting. Dave is nice, but sometimes he thinks he's more important than he is. He's Nancy's son, so he kind of feels like he's the boss of everyone, despite Nancy making it very clear that he's not.

"Hey, little lady," Dave says.

Oh, yeah. And he calls me little lady.

"Hey, Dave. Your mom said you need help out here?" I like to remind him that we all know he's related to Nancy.

"Yes. Over there. I need you to help Brian pack and organize a few shipments," Dave says, pointing at a young guy—who, apparently, I'm supposed to know is Brian—before disappearing into his office.

As I get closer to Brian, I realize I *do* actually know him.

He's in my art class. He's one of those people I've gone to school with for a while and know *of* but don't really *know*. I had no idea he even worked here.

But when you go to the same school in the same town with the same people in the same corner of Connecticut for your whole life, you tend to have at least *some* opinion about everybody. So if you asked me about Brian, I would probably say he's quiet, nice, a little nerdy, and pretty cute (because hello, I'm not blind). He's stocky, with a bit of a belly, and tall—like, maybe even a good six inches taller than me—which is never a bad thing.

"Hi," I say, adjusting my glasses. Being around boys tends to make me nervous, especially if they're good-looking.

Brian looks up from the paperwork he's reading and smiles, and suddenly he's even cuter. He's got high cheekbones, his grin is a little crooked, and his dark eyes crinkle at the corners. My stomach does a little whirly-loop because I'm a hormonal teenager and this guy is looking right at me as if he's known me forever and already thinks I'm great.

"Hey," he says, holding out a hand. "Charlie, right?"

We shake hands. He has a nice handshake—firm, but he's not squeezing my fingers to pulp like a lot of dudes do.

"Yeah, hi. I think we both go to George Washington High," I say, even though I know we do.

"Yes! Same art class. I'm Brian Park."

"That's a good name."

He laughs at that. "Is it?"

"Yeah. Names are one of those things you have no control over, but they can change everything. Imagine being, like, Atticus Mortimer the Third? You're rich, even if you're not. That's just how it is."

Thankfully, Brian's nodding as I talk. "Okay, sure. Like, if you were named Clarence McConkey, maybe life's not so great for you."

"Exactly! There's nothing *technically* wrong with the name Clarence McConkey, but people probably have feelings about it. I mean...yikes." I realize this conversation has probably gone on way longer than it should, but I spend a *ton* of time thinking about names. When you're writing, you're always trying to come up with the perfect names for your characters, and maybe I get a little carried away sometimes. Shrug emoji. "Anyway. Packages?"

"Yeah," he says. "Packages. We're grouping six small ones with each of these large ones. You take the small, I'll take the big?"

I'd normally want to argue about it. I'm no weakling just because I'm a girl, but the boxes *are* big, and I notice that Brian's muscular arms could handle them with ease. He's husky, you know? Like he could be a football player. He isn't, but I'm just saying. He's *really* not bad to look at.

I smile and agree, and we get to work.

"How long have you worked here?" I ask as we sort.

"Just started this semester. I found the job through the guidance counselor at school. I like it so far. Pretty painless. What about you?"

"I started in the fall. I like it, too. Everyone's really nice." As I talk, I shift boxes. "I just wish I had a clue what they actually make."

Brian laughs. "You neither? That makes me feel a little better. It's stuff for hospitals, that's all I know. I'm not out here trying to become a doctor, obviously."

"Same here. No thanks. I have a hard enough time thinking about how I'll have to dissect a frog in bio." I pretend to gag.

"Who was it that decided dissection would be a useful skill to have? Cool, I have no idea how loans work and I'd love to learn more about that whole '401K' thing, but yeah, let's dig into this frog!"

I laugh at that. He's totally right, and I'm pleased with how easy our conversation is as we work. Before I know it, we're done. I check my watch (an activity tracker that my mom bought for me so she can track my steps) and realize it's almost time to go.

"All set?" I ask.

"All set. Man, that went way faster with your help," Brian says, looking over at me. Then he chuckles. "Oh. You've got a little something." He points at his forehead. I rub mine with my sleeve.

"Did I get it?" I ask, feeling embarrassed.

"You got it. Happens to me all the time," Brian says. "It's dirty back here. Sorry you had to help while wearing your nice clothes."

I feel a smile involuntarily tug at my lips. I like that he thinks my clothes are nice. "It's no problem. Glad I could be helpful." I turn to leave. "See you in...art class, right?" I pretend I'm not sure he's in my art class even though I know he totally is.

Brian smiles at me. "Yeah! I'll definitely see you in art class, Charlie. Thanks again."

* * *

When I get home, my mom's car is missing from the driveway. Small miracles. Inside, on the kitchen counter, there's a note that just says *Enjoy*. It's propped up on a meal-replacement shake, and suddenly my good mood dissipates.

My mom swears by these shakes. They're what got her thin, she says to anyone who'll listen. She loves them so much that she's become a consultant for the company, and now she sells them on Facebook as part of what's definitely not a pyramid scheme (it's a pyramid scheme).

For a while now, she's been trying to get me to drink them, too. She tells me if I just replace one meal a day with them, I can really start to see some results on my body—my unruly body that needs to be controlled, I guess—and I can finally start *living*. Like it's impossible for me to live now in this body I have.

I'm ashamed that I often look at my body and secretly agree.

See, the thing about my mom is that she was fat until, suddenly, she wasn't. Or at least that's how it felt to me. I feel like I woke up one day and the Mom I knew was gone and replaced with a newer, thinner model.

But the change didn't actually happen overnight. Perhaps I didn't want to see what was right in front of me—that my mother's body was slowly shrinking, looking less and less like mine every day, because I couldn't (or wouldn't) acknowledge that she was achieving the very thing I waste so much time longing for.

It went like this: my dad got sick and died, my mom wallowed for a long time, we both got fatter together in our sadness, she had trouble feeling good about herself, she decided to throw herself into losing weight, and then—*bam*. Things were different.

I guess there were a few other things that happened in between, but that's the gist.

It didn't help that my mom and I were never especially close. People always said I was Héctor's girl, through and through. I inherited Papi's brown skin, dark eyes, curly hair, and sense of humor. My mom—white, with light-brown eyes and straight hair, not as easily amused as us—would sometimes grumble about the fact that she felt left out of our jokes.

My dad and I just *clicked*. Our relationship was easy in all the ways that my relationship with my mom is hard. It was like he got me right down to my core from the moment I could talk.

Though he worked construction, Papi's heart really belonged to storytelling. He wrote in his spare time—he loved mystery novels and the art of a good thrill—and passed that admiration for language on to me (though telling stories about ordinary people falling in love is more my cup of tea). Storytelling was just something we did together. When I was a kid, he read me stories at bedtime until I was old enough to read some to him. Then we ditched the books altogether and started making up the stories together. It was our thing, and he even wrote a few of his favorites down so we would remember them. My favorite was "Charlie and the Rainbow Shoes," which we based on a pair of Mary Janes I owned that had rainbow stitching around the edges. In the story, they were magical and let little Charlie do things like swim with whales and fight monsters and ride unicorns and fly. I still have the story in a box under my bed.

Papi had a thing for the spoken word, too. He was bilingual and always seemed to be talking—he just always had stories bursting out of him. He couldn't (or didn't want to?) contain his big imagination, and sometimes that meant he got too invested in new projects that would never go anywhere. If we needed a little extra cash: What if we started a dog-walking business? If we were bored of the same meals: What about a night of homemade sushi and gyoza? If we were seeking some adventure: What if we drove to the coast and explored the shoreline?

I liked to think of my dad as a balloon always drifting toward the sky, and my mom as the anchor always keeping him tethered to the ground—not enough so that he couldn't dream, necessarily, but enough so that we didn't go broke or end up at the beach in the middle of the night when it was freezing cold out.

Even though sometimes my parents were like fire and ice, for the most part, they worked together. She never let him float away, and he helped her keep her joy alive.

That's why it was better when we were three. There was a sense of stability, and when things got tough between me and my mom, my dad could serve as the buffer between the two girls he loved most. Because if I got my love of words and laughter from my dad, I got my stubbornness and tenacity from my mom. We aren't so much oil and water as we're just two straight-up firecrackers who both like to be right and have the last word and are—ultimately—incredibly sensitive.

So Papi had to help keep the peace, and he made us both feel heard. Mostly, I think he just wanted us to be happy together, our little family, and he'd do anything to make it so.

It's not that we never had nice moments, my mom and I. We did. We both loved reality television. We were always singing old-school Mariah Carey. Shopping brought us together, too, especially when it came to clothes: Mom liked to say she never met a sale she didn't like, and she taught me to dress well, to appreciate the thrill of finding a good garment—which was especially tough to do as fat women.

We also had fun cooking together, dedicating ourselves to delicious food and savoring our creations. My mom was an amazing cook; her love language was food—lots and lots of it, seconds, thirds, even fourths—and she took great pride in feeding others good meals until they wanted to burst. I developed such a joy for eating when I was standing next to her in the kitchen, concocting a meal and delighting when Papi loved what we'd made for him. There was something so pure about the taste of a scrumptious recipe, something so simple, and it brought us happiness together. As a family, we were fat, and maybe we didn't love that about ourselves, but we accepted it.

But then we lost him.

Without him, the balance and the joy in our home were lost, too. Without him there to separate us or draw us together when we needed it, my mom and I couldn't stop fights before we said things we didn't mean, couldn't fill a silence before it got too big.

I was thirteen when my dad died and I was fourteen when my mother's body changed. Mine was changing, too, but not in the way I wanted. I developed, but also widened, going from having "baby fat" to just being "fat-fat." At a time when I was becoming interested in boys and men, I realized how interested boys and men were now becoming in my mother.

As my mom shed her old body and habits like a snake shedding its skin, the things that brought us together began to disappear: no more sitting on the couch watching reality TV; no more shopping for clothes together (we couldn't patronize the same stores); absolutely no more cooking together unless it was grilled chicken and broccoli, no delighting in indulgent meals or whipping up decadent desserts—no, nope, never. Food was no longer a celebration. We ate to survive and nothing more.

I tried it her way for a while. I really did. But I missed my dad, I missed my mom, and I missed my old life. I missed food.

So she shrank. I didn't.

Instead, I refocused. I amped up my writing, which helped me escape my brain. I went online and began to share stories of beautiful girls with happy endings, which made me feel joyful and whole, even if only for a bit. And then, slowly, through those writing communities, I ended up finding feminism and the fat acceptance movement, and I moved on to writing stories about girls of all sizes, from all backgrounds. It started to impact the way I thought about bodies, about nourishment, about diets, about myself.

And that was maybe the final wedge between me and my mom. When I tried to talk about some of the things I was learning or questioning, I was swiftly shut down. Her body had been a "prison," she said, and mine was, too. I could be "free," if only I could commit to being thin.

She started looking at me critically, saying things like, "Do you really want to eat that?" "Are you sure you should go back for seconds?" "*That's* what you're wearing?"

I try not to let it get to me. I recognize that my mom's thoughts about her body and mine are not healthy. And yet...

My own relationship with my body is so complicated. I am endlessly surrounded by messages that tell me to love myself, to celebrate stretch marks and soft rolls, to take charge and take up space, to be unapologetically me. Show off that visible belly outline! Rock a fatkini! All bodies are beach bodies! I get that. I celebrate that. I *believe* that.

But I'm also surrounded by messages that tell me I need shapewear, I need to lose weight, I need to fit into straight sizes, I need to look like an Insta girl, I need to be tiny to be loved. Even my lived reality seems to support this. I don't mean to seem shallow, but it's like, when *everyone* goes out of their way to tell you "what a pretty face" you have, you notice.

Is it any wonder, then, I still find myself wishing so badly for this body of mine to be smaller?

I've quietly tried the diets and the shakes and the workout plans and the control tops and the wasting-birthday-wishes-on-thinness— and simultaneously, I've gotten involved in the fat acceptance movement, celebrating Fatness and following the #fatfashion hashtag like it's my religion. I believe that people can be healthy at any size. I think other fat girls are absolutely beautiful.

But my mind struggles to bridge the gap between the two ideologies. I'm fat, and I celebrate other fat people, but I don't quite celebrate me. It makes me feel like a fraud.

My mom says I'm unable to lose weight because I don't want it enough, but she couldn't be more wrong: I would secretly give anything to be thin, while outwardly and openly rebelling against the idea that anyone should have to.

Food comforted me then and still comforts me now. The rush of happiness I feel when I bite into a chocolate chip cookie, the ache of a belly that's a little too full, the anticipation before digging in to a meal—these things bring me joy.

Because of that, I guess I can see why my mom doesn't believe that I try to eat better and exercise, even though I do. It's just that sometimes I look at my mom's lithe body and all the enviably thin bodies around me and my efforts feel futile. It's hard not to turn to food, which is so reliable and so easy.

I return my gaze to the shake on the counter and turn it around in my hand a couple of times. The label boasts ONLY 210 CALORIES AND 24 GRAMS OF PROTEIN, and for a brief moment, I consider giving it another shot.

But no. I throw the shake in the trash and pull out my phone to order some food instead. If I hide the evidence of what I'm about to do, my mom won't scold me—and what she doesn't know won't hurt her.

Chapter Four

I do nothing all Saturday except read, write, and mess around on the internet. Mostly, I post new pieces of writing and chat with my community of online friends who help critique my work and offer support from the sidelines, which is really nice. In my real life, only Amelia knows I write, and sometimes even *that* feels scary; sharing my writing is one of the most vulnerable things I can imagine.

But there's something thrilling about it, too, especially when it's well received. I'm addicted, and my hobby often keeps me so rapt that I don't even feel time passing.

When my phone buzzes midday Sunday, I see a text from Amelia.

Jake's? it reads.

She's referring to the small coffee shop downtown where we (and, I'll be honest, most people from my school) hang out. I glance down at myself—still wearing pj's even though much of the day has passed me by, my curly-now-frizzy hair piled on my head, a mess from excessive lounging around—and feel the brief temptation to pretend I didn't see the text at all because it would require me making some kind of effort.

And to leave the sanctuary of my room—which *is* a sanctuary, by the way, from the twinkling white lights to the mountains of books to the window seat where I love to read. I've worked really hard to curate this very particular Instagram aesthetic and I only leave it when I absolutely must. It's the introvert in me.

I weigh my options: say goodbye to the warmth of this blanket and the easy banter with my online friends, or venture out into the real world with my bestie and feel like an actual person?

When my phone buzzes again (**Helloooo?**), I sigh and decide on the latter.

Just need a few minutes to get ready, I write.

I'll wait. You're picking me up anyway!

With long hair like mine, there is no such thing as a quick wash, so I opt to keep it up in the shower and am careful not to get it wet. Once I'm out and dry, I braid it into two plaits, pin it to the back of my head, and slip into a sweater dress, some tights, and boots.

I grab Amelia and we head to Jake's. It's a quirky little coffee shop with delicious lattes, fresh-baked goods, and eco-friendly compost bins where they recycle the used coffee grounds. The mismatched decor makes the place feel cozy and lived in, like maybe you're having coffee at your hippie aunt's house. There's tons of natural light, which makes for getting the perfect Insta pic of your drink, and a tiny section of used books they sell for a dollar each. Obviously, I'm all about it.

It's late January in New England, and the best place to sit is by the fireplace. Unfortunately, that spot is always taken, so Amelia and I settle in two comfy chairs by the window with our large hot drinks instead—chai latte for me, hazelnut coffee for her.

"I saw you posted a new story this weekend," Amelia says, propping her legs up on the small table between us.

"Eesh, I did. I don't know about it, though," I say. "This is the first time I've written from the perspective of a boy. And what do I know about boys and how they think?"

Amelia laughs. "Yeah, but what does *anyone* know about boys and how they think? So come on, Charlie. Give yourself a little credit. I thought Clive and Olivia were really cute together!"

I smile at her. "Thanks. But be real with me: Would you change anything?"

"Well…" She taps her chin thoughtfully. "Since you asked—I was curious why Olivia was so scared to hold Clive's hand. She's sixteen, not a nun."

I wince a little internally, if only because Olivia's nerves are totally based on mine. "I mean…not everyone is comfortable just going for it…."

Amelia takes a sip of her drink. "You just spent, like, a *really* long time explaining how terrified she was and I wanted to be like, ugh, just *do* it, girl! It's just holding a hand!" I chew on my lip a little, letting her critique sink in. I maybe take it a bit more personally than I should, and she notices, adding, "I mean, don't stress. Everything else was perfect."

"Okay, yeah." I give her a smile. "I'll work on that next time."

A thoughtful look comes over Amelia's face. "You know, it's really impressive that you just, like, come up with these stories from your brain. You *make people up*. Whole-ass people!"

I laugh. "Guess I've never thought of it like that. Amelia, honestly, writing is super hard—it makes me feel so vulnerable. I mean, you know how reluctant I am to share my stuff. But my dad always used to say that to be a writer, you've got to be fine 'writing naked'—like, baring your soul, being *real*—so I think you're just supposed to power through the fear. It's hard, though! It feels so personal that I can't help but be fiercely protective of it, and then there's this little voice that's constantly concerned it's not quite ready for other people's eyes yet, but then it's like…if I'm not going to share my writing, what am I even doing? I don't know. I sometimes think I should totally switch dream jobs and just do data entry at a novelty mug warehouse."

Then I feel a little sheepish for sharing so much and add, "I fully realize how dramatic I'm being."

"I think it's cute. You *should* get dramatic about things you care about," Amelia says. "I *wish* I were that passionate about track."

I frown at her. "You've been unhappy with track all year. Why don't you just quit?"

She wrinkles her nose at that. "My mom really wants me to stay on. The *legacy*." An eye roll. Mrs. Jones was a track star. "She also says it looks good for my college applications."

"I wish I could say she's wrong, but everyone keeps saying you need to be super involved in a trillion extracurriculars to even be *considered* for college these days." It makes me think of how sparse my own résumé is. There's my job, sure, but writing online probably doesn't count as an extracurricular, right?

"I know, that's what blows. She's right! I just don't want her to be!"

I shoot her a sympathetic glance. "You shouldn't have to do something that doesn't make you happy. Maybe you can talk to your mom and just be super honest with her about it. You're already doing volleyball and your grades are good. I think she'd understand."

Amelia looks unconvinced. "Yeah, maybe. But I don't want to disappoint her."

"You wouldn't."

"I think I'll stick it out for the rest of the year and just not sign up next year," she says. "At least I've met some cool people on the team."

"That's true." I nod, but I'm bummed for her. While I'm used to disappointing my mom, I realize others probably aren't—especially not Amelia. Her mom is so great I'd be scared to disappoint her, too. "Oh, I know what will make you feel better! I meant to share this with you. I'm obsessed with this new playlist I found on Spotify. It's called 'Lovesick.'"

"Please tell me there's at least one Spice Girls song."

"There are multiple, which is why I know this playlist is meant for you." I whip out my phone and dig through my bag to get my AirPods. I hand the left one to Amelia and stick the right one in my ear. "Here." I settle back in my chair as we listen.

"Ah." She sighs happily.

"Yeah. Pretty great, right?"

We sit and listen until we finish our drinks, then head home. Amelia has homework to do and I, feeling inspired by the playlist, have some writing that's calling my name.

Also: I want to put off going to bed as long as I can so that I can pretend Monday isn't coming.

* * *

Weirdly, no matter how late I stay up writing on Sunday nights, Monday always comes around again. So then, on top of it being the start of another week, I'm super tired. Sigh.

At least my first class is English—my favorite, obviously. It's a bunch of quiet, nerdy seniors. I'm the only junior, which makes me feel special, TBH.

I admire the teacher, Ms. Williams. She's whip-smart and worldly, and in between each book we're mandated to read by the school curriculum (aka a "classic" written by a white dude), she also picks a book written by an author from a marginalized group. For every *Animal Farm* and *The Great Gatsby* we've read, we've also read *The House on Mango Street* and *The Bluest Eye*. It's incredible, and it's in this class I've been exposed to some of my favorite books.

Plus, Ms. Williams gives us time in class to write, and unlike my online writing, *this* writing gets attached to my actual name, which is terrifying but exhilarating. Not that we do anything too rigorous, but we do spend the first ten minutes of each class free-writing in our own notebooks. We're not graded on what we put in there; the only rule is we have to write for the full ten minutes. I really let myself go and spill my thoughts—sometimes about my life, sometimes about what I'm reading, and sometimes just little snippets of story ideas floating around in my head.

Ms. Williams often leaves me little notes on my writing, too, asking questions, adding comments, and underlining and putting smiley faces next to her favorite lines. I love that.

Today, though, we're talking about *The Catcher in the Rye*. I don't love that.

"So now that we've finished the book, I want to hear your immediate takeaways. What did you all think?" Ms. Williams asks.

I wait a second before raising my hand. She calls on me.

"Honestly? I thought Holden was kind of a jerk," I say. Ms. Williams smiles at that. "I felt he was incredibly judgmental about the world around him. He hardly gave anything a chance. And he felt like he was better than everyone. I understand he was depressed, and I want to be mindful of that, but it also sometimes felt like he was just a whiny white dude who hated people for trying to make their way in society."

At this, Chad, the Goody-Two-shoes who hates when race comes up, raises his hand. I know what's coming.

"I disagree with Charlie." There are a few giggles, because honestly, Chad *always* disagrees with me. "I loved Holden. I found him incredibly sympathetic. And he's right; it *is* stupid that most people try to blend in with society. I think he was relatable regardless of his skin color."

I try not to roll my eyes. Technically, like, US Census technical, I'm white, but I'm also Puerto Rican, and Chad's always trying to invalidate my criticisms about race and race relations. But I don't take the bait.

"Holden takes a typical privileged perspective here. It's not always possible or even safe for everyone to stand out—not when their identities are villainized, questioned, discriminated against, or attacked," I say. "Some people *need* to conform rather than stand out."

"How can you say Holden is speaking from a place of privilege?" Chad's face looks both annoyed and disgusted at what I've said. "He's talking about embracing being an individual! That's the least-privileged thing ever. He's basically saying be you, whoever you are, and I agree with Holden. Anyone who chooses not to is just looking for an excuse and, yeah, is kind of a phony."

Before I can interject and run down the laundry list of ways in which Chad is wrong, Mrs. Williams swoops in. "Thank you, Charlie and Chad. Two fair and thoughtful perspectives. Let's dig into this."

It's an hour of literary bliss.

As the bell rings, Ms. Williams reminds us to grab our notebooks from her desk on our way out of the classroom. When I reach for mine, she smiles at me.

"I loved what you wrote about *The House on Mango Street*. I'm glad you could relate to Esperanza. She's one of my favorites, too," she says. "Keep up the great work."

I leave the class beaming.

Outside, Amelia is waiting for me. Her first period is right next to mine, and she's always the first out the door.

"Why are *you* all smiley on this dreary day?"

I shrug. "Just a great class."

"Nerrrd," she teases.

We start walking toward our next class. As we do, Cal passes us, surrounded by his flock of football bros. They take up more than half of the hallway—they're all so big and muscular, I bet they could collectively pull an eighteen-wheeler without much effort. Most of the boys nod at or say hello to Amelia, and she offers polite smiles back. But Cal grins at both of us.

"Hi, ladies! Looking beautiful today, as always!" he says.

Amelia ignores him, but I smile big and take a step toward him instinctively. "Hi, Cal!"

"Oh my gosh! Watch out!" Cal's friend Tony shouts, dramatically putting an arm in front of Cal as if protecting him. Cal looks puzzled, and Tony stares at me, a smile spreading slowly across his lips. "Oh, sorry, man. Thought that was an elephant stampeding toward you."

You know how the movies always show moments where time seems to stop and everything goes in slow motion?

This is kind of like that, only worse.

Because it's happening to me.

I was just called an elephant in front of my crush, all of his popular friends, and my beautiful and perfect best friend.

Some of the boys around Tony yell *"Ohhhh!"* and *"Shit!"* but most of them are just laughing, and so are a few randoms in the hall. I wish an asteroid would hit our school right now or, at the very least, that I could say something witty back, but I do something worse: I laugh, too.

Cal frowns at Tony and says, "Come on, man," at the same time that Amelia lunges toward him yelling, *"What the fuck did you just say?!"*

I grab her arm and pull her back. "It's fine," I manage, even though my insides are trembling.

"Let's go," Cal says, motioning with his chin toward the stairwell and signaling to his friends to get walking. He starts to move after them but then turns around. "Sorry," he says, looking between me and Amelia. "See you in history?"

I nod and say nothing.

"Fuck that guy!" Amelia says, turning to me. "Are you okay?"

"I'm fine. It's no big deal." I ignore the water that's welling in my eyes. The last thing I want to do is start crying in front of everyone.

She shakes her head. "You're not."

Through gritted teeth, I say, "I'm fine. Can we just drop it?"

Amelia stares at me for a second and I can tell she wants to press, but she doesn't. "Okay," she says, relenting. "I get it."

Only she doesn't. That's the thing. She has no idea what this feels like.

Still, I cling to the fact that Cal didn't laugh at the joke. I guess that's why I like him. Even though his friends make fun of me and he could easily join in, he doesn't. He's nice to me. Maybe that makes my standards too low, but I don't care.

"Babe, you want to go shopping later?" Amelia asks softly as we head into our next class. She knows that I like to shop to make myself feel better when things are bad.

"No Sid today?" I ask. Because I'm still tense, it comes out snarkier than I intend.

"He's meeting up with his band. And I'd rather shop with you anyway," she says calmly.

"Okay. Fine. Yes," I say. "That would be nice."

My insides are still jumbled, and I know that this is a moment I will probably remember, think of, and turn over in my brain again and again. But my hope is that we won't ever talk about it. Pretend it's fine and it will be.

Even if I know that's a lie.

* * *

After school, I drive us to a nearby plaza with a few different stores. We go into Amelia's favorite, and I look through the clothes with her, making idle chitchat about her ten-year-old sister, Tess (who annoys her, as sisters do, and keeps trying to steal from her closet).

As I look through racks of clothes I can't fit into, I try to stop the voice in my head that keeps replaying Tony's comment over and over. When I fail, I give up pretending these clothes will fit and wander over to the accessories. At least I can wear a purse.

The truth is that I'd need to be shopping at a plus-size store—or, at the very least, a store that carries a plus-size section—to buy anything. I haven't ever really pointed this out to Amelia, and I like to think I've gotten pretty good at blending in during our shopping trips—here and there scoring a couple of straight-size items that run big, stocking up on so many accessories that I'm always buying something, even if it's not clothes. It's entirely possible that Amelia totally knows what's up and is too polite to say anything, but I don't necessarily live for the conversation that is *Hey, I can't shop here, can we go somewhere else?*

Amelia buys a few tops, I buy a pair of socks with little notebooks on them, and then we walk to the burger place across the way.

"Don't tell my mom about this," I say once we sit down with our food.

"Ugh. She's so weird about eating," Amelia says, pulling the pickles off her burger before taking a big bite. She chews for a moment before saying, "I know she lost all that weight or whatever, but she shouldn't put her food issues on other people—especially not on you."

I nod but say nothing. Instead I think about how, when my mom was fat, she, my dad, and I used to come to this burger place all the time, especially when one of us had a bad day. My mom and I definitely don't do that now. We barely even eat together anymore.

"So, you know, while we're here, I was hoping we could talk," Amelia says.

"Isn't that what we're doing?"

"Seriously, Charlie. About earlier. Tony, he's—"

"Don't."

"But—"

"Please. I *can't*." My eyes plead with her: *Just drop it. Don't make me hear it again. Don't make me say it again. Don't make me* think *it again.*

She looks at me for a long time, then finally says, "I'm just sorry, then."

"Thanks."

After a few minutes of eating in silence, she speaks again. "If you're sure you don't want to talk about it..."

"I'm sure."

"Okay. Then there's something else. I could use your advice. About Sid."

I look at her and put my food down. I think it's really sweet that Amelia sometimes comes to me for boy advice. And she always takes me seriously, even though I have no experience to back anything up—unless reading excessive amounts of romance books counts.

"Of course," I say. "What's up?"

"I think I'm in love," Amelia says.

I nearly choke on my food.

"Really? You're in love with Sid?" I hope the surprise shows on my face more than the disappointment. (Like I said before: Amelia is *way* too good for him.)

A wistful smile overtakes her face. "Yeah. I am. He's so sweet to me when we're together. It's like it's just the two of us, you know? He trusts me and, like, isn't even threatened by the other guys that come on to me, which is nice. And he makes me feel special without fawning over me. He's just...amazing."

"And hot," I add.

"That helps." She bites her lip. "But I'm not sure I should tell him I love him. I mean, we've only been dating for a few months. I want to, but I also think maybe I should wait for something special. Like our six-month anniversary. It's on Valentine's Day."

"That's really cute." It's adorable, actually, but I still can't stop the pang of envy in my gut. I push past it and say, "Honestly,

Amelia, if you love him, I think you should be real with him. Who wouldn't want to hear that their girlfriend loves them?"

"But I feel like he should be the one to say something first."

"Says who?" I ask. "You can totally tell him you love him first."

"I know I *can*, it's just—I don't want to be seen as clingy or anything." She plays with her fries. "You know what people say about girls who say they love the guy first. Dudes will ghost you or break up with you or whatever."

"Well, I think you have to be okay with him not saying it back right away. You have to feel good enough—strong enough—in your feelings that it'll be okay if he needs more time." I take her hand. "But he probably will say it right back, because how could he not love my beautiful, wonderful, amazing best friend?" She gives me a gentle smile, but I can tell I haven't persuaded her. "Riiiight?" I prod.

"Yeah, I mean. It's just. There's more, too."

"More than just telling him you love him?"

She nods. "I think I'd also like to..." Amelia leans in closer to me. "You know. Sleep with him."

I can feel my eyes widen, though I don't mean for them to. "Oh!"

"It's just that, in my head, I have it all planned out. It would be super romantic. Like, we go out to celebrate our anniversary, I finally tell him I love him, things feel really right, and then we just...have sex. It seems pretty perfect."

I'm nodding as she speaks, but my head is swirling—Amelia is ready to profess her love *and* lose her virginity and I can't even fall in mutual like with a boy. It's a selfish thought, I know, but it's hard for me to deny the jealousy I'm feeling right now. I can't even imagine having sex with someone. (I mean, I'm no prude, *of course*

I can imagine it, but I can't really picture me—clothes off—with another person with their clothes off.)

"Yes, it sounds like it could be romantic," I say tentatively.

"But I also don't want to build it up too much in my head or anything. I might be overthinking this. I don't know. I don't know!"

She buries her head in her hands and sighs and I know that I've got to put my own stuff all the way aside to help. Plus, the hopeless romantic in me wants this to happen for her sake. "It honestly does sound pretty perfect, Amelia. I think if you feel ready—like, *really* ready, on both counts—then that's what's important. I don't see a better day than your anniversary-slash-Valentine's Day to share how you feel. It's so perfect that it's like, who even are you, the main character in a rom-com?"

She laughs a little at the last part and looks up at me. "So I'm not overthinking it?"

"Oh, you're totally overthinking it. But you want this, right?" I ask. Amelia nods. "Okay, then. Love plus special date plus Valentine's Day seems like a great reason to get naked."

She tosses a fry at me. "Damn, Charlie!"

"I'm just saying!"

"I hate you and I love you," Amelia says, smiling.

I smile back. "Hate you and love you, too."

Chapter Five

"*I like that it's* tropical."

It's the only thing one of my classmates can think of to say when we're critiquing my triptych in art class.

As I recently learned, a triptych is a work of art made of three linked panels. I decided to do a beach scene, based on a photo from a trip my mom and I took awhile back. In the left panel, the day is sunny; in the middle panel, the sky looks a bit less blue; and in the right panel, I've got some dark clouds rolling in. I thought it was deep, but as I look at it now, I'm not so sure.

Art class is probably my second favorite after English. I try really hard in this class, but I'm not naturally gifted. My mind is much better at visualizing my creations than my hands are at creating them. Thankfully, our teacher, Mr. Reed, is super nice and passionate about the subject and seems to recognize that you don't need to be perfect at art to appreciate it. He's also a tad on the dorky side, which I like. (Confession: I actually used to have a major crush on him in ninth grade.)

But whenever we have to show off our art for critiques, I find myself wishing I had more talent.

"Good," Mr. Reed says, responding to the critique, even though we all know that what my classmate offered up is not quite the thoughtful response he's looking for. "Anyone else?"

No one budges.

"Come on. Someone must have some thoughts, especially based on the things we've covered over the last few weeks."

"I like the difference between the left and right panels. It's cool that the weather is different," Amelia offers. "On one side, you have this beautiful beach, and on the other, it looks dark, maybe rainy. It could change the whole day, and the whole painting."

She looks at me and I nod with appreciation.

"Excellent! Very good, Amelia. Charlie, why don't you walk us through your thoughts?"

"Sure. Well, Amelia was pretty spot-on; I was sort of trying to use each of the three panels to depict different moods, so if you viewed them separately you'd have a different feeling, but together they'd still work. I also kind of wanted to create this serene beach scene that is on the cusp of changing for the worst—which I realize now sounds depressing."

"No, no, it's good," Mr. Reed says. "It's a great use of color, Charlie, and I appreciate the mood you're conveying. For next time, let's work a little on our shadows and ensure they're coming from the same light source, okay? Otherwise, nice work! Now. Who wants to go next?"

I take that as my cue to remove my art from the easel we're all crowded around, and as I'm bringing it back to my seat, I see Brian stand. Now that I've hung out with him at work, I notice him a lot more around school, and I'm curious to see his project. He puts his piece on display.

Brian's triptych is good. It's more abstract than anything we've seen so far: it's red and white and black, and the style is loose.

I love it.

"Before we have Brian say anything about the painting, let's share some initial thoughts," Mr. Reed says. "What do we think? How does this make us feel?"

The first hand to shoot up belongs to Layla, one of our class-mates. She's part of a group of sophomore girls, including Bridget and Maria, who sit at Brian's table. I'm realizing that Layla has the *biggest* crush on Brian, and I get it. I used to think he wasn't much of a talker, but now I realize he only speaks when he has something to say. He waits until the perfect moment to deliver a punch line and then he'll really get you. The guy's hilarious, which explains why Layla and her friends spend most of the art period giggling. I can't really judge them for getting the giggles around a boy they like.

"With this painting, I feel like Brian is really baring his soul. I think the red reveals a bit of anger, maybe frustration. The clock—that's representing the passage of time, like maybe he's angry at how slowly time passes. The untied shoe...I think that's kind of about feeling undone, and a little lost," Layla says, looking thoughtful. She's always measured and reflective in her critiques, often noticing things in each student's art that might otherwise be missed. I can see exactly how she's arrived at this analysis and would normally nod along in agreement, but because Brian and I have had a few conversations now about college and the pressure of school, I see this painting a little differently, which is part of what makes art so fun. There's room for all interpretations.

"Wow. That makes me seem deep. Honestly? I just really like shoes," Brian says, playing.

"Brian," Mr. Reed says, giving him a warning look. He turns back to Layla. "Excellent work. Very astute. So what about the fact that it's blurred at the edges? Is that time moving slowly, or something else? What do we think?"

When no one offers their perspective, I raise my hand and wait to be called on. "Yes. Charlie. What do you see?"

"I see something a little different," I say tentatively, hoping not to offend Layla. "When we were talking about color theory last week, we talked about how red could be anger, but that it could also be a symbol of power. So I'm sort of seeing this as being less about anger and more about the importance of the clock." I glance at Brian to see if I'm on the right track, and he smiles at me, so I continue. "The clock is blurred because it's moving so quickly we can't even tell what time it is. And the shoes, well, that's sort of like running and movement, too, right? So maybe his piece is more about running out of time—there's that little graduation cap in the corner, which I'm sure we can all relate to—and the enormous pressure that causes?"

Mr. Reed is nodding, hand on his chin. "Yes, yes, I think you're onto something, Charlie. Brian?"

"Yeah, it's sort of supposed to be about how anxious junior year can be. There are so many things to worry about as we're getting ready for college—so, like, you're trying your best but you also want to live your life and that's hard to balance. There aren't enough hours and everything matters. I included some texture in the piece also—those sheets of paper that are decoupaged on are different exams I've taken this year that, for better or worse, are shaping my grades and future."

He adds the last part a bit shyly, but I think it's brilliant he thought to do that.

"Excellent, Brian! That's excellent!" Mr. Reed says, getting excited. He gets up close to the painting and touches one of the exams. "We can even see the grade at the top if we get closer. This is wonderful—great, great work."

"Thank you." Brian smiles wide, removes the painting from the easel, and looks directly at me. "I appreciate everyone's thoughts."

And I feel a little warm inside. I can tell he really does.

I see Brian again later when I stop by the warehouse at work. My shift is basically over, but I have to deliver some paperwork to Dave, and as I'm leaving, I give Brian a wave.

He starts to walk toward me. He's wearing something different now, having shed the flannel he was wearing in favor of a black T-shirt that was probably underneath all day. I note that he looks extra good.

"Hey, Charlie," he says, breaking into a smile.

"Hi, Brian," I say, smiling back. "Great work earlier in art!"

His cheeks flush a little. "Thank you. It's always a trip to get critiqued like that."

"It's my least-favorite part of the class. But your piece was so good."

"I appreciate that, thank you. And hey, yours, too! I really liked what you did today." He shoves his hands in his pockets. "I should've spoken up to say so."

I wave a hand. "Oh, no worries. I don't like to contribute to those critiques unless I'm certain what I'm going to say is right—and I felt like Layla was a little bit off this time, so..."

"She was! I mean, I see where she was coming from, and she's so great, but yeah. I owe you." Brian bows down as if worshipping me. "I am not worthy." I laugh, and he grins at me. "So, what brings you back here?"

"Nothing. Just had to drop something off for *Dave*." I shudder as I say his name, and Brian chuckles. "For some reason, Nancy wanted Dave to look over the thank-you letters I wrote for some board members—as if he'll contribute much."

"Whoa now, you're writing thank-you letters to *board members*?" Brian lets out a low whistle. "Well, shit. Look at you."

I give him a sheepish grin. "It's nothing. I love to write, and Nancy knows it. It's really cool that she lets me put that skill to use. Definitely beats counting brochures."

Brian laughs. "Yeah, I imagine pretty much anything would. Even watching the grass grow, because at least then you're out of the office. Bet Dave has nothing to offer your letters, though."

"I don't know. What I do know is that he kinda annoys the

crap out of me. He purposely refuses to call me by my name!" I say. "It's always 'little lady' instead. I hate it."

"Yikes. Well, if it makes you feel any better, Dave keeps asking me where I'm from. Like, he won't accept that I was literally born and raised here. He once got straight to the point and asked where my family's from in China. I'm Korean."

I laugh, even though that's terrible. "Oh my God. Yeah, you win." Brian looks at his watch, and I take it as a cue to go. "I should head home."

"Wait," he says. "I'll walk you out."

"Okay," I say, surprised. "Great."

I smile to myself as Brian pops his head into Dave's office and says good night, grabbing his coat. He nods toward the door. "Let's go."

We walk into the office, where I grab my bag and coat and say good night to everyone before heading outside with Brian.

"So," Brian says, holding the door for me as we go—a gesture I make note of. "In between all the working and the school stuff, you do anything for fun?"

"Me?" I ask, and wish I hadn't.

Brian laughs. "Yeah, you."

"I don't know. I hang out with Amelia."

"I do see you guys at school together all the time."

"Yeah, but we're not, like, joined at the hip or anything," I lie.

"Right, sure, sure. But besides that. Do you ever, I don't know, go places? Out? Downtown? To Jake's?"

"Yeah, I love Jake's! They have the best coffee." We're at my car now, and I stop walking. "This is me." I point at the car. "But you were saying?"

"Oh, nothing. Just that…maybe I'll see you at Jake's sometime."

"That'd be really great, actually," I say. "And until then, see you at school?"

He grins at me. "Yeah. See you at school."

I climb inside and drive away wondering: Did I just make my first boy friend?

Like, male friend. Not *boyfriend*. Ha.

Chapter Six

I might daydream about handholding almost as much as kissing. There's something so intimate and sweet about it. (That's probably why it makes my characters all sweaty.)

But honestly, it's hard *not* to think about it when I'm surrounded by couples in love. They're laughing together, and walking through the halls, and kissing, and shooting each other meaningful glances, and—yes—holding hands.

I blame it on the time of year. We're nearing Valentine's Day, and that surely plays a role, but at my school, the thing that's really pushing couples together is the George Washington High School Annual Football Awards Ceremony and Dance.

We just call it the dance. As you do.

The event honors football players for their accomplishments throughout the prior season, mostly because if my town can think of a way to prolong football season, they're absolutely going to.

The players are supposed to bring a date who will accompany them to the dance that takes place afterward, and they often ask in big and public ways, kind of like promposals. The boys can ask their date to the ceremony as early as they'd like, but most start asking when February starts, and it really ramps up a week before the event.

Two years ago, people lost their minds because Grey, our best quarterback, invited his longtime (but kind of secret) boyfriend, Logan, to the ceremony in front of the entire school. He presented Logan with a dozen red roses, which were each tied with a strip of paper that listed a reason why Grey loved him. Grey read each of the reasons aloud before giving the roses to Logan one by one.

It was beautiful. I cried.

I hate to admit how romantic I think this entire thing is, and I'm embarrassed by how lonely it makes me feel.

Cal is a football player, so I know it's only a matter of time before he asks someone who isn't me to the event. Last year, he waited until the day before the dance to ask Elizabeth Myers, painting the words *Football Ceremony?* on his bare, beautiful, muscular chest.

This year, Cal is into Amelia, and I'm convinced he'll ask her. I know when it happens, it'll crush me, probably for days, and I'll need to reevaluate my life.

But at least maybe I'll get to see his chest again.

I usually spend the few weeks before the ceremony feeling dreadfully lonely, and this year is no different. I try to throw myself into my online writing communities, which works temporarily, but here's the thing: I mostly write about love, dreaming about boys and their soft lips and all the ways they can kiss whichever main character I've created (who is always some version of the person I wish I could be). Then, once I stop writing, I remember that I'm alone and haven't been kissed and it stings all over again.

Between that and watching all my peers couple off, I find myself transformed into a full-blown grouch by the time we're a week away from the dance.

My grouchiness comes out in physical form in bio lab when I'm partnered with Benjamin and I put down the slide under our microscope a little too hard and crack it.

"Careful, Charlie!" Benjamin says.

"Oh, sorry," I say. "It's still usable, isn't it?"

He slips the slide out from under the microscope and lifts his glasses to the top of his head to closely inspect the damage. "I think we're good. We should still be able to see the heart tissue all right."

He looks at me as he moves his glasses back in place. "But maybe I should be the one that sets our microscope up."

"Yeah, maybe. Sorry. I'm just tense today."

Benjamin grunts a little, and I'm not sure if it's a sympathetic or annoyed grunt. He can be a tough one to read, his brown eyes rarely giving an indication of what he's thinking, his mouth often pursed into a thin line. I'm embarrassed to admit that sometimes I look at him and think that if he just fixed his hair a little (like, curl cream is calling his name) and wore better clothes, he'd be cute—he's got nice scruff and a good face. But that's Judgmental Charlie coming out. I'd hate to know what people think about me. *If she'd just* blank, *she'd be so much prettier....*

Wordlessly, Benjamin takes his time to carefully set the slide in place and focus the lens. Then he looks up at me, rubbing the stubble on his face, and surprises me when he simply asks, "Why?"

"Oh, you know. All this dance and love stuff has me on edge, I guess," I say dejectedly.

He snorts. "Everyone gets pretty daft this time of year."

At that, I smile a little. Benjamin sometimes comes out with things I don't expect.

"They do, don't they? It's so annoying. They just go totally gaga and it's like nothing else even matters except for the dance." Benjamin nods but goes back to squinting into the microscope, so I continue. "They even make a mess of the hallways with their over-the-top proposals. Did you see that Jamie Gale used confetti cannons to ask out Lainey Christensen? It made a huge mess. Janitor Sal's going to have to clean all that up, which is super rude."

"Yep," Benjamin says.

"And Nick Williams literally *painted* on Ericka Hall's locker. Basically vandalism! I just feel like maybe these proposals are getting a little out of hand." Why am I so worked up about messes in the hallway? "Plus, Perry Bell hijacked the morning announcements to profess his love to Alyssa Choi. Like, what next, right?"

Benjamin backs away from the microscope and clears his throat. "Charlie, I can appreciate your irritation, but we really need to get on with it. Mrs. Robinson won't be happy if we spend the whole class just dunking on our classmates." Then he adds, with a chuckle, "Not that I don't enjoy that."

I smile. "That's fair. I was getting a little carried away."

"I mean, yeah, the way the school treats the dance is pretty absurd," he says. "But you know, the best way to show them is to forget about the stupid high school romances and just focus."

Forget about the stupid high school romances? I live for the stupid high school romances! I want to be in my own stupid high school romance, and that's the problem!

But all I keep imagining over and over again is Cal asking Amelia to the dance and me standing next to her while this amazing thing I've been wishing for happens to her. I'm there, but not there at all, a background character. I can see the scenario so perfectly in my head that I've even sometimes found myself acting a little cold toward Amelia.

It's irrational bullshit and it's totally my own problem, I know, but I even recently turned down an invitation to go to her house and watch a movie because I knew I'd get mad at her if we were both in sweats and she looked beautiful while I looked like a lump.

I've got to get out of my own head somehow, but I can't.

When I see Cal that afternoon, my heart sinks as if he's already gone and picked Amelia over me, which, no surprise there. But why not me, Cal? I swear I can be what you need!

I think this bitterly as I'm shoving books into my locker, and I barely notice when someone sidles up next to me.

"Hey, Charlie," a voice says, and when I look up, I'm surprised to see Cal. Cal! As if I was thinking about him so feverishly I made him appear! He leans against the locker next to mine.

"Hey, Cal," I say, nervously adjusting my glasses.

He smiles at me and runs his hands through his beautiful hair. Again with the me-wishing-I-was-his-hand thing. "You got a sec?" he asks.

I giggle a little. "Sure." I close my locker.

"So," Cal starts, then reaches into his book bag for something. He retrieves a single red rose and holds it out to me. On the stem, there is a ribbon that unmistakably reads *CHARLIE* in messy block letters. My heart is in my throat.

"Let me start by saying that you're one of my best girls," he says. "You *know* that. And I just wanted to show a little appreciation." He pushes the flower closer and I realize I haven't done anything but stare at him, so I reach for the rose and hold it as delicately as if it's made of glass.

"Cal, I—thank you," I say.

"You've been real good to me, Charlie. Always happy to see me, always laughing at my jokes, always making sure I pass my classes—it's nice, you know? That I can always rely on you. So, I was wondering if you were free next Friday?"

My heart is thumping so hard I feel I could pass out. In fact, it is very possible I *did* pass out and everything currently happening is some kind of dream—because there's no way that Cal Carter has just asked me if I'm free next Friday, right?

"Um," I say, feeling my heartbeat speed up. "I am free next Friday, yes?"

It comes out like a question.

"Beautiful. It's the dance, you know?"

"I do know, yes," I say, feeling flushed. Is it hot in here? It feels hot in here. "That it is. The dance."

"Well, I was just hoping you would join me..." He hasn't finished his thought, but I can feel my giant smile and I find myself staring right at his beautiful face. This is happening. It's happening!

I can already see us at the dance together, his arms around me, my arms around him. We're swaying together to a slow song and our heads are close and suddenly Cal leans in for a kiss—*my first kiss*—and my breath catches in my throat. But in real life.

"Charlie?" Cal asks, and I realize he's been talking this whole time and I definitely haven't been listening. And now I've just made a weird throaty breathing noise.

I cough and try to pretend there's just something in my throat, which is super smooth, self. "Yes," I say. "What were you saying?"

"So, you think Amelia will be cool with this, then?"

"Oh," I say. Would Amelia be cool with Cal and me going to the dance? That's a great question. I think about how much Amelia has hated Cal and his incessant flirting (borderline harassment, maybe), but I also think about how obsessed with him I've been and I know, in my heart, that she'll be happy for me, even if she thinks I can do better and even if she thinks he's a jerk. I smile at him. "I think she'll be more than cool with it."

Cal's whole face brightens and he breathes a sigh of relief.

"Great," he says, smiling back. Those. *Dimples.* "So, it starts at seven in the gym. I won't be able to pick you up, unfortunately, but we'll meet there, yeah?"

"Yeah!" I say. "Definitely!"

"You're the best, Charlie." Cal reaches out and squeezes my shoulder. "I mean it."

"You, too, Cal. Just the best," I gush.

"I gotta get going, but you just made my day!" He starts down the hall backward, still looking at me. "It's going to be great!"

"Yes," I whisper to no one, still buzzing.

Because Cal Carter just asked me to the George Washington High School Annual Football Awards Ceremony and Dance.

Me.

Chapter Seven

CAL ASKED ME TO THE DANCE!!!!!!!!!! That's the exact text I send to Amelia. I use ten exclamation points, but even that doesn't properly convey my excitement.

She writes back immediately, **GET YOUR ASS OVER HERE RIGHT NOW!**

The whole way to Amelia's house, I sing along to the radio at the top of my lungs. I dance at the stoplights. I laugh out loud to myself like I'm losing my mind—because I am! I'm not even annoyed when I arrive and see Sid outside on the curb smoking. I actually wave at him, then practically float inside.

Amelia grabs me by the arms and starts squealing, and it's contagious.

"Tell. Me. Everything!" she yells, dragging me down the hall and into her room.

I do. I don't leave out a detail. I say it so fast, the words just come tumbling out, and I feel like I'm reliving the moment all over again, and I can't stop smiling.

"I can't fucking believe it. I mean, I can—you're amazing—but this is what you've been waiting for, and I'm so, so happy for you!" Amelia says, throwing her arms around me and squeezing. I squeeze back until I remember the flower.

"Oh, and!" I dig into my purse and pull out the rose. The single, beautiful red rose with the ribbon that says my name, and I hold it out in front of Amelia's face. "He gave me this, too."

"Just one rose, huh? Guy couldn't spring for more?" Sid asks. I realize he's been in the doorway of Amelia's room this whole time.

"Oh, come on, Sid. This is sweet!" Amelia says.

Sid grunts in reply. "Hmm."

I don't like the sound of that.

"What?" Amelia asks, giving him a look.

"Nothing," he says, shrugging.

"If you have something to say, Sid, then say it." Amelia stares Sid down as he crosses his arms. "Seriously. Out with it!"

He licks his lips before he speaks. "It's just that, from what you've told me, this is kind of a big deal. The guys do a huge thing or whatever to ask the girls, right?"

"Yeah, and?" Amelia asks.

"Just wondering why he didn't do something like that. Why he bought one rose and called it a day. Why he waited till he and Charlie were *alone*. And why he didn't bother asking till the very last minute." Then he looks at me. "I think the guy's an ass."

I consider this. Not the he's-an-ass part, because yeah, obviously Sid hates Cal since he knows Cal is into Amelia, but the rest of it. I look at Amelia, who is shooting wide-eyed, how-dare-you vibes over to Sid.

"Charlie doesn't like being the center of attention," Amelia says, though it doesn't sound super convincing. "She wouldn't have wanted a big proposal in front of everyone."

"That is true," I admit. The attention would have likely sent me into a panic attack. I'd honestly have assumed the ask-out was a huge joke.

"And Cal waited until the last minute last year, too, because he knew he could. Cal is so full of himself, he totally gets off on keeping everyone on the hook waiting to see who he'll invite. It's a thing. I swear it's a thing," she says.

"You trying to convince me or yourself?" Sid asks.

"Stop it, Sid!" Amelia says. "Don't ruin this."

Sid shrugs again. "I'm not trying to ruin anything. I'm just saying."

Amelia bites at her lip. The worry line between her brows betrays her, and I feel a pang. Like Sid, there is a piece of her that can't believe this is true.

Part of me is hurt and the other part of me can't blame her; hell, if I hadn't been there, I wouldn't have believed it, either. But it did happen, and it's arguably one of the best things to *ever* happen to me. I look away, wordlessly packing the rose back into my bag.

"No! Just don't even listen to him, Charlie!" Amelia says. Then she scowls at Sid. "God, why do you have to be so negative?"

I don't want them to fight on my account. "It's okay," I say. "He does have some good points."

"No, he doesn't, and you don't have to pretend like he does," she says, eyeing him.

Sid holds up his hands in defeat. "I'll get out of your hair. Meeting up with some friends, anyway." He leans down to give Amelia a kiss, but she won't kiss him on the mouth, so he settles for the cheek. Then he grabs his coat and he's gone.

"He's wrong, you know," Amelia says.

I shrug. "Maybe."

"No, Charlie. He is. He's wrong about a lot of things. Like, one time, he was convinced that Tina Fey was the blond one and Amy Poehler was the brunette. Con-*vinced*. We had to Google it."

I smile a little at that.

"Another time, he swore on his life that Froot Loops used to be spelled *Fruit Loops,* and I told him, 'They use the circular pieces of cereal to make the goddamn O's, Sid. How could that have ever been true?!'"

Okay, at that, I laugh.

"And!" Amelia is clearly pleased that I'm amused. "Just recently, he told me that the moon landing was probably all a hoax because his idiot best friend said that on the original broadcast, they accidentally left a Coca-Cola can on set. The *moon landing,* Charlie. He doesn't think *the moon landing* happened!"

We're both laughing now, and I start to feel better.

"I love the guy, but sometimes…he's just plain wrong," Amelia says.

"Clearly," I say, smiling.

"Cal went out of his way to ask you to the dance. He bought you a flower. He tied a ribbon on it. He wrote your name!" she says. "Your name! Not my name! Not someone else's name! Your name. Because it's you."

"Me," I repeat.

"Yeah, Charlie. You. *Charlie.* Charlotte goddamn Vega!"

I'm getting amped again.

"He asked me!" I say.

"Yes!" Amelia shouts. "He asked you! He leaned up on a locker all cool-like, and he smiled his dazzling smile."

"And his dimples were so, so cute, and he came in real close to me, and he touched my shoulder, and he asked *me!*"

We squeal some more.

Then Amelia clears her throat and says, "So, on to the really important stuff." A dramatic pause. "When are we going shopping for a dress?"

My heart drops. "Oh—I think my mom's taking me, actually," I lie.

At that moment, the music in Amelia's sister's room reaches an unnatural volume, and Amelia's face changes. "Tess, if you don't shut that shit off, I'm going to murder you!" she screams.

"I wouldn't have to make it so loud if you weren't being so loud!" Tess shrieks back.

In an instant, Amelia is off her bed and out of the room, no doubt about to shout at Tess for being a brat.

But I'm grateful for the abrupt end to the discussion.

I love Amelia. But I can't go shopping for a dress with her. I'd have to shop at a plus-size store, and I've actually been careful never to go to one with her before.

So this is one adventure I'll take on alone.

Chapter Eight

I'll admit that I'm timid when I step inside the plus-size dress store to shop for my first-ever formal gown.

I shop here all the time, but today feels different. Bigger. (Ha.) More important. I'm shopping for a dress to go to a *dance* with a *boy.*

For a while, I wander around, feeling completely overwhelmed. There are so many options. Sweetheart? Halter? Short? Long? Pink, black, blue? All I know is I refuse to get one that exposes my arms; I'm way too self-conscious for that.

Yeah, yeah. The #fatfashion comm would be like, *What the fuck, Charlie? Don't say that shit.*

But then I'd be like, *Guys, I live in the nasty, judgmental Real World, and that means I still sometimes think not-great things about my body. Sorry.*

It's not just unique to me, even. Most girls, no matter how hard they try, have some feature they're insecure about. Maybe it's just human nature; there's a reason everybody uses filters, right? Even Amelia insists she has chicken legs. I want to smack her every time she says it, but she fully believes it. There is nothing more infuriating than a privileged skinny person being embarrassed about their body. It's like they won the body lottery and they can't even appreciate it.

Still. For Amelia it's her chicken legs and for me it's my arms. It wasn't always this way; there was a time when I was younger where I didn't think much about my body aside from whether it could help me climb a tree or how far I could run without stopping, but things happen.

In middle school, I wore a sleeveless shirt on an especially hot day. One of my classmates, Rian, looked at my arms and said, "Wow, you've got some huge arms! They're bigger than mine!"

After that, I stopped wearing sleeveless clothing.

I'll also probably want a dress that isn't too form-fitting. I can thank my mom for that one. Once, she and I were on vacation, and we had someone take a photo of us in front of a statue; when we looked at the photo to make sure we both liked it, she quickly assured me she'd crop it at my chest. "I know what's it like," she said, giving me sympathetic eyes. I had actually felt kind of cute in that top up until that moment.

At least I like my legs, which is why I tend to opt for dresses or skirts. Flaunt what you've got, right?

So, okay: *sleeves* and *flowy* and *maybe on the shorter side*. But there are so many choices! Ahh!

I must look as lost as I feel, because the woman behind the counter makes her way over to me and introduces herself as Divya. She's beautiful—long black hair that reaches her waist, impeccable cat-eye makeup—and she's wearing a retro plum dress. She's also fat like me, so I can only assume she'll know how to suggest something I like.

"What can I help you find today?"

"I'm looking for a dress to my school's dance. I'm, um, going with this guy I really like, so I'm hoping for something kind of... nice."

"*The* dance?" she asks, and I nod. She smiles wistfully. "Lucky girl. And lucky boy."

I smile and tell Divya what I'm searching for but admit I'm a novice, and she reassures me I'm in good hands. She takes a look at me and then starts picking out a few things that might work, insisting her selections will look good with my body and skin tone. She tells me we're lucky to be brown because we look good in every color, and that feels nice.

Divya starts a dressing room for me and even hangs around near it when I'm trying on the first dress. Normally, I hate that, but I need someone in my corner for this and I just trust her. I come out and look at myself in the three-way mirror.

"Well?" Divya asks. "How do you feel?"

I gaze at myself skeptically. "Weird," I admit.

"Then that's not it. You should feel like a goddess. On to the next!"

It goes like that for a bit, and after I've tried on nearly a dozen dresses, there is one that brings me pretty damn close to that goddess feeling.

Divya sighs when I step out of the dressing room. "That color! It's made for you."

"You think?" My eyes fall on the emerald dress my reflection is wearing. It's lace with a sweetheart neckline and flares at the waist. The lace continues over my neck, shoulders, and arms to make three-quarter-length sleeves. It really is *lovely*.

And honestly? My body looks kind of good in it. Those legs!

Maybe I don't feel *exactly* like a goddess (whatever that means), but I do feel *pretty* in this, especially when Divya helps me pin my hair up and pairs it with some pearl earrings and some green sling-back heels.

I take it all (and wish I could take Divya, too).

When I get home, my mom is doing yoga in the living room. While she's in downward dog, she spots me in the doorway and wrinkles her nose when she notices my shopping bag. She's made a vow never to step foot in a plus-size store again.

"Shopping trip?" she asks.

"Just for a few things," I say, tucking the bags behind my back.

"Get anything good?"

"No."

"Well, we'll get you out of that store someday." Mom switches to the hare pose. "In fact, why don't you join me?"

I actually like yoga, but I pass and head to my room instead, where I pull the dress out and hold it up to my body, marveling at the smooth, shiny fabric and the way the jewel tone looks against my skin.

I find myself daydreaming of the dance ahead: me, in this gorgeous dress, all done up, swaying along to the music under the twinkling lights with Cal...

But then—without warning—I imagine Brian?

Truth be told, I've been finding myself thinking of Brian and his adorably crooked smile more often than usual. When he asked me about Jake's the other day, I don't know. It just made me wonder.

So I don't have much trouble picturing myself enveloped in his strong arms, savoring the faintest hint of his cologne, which maybe I've taken notice of, and enjoying the way he towers over me, tall and big and handsome, somehow making me feel petite.

Just for a second.

The absolute best part about daydreams is that you can have it all.

Chapter Nine

A three-day weekend (thanks, professional development days!) leaves me with far too much time to think. It's during this time that I begin to wonder: Did Cal *really* ask me to the dance? I have an excellent imagination, and I find myself fretting that this whole thing might have happened completely in my head.

Or worse: Did Cal ask me but as some kind of...joke? Maybe at Tony's encouragement?

These kinds of thoughts plague me, so, back at school on Tuesday, the first thing I do is try to catch Cal at his locker before classes start. He's alone—no Tony in sight—which I'm *supremely* grateful for, so I march right up and tap him on the shoulder.

He turns. "Hey, you."

"Hi." I'm less giggly and doe-eyed, more terrified and wide-eyed now. I can feel my heart beating in my fingertips.

"What's going on?" Cal asks.

I take a deep breath. "Right. So. I just wanted to check in after our conversation on Friday. About the dance."

"What about it?" Cal asks this with a smile that starts to make me feel a little better.

"Well, I—I wanted to make sure you didn't change your mind."

"Change my mind?" He laughs. "No. I haven't changed my mind, Charlie."

Relief washes over me, and I smile. "So we're still on, then?"

"Of course we are. You're good with that, right?" Cal asks. "Because if it's too much to ask…"

"No! I'm down. I'm so down," I say. "And excited! And honored!"

Cal chuckles. "Okay. Great. I think it'll be a really good time—all thanks to you," he says, shutting his locker and slinging his bag over his shoulder. "Don't you?"

I nod. "Yes. It'll be a really, really good time. I can't wait!"

My insides are jittery with the realization that Cal Carter really *did* mean to invite me to the dance. This might just be the greatest day of my life.

* * *

I feel like skipping to English.

And to every other class.

And to work.

And *during* work—which is fine, because today is the office's early Valentine's Day party (which I'd totally forgotten about). An amazing day at school and I only have to work for part of the afternoon and then I can totally check out and eat desserts I didn't have to make? Yes, please!

But first, I stroll up to Dora and smile obnoxiously big, bouncing on my tiptoes. I have to tell her my good news; she grew up in this town, knows how big of a deal the dance is, and knows all about my crush on Cal—and *I* know she'll freak.

"Well, someone seems happy," she says. "Is it because of the Valentine's Day party? I baked those chocolate raspberry cupcakes you like!"

"You did? Man, if I was smiley before, I'm even smilier now!"

"So what's the real reason you've got that big ol' grin on your face, dear?"

"Oh, no reason," I say, looking down at my nails like I'm not about to share good news. "You know, just that Cal invited me to the George Washington High School Annual Football Awards Ceremony. No big deal."

She leaps from her chair and throws her arms around me. "Oh, Charlie, I'm so happy for you! How wonderful!"

"So, so wonderful!" I say, beaming.

Dora pulls away from the hug with a huge grin on her face. "Good for you, honey. Now, tell me more!"

So I do: how he asked me to go with him; the dress I bought; how I envision us slow dancing. She listens intently. Before I know it, she's telling me all about the best ways some of the football players asked out their dates back in her day—and then, suddenly, Nancy has asked for everyone's attention and we both realize it's time for the Valentine's Day party.

Dora and I walk over to where Nancy is standing, wearing a white sweater with sequined red and pink hearts and some dangly red earrings. A group has already formed around her, including the folks from the warehouse. I spot Brian and wave.

"As many of you know, I *love* Valentine's Day," Nancy begins. "It has always been my favorite holiday, and it took on even more meaning when I met the love of my life, Gary, during a Valentine's Day party at a mutual friend's house decades ago. That's why we're so excited to share our love for the holiday with you all. And this year, Gary and I are trying something new: we're thrilled to be hosting today's festivities in our brand-new RV out in the parking lot!"

I briefly wonder how our office of thirty will fit into an RV, but I'm so enthralled by Nancy's love for the holiday and the way she looks at Gary and how great this day is going that I just roll with it.

Tish makes a beeline for Dora. "Can't wait to get a little buzzed," she says with a wink. "Come on!" She grabs Dora's hand and drags her outside.

I trail behind, pulling my pea coat tighter against the cold air and pausing for a moment to marvel at the RV ahead. It's shiny and massive and there are Valentine's Day decals decorating all the windows.

"It's...huge," Brian says, suddenly standing next to me.

I laugh. "Bigger than my house, I think."

"Seriously. Shall we?" I nod and we start to walk toward the RV.

"So apparently there's drinking at this thing," I say, leaning toward Brian and keeping my voice down. "Tish was talking about getting buzzed."

He arches an eyebrow. "Day drinking? This group?"

"I know, right?"

"Wow. Who'd have thought these people had such a wild side? Boozing in the middle of a Tuesday? At work? In an RV? In the name of love? Damn, I kind of dig it."

"Oh, yeah. I'm all in on this," I say, climbing up the RV steps.

Once we're inside, we can see that the RV is pretty big, but also... thirty people, like, really is a lot of people to fit in here. Some are sitting where they can, some are standing, and at the center of it all, there's a table that's covered with beautiful desserts and chips, as well as alcohol—*so much alcohol*—and classic red Solo cups.

Most everyone who beat us here is already holding a cup, and some have dug into the snacks, too. As the last ones in, there's nowhere for Brian and me to go, so we hover by the door.

"Should we get something to eat?" Brian asks.

"I don't even know if we can make it over there," I say, motioning around at the packed RV. "Are there even any regular drinks? Like, for us?"

"Stay here. I'll figure it out." And then he's gone, maneuvering between our colleagues-turned-boozehounds as he makes his way to the table of goodies. Once there, he grabs a heart-shaped plate and then looks at me as if to ask if there's anything I want.

Cupcakes! I mouth to him, and he gives me a thumbs-up, grabbing two and putting them on the plate. He snags a few other things, too, then surveys the drinks, shrugs, and comes back.

"Mostly beer and wine over there," he says, holding out the plate toward me so we can share. "There's a bottle of Coke, but I wasn't sure how I was actually going to balance two cups with the food. Here, I got a little of everything."

"You did great. Thank you!" I say, eternally grateful that I didn't have to try to squeeze by everyone to get to the food. "What should we try first? Cookies?"

"You go ahead. I only got those in case you liked them. Personally, I'd prefer a cookie with something savory inside. Why does no one ever put meat in cookies?"

"Meat in cookies?" I ask, appalled. "Like *hamburger*?!"

Brian laughs. "More like bacon."

I laugh, too. "Okay, Guy Fieri," I tease, reaching for a cupcake. "Anyway, these are where it's at. Dora's baking is no joke. It sounds like you're not a huge sweets person, but I highly recommend giving one a try."

"There's room in my heart for the occasional cupcake."

I survey the one in my hand—chocolate cake with a perfectly sculpted mound of pink frosting, topped with a raspberry and nestled in a super-cute red cupcake liner—and consider how I'll take a bite without making a huge mess. "The one problem with cupcakes, though, is that they're so hard to eat."

"You don't know the trick?"

I give him a look. "There's a trick to eating cupcakes?"

He pushes the plate toward me. "If you don't mind." I take it from him and watch as he carefully removes the cupcake's wrapper and then delicately breaks the bottom half of the cake off. He squishes the half cake on top of the frosting, effectively turning the cupcake into a cupcake sandwich.

"Ta-da!" He takes a big bite for dramatic effect.

I can't help but laugh at how proud he is of himself. "Okay, that's great and all, but total blasphemy."

Brian swallows hard. "Blasphemy?! I just showed you the perfect, mess-free way to consume a cupcake. Give the guy a little credit!"

"Fine, fine. Points for creativity."

"Thank you," he says, then finishes the cupcake with another big bite. "See? So clean. So easy. So delicious."

"It's an impressive trick, but is it really the *best* way? I think not." I hand him the plate back, and he takes it with an amused smile. "Now, pay attention. The best way to eat a cupcake starts the same way your trick does." I remove the wrapper of my cupcake, followed by its cakey bottom. "But then…" I take a bite from the cakey bottom, and then another.

Brian's eyes go wide. "You just…eat the cake? With *no frosting?*"

I nod, taking the last bite of the bottom and leaving the cake top and its frosting fully intact. "You have to suffer through the cake portion alone so you can get the real reward: a small bit of cake with mountains of frosting!" Now it's my turn to take a dramatic bite from my cupcake, but it doesn't go as well as I'd hoped: I can instantly feel the icing smear around my mouth, and Brian starts laughing so hard he nearly chokes.

"Elegant!" he says between laughs, then reaches into his back pocket and pulls out a heart napkin, which he hands to me. "So classy!"

I laugh, too, shielding my mouth with my hand and using the napkin to wipe my face, hoping I don't accidentally smudge any highlighter and leave my face real shiny in one spot and totally matte in another. "Okay, so, definitely messier than your technique…"

"But so good, though, I bet?" he asks.

"*So* good," I say, going in for another bite.

"Ladies, gentlemen! May we have your attention for just another moment?" A voice bellows over the noise. Brian and I turn to see Gary standing with Nancy in the hallway nook just past the food table. "Before the festivities get too far underway, we would like to thank you all for humoring Nancy and me in our little celebration. I also want to say thank you to my beautiful wife, who I've had the honor of being with these last thirty years. It's been wonderful celebrating these last thirty Valentine's Days with you, honey, and I must say: you get hotter and hotter each year that goes by!" He grabs Nancy and kisses her big and I hear Dave let out a giant groan.

"Enough, you two!" he yells, which only makes Gary dip Nancy into a kiss so hard that her hair nearly grazes the floor.

I turn to Brian, mortified, and he's shaking his head like this is the craziest thing he's ever seen as the others whoop and holler and cheer Gary and Nancy on. How drunk *are* these people?! It's, like, four-thirty in the afternoon!

I motion toward the door and Brian nods, tossing our goody plate into the trash can and pushing the door open. We're able to slip out completely unnoticed in the hullabaloo and we book it toward the office, unable to contain our laughter.

"Who are those people and what have they done with our prim and proper colleagues?" I ask.

"I don't know and I don't want to know!" he says, opening the door and letting me into the building. "What is it about Valentine's Day that makes people so loopy? First everyone at school—now this!"

I'm nodding along with him. "There is *something* about this holiday. I can't say it's my favorite, though. I mean, it's great when you're a kid—it's so simple and innocent and everyone in your class gets some candy and a sweet little valentine. But then you get older and you're lucky if you get anything at all."

"I feel like Valentine's Day always kinda sucks for dudes, too," Brian says. "You never get anything—there's just this expectation that you're going to deliver. It's weird, man."

"Yeah, I agree. Although..." I let my voice trail off.

"Although?"

"Well...something kind of cool happened that's making me think Valentine's Day might not be so bad," I say shyly.

"Oh, yeah?" Brian asks, smirking. "Like what?"

"I got invited to the dance on Friday."

"Oh. Wow!" Brian seems surprised, and I swallow my disappointment. He quickly adds, "Good for you, Charlie."

I try to push past it. "Thanks! I'm really excited."

"Who's the lucky guy?" Brian asks.

That makes me blush a bit. "You won't believe it."

"Now you've definitely got to tell me."

"Well..." I hesitate. I started this conversation feeling so light and self-assured, certain Brian would be one person rooting for me. But my confidence has wavered, and I end up stammering. "I—I'm going with Cal, actually."

Brian's face seems to fall. "Cal *Carter*?"

"Yeah, that'd be the one. I've had a thing for him for a while, so...," I say, my buzz fully wearing off at his lackluster reaction. Have I overestimated how friendly we are? "It's wild, right?"

"Yeah...that *is* wild." The way Brian emphasizes the word *is* makes me regret sharing this news at all. I get it: gorgeous, popular Cal with *me* seems way off base, for probably dozens of reasons. Still, I feel my neck start to burn with shame, and suddenly the sugar from the cupcake I've eaten tastes sickly sweet in my mouth.

"I mean, not *that* wild, though. He did ask me, after all," I say, feeling defensive. "But I get it."

"Wait, Charlie—no," Brian says. "That's not at all what I meant."

"No, it's fine. It's weird."

"No, that's not it. It's just—I mean—Cal's a...doorknob."

I give him a look. "What?"

Brian shakes his head. "Never mind. I'm sorry. I'm excited for you. Really! I hope you have a great time."

"Yeah, I hope so, too," I say. "But I'm going to head out. Night."

I don't wait for him to say goodbye, and I walk back out of the office door. Though I can tell Brian feels bad for what he said, I don't want to stick around. The last thing I need is more doubt. I'm already full of it.

Chapter Ten

If trying on your dress a million times is wrong, then I don't want to be right.

I just need to make sure that I look okay—good, even—if I'm going to pull off being Cal Carter's date to the dance. I need to feel and act the part, so if that means slipping into my dress, turning on a little music, and modeling in the mirror, that's fine, right? (And with Brian's less-than-reassuring response to my news, I just need to remind myself that this is really happening.)

But something about this Spice Girls song—yes, I'm *totally* listening to the "Lovesick" playlist I recommended to Amelia—gets me so hyped that eventually I'm not really trying on the dress so much as just straight-up singing and dancing in the mirror.

Just as I'm belting out the chorus, the door to my room swings open, and there's my mother.

"Mom!" I grab my phone and fumble with it, trying to pause the music. "Don't you knock?"

She's laughing when I finally get the song to stop playing. "I wanted to use your mirror and I didn't think you'd mind a quick interruption to your concert. You know I prefer the lighting in here." She motions at me. "What's all this?"

"Nothing. Just singing," I say, but I know there's really no way out of this one.

"In a new dress?"

I sigh. "Well."

"What?" she asks.

I sigh again. "It's for the dance."

"The dance," she repeats. Then her face lights up. "The George Washington High School Annual Football Awards Ceremony?!"

"That'd be the one," I say.

"Oh my God!" she exclaims. "But you?"

I feel my jaw clench a little. "Really, Mom? 'You?'"

She rolls her eyes at me. "Ugh, Charlie, that's not what I meant," she says. "I'm just surprised."

"Yeah, I can tell. But why?" I press.

"It's just that not everyone gets to go, so of course I'm surprised. Happy, but surprised."

"It's so surprising that someone would want to go with me?"

"You know what? Don't start." Mom puts up her hand as if to physically block any other words that might come out of my mouth. "Who are you going with?"

That I definitely don't want to share.

Cal Carter is such a big name on the football team that even my *mom* knows who he is—and okay, fine, she may have overheard me talking about him to Amelia before, so she knows not only that he's super popular and super cute but that I'm super into him.

"Well?" she asks.

There will be something a little satisfying about revealing it, though, right? For her to know that there are people out there who find me attractive just as I am? For her to have to eat her surprise? For her to have to acknowledge that I *have* been invited to this super-special dance?

I stand up a little straighter before saying, "Cal Carter."

My mom starts laughing. "Oh my God, Charlie. Come on. Seriously, who are you going with?"

My fists clench at my side. "God, Mom, I'm being serious!"

"Okay, okay! Jeez," Mom says. "I thought you were joking. But good for you!"

"Yeah, good for me," I spit out. "Do you want to use the mirror or not?"

"Yes, I do."

I step aside to let her in front of it, but I cross my arms and stare at her the whole time she's checking out her hair. She can, no doubt, see me in the mirror, but I don't care.

I watch as she takes in her appearance—her light brown eyes, which she delights in describing as hazel; her effortlessly straight ombré hair that goes from a chestnut brown to a soft blond; her skin so smooth it doesn't even need a touch of BB cream. She uses a finger to tidy up the rosy lip stain she's wearing and smooths her chin, a ritual she's developed as an attempt to will away what she calls her double chin (which it hardly is). I feel like she's doing all these things painstakingly slowly just to annoy me—especially as she turns to the left side, then the right, and adjusts the fitted wrap dress she's wearing on her small frame. I try not to let the sight of her body make me feel any kind of way about my own, not when I was just having such a joyful time and feeling so good, but it's hard.

"All right, Miss Attitude. All set," she says. "I'm going on a date, so I'll leave you to your little performance."

"Fine," I reply. "See ya."

She disappears from my room, shutting the door behind her, and I instantly turn the music back on in an attempt to resume my dance party. But when I look in the mirror and see my body reflected back at me, taking up at least twice the size of my mom's, I can't muster the enthusiasm. Not even the Spice Girls can save me.

So I turn off the music, peel off the dress, and get in some pajamas instead.

After the exchanges with my mom and Brian, I decide I'm not telling another living soul about the dance or about Cal or about anything, really.

Thankfully, the topic doesn't come up again with either of them, and there isn't even any weirdness with Brian the next time I see him. We talk about a killer history test we both had to take, that time Brian actually went to math camp (!), and *RuPaul's Drag Race* (which I'm obsessed with and trying to get him to watch), but not a word about the dance, for which I am grateful. I just want to stay positive about it.

And I am. In fact, thinking about attending the dance with Cal makes me feel giddy and light. I spend *a lot* of time daydreaming about what it will be like. I imagine Cal in a suit, smiling at me, his beautiful golden hair mussed like he's just rolled out of bed (My bed? Okay, Charlie, stop). I imagine all the slow songs we'll dance to. I wonder whether we'll kiss (and how many times and how great it'll feel).

These thoughts keep me floating toward the end of the week, closer and closer to Friday's dance. Amelia's support buoys me, too, and on Thursday, we use art class to work out the details of how she'll help me get ready as we work on our pointillism pieces.

"I still can't believe you haven't let me see you in your dress yet!"

"It adds to the element of surprise," I say.

"I think it's supposed to be a surprise for your date, not your best friend, but okay. I'm sure you're stunning." She points her paintbrush at me. "I'm at least still coming over to do your makeup and hair, right?"

"Yes, please. I'm hopeless without you!"

"No need to be a suck-up, lady." Amelia's brows furrow as she looks at her piece. She holds it up to show me. "My pointillist banana is looking a bit...expired."

I look down. My pointillist donut is looking similar, so I hold it up to show her. "Hard same. Probs shouldn't have chosen food for this piece." We laugh. "Anyway, what time will you be there?"

"Right. The important stuff. My track meet gets out at five, and I'll come straight to you. That should give us plenty of time to do hair, makeup, all of it. You'll barely need anything, anyway, because you're so pretty on your own."

I roll my eyes at that, but secretly, I'm pleased. I like when she compliments me.

We hear giggling from across the room, and Amelia and I turn to see what's what. The girls who sit near Brian are all gazing at tiny pieces of paper and seem to be swooning. We don't get a chance to question it because suddenly Brian's at our table handing Amelia a similarly sized piece of paper.

Amelia looks at it and grins. " 'You're great. Happy Valentine's Day,' " she reads aloud, then turns it so I can see. *Great* is spelled *grate* and there's a cute doodle of some cheese being grated. It's handmade, I assume by Brian, and totally adorable. With Valentine's Day this weekend, Amelia's already gotten plenty of valentines from admirers, but I can tell she likes this one. "This is so cute! Thanks, Brian!"

"You're welcome," he says. Then he holds one out to me. "And last, but certainly not least. Happy almost Valentine's Day, Charlie."

I look up at him. "For me?"

"Of course. Someone recently told me that Valentine's Day sucks as you get older because not everyone gets something. So I wanted to make sure everyone in this class, at least, would get something. That person especially." He gestures for me to take it.

My heart is thumping as I reach for the slip of paper, touched that he listened so openly to something I said and even turned it into action. I'm also just...floored that I'm receiving a valentine. A real valentine. From a real boy.

The valentine Brian's made for me has an intricate drawing of a typewriter, etched in ink and filled in with watercolor. It's beautiful enough to be a piece of art you'd find in a hipster gift store, one so irresistible you don't mind the hefty price tag. Beneath the drawing, in Brian's handwriting, it says, *Just my type.* I turn it over delicately to find that on the back he's written, *To someone who makes my workday wonderful. Happy Valentine's Day, Charlie.—Brian.*

"Wow. This is beautiful, Brian. And really sweet. I love it."

"I thought because you like writing, it might be fitting."

And at that, I feel a little choked up. "That's so thoughtful. Thank you. So much."

He smiles big at me. "Yeah, of course. I'm just happy you like it." He lingers for a minute, then does a little knock on our table and heads back to his.

Suddenly, I don't care so much that Brian and I didn't quite see eye to eye on the dance earlier in the week. And I'm reminded why I found myself daydreaming of slow dancing with him, too.

I'm truly moved by this gesture—by the time and the effort that went into creating this, an idea he said was inspired by *me*—and I swear I'll remember it forever.

Chapter Eleven

It's finally Friday and the dance is here and everything about me is all wrong.

My legs are suddenly too stumpy. My boobs don't look even. My glasses are nerdy. My arms are too wobbly, my belly too round, and all I can hear in my head over and over is Tony calling me an elephant. I'm not sure how I ever could have believed this dress was the One.

I start to voice these feelings to Amelia, but she won't hear any of it.

"Stop! You are stunning. Like, drop-dead gorgeous. Cal's gonna flip," she says firmly. "And tonight is your night!"

I look at myself in the mirror again. We're in my room and I'm getting ready for the dance. Amelia did my makeup—cat-eye, which I don't tell her is inspired by Divya, but it totally is—and my hair, which is curled beautifully and pinned back on one side.

I try to see what Amelia sees. Objectively, my dress is beautiful. Objectively, my makeup is impeccable. Objectively, my hair looks amazing. But it's still me.

And I guess it'll have to do.

"You ready to go?" Amelia asks.

"I'm going to barf," I say.

"You won't." She hands me a small silver clutch she's letting me borrow, then wraps a balloon I picked up for Cal around my wrist. (It says CONGRATS! on it because there's no way Cal isn't getting an award tonight.) She squeezes my shoulders. "You're going to be great."

I smile at her. "Thanks, Amelia." The alarm on my phone reminds me it's time to get moving. "I guess I'm ready to go, then. Wish me luck."

Amelia throws her arms around me dramatically. "Good luck, beautiful. This is your night!"

I repeat variations of this sentiment to myself over and over on my way to school.

When I arrive, the parking lot is overflowing with cars. I see couples dressed in their finest arriving in beat-up Suburbans, and I find the contrast a little amusing; others are dropped off, while still others arrive in limos. I briefly wonder why Cal didn't offer to pick me up like all the other football players seem to have done for their dates, especially because the lot is so full of the cars of attendees and their families that it's hard for me to find a spot. By the time I do, I'm running a little late, so I have to walk-run inside. I'm out of breath when I get into the gym, but the lights are dim and I hope no one notices.

The space has been transformed from a stinky, run-down, wood-floored gym to a stinky, run-down, wood-floored gym with beautiful decorations strung about in our school colors. A few rows of folding chairs are set up in front of the stage (the same one they use whenever graduation has to be held indoors), and they're reserved for the football team and staff. The rest of us will watch from the bleachers.

Unfortunately, the only empty seat I see is a couple of rows up and a few people deep...which means I need to hoof it up there and say "Excuse me" a bunch as I clumsily climb over my peers with my gigantic body. Sure. No problem.

It actually takes me a second to work up the nerve to walk up the bleachers and my anxiety brain even considers leaving, but I eventually muster enough courage to walk to the correct row.

"Excuse me," I whisper to the girl sitting at the end of the bleachers, and she looks over at me. "Can I squeeze by?" I see her eyes flit over my body and she elbows her friend, who looks over at me, too. "Can I sneak past?" I ask again.

"Sure," the friend says, and then they both stand up, like I wouldn't be able to just scooch by like most people if they just drew in their knees. (Fine. I probably couldn't.) I don't think they mean it in any kind of way except helpful, but it still bugs me, especially because most of the other people I ask to move have similar reactions.

Eventually, I have a seat, and after a few minutes of obsessing over the fact that I just had to do that, I can take in my surroundings. I mean, it's the gym. That isn't exactly the venue I'd have chosen for the awards ceremony portion of this event, but our actual auditorium is closed due to asbestos. (Seriously.)

But so what?

And so what if I had to ask a bunch of people to move out of my way so I could get to a seat?

And so what if most people seemed super inconvenienced by the fact that there was a Large Woman Coming Through?

Because I'm about to go to the dance with Cal.

This is my night.

I refocus. The ceremony itself is as exciting as these ceremonies usually are, which is to say, not at all. But the football players seem to be enjoying themselves. They cheer and yell every time a teammate is called up for an award, and they look nice in their suits—a big change of pace from their regular football gear. They seem much less intimidating, far more approachable—almost human-like.

Their families cheer loudly, too. I giggle at the fact that moms and dads are jumping up and down for their sons, even though they're all gussied up.

I even find myself getting into it, yelling and cheering for players along with everyone else (except for Tony—no thanks). Once I let myself loosen up a little, I realize how nice it feels to relax and be part of something.

When Cal is called up for the final award—he's MVP—I yell and wave like a fanatic. He scans the crowd for a few seconds, then notices me and gives me a smile. He turns and focuses on receiving his award, which he promptly puts on the floor, then grabs it with his feet as he goes into a handstand. Show-off. His friends eat it up, and so do I.

I'm so tempted to turn to the girl sitting next to me and say, "I'm here with him." But I refrain.

Then all at once it's over, and families are reuniting with their kids and I'm being jostled around. It takes me a bit, but I eventually find Cal in the corner of the gym with two people I can only assume are his mom and dad. Cal is a lovely mix of them both, I notice: he has golden hair and piercing green eyes like his mom, and a smile accented by deep dimples like his dad.

I make my way over, unwinding Cal's balloon from my wrist and holding on to the string so I can hand it over to him.

I'm nervous; I'm going to have to meet his parents, like, now, and I bet they'll wonder why Cal asked me to this thing. Hell, I'm still kind of wondering the same thing.

But I try to channel Amelia, and I walk with my head held high. *I will be confident,* I remind myself. *This is my night.*

As I get closer to Cal, he spots me and says something to his parents, who step away from him.

"Hey," he says once I'm within earshot.

"Hey!" I say back, and smile. "You look great. Really great. I loved the handstand." I'm gushing.

He chuckles. "Thanks. Give the people what they want, right?" He pauses, as if hesitating. "So, uh, where's Amelia?"

I'm confused. I can feel my face show that. Slowly, I say, "She's probably out. Why?"

Now he looks confused—maybe surprised. I don't know. "Out?"

"Yeah, of course. She's usually out on Friday nights. Well, not always, but a lot. I rarely get her to myself on Friday nights anymore," I say. Rambling. "Why?"

I see annoyance flicker across his face. "Well, Charlie, I *did* ask you to bring her along with you tonight. That's kind of the whole point."

"What?" I ask. My heart is pounding in my ears as I wait for his response.

Cal looks behind him at his parents, as if making sure they're out of earshot. They are, but he still lowers his voice. "Charlie, come on," he hisses. "This isn't funny."

"No, it's not," I say. "I don't understand? You asked me if I was free..."

"Yes, and then I asked you to do me a solid and *bring Amelia with you to the dance*. I knew she wouldn't come without you. I mentioned all of this to you last Friday. You said it sounded great!" He's getting mad, I can tell. "You even said a couple of days ago that you were so excited about it!"

I feel my face getting hot, and there's a lump in my throat.

So. That must have been all that extra stuff Cal had been saying to me when I was off in dreamland imagining him kissing me.

But the rose? The ribbon with my name? It doesn't make sense.

"Yeah," I manage to choke out, forcing a laugh. "Yeah. I'm just messing with you. She, um, couldn't come. At the last minute. Sorry."

His shoulders slump. "Not cool, Charlie. You should've told

me before now," he says, shaking his head. "I thought you could get her to change her mind about me, but clearly you weren't up for the task. Now I look like an idiot."

"Right. Sorry." I can feel my eyes sting as I hold back tears. "I didn't mean to disappoint."

He sighs. "It's whatever. Fine."

"I'm sorry," I say again, because I can't think of what else to say. "I should go."

"Yeah. You probably should," he says, and he turns away from me.

I let go of the balloon and walk quickly out of the gym. Once I'm in the hall, I sprint all the way to my car. I barely make it inside before I start crying. Loud crying. Ugly crying. The kind of crying where my makeup is off in seconds and gets right in my eyes and stings. That makes me cry more, and my face is wet, and there's black mascara and eyeliner and sparkly eye shadow all over.

I can't even go home and curl up in my bed, even though that's all I want to do. My mom will know what happened. I can still hear her laugh of disbelief when I told her about Cal. I shudder remembering it.

I can't go to Amelia, either, because I don't want her to know—not yet. In fact, part of me hates her right now, even though *none* of this is her fault.

So I drive.

I have to stay out until at least midnight. That's when I told my mom I'd be home. I drive really far with my music blasting, and I sing loud until my throat gets scratchy. Sometimes I'm just plain screaming along with the songs. I think about driving forever, but eventually I need to get gas (I feel like a freak getting gas in my dress). That sobers me up enough to turn the car around and go home.

* * *

By the time I get there, the house is dark. I rush toward my room, hoping my mom is already asleep.

Behind the protection of my locked door, I start to cry again. I drop my clutch on the floor and rip off my dress, shoving it directly into the trash. Then I take the rose Cal gave me—the one I thought was so special—and stuff that in the trash, too.

Cal didn't even say I looked nice.

He didn't even *see* me.

I cry harder at the thought of how wrong I was, at how wrong I've been. I thought Cal said hi to me because he saw me as a person, but he only says hi to me because I'm a way for him to get close to Amelia. I'm an idiot. An unlovable, sad excuse for a person.

I kick my stupid shoes across the room, I rip the stupid bobby pins out of my hair, and I toss my stupid earrings on the dresser so recklessly that they bounce straight off and skid across the floor.

Then I force myself to stare in the mirror. I don't bother rubbing my makeup off, even though there are black streaks all over my face. I look feral. I *am* feral. I stare at my fat, round belly and grab it violently with my hands and shake it. I don't even know why. Then I grab at my arm fat, and my leg fat, and my face fat, and it takes everything in me not to scream. I stare at myself until I'm so overwhelmingly disgusted that I can't handle it. I want to rip my skin off.

On the floor, I can hear my phone buzzing. I know it's Amelia. She's probably checking in, wants to know everything.

But if I pick up the phone I'll start sobbing. I'll tell her I hate her, when I *totally don't,* and ask her why she has to ruin everything, which she *totally doesn't.*

Boys do.

So instead, I throw myself into my bed, burrow into my pillows, and wish the ground would swallow me whole.

Chapter Twelve

I wake up the next morning with such a headache that I imagine this is what hangovers are like.

The idea of staying in bed forever appeals to me, but my temples are throbbing so badly that I need a cool shower. I look outside to find that my mom's car is gone from the driveway, so I feel safe going into the bathroom. I avoid my reflection in the mirror as I get into the shower. I can't quite handle the sight of me.

When I'm done, I put on my comfiest pajamas, climb back into bed, and drift in and out of sleep, my TV humming in the background.

It must be hours later when I hear a knock on my door.

"Yeah?" I say.

"It's me. Are you *still* in bed?" Mom asks.

"Yes."

"Don't you think you should get up?"

I grunt in response.

"Fine, then. How'd the dance go?"

I say nothing. I don't want to tell her the truth, but I don't have it in me to lie.

"Charlie?" she asks, a little louder. "I asked how'd it go?"

"Please leave me alone."

I hear her sigh. "Oh, Charlotte," she says, more to herself than to me. Her footsteps pad away from my door. I pull the blankets up over my head.

It's not long before there's another knock on the door.

"Just go away—please," I say.

"Charlie, it's me." It's Amelia on the other side of the door. "Can you let me in?"

I do, and when I see her, I'm not mad or jealous or frustrated anymore; I'm just glad she's there. I don't know how she knew to come, but that doesn't really matter. Amelia pulls me into a tight hug and I cry into her shoulder.

"He didn't want me there," I manage to say.

"He's an asshole," Amelia says, rubbing my back. "Come on. Let's close this door." We do.

I climb back into the bed and Amelia sits beside me. She strokes my hair and doesn't make me say anything. Instead, she says, "You are amazing, you know?"

But that just makes me cry more.

I cry until I can't, and then I fall asleep. Amelia is there when I wake up, and I notice my phone is now on my charger, and the clutch and the earrings are arranged nicely on my dresser; the emerald dress is no longer in the trash and instead hangs over my desk chair.

I look at her. "Hi," I say.

"Hi," Amelia says, keeping her voice soft. "You wanna tell me what happened?"

"There isn't much to tell. Cal didn't want me at the dance with him."

"But why? What happened?"

"He didn't want me to be his date," I say, and when I do, my voice catches a little.

"I don't understand. He asked you to be there. He gave you that rose."

"I know."

"So what, then?" she asks. Her voice is really soft and her eyes look glassy, like she wants to cry for me. Like maybe she already knows.

"He didn't want me there," I say. I know I'm being difficult, but saying it all out loud feels like...a lot.

"Did he say that?"

"No."

"Then what? Please, Charlie." Amelia is practically begging.

"Well, he did ask me to come and all, but there was an agenda. One I somehow missed." I swallow hard. "You."

"What?"

I take a deep breath. "I mean...he asked me to the dance. He did. And I went. I got there a little late, but it was fine, whatever. The awards went well. Cal won MVP, of course. But after...I don't know. It was clear he wasn't excited to see me...like, at all. He was standing with his parents and I walked up to him and he barely acknowledged me. He just asked where you were."

"Why would he ask where I was?"

I shrug one of my shoulders and toy with the edge of my comforter. "He said—" My voice breaks off and I feel my lip quiver, but I continue. "And this is so stupid, but...he only invited me to the dance because he thought I could get you to come with me. He was after you, not me."

Amelia's face drops. "Charlie."

I laugh, and the sound is a little sharp. "Yeah, I mean, *of course,* right? Of course he'd want you there, not me. I was an idiot for thinking otherwise."

"Charlie, no," Amelia says. She takes my hands in hers and looks right into my eyes. "I'm so, so, so sorry. That's awful. So, like, what was his grand fucking plan, anyway? Invite you and just hope I tagged along? God, what an idiot."

The embarrassment of the whole thing hits me all over again and a few tears escape. I take my hands back from Amelia's and wipe my eyes. "No, not exactly. I hate to share this—like, I'd almost rather die than tell you this part because it's so embarrassing, but...

Cal was actually up-front with me about this plan. I just—I guess I was just so excited by him asking me to go that I"—I hesitate—"I wasn't really listening when he said it. How's that for screwed up? I did this to myself."

"*No.* You did not do this to yourself. Cal is the bad guy, no matter how we look at it. Even if he was up-front about his nasty plan, it's still a fucked-up thing to do! He should never have asked you to get me to come! He knows that you like him and that I have a boyfriend and that I hate him and it's just *messed up.* And he gave you a rose, Charlie, a rose with *your name* on it—your name, not mine!" She's wringing my pillow. "No. Not okay. Screw Cal! I'm going to cut his dick off!"

"No. Amelia. It's fine," I say, even though it's not.

"I'm just so sorry," she says, in a voice that sounds desperate, as if her apology can make up for everything that happened.

I nod. "I'm sorry, too. You're right. It was messed up of him to use me to get to you, especially since you've made it pretty clear you're not into him. But honestly, that's part of why I'm so upset. I knew he liked you. I mean…this whole time. I knew that. You knew that. And I *still* liked him. How pathetic is that?"

"Don't. Please."

"But I knew," I continue. "I just couldn't see that Cal would never like me back. God, I'm so stupid."

She shakes her head so hard that her curls are bouncing. "No," she says, keeping her voice firm. "He used you. He confused you. I've seen him with you—he's flirty as hell! He knew what he was doing! Seriously—*fuck him.*"

I rub at my eyes. "I don't want to talk about this anymore."

"Okay," Amelia says. "Yeah. Of course."

We're quiet for a minute, then I ask, "How'd you know to come over?"

Amelia bites her lip. "Don't be mad."

"Tell me."

"Your mom told me to come."

I guess I'm more surprised by that than angry. "She did?"

"Yeah. I mean. Last night, when I was texting and I didn't hear back, I started to worry. I thought if it was going well, you'd be texting me. When I didn't hear from you, I started thinking something might be wrong. But I also didn't want to bother you just in case I was totally off base and things were actually going really well. But then this morning, I *still* hadn't heard from you. So I stooped real low: I called your landline. Your mom answered and when I asked if you were there, she said yeah but that something was up."

"How did she phrase it?" I don't know why this is the first thing I want to know, but it is.

"Well…she gently—very gently—said she thought you might've been stood up." Amelia's biting her lip again.

"Not quite, but close," I say. "My crush didn't stand me up—he just didn't want me there at all. Great guess, though, Mom. Real nice." It kills me that my mom was right all along.

"That's not how she meant it. She was just concerned. Like me. She didn't mean anything by it," Amelia says quickly. "She just wanted me to come over. She thought I'd have better luck talking to you."

"Yeah."

"Maybe she shouldn't have said anything, but I'm glad she did. I *want* to be here for you."

I try to offer her a smile. "Thank you."

"You don't have to smile on my behalf. This is bullshit and you get to be sad."

"I really am," I admit.

Amelia sighs. "I know."

We fall quiet again.

"I appreciate you coming, Amelia. I do. I needed this. But I think I want to be alone for a little bit."

I can tell she isn't thrilled at the idea of going, but she nods. "I get it." She pulls me into another hug. "I'm sorry," she whispers. "You're amazing." I nod like I believe her.

"My mom's going to ask you what happened as you leave," I say.

"Yeah, so?"

With another shrug, I say, "You can tell her."

She raises her eyebrows. "Are you sure?"

"Yeah. I'd rather not have to tell her myself."

Amelia nods sympathetically, then rises to her feet. She opens the door and starts to go, then turns back to me. "Please keep the dress. You really looked beautiful."

I look over at it hanging smooth and green on the chair. "I'll think about it."

Amelia leaves, but the door doesn't quite latch behind her, so I hear her start to tell my mom about what happened, a story I'm not keen on hearing. I get up to close and lock the door, but not before I hear my mom say, "I tried to tell her..."

* * *

I watch TV for a bit. I can't focus, but the noise is a nice distraction. I fall asleep again. I stare at the wall. I stare at the dress. And at some point, long after Amelia has left, I can swear I smell rice and beans. But I must be imagining things, because we don't do carbs in this house, not anymore.

Then there's a knock at the door.

"Yes?" I ask.

Through the door, my mom asks, "Hungry?"

I am.

"A little," I say.

"Come on," she says.

I get out of bed and follow her to the kitchen, where the caldero is on the stove. I haven't seen it out in ages. She pulls off the lid and I see the steam disperse into the air. Inside is a pile of vibrant yellow rice with pigeon peas. My stomach grumbles. She piles two scoops onto a plate and hands it to me, then takes one scoop for herself, and we sit at the table.

"This is delicious, Mom," I say after my first mouthful. Each bite feels a little like a warm hug.

"Thank you." She always took pride in being able to cook well, at least before the whole shakes-and-weight-loss thing. When she and my dad met, my mom only knew how to cook Polish and Italian food, a product of her parents' backgrounds. But my dad showed her how to cook some traditional Puerto Rican dishes—rice and beans (both yellow with pigeon peas and white with kidney beans, of course); empanadillas; pernil; tostones—and those also became the staples in our house, the food I grew up on. Eventually, my (white) mom could cook these meals even better than my (Puerto Rican) dad, and my dad wouldn't have it any other way. These were my comfort foods. And comfort is what I really need right now.

"Amelia told me what happened," Mom says.

"Yeah," I say. "It sucks."

She sighs. "Yeah. It does. If you need anything…"

I look down at my plate of food. "This was just what I needed."

At that, my mom smiles. "I'm glad."

We eat the rest of the meal in peace, and then my mom starts to clean up. It almost feels like old times, which I appreciate. I thank her again and then I go back to my room.

I decide to turn on my phone, and when I do, I see the flood of texts and missed calls from Amelia from the night before. I browse through the messages, then clear the notifications and get to the most recent text from her.

Just checking in. Love you.

I lock my phone without replying, then notice the date on my home screen: February 13.

Tomorrow is Valentine's Day—Amelia's six-month anniversary with Sid and the day she's planning on telling him she's in love with him. I haven't asked her about it much since I've been asked to the dance, too preoccupied with my own stuff.

I text her back with **Love you, too. I'm good. I'm a jerk and I forgot to check in about your anniversary. What did you decide?**

We don't have to talk about this, she writes.

I want to. Fill me in! What's the plan? (I'm thankful that I can sound more chipper via text than I can in person.)

Going to take your advice, she writes. **I love Sid. I want him to know. I hope he says it back.**

He will, I write. **Keep me posted!**

I'll text you. We're meeting up at 6 for dinner. If all goes well, I may not text you until much later :)

I start to reply but can't really think of anything to say. So I just write, **Love you! You got this. xoxo**

Then I put my phone on my nightstand and go to bed.

Chapter Thirteen

By Sunday, I've felt a lot of things, and I'm nearly all feeling-ed out, except for one emotion that I've just added to my list:

Anger.

I'm mad because today is Valentine's Day and I thought I might have a valentine for the first time *ever*.

I'm mad at Cal for using me to get close to Amelia. I'm mad at the way he treated me, at the way he discarded me, at the way he may not even fully *realize* he was unkind to me—or, worse, knew exactly what he was doing and was willing to hurt me to get what he wanted. God, that sucks.

I'm mad at my mom and Sid and Brian, for being right. They knew going to the dance with Cal was too good to be true.

I'm mad at Amelia. Yeah, I'm back to being mad at her. It's not fair, but whatever, I can't help it. I'm mad at her for *always* being everyone's first choice. Cal's. My mom's. The litany of boys we've known—boys who started out being both of our friends but eventually gravitated toward her, for all the reasons *I've* been drawn to her: she's kind and thoughtful and always knows the right thing to say and is somehow perfect and always has been. How is that even fair? No wonder I'm always coming in second to her. Girl's a goddess.

But mostly, I guess I'm mad at myself.

I never should've agreed to go to the dance with Cal in the first place—even without knowing what was going to go down. I knew

Cal liked Amelia. Not to mention that fact that he treated her terribly, constantly pursuing her long after she made it clear she had zero interest.

And if I'm being honest with myself, Cal and I never had any kind of real bond. Like, looking back, I'm embarrassed to even take inventory of our so-called friendship, the one I cherished so close to my heart. Things I took as evidence that he liked me weren't actually "signs" at all. Cal mostly talked to me whenever he needed my homework or my notes or my money. (I'm ashamed to admit I've given him money on more than a few occasions. Of course, he's never paid me back.) I thought if I treated him well enough, he would eventually realize I was the one he should be with. The classic be-with-the-one-who-was-standing-in-front-of-you-the-whole-time trope. As a self-proclaimed writer, I should *know* better! But I *hoped*—and thinking of that now, I cringe.

Also, looking at the clock, I know it's dangerously close to the time when Amelia and Sid are celebrating their anniversary. That also means it's dangerously close to the time when Amelia takes the plunge and leaves me virginal and alone while she gets to ascend to the astral plane that is Totally in Love and Sexually Active.

Okay, that's not really how I think of it, but is it wrong to feel like having sex is something I might never experience? Not when I've made it sixteen long years without so much as a peck on the lips.

Most of my classmates, it seems, have crossed over into that realm—first falling in love (though not always, obvi), and then having sex. It feels like they're *all* having sex. I'll never forget a conversation I overheard between Amelia and some of her friends at the end of eighth grade. Tyler, one of the guys she met on the track team, had asked: "Think you'll go all the way next year?"

Amelia, cool as a motherfucking cucumber, just shrugged. "Probably not. But maybe the year after."

Like it was the most casual conversation on the planet! The others chimed in, too. Jessica said she already had (she and her boyfriend had been dating for a whole year at that point), while Maddy shyly shrugged and said maybe. Then John and Khalil high-fived and said yes, and I just sat there, totally dumbfounded at how they could even be thinking about this.

I mean, yeah, fine, I was thinking about it, but I had *just* started my period and was still navigating that; sex wasn't even on the radar for me, and now I had to add it to my list of things to worry about.

Maybe I'm a little bitter. I can't help but feel like...well, like a loser. I know I'm being hard on myself and that I've got to be better about that, but I don't know how, and I'm not going to solve that tonight, so I decide to write instead.

I need to get out of my own head, and writing always helps me do that. For a few minutes or hours, I can get swept up in another life, another place. Today, I decide to write about something happy. It's a short story about a lovely girl traveling the world and having a really nice moment with a stranger who happens to be wearing the same dress as her. I'm typing so feverishly that I almost don't hear when my phone buzzes.

But it does, twice, indicating a text. I check it. It's from Amelia. I'm expecting her to be offering details of her hookup or telling me she feels like a changed woman or something, but instead, it reads:

Sid broke up with me.

I gasp. Then I call Amelia immediately, and she's sobbing on the other line.

"Let me come get you," I say, already grabbing my purse and heading outside. "Where are you?"

"Outside his house," she chokes out.

"I'm on my way, Amelia. Stay put."

I get to Sid's way faster than I should, and Amelia hardly

gives me time to stop before she's yanking at the car door handle. "Drive!"

"Where?" I ask.

"Just go!" she yells.

I do. I drive around and let her cry, because it's all I can think to do.

We end up at my house. I make Amelia text her mom to tell her she'll be at my place, probably staying the night. I'm not sure what makes me act so logical at that moment because inside, I'm totally freaking out over this, but I need to do *something*, and telling Amelia to reach out to her mom feels like that. Plus, it offers a brief, if fleeting, distraction that lets me put my game face on. My best friend needs me. Let's do this.

I bring Amelia into the living room and we sit on the couch.

"I'm so, so sorry," I say.

She looks at me and her face crumples. I pull her to me, let her cry. I try to say things to make her feel better, but I know she's hardly hearing me.

"Everything was going perfectly, Charlie. We had a great dinner. We were laughing, flirting. I told him I loved him. He said it back. And we started, but then I—I couldn't go through with it!" she cries. "I just couldn't."

"That's okay," I say, rubbing her back.

"It's not. It's not! What's wrong with me?" she asks.

"*Nothing* is wrong with you," I say. "It's totally fine not to want to have sex yet."

Amelia furiously rubs at the tears wetting her face. "*Everyone* else has sex, Charlie. And I love him. Yet here I am. Not 'ready' and with no good reason." She lets out a sob. "He just kept saying, 'But I thought you loved me?'"

"Well, that's really shitty of him."

"It's not; he's right!" she says. "Who on earth dates a guy for six months in high school and doesn't sleep with him? I can't even blame him for dumping me!"

I let her cry for a little without trying to interject.

It's rare that I see Amelia this way, and I'm always shocked when it happens. I don't think of her as particularly vulnerable or insecure—but that's stupid, isn't it? Because we're all kind of a wreck inside, at least sometimes.

And imagine my complete shock to find out that my very best friend is struggling with some of the same feelings around sex that I am; that in the same breath that we can say it's fine and theoretically not a big deal and we want it, we can also be feeling like we're just not there yet, for whatever reason, and it's hard not to let that make you feel like a total freak.

I can only imagine the heartbreak of telling someone you love them, hearing they love you, too, but then having them throw that so-called love in your face moments later.

I keep my voice quiet when I speak. "I'm sorry, Amelia. So sorry. If he would try to guilt you into sleeping with him after you told him you loved him, that's fucked up. You're incredible and you deserve better."

"I *hate* him!" Amelia cries.

I squeeze her hand and say, "I know."

Softer, she says, "And I love him."

Another hand squeeze. "I know."

I wish I could do more than dote on her, but I can't, so instead I get her a glass of water, the blanket from my room, and some comfortable clothes (my mom's) to change into. She was doing the same for me just yesterday and yet it feels like eons ago.

"Hungry?" I ask. She nods. I go online and order too much food from our local pizza place. Then I settle next to her on the couch, where she's rubbing her puffy, red eyes. "Do you want to talk?" I ask. "Or we can not talk. We can watch a movie."

"I don't know," she says, and I know that's my cue to take the lead. Sometimes when you're feeling too many things you need someone else to grab the reins. I can do that.

I grab the remote, turn on Netflix, and pick a scary movie. I find it a little hard to concentrate at first (and I'm sure she does, too), but then I get sucked in and nearly jump out of my skin when the doorbell rings and our meal arrives.

I take the food and spread it out on the coffee table in front of us. Food always makes me feel better; I hope it makes her feel better, too.

"You know what we need?" I ask.

Amelia bites into a mozzarella stick. "What?"

"Booze," I say.

She lifts her eyebrows. "Yeah?"

"Yeah! Just a little. I'll be right back."

Despite the fact that Amelia and I are woefully underage, we occasionally sneak into my mom's minibar in the basement and take a few drinks. Nothing serious, and my mom never seems to notice, so now seems like as good a time as any.

I grab four of the Skinny Mini wine coolers and then run upstairs, grinning. I'll admit that stealing these always feels a little thrilling, even if they're just from the basement. I hold them up to show Amelia.

"Yes," she says. "Gimme!"

I throw her a strawberry one and take a raspberry for myself. We twist off the tops, clink them together, and drink. I know that wine coolers are barely alcohol, but Amelia and I always end up with flushed cheeks and feeling a bit more relaxed.

It must work, because soon Amelia seems more willing to talk.

"Boys are the worst," she says.

"They are! All of them."

"Like, you do everything for them, and for what?"

I shake my head. "They don't appreciate anything."

"No. They don't." Amelia frowns. "I'm sad."

I nod. Then I hear a set of keys in the front door. I instinctively grab the empty wine coolers and shove them underneath the couch just before my mom walks in.

And she looks mad.

"Mom, what are you doing home? I thought you had plans," I say, hoping I sound cool, even though my heart is racing.

She ignores me. She throws her purse onto the side table, walks into the living room, and motions for me to move over on the couch. Then she flops down and grabs a slice of pizza.

Amelia and I exchange a look.

"Everything okay?" I ask.

"It's fine," she says.

"Mom. Come on," I say. "What's wrong?"

She shakes her head. "Nothing."

I fight the urge to say that her storming into the house and sitting in the living room but refusing to talk is the real-life equivalent of posting that you're mad but then saying "I don't want to talk about it" when someone asks what's wrong.

"Doesn't seem like nothing," I say.

"Yeah. Tell us," Amelia insists.

My mom takes a bite of the now-room-temperature pizza in her hand and considers this. Then she sighs. "It's just not like I remember it."

"What's not?" Amelia asks.

"Dating." At the sound of the word, I feel myself stiffen a bit. I know she's dating—she has often told me she'll be home late because she's on a date—but I don't like to think about it more than necessary. Not when *I'm* not dating.

"It's all so different now," my mom says. "Texting and Facebooking and Tinder."

"Mom, are you on Tinder?" I ask.

"You have to be these days! If you're not on every single thing, it's like, why bother?" Amelia and I exchange a look and smile. "It's hard. I just don't know."

It's a little cute, if sad, what she's saying.

"I think you're a catch," I say, hoping that bolsters her confidence.

But she just sighs again. "I'm just over all these men! They want so much from you. Be beautiful but not too beautiful; thin but not too thin; feminine but not too feminine. On dates, it's the same thing—talk, but not too much. Ask them questions about themselves, but not too many questions. I'm exhausted."

Amelia looks over at her. "What happened?"

Mom closes her eyes and rubs one of her temples, pizza still in her other hand. "It was a particularly bad date. First of all, this guy, *Keith*"—she says his name like it's a bad disease, and maybe it is—"asks me to meet him at a restaurant an hour away from here, which, fine. Not great, but fine. So I do. I drive all the way out to Fairfield and sit through a date with this guy who can't even string together two sentences that aren't about himself. Or his mom."

"Excuse me?" Amelia asks.

"Yep. Just on and on and on about how his mom is his best friend, his idol. They do everything together, apparently. They've traveled the world, in fact—Paris, Bali, Rome."

I'm sufficiently wigged out by this mother-son closeness. "What on *earth*?"

"I don't even know. And he was so full of himself he didn't ask one thing about me. Every time I tried to talk, he'd either cut me off or turn the conversation right back on him. It was like I wasn't even there. It was an excruciating hour-long dinner—and as we're wrapping, he tells the waitstaff we won't be ordering coffee or dessert without even asking me." My mom rolls her eyes.

"What happened to all that money he supposedly has? Whatever, though, right? But then. Then! Rather than try to make polite conversation while we're waiting on our bill, he's checking his phone. He'd been doing this since at least midmeal, which I thought was *so* rude."

"Was he texting his mom?" I tease.

"I wish," Mom says. "Because before we even get the check, he gets up to excuse himself and I see him walk over to another woman at the bar! He had lined up another date!"

"What?!" Amelia and I exclaim.

"I know! I was not having that. I walked over there and tapped her on the shoulder and told her he had just finished a terrible date with me and she should save herself the trouble and go home." Mom shakes her head. "He was livid, raising his voice in the restaurant and telling her I was lying, like he hadn't literally just wrapped dinner with me mere feet away. I just dropped his credit card and bill down in front of him because Mr. Smartypants hadn't bothered to pick them up and then I stormed out. It was just like, seriously? This is my dating life?"

"Oh my God, Mom. That's horrible!" I say. "I'm so sorry that happened."

"That might be one of the worst dates I've ever heard," Amelia says.

"Right? And it's always me, it feels like. I don't know. I've been really striking out. The guys I've been going out with have just been one bad guy after another. It's like they forget to have manners. I don't even think I'm asking too much, but maybe I'm too old-fashioned now. I just want someone to be nice to me and to make me laugh and to maybe do things like pull out my chair and ask how I'm doing." Mom takes another slice of pizza and takes a bite, looking thoughtful. After swallowing, she starts again, her voice softer now. "Your father *never* would have treated me the way these men are treating me. He was so good to me. Always going out of his way to do little things that meant so much."

The mention of my dad is unexpected and immediately makes me feel a little emotional. I think back to all of the ways he would show my mom he cared, like by doing the chores he knew she hated, and by always letting her win their arguments even when she wasn't right because he knew it meant way more to her to be right than it did to him.

"He was such a good listener," I say.

"Yes! He would give you his undivided attention. It was really something."

I nod. "It was. I loved that. And he really was so goofy and funny."

"You two had the exact same sense of humor," Mom says. "Sometimes I didn't get it at all, but that didn't stop him from going out of his way to make me laugh. He was always just trying his best, and that's what I loved." A wistful smile comes over her face. "I know I will never replace him, *ever*, but I would like someone to treat me a fraction as well." Then she turns to me. "Just— promise me you girls won't devalue yourselves for anyone. And I mean anyone." She takes a good, long look at me and at Amelia. "You can't. You have to really be kind to yourself and look out for yourself because the world can be cold and cruel. Don't feel bad, ever, about putting yourself first. Promise!"

"I promise, Mom."

Amelia casts her gaze downward. "Yes. Promise."

Mom takes notice of Amelia's change in demeanor and sighs. "Sorry. I didn't mean to bring the party down."

Amelia shakes her head. "No, it's okay," she says. "We were already pretty down."

"Oh, no." My mom frowns, then looks over at me. "You doing okay?"

"I'm okay, Mom. Thank you."

"It's actually me," Amelia says. She pauses, as if bracing herself for the next sentence. Quietly, she offers, "Sid broke up with me. On our anniversary."

"What? No!" My mom hugs her. "Oh, Amelia. I'm so sorry."

"Yeah, well, apparently that's what you get when you tell someone you love him but you won't have sex with him," Amelia says, her voice cracking.

I'm shocked that she's shared this so openly, but if my mom is fazed, she doesn't show it. Instead, she wraps Amelia in another giant hug.

"I'm so sorry, honey," she says. "You don't deserve that. Not at all. And any boy who's going to put that kind of pressure on you is a dirtbag. Just an awful, terrible person who you're better off without."

I nod. "You were too good for him, Amelia."

My mom is nodding, too.

"But it hurts. I do love him," Amelia says. "I wish I didn't, but I do."

"You do now, but I promise that'll fade," Mom says. "You know, when I was your age, I fell in love with a boy, too. Jack. Kind of a bad boy. My parents hated him. But just three months together and I was ready to run away with him and get married. We even talked about it. But then I caught him cheating on me with one of my best friends! Scumbag."

"Mom, that's awful!" I say.

"I cried, and cried, and cried for what felt like days. And then one day, I just didn't. I stopped crying. I stopped feeling bad about it. I stopped missing Jack and I moved on. And I promise you, Amelia, you will, too," Mom says. Then she looks at me. "And same with Cal. It stops hurting. It does." With a sly smile, my mom adds, "Besides, Amelia, Sid had terrible hair."

It's so unexpected I burst out laughing and I can't stop. I'm laughing so hard that Amelia starts to laugh, too. My mom full-on grins.

"He *did* have terrible hair," Amelia agrees, still laughing.

"And why so much product?" I ask.

"I always had to wash my hands after I touched his hair," Amelia says. "It was slimy!"

"Ew!" My mom and I say in unison, then laugh some more.

And we keep laughing. We laugh until we're clutching our stomachs, and our eyes are watering, and we can barely breathe, and it's not even that funny, but we still laugh.

Life may be shitty. But in moments like these, everything feels like it might just be all right.

Chapter Fourteen

When I wake up the next morning, it's like last night never happened.

It's like my mom didn't change into her pajamas and join Amelia and me on the couch. It's like she didn't feast with us and then wash it all down with a late-night run for milk shakes. It's like she didn't stay up way too late with us watching scary (terrible) movies. It's like she didn't fall asleep on the chaise, with me on the floor and Amelia on the couch. It's like my mom didn't share a piece of herself with Amelia and me. It's like our impromptu girls' night never happened at all.

It all feels like a dream. I know it happened, yet all evidence of our evening has been scrubbed clean. The living room, except for where Amelia and I were asleep, is back to pristine condition. My mom is nowhere to be found.

And there's one of her meal-replacement shakes waiting for me on the kitchen counter.

I shouldn't be surprised, but I am. Hurt, really. I want to throw the shake through the window. Instead, I open it up and pour its contents in the trash, followed by the bottle, where I hope my mom will see it.

Then I fumble around under the couch, pull out the empty wine coolers, take them directly outside, and put them in the bin beneath another bag. Those I hope my mom won't see.

By then, it's time for school, because yeah, last night was a *school night*, so I wake Amelia and we get ready. We need to make a pit stop at Amelia's house so she can change into some of her own clothes, and as she does, I wait in the car. Through her living room window, I can see Amelia's mom give her a big hug and undoubtedly some comforting words, and I feel a pang in my gut.

Amelia and I don't talk much on the way into school, but as I park the car, I turn to look at her. "You're going to be okay," I say, giving her a smile.

She smiles back at me and says, "Yeah. You too."

It's then that I'm reminded that, oh, yeah. This is my first day back at school since the dance.

And if I hadn't remembered that in the car, I'd have been reminded the moment I got into school because I can hear *everyone* talking about that night. Yet no one is talking about me. And it's then that I realize the stuff between me and Cal was so inconsequential that it didn't even register for most people.

The truth is, if you didn't know I'd showed up to the dance mistakenly thinking I was his date, then what happened on Friday would hardly be notable at all. Maybe a little odd—an overeager junior showed up to support a popular senior at an awards ceremony she was sort-of-but-not-really invited to—but nothing too gossip-worthy. Everyone is preoccupied with their own good (or bad) time at the dance and not at all concerned about me.

For once, I'm grateful to kind of be a nobody.

Nevertheless, it's not a great day.

First, I overhear some seniors talking in the hallway about how Cal Carter and Nova Sanders (the girl who ended up accompanying him to the dance) looked *sooooo* cute together. Turns out, he had quietly asked her to "hang out" with him at the event in case the Amelia thing didn't work out, and she'd accepted! (I want to tell her to have a little dignity, but given that I wanted to go to the dance with Cal so badly that I somehow blocked out the fact that he wasn't actually asking me, I have no room to judge.)

Second, I end up having to participate in gym class. And I hate gym class. Not only am I terrible at it, but I sometimes feel like my gym teacher takes special pride in judging me because I can't run a seven-minute mile. (It's more like a twenty-minute mile because I end up walking. Sue me.)

Third, not only do I have to participate in gym class, but there, in the gymnasium, bobbing up in the rafters, is the balloon I purchased for Cal on Friday. CONGRATS! it reads, taunting me through my worst game of badminton ever.

Fourth—and this is the worst part of all—Cal shows up to my art class and just casually grabs a seat at my and Amelia's table.

"Hey!" he says. He's smiling at us like nothing is wrong.

Amelia practically snarls at him. "What the fuck are you doing here?"

"Whoa, whoa. Can't a guy say hello?"

"No, he can't," she snaps. "Not when he's a fuckboy like you."

It's like watching a tennis match.

"*You're* mad at *me*?" Cal looks bewildered. "If anything, I should be mad at you two. Amelia, I thought you were coming on Friday."

"Why on earth would you think that? You didn't ask me," Amelia says. "You asked Charlie, and then it meant nothing to you that she showed up!"

"I asked Charlie to *bring you*. The plan was always that you and I would go to the dance together." He looks over at me. "Tell her, Charlie."

As if I'm going to defend him.

"You're a coward," Amelia says coldly.

"For fuck's sake, Amelia, what's your problem?" Cal asks, but I have a feeling he's not looking for an answer. "Look, I get it. You made it loud and clear when you didn't bother to show up for the dance. You don't want to date me."

"Of course I don't want to date you! I've been telling you that for months. I have a boyfriend!"

Then Amelia looks at me, realizing that she's actually single, and I know I have to get Cal out of here.

"Enough, Cal," I say. "Please leave."

"What? Charlie, not you too," he says, cajoling.

"Cal," I repeat.

"Can't I just get your history homework first? I didn't have time to do it this weekend."

Ugh. SERIOUSLY?! This no-good, selfish, floppy-haired *motherfucker* who is *obviously* peaking in high school! Fuck. This. Guy.

"Just get the hell out of here, Cal!" I yell. "And don't bother Amelia or me again. I mean it!"

Mr. Reed has made his way over to our table now. "Everything okay here?" he asks, looking at Cal. "Calvin, this isn't your class."

"Cal was just leaving," I say.

"Please. Or I'll be forced to write you up," Mr. Reed says.

"This is bullshit," Cal mutters, getting to his feet.

"What was that?" Mr. Reed asks.

"Nothing," Cal says. He slinks out of the room.

Mr. Reed looks at Amelia and me. "You sure everything is okay?"

We nod. "Yes," I say.

"All right. Just watch the language, okay?"

I nod some more. "Yes. I'm sorry."

Mr. Reed walks away from our table, and Amelia stares down at the watercolor paints in front of her. "I don't have a boyfriend anymore."

"No," I say. "But you're going to be okay."

She sighs. "Maybe."

* * *

I wish I could say that after art class, my day started looking up.

It did not.

At work, Dora immediately asked me how everything worked out with Cal. And I had to make up a lie about him being sick, about us not getting to go together. She seemed crushed, probably because she was really rooting for me—a fat girl getting the cute, popular boy. That's like the storybook dream for fat girls everywhere. I get it. I feel bad that I've disappointed her.

But at least I get to hang out with Brian at the end of my shift. Nancy tells me they're swamped in the warehouse and could really use my help today. I don't even mind that I'll be working really hard; I could use a friend.

"Hey," he says as I walk through the warehouse doors, waving as if he's been waiting for me.

"Hey."

"So, we don't really need the help back here."

"What?"

A proud look overtakes Brian's face. "I lied. I told Nancy we did, but yeah, we definitely don't. I just thought…you know…we could goof off for a little bit."

I grin. "Well, I'm in. I really need the distraction."

Brian smiles. "Good. Me too. I told Dave that you're helping me with inventory and I'm pretty sure he was all, 'What's inventory, again?'"

I do an impression of Dave. "Work? Never heard of it."

We both laugh as we head to the storage room. Brian grabs a seat on a stool and lets me take the swivel chair. I immediately start to maneuver the chair back and forth.

"Want me to spin you?" Brian offers.

"Like, in a circle?"

"Yeah, of course!"

"What? Really? No!" I say with a laugh, but I don't stop moving the chair left and right.

"Are you suuure? It's pretty awesome."

I grin. "Okay. Yes!"

I tuck my legs beneath me on the seat. Brian grabs the arm of the chair in one hand and starts to run in a circle, spinning the seat with him, faster and faster, before letting go. I spin a million times in a row and erupt into laughter.

It's silly, but I feel so light and airy in that moment. Brian's laughing as he watches me spin around and around, and when I start to slow down, I offer him next up.

He shakes his head, but he's smiling. "All you," he says. "Want to go again?"

"No," I say, smiling back. "I might throw up if we do that again."

"Fair enough. Hey, so, how was the dance this weekend?"

I give him a look. "Ha ha. Very funny." There's no way he hasn't heard about the amazing Cal Carter and Nova Sanders.

He furrows his brows. "What? Did it not go well?"

"Are you messing with me right now?"

"I'm genuinely asking."

"Oh." I swivel back and forth in the chair some more. "I thought you might have heard what happened. Especially in art class?"

Brian shakes his head. "I missed art class today. Dentist appointment."

"Oh, yeah."

He chuckles. "Gee, you didn't even notice I wasn't around?"

"No, no. I'm sorry. On any other day, I would have noticed. I swear. Today was just an exceptionally bad day." I look over at Brian, and he's turned his body to face me completely, giving me his full attention. I can't *not* share what happened with him. "I guess I'll start with the dance? Spoiler alert: it was awful."

Brian frowns. "I'm sorry. What happened, if you don't mind me asking?"

"So, in one of my most embarrassing moments yet, it turns out that Cal didn't exactly intend to invite me to the dance as his date. He only invited me so I'd bring Amelia."

"*What?*"

"I know. Apparently, in my excitement, I didn't hear that part, which sounds more unbelievable each time I say it. So then, when I got there, Cal just kept asking me where Amelia was. He couldn't have cared less about me. It was awful. He was sort of envisioning the dance as the moment he finally got the girl—Amelia, not me."

"My God," Brian says quietly. "That's brutal."

"Yeah. I just feel *so* stupid. I was just so caught up in the thrill of being asked out by Cal Carter that I couldn't see the truth: that he'd never in a million years date someone like me." I bury my face in my hands.

"Hey, no."

"I fell for the whole thing without question," I say, looking up at him. "I guess...in fairness to me...he really turned the charm up to the next level, especially leading up to the dance. He even gave me a stupid rose with my name on it to ask me to be his date—or fake date, whatever."

"Honestly, Charlie," Brian says, concerned, "it sounds like he led you on. How is that your fault at all?"

I groan. "I don't know. I should've known better. But it makes perfect sense, you know? *Everyone* prefers Amelia."

"That's not true at all."

"I mean, yeah, it kind of is. It's been true since I've known her. If you knew how many times guys have picked her over me, you'd pity me. If you knew how many times my own *mom* has picked Amelia over me, you'd lose it. Literally my mom's job once had a Take Your Daughter to Work Day and instead of just taking me, she took me *and* Amelia. Who does that? But, I mean, I get it. Amelia is this perfect, beautiful, ethereal being, and I'm just..." I refrain from letting all the adjectives I think about myself spill out and instead motion toward myself. "I'm just me. Honestly, given the choice between the two of us, I'd pick Amelia, too. *Every* time."

Brian looks taken aback. He emphatically says, "Don't say that."

I double down. "Well, it's true. And on top of all that, in art class today, Cal waltzed up to me and sat at our table. He asked if he could have my history homework. Like nothing happened!" I laugh, a little bit to keep from crying. I feel like I want to, so I look away from Brian. "So stupid, right?"

"*Shit.* I'm so sorry, Charlie. What an asshole," Brian says, a tone to his voice I haven't heard before. I look over at him. His jaw is locked, nostrils flared. "I could punch him."

"You and me both," I say. Then I take a breath, regaining my composure. "Anyway, the good news is I got to yell at him publicly. That felt pretty good."

"I bet," Brian says with a small smile. "But still…fuck. That is…a lot."

"Yeah," I say, sighing. "And you were right, you know. He *is* a doorknob."

His expression softens. "I'm sorry. I wish I hadn't been right. You deserve better."

I shake my head. "I'm not sure I do." Against my wishes, I feel a tear squeeze out and roll down my cheek. "You know, even my mother had suspicions about the fact that Cal asked me to go with him."

"That must've felt terrible," Brian says, putting a hand on my shoulder. "I'm really sorry this all happened, Charlie."

I dab at my eyes with my fingers and sniffle. "Thanks, Brian. I'm sorry I unloaded on you like that."

Brian waves a hand "Don't be. It's clearly been a hell of a few days for you. You can't keep that all bottled up."

"I really appreciate it," I say. "I'm sure nothing as horrifically mortifying has ever happened to you."

"Well, I'm not the kind for one-upping, but I did wet my pants in the first grade," Brian says, and it's so unexpected that I laugh.

"But you were just a kid! That really doesn't seem so bad."

"You weren't the one that peed in front of your classmates while giving a presentation on bears." Brian laughs. "But truthfully, I've had my fair share of mortifying moments. Maybe not like what happened to you, necessarily, but I *did* once try to shoot my shot with an older girl—Marissa Thompson—and it was awful. I was in ninth grade and had somehow ended up friendly with her and her friends and decided the absolute best thing I could do was ask her out in a big way. A public way."

I suck in a breath through my teeth. "Oh, no."

"Oh, no, indeed," Brian agrees. "I was inspired by all those football players asking their dates to the dance and decided to just go for it. She was obsessed with really old movies and loved this one called *Say Anything*…where apparently this guy in, like, a trench coat holds up a boom box and plays a song to get a girl. Cut to me, also in a weird trench coat, holding up my phone, playing that same song in the parking lot as I waited for Marissa and her sophomore friends to get out of class."

My eyes go wide picturing this. "Oh, *no*."

Brian's cheeks flush a little red. "Oh, *yes*. They show up, I literally fumble with my phone before I can even get the song to play, *finally* get it to play, and Marissa and her friends just bust out laughing. One girl even made a crack about how the guy in the movie wasn't Asian."

"Seriously? A nice, healthy dose of racism on top of everything?"

He sighs. "Yep. Totally crushed my spirit."

"That's terrible, Brian. I'm so sorry!"

"I was, too. But I'm still here, right? And Marissa Thompson is...God knows where."

"Well, who cares?"

"*Exactly*. Who cares?" Brian looks over at me. "All I'm saying is that even though it feels horrible now, soon it won't. Soon Cal and his shitty behavior won't matter and anyone who might've witnessed what happened will forget and you won't feel so bad for putting your heart out there. Most people refuse to give things a shot, but you tried, Charlie. That's something."

I smile at him. "I don't think you understand how badly I needed to hear that."

In response, he smiles back with that crooked little grin, and I can't help it: my heart—my broken, torn-up, never-going-to-feel-again heart—flutters a little.

Chapter Fifteen

I'm grateful when it's the weekend again.

A week of emotional turmoil has left me feeling really raw, so I'm very much looking forward to spending some time being an introvert in my room—scrolling through Insta, writing, maybe snacking on food that's not super great for me.

Imagine my surprise when I check the fridge and pantry to find that they contain chicken, spinach, cottage cheese, seltzer water, and my mother's beloved shakes, but barely anything else. Can't a girl just indulge in some stress eating? It's been a *week*!

I want to ask my mom what's going on and end up finding her down in the basement doing Zumba along with a YouTube video she's pulled up on the downstairs TV.

"Everything okay, Mom?" I ask.

She turns to look at me, then goes back to her workout. "Why wouldn't it be?"

"I don't know. Just asking."

Mom turns the question on me. "Are *you* okay?"

"Yeah, I'm fine," I say slowly. "But I *am* pretty confused about what happened to all the food in the house. We barely have anything."

My mom stretches. "We have plenty of food in this house."

"Not sure you and I share the same definition of *plenty,* but all right."

"Lots of healthy, delicious things to eat. Spinach, arugula, kale, chicken…"

I sigh. "I want Pop-Tarts."

She looks at me and wrinkles her nose. "Really, Charlie?" Then she returns to her workout. "How about a shake?"

I make a gagging noise. "I'm good."

"I had a feeling. Found the shake I gave you earlier this week in the trash, poured out. What a waste."

"Oh," I say. "That."

"Yeah. That." In between air kicks in time to the Zumba music, she says, "I pay good money for those shakes and I don't appreciate you throwing them out like that. If you don't want to drink them, fine, but no need to waste them."

"All right. It's just that I didn't really appreciate you leaving me a shake to drink after what I thought was a nice night, but okay."

"The company was nice. The food was not." Mom shakes her head. "I can't believe I let myself eat like that, let *you* eat like that. We put so much garbage in our bodies that night. It's gross."

"Right. So gross." I turn around and start heading upstairs. "Okay, Mom."

"Okay is right," she calls after me. "We're turning over a new leaf in the Vega household! I'm calling it Fitness First!"

I walk away before she can continue.

* * *

Only, the next day, I realize my mom is not letting this turning-over-a-new-leaf thing go. She comes home from a shopping trip with a giant whiteboard calendar. She puts it on display in the kitchen and writes *Fitness First* across the top, then her name in one color and mine in another.

"What's this for?" I ask.

"We're going to keep track of our weights!" Mom says. "We'll weigh ourselves each day and we'll write it down."

"No," I say.

"Yes!"

"Absolutely not."

"Charlie, yes. It will keep us accountable," she insists. Then she reaches into her bag and pulls out a scale. "I even bought a new scale to go with it."

I can feel my heart thumping just looking at it. There is no way in hell I am going to subject myself to this humiliation. What, so my mom can have concrete proof that I'm not losing weight and throw that in my face? No way.

"You can have fun. But I'm not doing it."

By the look on her face, I can tell she's annoyed. "You're doing it. We're not going to just keep eating poorly and not working out. Not anymore." She pulls the scale out of its box and puts it on the ground. "I'll go first."

"No," I say, trying to keep my voice firm, but I can't look away from the scale as it reads her weight, and I feel gutted when I realize she weighs less than my (secret) dream weight.

She shakes her head. "Not where I want to be." Sighing heavily, she looks at me. "You see? We both have work to do."

I feel queasy watching her write the numbers on the whiteboard.

"You can take care of that work on your own," I say. "I'm not going to be part of this."

"And why not?"

"This feels like a sick mind game."

"Mind game? What do you even mean by that?"

I scowl at her. "I'm not going to be part of this weird routine where we display our weights publicly to shame ourselves. Are we supposed to wear scarlet letters, too? That's messed up, Mom, and I'm not going to do it!"

"Why do you always have to act like this, Charlie? You always overreact. Always!" She crumples up the plastic bag and aggressively shoves it into the weird collection of plastic bags we have hanging from the pantry door.

"I'm overreacting?! You're the one freaking out because you ate a fucking mozzarella stick! Jesus, Mom, live a little!"

She shoots eye daggers at me. "Language! Show a little respect here!"

"I don't really feel like you're respecting me right now, so I'll pass."

"Oh, you'll pass, huh? I'm so sick of that mouth on you."

I give her a sarcastic smile. "I'm sick of literally everything about you, so great. We're even."

"You think you're so goddamn smart, Charlie, but I've had it!" she says. "I'm trying to do something nice. Something good. And *this* is how you repay me?"

"Nice? Good?" I laugh, and it comes out like venom. "You just want to embarrass me! You're delusional."

"And you're in denial! You try to pretend you're happy, but I *know* you're not. You're not doing well."

"I'm not sick, Mom, I'm just fat!"

Mom visibly recoils at the *f-word*. "Don't say that."

"But I am! I'm fat!" I gesture toward my body. "And it's okay, Mom. I'm allowed to be fat!"

"No, Charlotte. It's not okay. It's not *healthy*. I would know."

"Don't you dare try to lecture me about what's healthy. You peddle weird pyramid-scheme shakes for fun. You don't eat actual food and you try to force your messed-up views about bodies on me, too! All I ever hear from you is that I look wrong, eat wrong, dress wrong! You didn't even believe a boy would ask me to a dance! *You're* the one who's not happy with me! So congratulations! You're a terrible mother!"

The silence that falls between us is deafening.

My mother takes a breath. "I think you need to go to your room," she says.

I try to protest. "Mom, I didn't—"

"Now. Go."

Chapter Sixteen

I'm grounded. Understandably. I want to apologize to my mom—I went *way* too far—but it's not really the kind of thing we do.

Instead, she lays out the rules of my punishment and I quietly listen.

No going out—except to my titi's upcoming gender reveal party, which I wasn't planning on going to but am now being forced to attend.

No internet, except for homework. Ugh.

No phone. So I can't even sneak on the internet! Or talk to anyone! Or do anything!

And no work. That one makes me mad. No work means no money, and absolutely zero time away from the house (or Mom) except for school. It feels *mean*. What does she even gain from that? Does this qualify as cruel and unusual punishment?

But I suck it up, and first thing on Monday, I call my boss… using the *landline*. I need to tell Nancy I won't be in the next day, or maybe the next few days. I'm unable to come up with a good excuse, so my plan is to keep it vague. When I tell Nancy I won't be in for a while, she gets incredibly concerned and starts asking me if something happened at work, so I end up telling her that I'm grounded, and for whatever reason, I start crying. Thankfully, Nancy is endlessly kind to me and tells me not to worry and she hopes I'll be back soon, but to take as much time as I need.

I have to wait to tell Amelia what happened until I see her *at school*. Like this is the goddamn 1900s or something. I rattle off my punishments, counting them off on each finger. Amelia gasps at each.

"No *phone*?" That elicits the loudest gasp. Obvi.

"No phone," I repeat, shaking my head. "And lastly, no work."

At that, her brows furrow. "Wait, what? Seriously? No work? Charlie, that's weird, and…well, fucked up. Like, really fucked up. Jobs aren't for *fun*. You shouldn't be grounded from a *job*. It's not normal for parents to do that."

I sigh. "Don't get me started."

Her face doesn't clear, but she says nothing. She knows when I'm done talking about my mom.

In study hall, we get on the topic of movies and we struggle to remember an actor's name, so Amelia tells me to just Google it and I have to dramatically hold up my empty, phoneless hands.

"Oh my God. I forgot!" she says. "God, what's it like?"

"Terrible," I say. "You know, my mom is actively keeping me from becoming a more knowledgeable person."

"I can't believe she's doing this to you. No phone? Why not just murder you and call it a day?"

"I know." I pick at my nails. "I *do* wish I hadn't called her a terrible mom."

"Yeah, well, she's not innocent, either. She said some incredibly hurtful stuff, Charlie. Stuff that's not at all true."

"I guess," I say, unconvinced.

"No, I mean it." She lowers her voice and leans closer to me. "The way she talks to you sometimes—you know that's not okay, right?"

I don't look at her but shrug. "That's just how she talks."

"It doesn't matter. My mom would literally never say that stuff to me—ever!"

"Your mom is also one of the sweetest people on the whole

planet," I say, busying myself by flipping through one of my note-books. Amelia thinks families do things like "communicate" and "be kind to each other" and "show mutual respect," because *her* family (and her whole life!) is freakishly perfect.

"No one's mom should talk to them the way your mom talks to you. Moms are supposed to, like, build you up. Make you feel good. At the very least, they're not supposed to make you feel *worse* about yourself."

"Can we just drop it, please?" I ask.

"I'm just saying it's not okay, and you should know that."

"Yeah, it's not okay," I say briskly. "But it'll be fine."

. * .

At lunch, Brian flags me over to his table, and I'm grateful that we saw each other so I can let him know he won't be seeing me at work. He's surrounded by guy friends who smile and greet me warmly.

"Got a sec, Brian?" I ask.

"Oh, yeah, for sure," Brian says. "Want to go for a quick walk to the vending machines?" There aren't a lot of places we're allowed to go without a pass, but the vending machines just outside the cafeteria offer one option.

"That'd be great."

"Be back," Brian says to his friends; then he hops up from the table and motions for us to go. When we're out of earshot, he asks, "Everything good?"

"Yes and no," I admit. "I'm grounded."

"Grounded?! You steal a car or something, Charlie?"

"God, I wish. That'd be pretty badass, at least. No, I just got into a huge fight with my mom, so I'm banished from pretty much everything, including work."

He arches an eyebrow at me, slowing down his pace as we walk. "Grounded from work?"

"I know. My mom is an interesting lady," I say. "She's just really hard on me and knows how to push me right to the edge, and, well…she said some things and I said some things and it wasn't my finest moment." I hesitate, then add: "I told her she was a terrible mother."

Brian gives me a sympathetic look. We stop in front of the vending machines and he turns to me.

"I'm sorry that happened. But you aren't the kind to just lash out without a good reason, Charlie. You're a good person," he says quietly.

"You are, too. Always giving great pep talks. I don't know what I've done to deserve it." I smile at him. "And…since I *am* abandoning you at work and all, you can at least let me buy you a snack. Are you more of Snickers or Doritos kind of guy?" He gives me a look. "Oh! Right. Savory snacks. You told me that already. Doritos it is." I swipe my card on the machine and buy two bags, which we start to munch on as we walk slowly back into the cafeteria.

"How long are you grounded for?"

I roll my eyes. "That's the best part. It's delightfully ambiguous!"

Brian returns the eye roll. "Oh, wonderful. Well, thanks for the heads-up. I'd have been looking for you."

I nod, taking some joy in that, at least. "So until I'm out of exile, I guess we'll just see each other in art?"

"Try and stop me," Brian says with a grin.

I go straight home after school rather than doing, oh, I don't know, anything else. I know I have to show my mom I'm sorry if I want things to eventually go back to normal for me. And I am remorseful over the fact that I hurt her. But the way we fight just doesn't seem right. The way we make up could use some work, too. We don't apologize; once my mom has stopped talking to me, I just have to deal until one day she decides we're fine and acts like nothing happened. I hate it, but it's just how it is.

So I do my best to repent by taking on chores: doing the dishes, making a healthy dinner, and even cleaning my room. Mom's excellent at giving me the cold shoulder, though.

For days, I'm exiled.

But things aren't all bad. Writing, Amelia, and sleep help keep me sane.

At school, it seems as if Amelia and I have fallen off Cal's radar completely. No more hellos in the hallway. No more whispering in history class. He doesn't even ask me to copy my homework. In fact, he pretty much acts like the two of us don't exist, and that's fine by us. I'm actually thankful for it, mostly because I worry I'd be such a pushover that if he tried to talk to me again, I might give in. Better that he doesn't tempt me.

Amelia is trying to move on from Sid, which I think is wise. Word eventually gets out that she's single, so there's plenty of flirting directed at her. She even flirts back a little. Not because she's really over him, but because she's too goddamn stubborn to let him get the best of her.

* * *

In art class one day, as I'm gathering the acrylic paints Amelia and I need from the art supply closet, Brian finds me. The two of us haven't really spent much time together since I've been grounded.

"Hey!" he says.

"Hey, Brian!" I say, excited to see him.

"Back to work soon?"

I sigh, reaching for the white paint bottle. "I wish."

He starts to look through the paints, too, selecting the ones he needs and balancing them in his arms. "Still no luck getting through to your mom, huh?"

I shake my head. "Hopefully soon."

"Hopefully," Brian says. "Oh! So, I'm kind of a big deal."

"Oh, yeah?"

He grabs the last paint bottle he needs and adds it to the bundle he's carrying. "Yep. I get to pick what we listen to today."

Getting to select the music in our art class is kind of a thing. It started with this old, junky stereo that Mr. Reed brought in. He'd put on one of his ancient CDs on days we were all working on our projects rather than listening to him teach a lesson. It was mostly oldies—like from the eighties and nineties—but every now and then, he began to let someone from class pick the music. He told us we could bring in our CDs, but hardly any of us owned any. (He got weirdly upset, actually, when one of the students jokingly asked if they still made those.) Instead, he eventually gave up and let us play music from Spotify.

"Amazing! What are we going to listen to?"

Not missing a beat, Brian says, "I'm thinking the Smiths."

I smile and roll my eyes. "Of *course* you are."

"What's that supposed to mean?"

"Nothing! It's just that it's a total boy thing to like that band."

"They're a great band!" he insists.

I shrug. "They are. I'm just saying."

"Yeah, yeah," Brian says, smiling. "You have a better suggestion?"

"Hmm. Lion Babe?" I offer.

"I wouldn't say it's a *better* choice, but it's good. I'll give you that."

"Brian?" a voice calls just before Layla pokes her head into the closet. "There you are! Mr. Reed needs help carrying the easels into the class. They're in the storage room."

"Sure. Be right there." Brian looks at me. "They only need me for my brute strength," he says, and I laugh. "See you in there."

I finish picking out the paints for a painting of Central Park in winter that I'm about to embark on, and then I head back into the art room.

When I get to my table, Amelia's already got our canvases set up on our easels and Brian's music is playing. Only it's not the Smiths. It's Lion Babe.

Chapter Seventeen

Try as I might to get out of going to Titi Lina's gender reveal party, Mom won't budge. Not even after I caved and said I was sorry.

It's been a while since we've seen Titi and the family, she says, and she keeps reminding me that I'm grounded and I need to be on my best behavior if I ever wish to be ungrounded.

I'm not big into parties in the first place, even though we used to go to parties all the time when I was little. My dad only had one younger sister, Titi, but they had a huge extended family with dozens and dozens of cousins, mostly from Puerto Rico. (I think half of the people he called his cousins weren't really his cousins at all, just friends who had become like family.) They had carved out their own little community in this—let's be honest—otherwise pretty white area of Connecticut, and someone was always finding a reason to get together, eat, and drink. My mom liked to joke that they'd throw a party whenever someone sneezed. ¡Wepa!

As a kid, I always felt super out of place at these parties. Though I was surrounded by people who looked like me, I still felt like an outsider. They all spoke English *and* Spanish, for one. (Papi almost never spoke Spanish at home, so I only ever picked up on a few words here and there.) Plus, they all seemed so comfortable together, laughing and dancing to Latin music. The adults drank and traded chisme, the younger kids did a lot of running around and playing games, and the older kids would just kind of hang out.

I'd sometimes try to join my cousins who were around my age, but I always felt awkward. It's not even like they were mean to me or anything. I just felt too embarrassed for liking One Direction and Taylor Swift, for speaking like a "white person" (their words) rather than with an accent, for going to school in a super-white town and having mostly white friends. Truth be told, I sometimes even felt like I was better than them—getting a better education in my white-ass town, speaking perfect English. How messed up is that? They knew two languages and there I was thinking I was hot shit because I knew what an Oxford comma was. Hey, internalized racism. How you doing?

It was especially ironic because it's not like I felt like I fit in super well with my white peers, either. (They always asked me things like "Can I touch your hair?" or "What are you doing for Cinco de Mayo?" or "Do you know So-and-so?" in reference to anyone who shared my last name or also happened to be Puerto Rican.)

After Dad passed, Mom and I stopped going to as many parties with his family, though we were always invited. To the few parties we did attend, she'd often let me bring Amelia so I'd have a buddy.

And that's when genius strikes: I need to ask if Amelia can come to *this* party with me.

I casually mention it to my mom, who lights up at the suggestion. So I call Amelia (again, on the *landline*—when will I be free of this torture?) to extend the invite.

She answers and says, "I can't believe I have to talk to you on the phone rather than text. That's friendship."

"No, true friendship is coming with me to my aunt's gender reveal party!"

"Lina?" Amelia asks, surprised.

"Yes, it's this weekend, and I know you want to come." I sigh. "My mom's forcing me to go."

"I didn't even know Lina was pregnant. Thanks for sharing."

"Sorry! You know I'm not super close with them anymore. But will you come?"

"Maaaaybe. When is it?"

"Saturday. We can come pick you up. Please come, Amelia. It'll be just like when we were younger! I'll even dance!" Amelia would always try to get me to dance with her, but I would hang back and let her dance with my cousins instead.

"You will?"

"I mean...I'll *consider* it," I say, backtracking.

"Well, then, I guess I'll just *consider* going."

"Okay, fine. I'll do it. I'll dance!"

"Yes! Then I'm in!"

* * *

On Saturday, Mom and I swing by Amelia's house to pick her up and head to Titi's. We don't bring gifts, because in a few weeks there will be a formal baby shower where we can buy and give the appropriately gendered toys (insert eyeroll here). But we do wear pink or blue, which we've been asked to do to show whether we're #TeamGirl or #TeamBoy. I wear a pink cardigan, but Mom and Amelia both go with blue—Mom because she's convinced Lina will have a boy, and Amelia just because she has a new blue dress she really wanted to wear.

When we get to Titi's, we're greeted by pink and blue balloons on either side of the front door, and when we step through into the Cape Cod–style house, it's like a party store (albeit a classy one) has thrown up all over their home. The sleek and modern furniture has been covered in pink and blue: streamers, paper lanterns, garland, artfully placed confetti.

We're barely into the living room when one of my cousins, Ana, exclaims, "Well, well, well, look who's here!" She gives me and Mom and Amelia a kiss on each cheek—a tradition for us when entering or leaving a party—and then yells for Titi, who appears in the room looking tiny as ever, short, slim, her pregnancy nearly imperceptible except for a sweet little bump.

"Oh my goodness, hi! How are you?" Titi asks, rushing to plant kisses on my cheeks. Even pregnant, Titi is so beautiful—petite, with the cutest round belly; soft brown skin, shiny with that pregnant-lady glow; long, wavy, black-brown hair, thick and textured (note to self: ask what products she uses!); and long black eyelashes I wish I'd managed to inherit, too.

"Good, how are you?" I ask. "You look great!"

Titi rubs her belly and laughs. "I feel huge," she says, her adorable accent coming out on the word *huge*. She turns to Amelia and gives her two kisses as well. "Good to see you!"

"You too, Lina. Thanks for having me," Amelia says with a smile.

Titi waves her hand. "You're always welcome! *You* dance with us. We like that," she says, laughing. Then she gets to Mom and doesn't just give her two kisses but wraps her in a big, long hug as they rock back and forth.

"It's been too long," Mom says.

"Yes, it has!" Titi says, pulling back. "Look at you! So small now!"

I can tell my mom is pleased with the compliment by the big smile that spreads across her face. "Oh, no, not really," she says.

"Yes, really. Beautiful," Titi says. "But you need to get your asses over here more. All of you. Or else!"

We laugh, and Mom motions toward Titi's belly. "Can you believe it?"

Titi grabs my mom's hand and places it over her stomach. "No, but José and I are so excited. And with you three to celebrate! Come, come." She leads us beyond the foyer and farther into her home, which is packed with people.

The music is already bumping, and I glance around to see that no detail has been overlooked: in the adjacent dining room, the table has been pushed all the way to the side and is covered in pink and blue cups and utensils and treats (like glass bowls filled with colored candy and a massive pink and blue cupcake tower). There's also a white backdrop hanging from one of the walls, adorned with twinkling lights and pink and blue balloons that spell out OH, BABY (obvi the dedicated selfie spot). And I can smell the delicious Puerto Rican food, undoubtedly brimming in all-too-familiar aluminum trays, from here.

"Want a drink, Titi Jeanne?" Ana asks.

Mom nods. "I'll take a Corona," she says, which I haven't seen her drink since the last party here. I kind of wish I could have a drink, too, because I'm full of nerves being back around family I haven't seen in ages.

Instead, Amelia and I find some more of my cousins—Marisol, Carmen, Mateo, Junior, and Maritza—all crowded in the kitchen at the island, hovering over their phones. We start talking about a new song Mateo is obsessed with, which he's currently playing on his phone over the *other* music that's already blasting.

"I wish they'd let me DJ," Mateo says. "*This* is music."

Carmen, Mateo's sister, rolls her eyes. "You're so dumb sometimes."

"Don't call me dumb, stupid," Mateo says.

"Well, don't *be* dumb, stupid," Carmen shoots back.

"Guys, enough," Ana says, shaking her head.

"I *live* for the new Cardi B song," Amelia says, returning us to the topic of music.

Maritza perks up at the mention of Cardi. "Oh my God, same. Put it on!" she says, and just like that, Mateo switches the song. Maritza immediately jumps off her stool and starts to dance to the opening notes.

Marisol and Carmen join in, and so does Amelia, and I find

myself envying the way she so easily makes herself part of the conversation *and* the action. Meanwhile, I'm standing near them, sort of but not really bobbing along to the music and singing along to only the parts I know (the chorus mostly).

But the dancing is contagious, and a few of the adults start to dance, too, to the mix of songs playing. Even as the music shifts, people keep dancing and laughing, and Titi Lina and Mom start to dance, too.

I smile at everyone but use this as an opportunity to slip away to get something to drink. I've fulfilled my promise to Amelia: I danced, sort of, and all within the first twenty minutes after arrival. So I slink off to the corner of the kitchen, where I don't have to watch as Mom and Amelia dance together, looking more like mother and daughter than Mom and I ever have. I go on my phone for a bit instead. (Mom is letting me have it 'for the night'—very generous.)

Awhile later, Titi Lina spots me as she prepares a plate of food for herself. "What are you doing in here all alone, mi'ja?"

"Nothing," I say. "Just taking a little break."

"Can I get you something to eat?"

"No, I'm good. But thank you."

She piles some rice onto her plate as well as a few tostones and I expect her to return to the living room, but instead she joins me at the counter where I've been standing.

"You know, I sometimes get overwhelmed at these things, too."

I'm surprised. "You do?"

Titi Lina nods, then points at her belly. "These days especially. I get tired so quickly. I can't get down like your tío can."

"Who could?" I ask, and we both laugh.

"Sometimes you remind me so much of your papi. Both so quick," Titi says, and there's a tug at my heart. "It's hard to believe Héctor won't burst through the door and tell us some out-of-control story of his."

"He did always have the best stories," I agree. "They came with their fair share of embellishments, maybe, but that's what made them so good."

"Of course. We didn't even care if they were true half the time because they were just so fun to listen to. I miss him."

"I miss him, too," I say, giving her a soft smile.

Titi reaches over and squeezes my hand. "You know, we love having you and your mom here. You know you can come by any-time. We're still family."

"Thanks, Titi."

She smiles at me. "I'm going to get back out there before your tío comes looking."

I wish I could say this is the part where I find a way to break out of my shell, say screw it, and go over and start dancing with everyone—or start having an enthralling conversation with one of my cousins, or even start telling some funny stories that make other people laugh, but none of that's true. It means a lot that Titi Lina has extended an invitation to me to visit more, but it's still a little painful to be in these surroundings without my dad, and to feel so woefully out of place in my own family while my best friend fits in like magic. So as those around me have fun dancing, drinking, playing party games, and eating, I find myself sneaking away to corners where I can mostly be alone.

Even when Titi Lina and Tío José finally pop a giant balloon and blue confetti flies everywhere, I can't really enjoy it because Tío makes the sign of the cross on his head and chest and starts telling everyone how thank *God* he's having a boy and not a girl, and that's so rude to me.

But mostly, I just sort of watch as Amelia is a perfect hit with everyone, picking right up where we left off like no time has passed since we were last here. My girl cousins dance with her like there's no tomorrow. My boy cousins laugh at her jokes and sneak her booze. Junior hits on her and she giggles.

I'm miserable and sad and envious and all too grateful when we finally leave. I have to drive us home (I'm the only one sober), and after I drop Amelia off, my mom turns to me. "Well, that was fun, wasn't it?"

"Yes," I say, backing out of Amelia's driveway and into the street. "A blast."

Chapter Eighteen

Titi Lina's party aside, there isn't much excitement in my life these days. By week three of being grounded, I'm bored. Really bored. Mind-numbingly bored.

The days pass by well enough, but the nights are slow. And the weekends *kill me*.

I can't talk to Amelia—not that she's home much, anyway. She's been casually dating a few people, including my cousin Junior, because *of course* a person that perfect doesn't stay single for long.

I can't go anywhere, except for walks around the block, which I do, often, especially now that the weather is warming up and we're inching closer to spring. (Forty-degree days definitely feel like spring after months of frigid New England temperatures.)

I can't even kill time by messing around on the internet, which depresses me because I love the internet and I know I'm just missing so many good jokes on Twitter. So my riveting Saturday afternoons mostly consists of me lying on the couch watching Kardashian reruns.

I'm rewatching one of the old episodes—back when Kylie and Kendall were just kids—when my mom walks into the room.

"Hey," she says. After the party, we've resumed our routine of barely uttering a word to each other, so I'm surprised by this.

"Hi." I sit up.

"I'm heading to the gym. You wanna tag along?"

Normally, I'd be offended by this. We did just get in a fight about my weight, after all.

But I'm bored. So bored.

"Okay," I say.

"I'm leaving in ten minutes. Think you can be ready?"

"Absolutely."

I turn off the TV and go into my room, where I change into a sports bra, leggings, a T-shirt, and some sneakers. I also grab a water and my ancient iPod, which I haven't used since I was a kid, just so I can have something to listen to while I work out.

By the time I'm ready, my mom's already in the car. She's wearing pink athletic gear, all of which matches, and she looks amazing, which makes me second-guess my thrown-together outfit.

We don't talk much on the way to the gym. As we walk inside, two women my mom's age wave at us.

"Hi, Jeanne!" the shorter one says.

"Hi, ladies!" my mom says in a chipper voice.

"Is this Charlotte?" the taller one asks.

"Yes, it is! Charlotte, this is Jen." My mom points at the tall redheaded lady. "And that's Becca." She points at the short blond woman. "Becca got me into the shakes."

My eyes narrow at her, but I say nothing.

"So good to meet you!" Jen says, shaking my hand.

"We've heard so much about you!" Becca says.

I give them a smile. "I've heard a lot about you guys, too." It's not exactly true, but I do know of them. Jen and Becca are my mom's gym buddies. They meet there a couple of times each week, and they help motivate one another to work out. I think my mom knows Jen from work, but I have no idea where she met Becca. Probably Facebook. The three of them love yoga and Zumba.

"You ladies ready to dance?" Jen asks, smiling over at me.

"Oh, no, I'm just going to work out on the treadmill for a bit," I say. Workout classes sound like gym class, only with silent judgment from adults rather than noticeable giggling from classmates, so it's a hard pass from me. "But thank you."

Becca looks surprised by my answer. "But you have to join us! It's so much fun!"

"Yes! It's such a great workout, and they play the *best* music," Jen says. "I used to be terrified of Zumba. The instructor is fabulous, though. She's all about getting moving and keeping your heart rate up, which is great for me, because I'm awful at dancing."

"It's a nice class. But no pressure," Mom says.

I look down at my iPod, which I'm not even certain works anymore. Then I look up at the three women, who are staring at me with hopeful eyes.

"Okay," I say. "Sure."

Becca claps her hands excitedly, and my mom breaks into a smile. "I think you'll like it."

"Let's do this, ladies!" Jen leads the way to the class.

I regret my decision the moment I see that there are mirrors lining the room. Literally who thought that would be a good idea? Why would you want to watch yourself work out?

But I don't want to disappoint my mom, so I stay. A few people in the class start by stretching, and my mom, Becca, and Jen start that way, too. I follow their lead.

Then a young, lithe, dark-haired woman bounds to the front of the room and asks if everyone's ready. The cheers back indicate that yes, they're ready (and remind me that no, I'm totally not). I steal a glance around the room and it feels like everyone is much thinner than I am, except for one woman in the corner who's maybe my size. All right. If she can do this, I can do this, I tell myself. Secret solidarity.

The music starts and we follow the instructor's lead. Everyone else in the classroom seems like they know exactly what to expect, but I'm watching the instructor like a hawk, a full two or three seconds behind everyone else, who already knows the routine. The instructor is so bubbly and energetic, yelling out instructions like "Left!" and "Right!" and "Spin!" and "Back!" to help us along. I'm so caught up in trying to get the moves right that I (thankfully) hardly have time to look at myself in the mirror.

Jen's right that at least the music is good. She's also not super great with the dancing and she giggles a lot, which helps put me at ease. We're basically Zumba kindred spirits.

The forty-five minutes pass, but not easily. By the end of the workout, I feel sweaty and gross, and I'm relieved we're done.

"See? That was fun!" Becca says, glowing.

"Yeah. Fun." I take a big swig of water, and my mom hands me a towel from her bag. "Thanks."

"Did you like it?" Mom asks.

"It was exhausting," I say, still out of breath. "I can't believe you guys do that three times a week."

Jen laughs as we walk out of the classroom. "We sometimes opt for yoga instead. Much more relaxing."

"I need to run to the ladies' room. Can you hold my stuff?" my mom asks me. I nod and take her bag as she scurries off.

"I'm glad you came, Charlotte," Jen says. "Your mom is always talking about you."

"Yeah?"

"Yeah! We heard you just went to the George Washington High dance with the most popular boy in school. Good for you!"

"Totally jealous," Becca says. "I went to George Washington High growing up, and I'd have *died* to go to that dance! Your mom also tells us you're an amazing writer."

"Oh," I say, flushing. "I don't know about that." I'm trying to think of when Mom would have even read my writing, and all I can come up with are the old stories I wrote as a kid with Papi and maybe some of my book reports.

That would've been ages ago...but still.

"Nonsense! Your mom says you're great. What kind of writing do you do?" Becca asks.

"Nothing really. A little fiction here and there," I say, but I'm smiling. I can't believe my mom has talked about me, and in what sounds like a positive way. I didn't even know she liked my writing, let alone thought I was good.

"Well, I'm impressed. Great student and great writer. That's pretty fantastic!" Jen says.

By then, my mom is making her way back to us. I smile at her, and she smiles back.

"Ready to go?" she asks. I nod, and she looks at Jen and Becca. "I'll see you two on Monday, then."

"See you then. And so good to meet you, Charlotte!" Becca says.

"Yes. Come back sometime!" Jen says. "We'd love to have you."

"I will. Nice to meet you both."

Mom and I walk out to her car. She puts her key in the ignition and starts the car. Although we aren't exactly chatterboxes on the ride home, we do listen to the radio and sing along when an old-school Mariah Carey song comes on. (We both still have a soft spot for Mariah. We used to play her old albums over and over in the car until my dad begged us to pick something else.)

Back at the house, I take a shower, and when I get out, my phone is sitting on my nightstand. I carry it to Mom's room, where she's folding laundry, and hold it up to her, grinning.

"Does this mean I'm not grounded?" I ask.

"It means you can use your phone. And go back to work. But let's not push it," she says, though she's smiling. Progress.

* * *

"She's back!"

It's what Brian says when he runs into me in the parking lot on my first day returning to work.

"I'm back!" I say, grinning at him. He grins, too, and I realize how much I've missed seeing him outside of school.

In school, you've got to keep all the social politics of your classmates in mind as you behave. I'm too self-conscious to be my full self when I'm surrounded by people who've known me since I was five years old, already have an idea of who I am and where I fit, and can be pretty judgmental. I've seen what's it like to be a true outcast, and I just don't want to give anyone ammunition to make that my reality, so I only let them know a perfectly controlled version of me and my life.

But hanging out here and there with Brian means I let him in a little, more than I would the rest of my classmates. He knows things about me I haven't shared with anyone except for Amelia. Like, he knows that *The House on Mango Street* is the first book that made me feel seen. He knows I cry when I listen to the *Hamilton* soundtrack. He knows life with my mom can sometimes be tough, and he knows how hard I am on myself. Brian knows these things and he still enjoys being around me, and that's something.

And I know things about him, too, things I wouldn't have known if he was just that guy in my art class. I know that he thinks he's a bad writer but he enjoys writing anyway. I know that one of his life dreams is to watch all of Star Wars in machete order but that he hasn't done it yet because he's worried it'll disappoint him. I know that he's really into gaming with his friends and—he even sheepishly admitted—sometimes plays Dungeons & Dragons.

"Not sure I could have handled another day without you," he says, holding the office door open for me.

At that, I smile even bigger as I walk through the entryway. "Then I'm extra glad I'm back."

"Me too," he says, following me inside. "Maybe I'll see you later?"

"Yes. Definitely," I say.

In the office, I'm welcomed cheerfully, and I feel a little bad that I didn't miss them more, especially given how kind they've all been to me.

"So good to have that smile around again," Dora says, giving me a hug. "Hope things are better," she adds in a whisper.

I nod. "Much, much better, thank you."

But not everyone is excited to see me. My natural-born enemy Sheryl simply points at the giant pile of filing that hasn't been done in my absence.

"When you're done with that, you can get us ready for our next trade show," she says.

"Happy to," I say, even though I really just want to roll my eyes at her and her dumb face.

The projects keep me busy, but I get to replay the conversation I had with Brian over and over. He missed me! Hearing that made my pulse quicken, and I find myself daydreaming about walking out of work, just the two of us, me asking if he'd like to hang out sometime.

I think I could do it. Maybe.

Unfortunately, I don't get to find out. By the time I've finished up with my work and rushed to the warehouse, Brian's already gone for the day.

It's probably just as well. I know what happened last time I let my daydreaming get the better of me.

But when I get to my car, there's a Post-it note tucked under my windshield wiper. I pick it up to see a tiny doodle of Brian, with a word bubble over his head, saying, *Missed ya today!*

I smile to myself, and it's then that I realize:

I might have a crush.

Chapter Nineteen

I know things with my mom are good again when she casually mentions that we should have a party for my upcoming seventeenth birthday.

I joke that it'll be a little hard to have a party while I'm still grounded, to which she rolls her eyes and tells me it's fine, I'm not grounded anymore, did she forget to mention that?

On a sheer high from the newfound freedom, I agree to the party. My mom says I should start thinking about who to invite and that she'll take care of the rest, but I decide to focus on something more important first: What will I wear?

I'll want something less formal than what I wore to the dance, of course, but I still want to look cute. I turn to the #fatfashion community on Insta for inspiration.

Since the fight with my mom, I've been trying even harder to immerse myself in the fat acceptance community, both on Instagram and on Twitter. Something about the fact that my mom and I always seem to have the same fight over and over about diet and bodies and happiness has made me see that I desperately need to start thinking about it all in a new way. I can't let her rile me up as she has, and I think part of why I get so heated is because deep down, my mom has something I yearn for deeply. So maybe if I can start to apply some of these principles from the fat acceptance movement to myself, I'll be a whole lot happier. If the body she has becomes less of the ultimate status symbol, perhaps it can't be used as a weapon against me.

I've started by following a ton of women who post photos of

themselves proudly and free from Facetune. They are not apologetic about their bodies; they don't hide beneath a million layers. Some wear fatkinis and crop tops. Others don't necessarily show off skin but embrace the kind of beautiful, high-fashion looks I've always coveted. I do my best to participate, too. I comment with others who are active in the movement and, at the encouragement of one, have been trying to take and post more pictures of myself on my own Insta when I can, hoping to normalize what my own body looks like. It's been nice to follow some people who have bodies that look like mine, especially when they're often the first to leave an encouraging comment on my posts.

It's a slow process. But I'm trying.

During study hall one day, I've fallen deep down the rabbit hole of #plussizefashion posts when suddenly Amelia leans over and peeks at my phone screen.

"Whatcha looking at?" she asks.

Instinctively, I pull my phone toward my chest so she can't see the screen, as if she's caught me doing something I shouldn't be doing. Then I realize I should probably share this with her. My body is not a secret, right?

I try to play it off by teasing, "It's not polite to look at other people's phones." She sticks out her tongue at me as I turn the screen toward her. "But I'm looking for some outfit inspiration for my birthday party."

"Ooh, what are you thinking for it?"

I pull up a few of my saved posts and hand her the phone so she can scroll through. "Not sure yet. Just kind of looking for something that might look nice on me."

"I feel like everything looks nice on you," Amelia says without hesitation.

"Oh, please."

She scoffs. "Your complexion, those curves? Come on." My cheeks flush at the compliment. This is probably the first time she and I have really had much of a conversation about my body, which is…weird to think about. But it doesn't feel shameful or wrong or anything. Just feels normal. Why haven't I tried this before? "Oh, this!" Amelia hands me back the phone and points at the photo she's pulled up. It's a lovely brown woman, a little smaller than me, wearing a fitted, high-waisted midi skirt and a simple white tee, with mustard-yellow heels.

"That was one of my favorites, too!" I exclaim, earning me a "Shh" and a stern glance from our study hall teacher. I wave my hand apologetically at him.

"You would look awesome in that," Amelia says. "When do we go shopping for it?"

I read the description of the outfit and realize, sadly, that most of the pieces are really expensive. "Never. Pricey, pricey."

"Well, we'll keep looking then. Nothing says you have to get those exact pieces. But if we have an idea of the look, we can easily find some similar things, no?"

I nod, though I'm not so sure. Shopping can be such a source of frustration. I just wish I had as many options as everyone else. "But, I mean, before I dive headfirst into what I'm wearing, I guess I should come up with a guest list."

Amelia points at me. "Right. That would help."

I tuck my phone away and pull out a notebook, splaying it open on my desk so she can see. At the top of the page, in calligraphy, I write:

Guest List for Birthday Party I'm Not Interested In

"So? Who do I invite?" I look over at Amelia, expecting her to have the answer. She sees what I've written on the page and rolls her eyes.

"Seems like you *are* kind of interested in the party, given how much time you just spent on outfit inspo."

I wrinkle my nose. "Maybe I'm just really into cute clothes."

"Well, we already know that," Amelia says with a grin. "You could just buy some cute clothes and tell your mom you'd rather skip the party?"

"And risk getting my phone taken away again? Yeah, right," I say. "Let's just be rational and tackle the invite list."

"All right. Well, you should invite me, of course," she says. "You."

"Gee, thank goodness for your help with this list. What would I do without you?"

"Oh, just write it!"

"Okay, okay," I say, writing Amelia's name, then mine.

"I like that you're second on the list to your own birthday party."

We both laugh at that. I wouldn't even *be* on the list if I could help it.

"We should add your cousins, probably," she suggests.

"You just want me to add Junior," I say.

"God, no!" Amelia says, then quickly adds, "I mean, no offense. He was nice for that one date, but not for me."

I laugh. "It's fine. I can't believe you even went on a date with him in the first place. Who else?"

"Um...probably Liz and everyone—Jessica, Maddy, John, Khalil, Tyler. I think they'd have a good time."

Aside from me, these are definitely Amelia's closest friends, fellow athletes who are either on the track or volleyball team with her. And yes, they're the same people responsible for the traumatizing sex talk from eighth grade, but they're actually pretty cool. They're always very friendly and kind to me, but they're not exactly *my* friends...and I'm not sure if their kindness extends to "willing to go to a friend of a friend's birthday party."

"I don't know, Amelia...," I say.

"Why not?" Amelia asks. "You like them, don't you?"

I suppress an eyeroll. Sometimes she doesn't get it. "Yes, of course I like them. I mean, mostly. I could take or leave Tyler."

Amelia nods. "We could all take or leave Tyler."

"Yeah. It's just...do they really want to come to my party? They're kind of, you know...your friends."

"Don't start with that. Not again!" She shakes her head. "They're your friends, too, Charlie!"

"Not really. They like *you*, Amelia."

"*And* you. We're kind of a package deal."

I smile at that. "Okay. I'll add them," I say, scribbling down the names.

"What about Marcia?" Amelia asks.

I scrunch my nose. "She talks nonstop about Bible camp. Hard pass."

"Good point."

I add, "She *is* nice, though."

"Yeah, totally. But you didn't lie." Amelia taps her fingernails on the table. Then perks up. "Oh! Benny! From your bio class!" I give her a look. "What? You like Benjamin."

"Yeah..."

"Add him."

I do. It's not as if I have to invite him just because I write his name down. I also add Kait, a quiet but really sweet girl from my English class, and Kait's best friend, Alexis, because why not? Now I'm just adding names to add them.

Then I think of Brian. I want to add him for real. But I'll be honest; I'm afraid he might say no and I'll realize that our friendship is just something I've built up in my head. It's not like it hasn't happened before.

Amelia's reading my mind. "How about Brian?"

"I don't know...."

"I feel like that shouldn't even be a question. He's your friend. He should absolutely get an invite."

I shrug one shoulder. "He'll probably be busy."

"You can't possibly know that, and you won't unless you ask." A pause. "Just add him to the list. You can always change your mind."

"Okay." I write his name, including a little question mark after it.

"And I've got one more."

"Yeah?"

"Yeah," Amelia says. "Kira."

"Kira?"

Amelia nods. She's mentioned Kira a few times over the last few weeks. Kira is in Amelia's English class, sits right behind her. They've always been friendly (Kira runs track, so they're in the same social circles). Recently, though, Kira's name had been dropped in exponentially more conversations.

"*Kira*," I say with emphasis and a grin. "So *that's* why you don't want Junior there!"

Kira O'Connor is good people and I say that with confidence. A blond, freckled athletic girl with enviable green eyes, she's a killer track star who is always kind to everyone. When I forgot my lunch money on a field trip once, she loaned me cash without even making it into a thing. Sweet girl, big heart, and much better suited for Amelia than Sid ever was.

Oh, *that's* why Amelia suddenly doesn't mind track so much. Cute.

"Just write the name!"

"Oh, I'll write it, all right." I write *Kira* in giant letters and draw hearts on either side, then show Amelia. "Good?"

"Don't!" But she's smiling.

And I am, too. Amelia and Kira? I totally ship it.

Chapter Twenty

My car won't start.

And it's probably because it's a beat-up 1999 Toyota Corolla. But it's *my* beat-up 1999 Toyota Corolla, you know?

Unfortunately, my soft spot for my car does nothing for me. The fact is, I'm stranded in the parking lot at work without a soul around. The rest of my coworkers were all gone at 5 p.m. on the dot, but I stayed behind to finish editing a letter for Nancy.

I text Amelia for help. She responds quickly and offers to come get me. When I tell her I have no way of getting my car home, she tells me not to worry, once she finishes track she'll pick me up and we'll figure the rest out later.

Before I can reply and accept her offer, there's a knock on my window that startles me so badly I drop my phone.

It's only Brian, though, and he's laughing when I look up at him. I give him a look, reach down to retrieve my phone, and roll down my window.

"Don't do that!" I say.

He's still laughing. "Sorry! I didn't know you were so jumpy."

My heart is still pounding, but I let out a little laugh, too. "I'm a girl alone in the parking lot and it's getting dark! Have some self-awareness, my guy!"

"Yeah, you're totally right. Sorry! I wanted to say hi," Brian says, smiling sheepishly. "I just—I barely saw you today."

"I know. I was working on some writing for Nancy."

Brian whistles. "The big time, huh?"

I roll my eyes, but I'm pleased. "It's nothing. What were *you* doing here late?"

Now he rolls *his* eyes. "Finishing a big order alone because Prince Dave couldn't be bothered to stay past four. Typical."

"A prince never mingles with the court jester, so I'm not surprised."

"Wait, am I the court jester in this scenario? Charlie!"

"What?" I ask innocently.

Brian shakes his head, laughing. "Well, *traitor,* I'm going to head out. You have a good weekend."

"You too, Brian." He waves and begins to walk away. I'm watching him go when a thought occurs to me. "Hey, wait!"

He turns. "What's up?"

"Can I ask a favor?"

"Insult, then a favor?" Brian gives me a solemn look. "Yikes, Charlie. Yikes."

"Seriously, though. Know anything about cars?" I ask. Brian lifts an eyebrow, intrigued. "Mine won't start. Can you help?"

But when he shoves his hands in his pockets, I'm certain he doesn't. "God, I wish I could. I'm actually not that great with cars." His cheeks look at little pink as he says it, like he's embarrassed by that.

"Oh, yeah, no problem," I say. "I'll figure something out. Thanks anyway!"

"Well, wait. Just because I can't personally help doesn't mean I don't know someone who can. My mom could take a look."

"That's really nice of you, but I definitely don't want to inconvenience your mom. Or you." I hold up my phone to him. "I was literally just texting with Amelia and she offered to pick me up."

"It's not an inconvenience. My mom *lives* for this kind of stuff."

"I don't know...."

"We live, like, two minutes from here," Brian says. "Seriously, Charlie. Let me at least ask her and see what she says."

I'd love to not have to spend money on a tow...and Brian seems so adamant that he can help. Plus, hanging out with him for a little longer than I'd normally get to wouldn't be so bad, right? So I relent. "Okay. Yeah, thank you."

"And if my mom can't help, I'll give you a ride home. No big deal."

"That would be awesome."

As I watch Brian walk away to call his mom, I suddenly find myself feeling a little nervous. Brian and I are alone all the time at work, but for some reason, this feels different. And why are there suddenly some butterflies in my stomach? Is it my anxiety brain, just nerves, something else?

My phone buzzes and I check it to see that it's Amelia asking if I'm still there. Oh! Right. I text her back to let her know I'm good, but I won't need a ride, and I'll give her details later.

When I look up from my phone, Brian is already making his way back over to my car. He's smiling, so I think it's good news. "She'll be here in a few."

"Great!" I say. "Thank you so much."

"It's no problem. My mom is really good with cars. She once restored a 1954 Thunderbird convertible."

"Wow! I have no idea what that means, but it sounds impressive."

Brian laughs. "I wish I had no idea what that means. She talked about that car so much."

"You want to sit?" I ask, motioning toward the passenger seat of my car. It feels a little weird for me to be sitting in my car and not to offer a seat to Brian, too. "You should sit."

"Sure," Brian says as I reach over to the passenger door and unlock it. He lets himself inside. "Nice ride."

He's teasing, and I give him a playful look. "Don't. I know it's ancient." I glance at the empty water bottles I have in my backseat and frown. "And a little dirty."

"Like mine's any better." He forks a thumb in the direction of his car, and my eyes follow. It's a black convertible.

"Looks pretty nice to me," I say. "The top goes down!"

"Yeah, but it's pretty beat up inside. It's a Sebring. We got it secondhand and my ma restored it," Brian explains. "Also, not to sound ungrateful, but who wants to drive a convertible in Connecticut? The top leaks! Like, all winter long! I'm just glad it survived the season."

"Well, it looks pretty impressive on the outside, if that makes you feel any better. For pure aesthetics, I feel like you can't go wrong with convertibles. They just seem...I don't know. Cool."

" 'Cool,' huh?" Brian grins. "Yeah, I guess it is. In warm weather, anyway. It's kind of nice to put the top down during summer and drive around."

"You just love feeling the wind in your hair, don't you?"

"Ya got me, Charlie. You know how much I love to feel the wind in these long, beautiful locks of mine." He shakes his hair dramatically, but it's short so it barely moves at all. I giggle. "Hey, we should go for a ride sometime. When it's nicer. You actually might enjoy the feeling of the wind in *your* beautiful hair."

I feel my cheeks get hot at the compliment, and my hand reaches for a curl, which I give a little tug. "Yeah, that could be fun."

"Yeah." He's looking right at me. "It could be."

Nervously, I push my glasses up my nose, looking away from him and out the front window. My heart is beating fast and I'm scrambling to change the subject, like, *now.*

"So, my mom is being a jerk," I blurt out.

"Again? Everything okay?"

I laugh, probably a little awkwardly. "I mean, all right, she's not being a jerk. But she *is* forcing me to have a birthday party. And I told her I'm way too old to have a birthday party and nobody even does that anymore, but..."

Why am I even telling him this?

"Is it a birthday party with, like, Pin the Tail on the Donkey?" Brian asks. "In that case, yeah, sure, you might be too old. But if it's a birthday party where you get to invite some friends to do something fun, that might not be too bad."

I shrug a little. "Yeah. I don't know...." As my voice trails off, I see that Brian's looking at me, patiently waiting for more. "Well, Amelia and I were putting together a list of people to invite. And it's mostly her friends on the list. I just..." I hesitate to say the next thing. "I don't have many friends."

Brian shakes his head. "Everybody likes you, Charlie. You're, like, the nicest person in school."

"I don't know about that," I say.

"Well, I think you're well liked. And if nothing else, I'm definitely your friend."

My lips curve into a smile. "Yeah?" A pleasant feeling of relief washes over me as I hear that, like when your toes are bitingly cold and suddenly they start to thaw with warmth. For weeks, I've been in my head over whether we're actually friends, so afraid of my own judgment after the mess with Cal. But this confirmation, albeit small, gives me reassurance. What a kindness Brian has just extended to me without even knowing.

"Well, aren't I?"

"Of course!" I say enthusiastically. Then, after a beat, "So?"

"So?" he asks.

"Is this you offering to come to my birthday party?"

"No," Brian says, and my heart sinks. "This is you inviting me to come to your birthday party."

I laugh at that, relaxing.

"I'd love to come," he continues. "Thank you for asking."

"You're welcome," I say. "Aren't I thoughtful?"

"Absolutely. Can you actually make sure we can play Pin the Tail on the Donkey, though?"

"I'll see what I can do."

It's then that Brian points at a car pulling into the lot. "There's my mom. Uh, so, full disclosure: I look nothing like her."

I make a face. "I barely look like my mom, either. My dad's genes definitely won out."

"Right. But, like, my *other* mom is the one I look like. She's the one who carried me and all. I mean—some people are put off by it. I just wanted to get that out there so you didn't feel weird."

I can tell this is probably something he's had to explain before. I understand. When you don't look like one of your parents, sometimes you get funny stares, sometimes weird questions, and sometimes—best-case scenario—no reaction at all. I'm aiming for the latter here.

"You didn't have to explain that to me," I say gently. "But I totally get it."

He smiles, looking visibly relieved. "Come on."

We get out of the car and wave his mom over, even though the parking lot is empty otherwise and I'm pretttttty sure she would have found us. She pulls her car right next to mine and gets out.

Like Brian, his mom is tall and a little pudgy, but the similarities stop there. She's got red hair chopped in a bob, freckled skin, and bright blue eyes. He's right; she looks absolutely nothing like Brian, with his dark hair, clear skin, and black eyes. But she's lovely.

"Hey, Ma," Brian says.

"Hey. I hear we're having some car trouble?" She looks over at me and gives me a sweet smile. "I'm Maura."

"I'm Charlie. Nice to meet you." I hold out my hand for her to shake, feeling like a grown-up.

She shakes it. "And you. How can I help?"

I tell her that my car won't start and she asks me a few questions, then instructs me to get in, roll down the window, and start the engine. When it won't turn over, she tells me to pop the hood.

Embarrassingly, I have to ask, "How do I do that?"

Maura grins. "There's a lever on the lower left below the steering wheel. It should have a picture of a car with its hood open. Pull that up."

I search for the lever she's talking about and, when I find it, pull. But my trunk goes up.

"Not that one," Brian says, laughing.

"Oh, oops!" I laugh, too. I reach until I find another lever beside it and pull. This time, my hood makes an unlatching sound. "Is that it?"

"You got it!" Maura props the hood up. After a moment of inspection, she walks over to my window. "Good news and bad news."

"Oh, boy. It's dead forever, isn't it?" I ask anxiously.

She chuckles. "No. Good news is the car just needs a charge and you should be able to get it home."

"Oh! Great!" I say.

"Bad news is you'll need a new battery," Maura says. "This one's on its way out. Should run you less than a hundred dollars, and I can put the new one in for you."

"Really? That wouldn't be too much trouble?"

She waves her hand at that. "Not at all! I'd be happy to do it. You just connect with Brian and figure out where and when, and we'll get it done. Sound good?"

"Sounds amazing!" I say, grateful to avoid paying a mechanic on top of the hundred bucks I'll be out. "Thank you!"

Brian's grinning. "See? I told you she could take care of this, no problem."

"Can you grab my jumper cables from the trunk?" Then Maura looks at me and says, "We can get it hooked up and you'll be right on your way."

It takes only a few more minutes to connect our two cars and get mine to start. I'm so excited when the engine turns over and my car turns on that I get out and give Maura a hug.

"Don't forget to get that battery, though, okay?" she says. "And let me help you install it!"

"She means it," Brian says.

"I will, I promise. Thank you." I look at Brian. "Both of you. So much."

I get in my car to leave, and there's a little jolt of excitement inside me.

Because I now officially have a reason to see Brian outside of work or school.

Chapter Twenty-One

He likes you. I reread the text Amelia has sent me. I'm in English class, and I should be paying attention, but Amelia won't stop texting...and okay, I won't stop texting her back, either.

When I got home last night after Brian and his mom helped me with my car, my mom asked me to go to the gym with her. Her friends would be there, she said. So I agreed. We had a decent time and the workout left her in such a good mood that I used the opportunity to ask if she could take me to buy a new car battery. At the auto parts store, Mom was flirting with the sales guy so bad that he gave us his own employee discount of *fifty percent*. I've got to hand it to her: girl knows how to get what she wants.

Between all that and my homework, I barely had time to text Amelia those details I promised, so I'm doing it now. Amelia insists that the combination of Brian (1) helping me with my car, (2) saying I had pretty hair, and (3) inviting me to go for a drive with him means he likes me.

It's so obvious. Do you like him back? she writes.

I know the answer is yes. Because he dropped everything to help me with my car. Because of the valentine. Because of the way he makes me laugh. Because of the way he makes me feel heard. Because my chest is pounding just thinking he might like me, too.

But I'm not sure I'm ready for anyone else to know.

I don't know, I write back.

Let's figure it out.

Fine. But not in class. Ms. Williams is getting mad. Coffee after school tomorrow?

Yes!!!

Then the bell rings and my classmates dart out of the classroom.

I wasn't paying attention, so of course I missed the fact that everyone else had started packing up their bags. I've begun putting my notebook away when Ms. Williams heads toward me. My phone is in plain view on my desk, and I worry she's going to scold me (or worse, be disappointed that I didn't participate at all in class today), so I try to beat her to the punch by being super friendly.

"Hey, Ms. Williams!" I say.

"Hi, Charlie." She stops just in front of my desk and puts her hands on her hips. "We didn't hear much from you today. Everything okay?"

I nod. "Yes. Definitely."

She smiles. "Good. So listen, I've got something I'd like to show you. Can you hang around for a second?" I look at the clock on my phone. If I stay, I'll be late for my next class. As if reading my mind, she adds, "I'll write you a pass."

"Okay, sure," I say.

"Great." Ms. Williams starts walking toward her desk and I follow, slinging my bag over my shoulder. "So, I've been very impressed with your writing this semester."

"Thank you, Ms. Williams." My face flushes with pleasure. "That means a lot."

She reaches across her desk to pick up a sheet of paper. "I'm glad to hear you say that because I wanted to share something with you." She holds the printout toward me. "It's a writing contest I recently heard about. It's specifically for high school students, and they accept short stories. I think you should enter."

This feels like a *very* high compliment. At the start of the semester, I Googled Ms. Williams and I found a book of poetry she'd written. It had even won an award. So I know she knows her stuff. I'm beyond flattered. A published author recognizing me as someone with potential? That's huge!!!

"Wow! Thank you for thinking of me, Ms. Williams!" I look at the paper she's holding, skimming the details but feeling so excited and overwhelmed I can hardly process. "Tell me more!"

"It's a pretty open-ended contest, so really, this is about you and what you feel comfortable writing and submitting. There are no real genre rules, but there are a few guidelines for word count and things like that. I've really felt captivated by some of the snippets of fiction you've turned in. I love the pieces from the story about the group of young witches of color you've revisited all semester long."

"That's easily one of my favorites!" I say excitedly. "I think it could be a whole novel eventually!"

She nods. "I do, too. But there's also something very raw and emotional about the familial relationships you've explored in other pieces—loss, dysfunctional relationships between mothers and daughters. That kind of stuff can really resonate with people and may be of particular interest to the judging panel. You even have a few essays from your free-writes that could work as a basis."

I am truly moved that Ms. Williams has given this so much thought and that she's been so receptive to the things I've poured my heart into. She hasn't even seen my online writing, which is chock-full of other passages, scenes, and concepts. I feel like I'm bursting with ideas.

"I'm so excited that I wish I could skip the rest of my classes and focus only on this," I say eagerly. "I mean, where do I even start? How do I narrow it all down?"

Ms. Williams chuckles. "Well, I can't write you a note to make that happen, but I'm really pleased you're excited, Charlie. I'd say take your journal home and flip through it and see what inspires you. I've marked a few of my personal favorites, but it's really about what speaks to you. I'm happy to look anything over, too, before you submit."

"When's this all due?" I ask.

"Ah, great question." She points to the bottom of the page. "Submissions are due in May, so we've got some time, but it'll come up fast. Think about it, okay?"

I nod eagerly. "I'll get started tonight. Are you sure you can't excuse me for the rest of the day?"

Ms. Williams grins, shaking her head. "I'm sure." She scribbles a quick note to excuse my tardiness to my next class and hands it to me. "Let me know how I can help, okay?"

"I will," I say. "Thanks again!"

I spend the rest of my day at school brainstorming ideas. I even research the contest at lunch and read through the winners from the last couple of years. Their writing is good, but I know mine is, too. Or it can be. If I can figure out what to write about.

That night, I tear through my regular homework as fast as I can so that I can try to narrow down my focus for my submissions.

When I'm writing, there's a whole-ass vibe I like to curate. I don't necessarily think all writers need to have a special space or notebook or pen or whatever to succeed, but it doesn't hurt. So I turn off the overhead lights in my room, leaving only the white twinkle lights on over my desk, and then I use a match on one of my favorite scented candles (it's "old books" and I found it on Etsy!). I pull out my oversized notebook, the one where I've scribbled dozens and dozens of ideas and pieces of inspiration over the years, then my favorite set of pens, and place it all beside my fully charged and plugged-in laptop. Sometimes I write better on paper, sometimes by laptop; it just depends on how quickly my brain is whirling around.

Finally, I open up a new Google Doc, fully ready to start writing.

Only . . . nothing comes.

Because I can't settle on an idea. Do I go with the witchy girl gang? Do I start something completely new? I have ideas for a story about two nineties girls who became friends on the old version of the internet, America Online, but it would take a lot of research on my end. I could go with a short piece about a society of people born knowing when they'll die, so they celebrate death days rather than birthdays, an idea I've been toying with. But I haven't worked out all the kinks in that one yet. Do I write something about my mom? Or maybe about my dad?

I sit and think and sit and think until I'm absolutely convinced that the blinking cursor in my Google Doc is mocking me. And then an idea hits me.

Ms. Williams said I need inspiration, so I decide I'll start by reading a story that helps clear my brain. (Sometimes my best ideas come after I've done some reading.) I snap my laptop shut, dig under my bed to grab a tattered set of poorly stapled construction-paper pages, and settle with them in the cushioned seat of the bay window, which serves as my reading-slash-daydreaming-slash-brainstorming nook.

It's been a while since I've sunk my teeth into "Charlie and the Rainbow Shoes," but now seems like as good a time as any.

Chapter Twenty-Two

While I wait for Amelia to arrive at Jake's, I keep trying to settle into *I Know Why the Caged Bird Sings*. Coffee shops are normally a great place for me to read. The clinking sound of cups; the ambient music; the grinding of coffee beans; the slurp of foam; the indistinct chatter—all that is weirdly soothing and I'm usually able to disappear right into my book.

But not this time. I've reread the same sentence at least ten times. My brain seems to be bouncing between the writing contest, my birthday, and Brian.

I've finally settled on an idea for the contest—okay, two. I'm going to start with the witches and see how it goes. My second option is based on a series of difficult-to-read but really important passages I wrote in Ms. Williams's class about my relationship with Mom. In my heart, I know that's probably the winner, but it's much harder to tackle, so…the witches give me something to warm up with. And that's good, too.

As for my birthday, I'm making slow progress. I sent out a series of group messages to let everyone know the details. The final guest list included my cousins, Amelia's group of friends, Benjamin, and Brian (sorry to the random acquaintances who didn't make the cut). My cousins are in, of course, and so far, thanks to Amelia's enthusiastic response to the group message, it seems like most of the people from school are willing to come, too.

Thank God for Amelia sometimes.

I spot her walking into the coffee shop and wave her over. She comes to the table and tosses her bag onto the chair, looking a little frazzled. "So sorry I'm late."

"No worries," I say. "You okay?"

"Oh, yes. Just couldn't find my phone." She rolls her eyes. "Food?"

I nod and we walk up to the counter, leaving our bags at the table. We each place our orders and then return to our seats and settle in.

"So, I have a new Insta that I'm obsessed with," I say.

"Are you stalling?" Amelia asks.

"Maybe—but you'll really like it, too! It features Barbies dressed up and posed like they're in iconic scenes from movies and TV shows. They just posted a whole triptych—"

"Ooh, look at you, using that art lingo," Amelia interrupts. "Mr. Reed would be so proud."

"Right? But seriously, it's a triptych from *Stranger Things*."

"What?! Okay, show me now." She does dramatic gimme hands toward me as I dig out my phone and pull the post up. She takes it from me to get a better look and zooms in. "They even have miniature Eggos!"

"So fun, right?!"

Amelia nods in approval. "*So* fun." Then she hands me back my phone. "Now, on to the good stuff."

"The good stuff," I repeat.

"Yeah—quit holding out on me, lady. Tell me about Brian."

I use the straw to stir my drink, partly out of habit, partly to continue my efforts to stall. "What's there to tell?" I'm trying to be nonchalant.

Amelia's not having it. "Oh, come *on*! You're hanging out a lot and he's being really nice to you and he offered to help you with your car..."

"Because he's *nice,* and he's my *friend*," I insist. "You were going to help me with my broken-down car, too. He just happened to be in close proximity."

"Yeah, and he seems to be in close proximity more and more! Like making it a point to come over to our table and talk to you every art class. And spending time with you at work. And telling you you have beautiful hair and inviting you to do things!"

"You tell me I have beautiful hair and invite me to do things."

She sighs dramatically. "Okay, yes, but it's only because you do have beautiful hair and you're my best friend. And when I do it, it's just, like, a friend enthusiastically supporting a friend. When Brian does it, it's because he *likes* you," she presses. "You're just being stubborn and won't admit it."

My stomach feels like it's doing flips at the mere thought that Brian might like me and that someone other than me is noticing. "I'm not sure I see it."

"Well, there's something more important that I still need to know," Amelia says. "Do *you* like *him*?"

I don't look at her and instead take a long sip of my drink. Then I look up and, with a shrug, say, "Maybe." It's an obvious yes, so of course it elicits a squeal from her. "But that doesn't mean we need to get all weird about it!"

"That's exactly what it means!" Amelia crows.

"We can't," I say. "I really just want to be cool about it. We saw what happened with Cal."

"But Brian isn't Cal. Not even close."

"I know, but it's important to me to just...I don't know. Enjoy being friends. I don't want to ruin anything. At least for now." I swallow. "I need to be sure. You understand, right?"

Amelia looks disappointed, but she nods. "Yes, I do. I'll try not to push it. Are you at least going to take him up on fixing your car?"

"I think so," I say. "I've already bought the part. So." Amelia seems satisfied, and I use that as an opportunity to change the subject. "What about you? How's *Kira*?"

Amelia lights up at the name, a smile spreading across her face. She's moved on from denial that they're a thing to admitting that they're "talking." Like, every night.

"Oh, you know. Same ol', same ol'...," she says, playing coy.

"Spill—*now*. It's only fair!"

Amelia grins, and it's a goofy grin, so I know what she's about to share is going to be good. "Well, since you asked: Kira and I are together now."

My turn to squeal. "Together-together?!"

"Together-together," Amelia confirms, unable to wipe the huge smile off her face. It's contagious and I feel myself grinning real big, too.

"Amelia! You were holding out on me! I'm so, so happy for you," I say, stretching across the table and giving her a hug. "Why didn't you tell me sooner?!"

"It *just* happened last night! I swear. I'd never hold out on you," Amelia says. "She and I were volunteering at that animal shelter. You know the one downtown?"

"Oh, yeah. Wait, you volunteer there?" I ask.

"No, no. I mean, not normally. Kira does, though—on top of everything else she does. She's amazing, Charlie. She took me to the shelter and we fed tiny puppies! It was incredible!"

"Do you have pictures?!" Then I add, "Not that that's the point."

"Of course I have photos," she says, fishing through her bag, grabbing her phone, unlocking it, and tossing it my way. I quickly scan through the pictures, appropriately cooing with Amelia at all of the tiny pups.

I hand her phone back and sigh. "Puppies! And a girlfriend!"

"I know, I know!"

"So, how did you guys have The Talk? Was it before or after you fed the little babes?"

"After. We left the shelter and then just kind of walked around and we ended up in this little park. It was warmer than usual last night, so we sat on some swings and were just kind of talking."

"And kissing?" I ask, rightfully earning an eye roll from Amelia. "Sorry, but in my head, you guys were totally also kissing. It's the writer in me, okay?"

Amelia takes a sip from her drink. "Okay, well, the writer in you is correct. It was really sweet, actually, being under the stars, just her and me. There was just something—I don't know—kind of magical. And I know it hasn't been very long since Sid, but...this feels different somehow. I told Kira I wanted to take things super, super slowly, given everything, but then last night I just couldn't help myself. I asked her to be my girlfriend."

I clasp my hands together in delight and hold them to my heart. "Oh my gosh! I just love a good romance!"

Amelia smiles at that. "Yeah, well, you should know, right? Clearly that's in your future with Brian!"

"Don't," I say, pointing a finger at her.

"Who, me?" she asks, batting her eyelashes. "But...things *did* take a turn after I got home."

"How so?" I ask.

"I got home kind of late and my mom was waiting up! And she wanted to know what was what—who was I with and where was I, you know, typical mom stuff. So of course I spilled!"

I take a second to try to imagine spilling the details of anything in my life to my mom and come up short. But that's what I love so much about Amelia and her mother. They actually share that kind of stuff.

"But then," Amelia continues, "that got her curious. Who is this girl? Now that it's serious, can she and my dad meet her? So now, of course, my mom is insisting I bring Kira by for a formal dinner." She twirls a strand of her curly hair around her finger. "Why can't my parents be normal and checked out of my life?"

I can't imagine either of Amelia's parents being like that toward Amelia or her sister, Tess, who are their sun and moon.

"Maybe it won't be so bad?" I suggest. "Your parents are pretty great. They know you're pan, right?"

Amelia nods. "That's the thing. They're going to be so cool about this being the first girl I've invited over that they're going to go overboard." She groans. "They're going to smother my first girlfriend ever!"

"Girlfriend!" I say, swooning. "I just love the sound of that."

"Me too," Amelia admits. "But can we focus here?"

"Right, right. Sorry. Okay, so, dinner. I think it'll be fine. If you eat fast, maybe you can make it last all of thirty minutes."

"I doubt it. You know how my parents are. They're going to have a million questions, and they'll want to sit in the living room after and hang out. And Tess is going to be a nightmare, probably, annoying the hell out of Kira, and Kira is going to decide I'm not worth the trouble."

"She wouldn't," I say. "What if I join you? Would that help?"

Her face brightens at the suggestion, and that warms my heart. It's good to feel needed. "Will you?"

"Of course I will! Whatever you want."

Now she gets up from her side of the table to throw her arms around me. "Thank you! Thank you, thank you, thank you!"

"You don't have to thank me," I say. "You're my best friend. I'd do anything for you."

Chapter Twenty-Three

My mom drops me off at school the next day because my car is still dead. She uses the drive as an opportunity to talk to me about my upcoming birthday and how she'd like to invite a few of *her* friends to the house, too. I'm a little annoyed, but to keep the peace I say it's fine.

She and I have been bickering a little here and there about my party. I wanted it to be super small, just a few friends and family eating good food in the backyard. She wants to make it bigger, better, flashier, and I'm kind of over it. I thought birthdays were supposed to be about the person celebrating the birthday, but I guess not.

It's a bummer I couldn't catch a ride in today with Amelia so I could have avoided this conversation with my mom altogether. But she's busy attending an all-day field trip with her public speaking class, which means I'm also on my own at school.

It's a weird feeling. Amelia and I have been friends for so long that most people expect to see the two of us together. We're always Amelia-and-Charlie, like one word, a duo joined at the hip. We do so much together, from getting lunch to walking to class, that Amelia feels more like an extension of me than another person entirely. Or rather, I often feel like an extension of her rather than my own person.

I wouldn't say I live in Amelia's shadow, but her life often feels a lot bigger than mine. When I'm on my own, it's like I'm a little exposed. And...without anyone to sit with at lunch.

So, in bio, when we break into groups to complete a study packet for our upcoming test, I use it as an opportunity to connect with my pal Benjamin, who said yes to coming to my birthday (yay!).

"As excited as I am to dive into mitosis and meiosis, before we do, I was wondering if you could do me a favor," I say.

Benjamin shoots me a look. "What kind of favor?"

"Well, you know my bestie, Amelia?"

"I know *of* her, yes," Benjamin says, and I almost laugh. He knows *of* her? Benjamin is probably one of the only people in the whole school not completely enthralled with her.

"Well, sadly, she's not here today, so there goes my lunch buddy. I'm not super thrilled about the idea of sitting at a table all alone, so I was wondering—"

Benjamin holds up a hand to stop me. "Charlie, my friends and I decompress during lunch. We don't talk much."

"What do you think I'm going to do? Quiz you on mitosis?" I ask.

He shrugs. "I don't know. I wouldn't like that, though."

"I wouldn't, either. I just need a place to sit. Please don't make me be a complete loser." He looks at me for a moment, considering the offer. I pout as pathetically as possible. "Please? You won't even know I'm there!"

He breaks into a small smile. "All right."

"I won't bug you at all. I'm just a warm body." I hold out a pinky to him. "Promise!"

Benjamin glances around, looking a little embarrassed at what he's about to do, and then locks pinkies with me. "We sit on the east side of the cafeteria. You'll find us. Now, can we get to this study guide, please?"

A few periods later, I'm pleased to be walking into the lunch room with a plan, without having to worry about where I'll sit or who I'll sit with.

Honestly, I probably should be having lunch with Kira, Liz, Jessica, Maddy, John, and Khalil—all people who have graciously agreed to attend my birthday in a few weeks. (Through a stroke of luck, Tyler already had plans that night.) I should be trying to be friendly with them, get to know them a little better, show them I'm a person, too.

But, like Benjamin, sometimes I just want a little quiet. So I find him and his friends, we give each other a polite nod, and then I sit wordlessly and pull out my phone to start reading a book.

Before I can settle into it, another lunch tray clunks down across from mine. I look up as Brian sits down.

"Hi," I say, surprised.

"Hey," he replies. "How's the car?"

"Deader than ever."

"Well, if someone would take me up on my offer . . ."

I wave my hand dismissively. "I know, I know. I was going to! I had no way of getting in contact with you," I say. "And I didn't work yesterday."

"Instagram? Snapchat? Twitter? Hell, even Facebook?" Brian rattles all the ways I technically could have reached out. I can't help that I'm too shy to do so.

"I meant I couldn't text."

"Oh. In that case." He reaches for my unlocked phone. "Do you mind?" I shake my head, and he taps the screen a few times, concentrating. I hear his own phone vibrate in his pocket as he hands mine back to me. "There you go."

I look at the screen and realize he's texted himself. His name, as he's programmed it in, says *Brian* and there's the little flexing arm emoji after it. I laugh.

"What?" he asks.

But I don't respond. Instead, I write a message and hit send.

Hey. If the offer still stands, do you have time to help me fix my car?

Brian pulls out his phone and smiles when he sees the text. Then he writes back, **Of course. Tonight?**

Yes, I write. **Tonight.**

Chapter Twenty-Four

Brian and his mom are supposed to show up at my house at 5 p.m. At 4:30, I start looking out the window every few minutes to see if they're outside. I selfishly hope fixing my car won't take too long because I don't want my mom to come home while Brian and his mom are here. She's not a fan of unexpected visitors. And I'm not really a fan of *her* right now, so yeah.

Brian's car pulls into the driveway at exactly 5 p.m., which I appreciate, because I couldn't have handled any more time obsessively looking out the window. Plus, 5 p.m. should leave us enough time to get this done before the sun goes down. (At least I hope.)

I meet them outside. "Hi, Brian. Hi, Mrs. Park."

"You don't have to call me Mrs. Park," she says. "Maura is just fine."

I nod and smile. Before they arrived, I texted Brian to ask what I should call her, and he told me she'd prefer Maura over Mrs. Park, but I didn't want to seem presumptuous. (Technically, she and her wife are *both* Mrs. Park, which I think is pretty lovely and sweet.) I just struggle to call adults by their first names. I still call Amelia's parents Mr. and Mrs. Jones and it's been literal years.

"Okay, Maura. Thank you both for coming. I really appreciate it."

"No problem. Do you have the battery?" Brian asks.

"Yes! Let me grab it," I say.

"I'll help," he offers, following me as I walk toward the garage. I let us inside and go to grab the battery, but Brian's quicker.

"I can carry it," I say.

"I know. But do you want to?" He holds it out toward me. I wrinkle my nose in response. "Thought so."

We walk back to where Maura is standing beside my car, sleeves rolled up and hair pulled back. A toolbox is open at her feet and I can see that it's meticulously organized.

"Charlie, would you mind popping the hood of your car for me?" she asks.

"Yes! I'm super good at that now." I grab the lever that pops the hood, then see Maura motioning for me to come to the front of the car.

"Come here, dear," she says. "I'll show you how to get it open from here. Just in case you ever need to."

I join Brian and his mom at the front of my car. She explains that you need to stick your hand under the hood, palm up, and feel around for a latch to pull to fully release the hood. Once the hood is open, she shows me how to prop it up and lays an oil-stained towel over the front of the car.

"To protect it from battery acid that could drip," she explains.

Then Maura bends over the front of the car, talking about things like negative vs. positive ground, bolts and wrenches, and I'm trying to listen but I feel like it's all going over my head. I'm nodding but secretly thinking, *Oh, God, what?* Brian's watching intently but silently, too, so at least that makes me feel a little bit better.

Maura easily lifts the old battery out of the car, points to the place where it sat and says it's in good shape, then immediately gets to work installing the new one.

It's all over in a matter of minutes. She instructs me to try starting my car, and when I do, it turns on, first try. I'm amazed.

It must be clear on my face because Brian says, "She's good, huh?"

"Umm, she might be my actual fairy godmother. Of cars, of course."

Brian nods. "Right, of course."

Maura gives me an amused smile. "Now, if you want, I can get rid of this battery for you, Charlie. It should be recycled, not just thrown away."

"It won't be too much trouble?" I ask.

"Not at all," she says.

"Seriously, no problem," Brian echoes.

"It's so cool that you guys know how to do this stuff."

Brian points at his mom. "It's all her."

"Tig could learn if he wanted to," she says.

"*Ma,*" Brian says, shooting her a look that I recognize well. It says: *Mother, we've discussed this a million times, and you can't be cool?* To me, he says, "Childhood nickname," and I grin.

"What's it mean?" I ask.

"A story for another time," he replies, turning a little pink.

"Sorry." Maura gives Brian an apologetic shrug and does her best to reroute the conversation. "Like I said, he could learn. But he says it's boring."

He looks down sheepishly. "Not boring, just...not...fun?"

I try to rescue him. "Well, I can't tell you enough how much I appreciate all of your help! In fact, do you both mind waiting here a minute? I have to go get something from the house." Before either of them can reply, I run inside, grab a plate from the counter, and race back. I push the plate toward Brian. "Here."

He looks down, then grins when he realizes what's on the plate beneath the clear plastic wrap. "Cookies?"

"Chocolate chip. *With* bacon."

Brian's eyes go wide. "With bacon?!"

"Yeah! At the work party, you said, 'Nobody ever puts savory things in cookies.' So I looked this recipe up," I say, my cheeks getting a little hot. "I tried it and it's not half bad, you know."

"This is incredible," Brian says. Then he looks at his mom. *Bacon cookies,* Ma."

Maura just laughs, shaking her head. "That's very sweet of you, Charlie."

It's then that I see my mom's car pulling down the street. Way to ruin a moment, Mom.

"They're just a small thank-you, to both of you," I say, looking from Brian to Maura and trying to ignore the fact that my mom has slowed her car to a crawl as she nears the house. I can see her squinting at us, trying to figure out who I'm with.

"That's so thoughtful of you, Charlie," Maura says. "Thank you."

Then I hear my mom kill the engine of her car and she gets out, slamming the door shut behind her. We all look over at her, but she doesn't smile.

"Hi, Mom," I say.

She ignores the greeting. "What's going on?"

"My friend Brian and his mom offered to help me with my car. Remember?"

"Hi, I'm Maura." Brian's mom sticks her hand out to shake my mom's. My mom shakes it, then plasters on a smile.

"Jeanne. Nice to meet you," she says.

"Likewise," Maura says.

"This is Brian, Mom." I motion toward him.

Her eyes flick over Brian, head to toe. Then she forces a smile at him, too, and sticks out her hand. "Nice to meet you."

"Nice to meet you as well, Mrs. Vega," Brian says. "I hope it's all right that we're here."

"Absolutely. I was just surprised is all. My darling Charlie forgot to tell me we'd be having company." She reaches over and pats my shoulder.

I give her a thin-lipped smile. "Sorry, Mom. We were just wrapping up." Then I turn toward Brian and Maura. "Thank you both again for all of your help. My car is as good as new."

"You're more than welcome, Charlie. And if you run into any more car trouble, you just give us a holler, okay?" Maura says.

I know she means it. "I will."

"Thanks for the cookies, kid," Brian says, trying to make me smile. It works.

"See you soon," I say as they start to get into their car.

"And don't forget to return the plate," Mom adds.

"I won't. I promise," Brian calls before shutting the door.

I wave to them both as they pull out of the driveway. Once they're out of sight, I whip toward her. " 'Don't forget to return the plate'?"

She sniffs. "What? It's a good plate."

"I doubt he's going to keep our plate, Mom. It's not that serious."

"I was just reminding him!"

I roll my eyes and start walking toward the house. "Okay."

Mom is following me inside as I open the door. "You should've told me we were going to have company."

"I'm sorry, but the plans were last-minute. I made them at school." I push the door open and walk toward the kitchen. "And I did tell you it would probably happen when we picked up the battery. What's the big deal?"

"I would have neatened up the house," Mom says.

"They didn't come inside."

"But what if they had?"

I feel like she's just picking a fight with me, and I'm not in the mood to argue. "I don't know, Mom. I guess they would've seen that we're not perfect." I walk to the counter and start washing the handful of dishes I used.

"I'm not looking for an attitude." When she's in a mood like this, I know I can't say anything right, so I don't respond. "Who's the boy?"

"A friend, Mom. Brian. Like I said."

"Brian," she repeats, watching me wash the dishes. "Hmm."

"What?"

"Nothing." A pause. "Did you really need to bake him cookies, Charlie? Honestly. Now it's messy in here and I don't have time to clean it."

"I'm cleaning it right now," I say. "That was always the plan, Mom."

"But you know I hate it when you bake." She says that as if I bake constantly, which I don't, and she's acting like the kitchen is a disaster, which it's clearly not. But she's probably grumpy because, like me, she loves chocolate chip cookies. And the leftover cookies don't have bacon—just classic, delicious semisweet chocolate chips.

I turn to her. "There are a few cookies left over. I put them in a container over there. Help yourself."

"You know I can't," she snaps.

"Oh, yeah," I say. "I forgot."

She starts to sift through the mail I brought in and put on the counter, but I catch her glancing over at the container every so often. So when I finish drying the dishes and putting them away, I open the container, grab a cookie, and unapologetically pop it in my mouth.

Chapter Twenty-Five

It's not as if my parents are meeting *my* girlfriend for the first time, but out of solidarity, I'm still nervous about the upcoming dinner at Amelia's house.

I've gotta be strong, though, so all week long whenever Amelia asks if everything's going to be all right, I emphatically tell her yes and give her a play-by-play of how the night will unfold. The scenario is different every time, but it always ends with everyone skipping and holding hands, because the visual of her girlfriend holding hands with her parents grosses Amelia out and makes her laugh.

And then, before we know it, the night is here. Amelia and Kira swing by my house to pick me up so we can review the game plan.

I'm surprised when I climb into the backseat of Amelia's car and see what Kira is wearing. At school, she's normally pretty casual—hair pulled back in a bun, a T-shirt, leggings, sneakers, that type of thing—so it's hard not to notice that her long hair is expertly curled and she's wearing a dress.

"Is it too much?" Kira asks, and I realize I must have looked her up and down. I hate when I do that.

"Not at all! You look so pretty."

"Thanks," she says, touching her hair.

"You do," Amelia says, looking at her meaningfully for a moment. Then it's back to business. She starts to back her car out of my driveway and we head toward her house. "So let's talk game plan."

"We'll keep things casual, and I'll swoop in if a moment starts to feel awkward," I say. "Mostly, we will steer the conversation toward school and how great we're all doing academically, which your parents will be pleased about."

"And I can chime in with several mentions of track for your former track star mom—or sports, which your former football star dad will enjoy," Kira says.

"Above all, we'll work together to keep the mood light," Kira and I say in unison.

Then we all giggle.

"Okay, fine, so I've drilled this into your heads over the last week," Amelia says. "I just want to make sure all goes well!"

"It will. I don't know what Amelia has told you about her parents, Kira, but they are actual angels," I say. "Like, literally the sweetest people you will ever meet."

"That's certainly not the impression I've gotten from Amelia!"

"Charlie is exaggerating," Amelia interjects.

I shake my head. "I'm not! Amelia and Tess are the apples of their parents' eyes. They can do no wrong. And I know they'll like you, Kira."

"That's what I've been saying," Kira says. "Parents *love* me."

"We'll find out, won't we?" Amelia says as we pull up to her house.

Kira doesn't seem fazed. "I love a good challenge."

The three of us get out of the car and head inside, where Tess is sitting on the couch watching TV. She looks exactly like Amelia did just a few years ago. At ten, Tess is shorter than Amelia, of course, but they look so much alike it's not even funny: same dark skin, same lovely eyes, same gorgeous hair. The only difference is that Tess tends to wear her hair pulled back in two pigtail puffs, which I hope she won't grow out of—but I know in my heart that the days are numbered.

She looks up when we walk in. "Hey, Charlie!"

"Hi, Tess. Good to see you." Tess and I have always mostly gotten along. Amelia would often try to kick Tess out whenever we were chilling, but sometimes I'd argue to let Tess stay. I've secretly always wished I had a little sister, so I didn't mind her following us around as much as Amelia did.

"Amelia," Tess says.

"Tess," Amelia says through gritted teeth. Then she relaxes and smiles at Kira. "Kira, this is my little sister, Tess. Tess, this is Kira, who *you will be nice to.*"

"Calm down," Tess says, rolling her eyes. "Hi, Kira."

"Hi, Tess. Nice to meet you." Kira walks over to Tess to shake her hand.

Tess can't hide how excited she is by this, no doubt feeling like a grown-up, and enthusiastically shakes Kira's hand. "Nice to meet you, too!" Tess says.

"Amelia, is that you?" Mrs. Jones calls out.

"Yes! It's us!" Amelia replies.

Her mom, Beth, aka Mrs. Jones, rounds the corner into the living room and smiles. Tall, slim, and striking, she looks beautiful as ever with her box braids pulled back in a low, loose ponytail, wearing a simple cardigan over some slacks and flats. It's easy to see where Amelia gets her good looks.

If I could be anybody when I grow up, it'd be Mrs. Jones. She's always so poised and composed, and she's also incredibly smart and driven. But it was kindness that was the first thing I noticed and loved about her. During my first-ever sleepover at Amelia's, back when we were kids, she could sense my nerves, and at bedtime she tucked me in and gave me a kiss on the forehead as if I were her own daughter. It meant a lot to me.

She comes over and gives me a hug, which warms me to my core. "So nice to see you, Charlie."

"You too, Mrs. Jones."

"And you must be Kira?" Before Kira answers, Mrs. Jones has already enveloped her in a hug, too. "It's so wonderful to finally meet you."

"It's wonderful to meet you, too, Mrs. Jones," Kira says.

Mrs. Jones stands back and looks at Amelia wistfully, and I see the edges of Amelia's lips twitch into a small smile. It's a tender moment that I feel I'm not meant to see, but I do, and I can't help but be simultaneously envious and touched.

"Well, are you girls ready for some dinner? Dad's cooked up his famous chicken piccata!" Mrs. Jones heads toward the kitchen, us girls in tow, except for Tess, who rushes ahead of all of us and is already sitting in her designated seat at the dinner table, fork and knife in hand, by the time we get there.

"Eli, our esteemed guests are here," Mrs. Jones calls toward the kitchen.

Mr. Jones—taller than Mrs. Jones, dark-skinned, muscular, with kind eyes—pops his head into the dining room.

"Ah," he says. "There they are." Then he spots the new face at the table, Kira, and walks over to her. "You must be Kira." He puts his hands on his hips, towering over her. "And what are your intentions toward my daughter?"

Amelia practically chokes. "Oh my *gosh,* Dad!"

Mr. Jones laughs like he's told the funniest joke ever, even slapping his knee. "I'm kidding, Mimi," he says, using Amelia's nickname. "Loosen up a little!"

"Yeah, Mimi, loosen up," Kira teases.

Mr. Jones laughs again, pointing at Kira. "You. I like you." He surveys the rest of the table. "Now, I hope you girls brought your appetites."

"I sure did, Daddy!" Tess says.

He reaches to tug at her hair, but Tess ducks out of the way. He sighs like she's gravely wounded him. "All right. I'll be right back with the food."

"Do you need any help, Eli?" Mrs. Jones asks.

"I'm all set, Beth, but thank you," Mr. Jones says, disappearing into the kitchen.

Mr. Jones leaves and returns to the dining room several times, each time with a new component of the meal. He places a simple salad, heaping bowls of garlic mashed potatoes and sautéed spinach, and a plate of chicken piccata on the table, while Mrs. Jones busies herself by pouring each of us a tall glass of ice water.

"So, Kira, Amelia tells us you run track, too," Mrs. Jones says. I give Amelia a small smile across the table, knowing what's coming, and she returns it. "Did you know I used to run track back in high school? I was one of the most accomplished in my high school's history."

Amelia looks at Kira and rolls her eyes. I full-on grin. Mrs. Jones loves to talk about her time on the track team. We've heard these stories about a hundred times already. But here's to a hundred and one, right?

"What are we talking about?" Mr. Jones asks as he settles into his seat at the table.

"My time as the fastest runner at Wakefield High."

"Ah, yes. One of my favorite topics. Faster than a cheetah, this one!" Mr. Jones says with a laugh. "We may be in for a long night once she gets started—better dig in now." Mrs. Jones playfully swats at her husband, and he grins at her.

We start to eat while Mrs. Jones regales us with her possibly embellished tales. Her storytelling has always reminded me of my dad, so I don't mind, and now that Amelia is okay being on the track team again, the stories feel less riddled with pressure for her to succeed and more amusing in the parents-am-I-right? kind of way. Plus, the food is impeccable. Mr. Jones is not a chef but a pediatrician; however, I like to tell him he *could* be a chef if he wanted, and that always makes him laugh as if I've said something hysterical.

Once Mrs. Jones has finished telling us about the glory days, we fall into an easy rhythm of conversation. We talk about Tess's upcoming play, where she'll perform as the second lead. The field trip Amelia took with her public speaking class. Kira's recent indoor track competition, where she placed. The plans for my birthday.

I catch Mr. and Mrs. Jones looking over at each other every so often, speaking to each other without having to say a word. It's so dreamy.

Finally, the conversation turns to how Kira and Amelia met. Kira fell during a meet and was convinced she'd sprained her ankle, and Amelia insisted on taking her to the nurse and staying with her until Kira's mom could come pick her up. The adoring way Kira looks at Amelia as she tells this story makes *my* heart skip a beat.

It's the perfect dinner with what I view as the perfect family. It doesn't even matter when Tess starts to test Mrs. Jones's patience by begging for a cat—a crusade she's been on for months now and to which the answer is always no—because it feels just like any other night at Amelia's, which is to say that Kira fits in like a missing puzzle piece.

I leave the house feeling pleased that I could be part of a night like that. Amelia and Kira drop me off at my house, and I hug them both, congratulating them on a job well done. I even gloat a little about being right that Mr. and Mrs. Jones are so wonderful.

Yet back in my quiet room, with my mom gone on another date and not a sound in my home, I can't help but feel a little lonely.

Chapter Twenty-Six

My birthday is less than a week away.

My mom is convinced we both need to go shopping for new outfits, and she offers to pay, so I'm not about to say no—especially because I ended up buying a few items from some online stores and not loving them. They've officially fallen to their untimely death at the bottom of my closet, may they RIP. So I don't really have an outfit and the clock is ticking.

We go to the mall, the faraway one that still has most of its stores in business and not the sad one close to our house that's essentially an empty shell of what it once was (it's too depressing to shop there). After a few last-minute looks at the #fatfashion tag on Insta for some inspiration, I make a vow to step outside my comfort zone and try some things on that I might not have before.

So I'm a little disappointed when our first stop is in my mom's favorite straight-size store. She knows I can't fit into anything here, and as soon as I walk in, I feel like the salesgirls are all looking at me.

Mom starts browsing through a rack of tops, while I start to wander over to the accessories.

"Where are you going?" Mom asks.

"I'm going to head to the purse section."

"We're not here to buy a purse," she reminds me.

"I know, but…"

"But what?" she asks.

I don't want to say it, especially with people around.

"You know," I say.

Mom puts a hand on her hip. "Know what? We're trying to find you a nice outfit for your party."

I sigh, then pretend to be looking through the racks of clothing, too.

"There we go. Let me know if you see something you like."

I can't tell if my mom is purposely being hurtful, or if she genuinely doesn't realize that literally none of these things will fit me. It's not worth it to argue, though. I try not to focus on the fact that each screech of the wire hanger against the rack is a running count of all the items of clothing I can't fit into. One, two, three, four, five.

Mom's already got a stack of clothes draped over her arm and slips off to the dressing room for round one. Shortly after she disappears from sight, an employee wanders over.

"Can I help you with something?" she asks. She's tiny and beautiful and I kind of hate her because I feel like I know what's coming next.

"No. Just looking."

"Oh, okay. Just to let you know, the biggest size we go up to here is twelve."

I start to get hot. "Oh, yeah, okay. I'm here with her. So." I point toward my mom, who has stopped near the dressing rooms to look at a dress. "She's shopping, not me."

"Ohhh, that makes sense. Well, if your sister needs any help, just let us know!"

I could die. How will I survive this afternoon?

After a few other stores (all unsuccessful for me), my mom suggests we try Old Navy and I feel a surge of hope. Sometimes I can wiggle into their clothes. We both select a few items to try and then head to the fitting rooms. I bring in a fitted midi skirt (similar to the one Amelia and I ogled a few weeks back), a V-neck top that would match, an A-line dress, a few pairs of jeans, and a blouse.

Mom grabs one dressing room and I snag the one beside her. I decide to try the jeans first and save the skirt for last.

As I'm taking off my clothes, I hear my mom loudly say, "So."

"Yeah?" I respond, holding up the first pair of jeans and pulling on them to see if they have any stretch. They do. Jackpot.

"I told you Jen and Becca will be coming to your birthday party, right?"

I make a face, and I'm glad my mom's not there to see it. "Jen and Becca from the gym?" I ask, pulling on the first pair of jeans. They fit, but the legs pool around my ankles. Too long. Why can't fashion designers ever get the proportions on jeans right?

"Yes. I thought you liked them?"

I tug the jeans off. "I do," I say, barely wiggling into the next pair.

"Good. They just want to swing by and say hello. They like you, too."

"Okay. Sounds good."

"Obviously I invited Titi Lina, Tío José, Titi Isabel, Roxy. And of course your cousins. I also invited Tío Armando." We haven't seen him in years. "And his wife, Amanda. You remember Amanda, right?"

"How could I forget Amanda?" One time, she made a snide comment about how my mom shouldn't set such a bad example for me. If she lost weight, Amanda said, I'd probably follow suit. I have no desire to see Amanda.

"A few others will be coming, too," Mom says. "Eva, Sarah, Lynn."

"Who?"

"Oh, you know them! The girls. Remember? I used to hang out with them all the time."

"The girls," I repeat.

"Yes. From . . . you know. The group I used to meet with."

It takes me a moment before I realize she's referring to the weight-loss group she used to attend. Eva, Sarah, and Lynn were part of that group. Mom would talk about them sometimes when she got back from her meeting.

"Oh" is all I say.

"Yeah. It's going to be great."

The third and final pair of jeans don't fit, either, so I leave them in a heap on the floor and grab a top. "That's kind of a lot of people, Mom."

"I know, I know. I got a little carried away," she says. "You don't mind, do you?"

What can I say to that aside from "No, it's fine"? I mull over my response while trying on the blouse. It fits, but it makes me look like a shapeless box. Pass.

"No." I pull the top off and let it fall to the floor beside the jeans, even though that means I'll just have to pick it up and hang it afterward. "It's fine."

"Good. It will be so nice to see everyone. It's been too long."

I pull on the dress, which is a little snug in the armpits. Ugh.

"Oh!" Mom continues. "And Fernando will be coming as well. I can't wait for you to meet him!"

Fernando is the guy my mom has been on a few dates with recently. And suddenly, I understand what this is all about.

My mom wants to show off in front of all her old friends.

New man, new body...it's all wasted unless everyone else can see it.

I yank the dress off, saying nothing. I will not respond. I will not let her get to me.

Instead, I take a deep breath and try to calmly slip into the T-shirt and skirt combo. Miraculously, both fit, but when I turn to the side to inspect the look, I feel my heart sink. It just doesn't look the way I'd pictured in my head. And that feels like a gut punch.

I begrudgingly put all of the clothes back on their hangers, leave the dressing room, and bang on my mom's door.

"We done here?" I ask.

"Jeez, you scared me," she says, pulling the door open. "Yes. Nothing's doing it for me."

"Great." I put the clothes on the return rack and turn quickly on my heel, speed-walking out of the store.

"Wait," Mom says. I ignore her and keep walking. I've had enough of pretending I can find something to wear in these stupid stores. And I've had just about enough of this shopping trip.

Once I'm outside the store, I start to head toward the mall exit. I can hear my mom rushing up behind me, her shopping bags rustling. "Charlie! Wait!" I stop and turn to her. "Didn't you hear me calling you?"

"Oh, I heard you," I say.

Annoyance flickers over her face. "Then what's the problem?"

"What gives you the right to invite all of these people to the party, Mom? It's supposed to be my birthday party, not yours."

My mom seems startled by this. But then she stands up straighter. "I'm the one paying for the party, and it's my house, so I'll invite whoever I please."

"*Whom*ever."

"Whatever!" Mom snaps. "You're so ungrateful sometimes, Charlotte, I swear to God. I'm trying to do a nice thing here by taking you shopping."

"Yeah, at stores where I can't fit into anything!"

"Well, I didn't know!"

I find that hard to believe, given that when *she* was fat, she would always talk about how shopping for special occasions was particularly stressful. She lamented that it was hard to see some who could waltz into any store they pleased and buy anything, knowing it would fit, while she'd have to go to specialty stores *and* try everything on. But maybe it's been so long since she's been fat that she doesn't remember. And anyway, I'm tired, so I just say, "Okay, well, now you know."

Her face softens, and so does her voice. "Do you want to keep looking? We can try a different store."

I shake my head.

"Okay," she says. "We can go."

We've started to walk toward the exit when I think I spot Brian coming out of a video game store. Cue tummy flutter. The boy looks up and yeah, it's definitely Brian.

"Brian!" I say, a little more enthusiastically than I intend.

He breaks into a big smile. "Hey, Charlie! Hi, Mrs. Vega!"

"Hello, Bryant," Mom says.

"It's Brian, Mom," I correct, trying not to sound too offended.

"Oh. Sorry." But she doesn't sound like she means it. I shoot Brian an apologetic look, and he just laughs.

"Good finds?" he asks, motioning toward my mom's bags.

"Yes," she says, and leaves it at that.

"My mom had a very successful shopping trip," I say. "Me, not so much. We were looking for an outfit for my birthday party, but I didn't find anything. You seem to have had some luck, though!" I point at the bag in his hand.

He pulls the game out and shows it to me. "Yeah, it's this new video game I've been waiting for! I mean, I was happy to wait because the first one was *perfect*—it was set in medieval times, but apocalyptic, with a super-creepy alien invasion. Story, combat, crafting—ten out of ten. In this one, you actually play as the sidekick from the first game, except she's grown up now." Then he stops talking and looks sheepishly at me. "I'm rambling. I've been reading about it for months and it's finally out. Picked up the collector's edition."

"Of course," I tease. "It sounds fun." I'm not super into video games, but the excitement in Brian's voice is enough to intrigue me.

"We've got to get going, Charlie," Mom says.

I give her a look.

"Oh, sure," Brian says. "Well, good running into you, Charlie. I'll see you at school on Monday." He looks at my mom and waves. "Nice to see you, Mrs. Vega." She nods in reply and starts walking toward the exit.

"See you at school, Brian," I say, smiling and following her.

When we're out of earshot, my mom says, "You mentioned your birthday to him."

"So you *can* speak."

"What?" she asks, irritated.

"You didn't say a word when Brian was around."

"He was talking about a video game!"

I ignore that and ask, "Why does it matter that I mentioned my birthday party?"

"It's impolite to mention things to people when they're not invited."

"He is invited," I say.

Mom looks surprised. "Oh. He is?"

I can tell she's dissatisfied by this, though I'm unsure why, so I smile. "Yeah," I say. "He is."

And for the first time, I feel a little excited about my birthday party.

Chapter Twenty-Seven

"**Would it be bad** if I showed up to my party in pajamas?" I ask.

Amelia and I are seated on her bed. Tonight's my birthday and we should be getting ready for it.

She is. I'm not.

Amelia stops applying her mascara to look at me and what I'm wearing—a matching top-and-bottom pj set with puppies on them. "You know I'm normally all about hanging out in our pajamas. But this is your first grown-up birthday party."

My eyes widen at her. "It sounds scary when you say it like that."

"It is, though! We're not doing a slumber party like we normally do. This is, like, people coming over to have a good time."

"I guess."

She wrinkles her nose at me. "Don't get all weird about it."

"Well, now I *feel* all weird about it! So much pressure. I definitely can't wear this. I need to wear something like what you're wearing."

I probably look at her longingly. But it's hard not to. While I never ended up finding the right outfit for tonight, Amelia—whose night it *isn't*—looks incredible. Her toned body is snugly wrapped in a black sheath dress; her coiled curls are perfect; and her winged eyeliner is so precise it seems more mathematical than artistic. She's the epitome of what I want to be. Especially tonight, when all eyes will be on me, at least while they're singing "Happy Birthday."

"What do I do?" I ask, feeling suddenly desperate.

"Well, I can't believe you didn't choose an outfit before now! What happened to all of those clothes we'd been looking at online? You never ended up taking me up on my zillion offers to go shopping!" She's right. Before the disastrous shopping adventure with my mom, I was too nervous, and after, too discouraged. Amelia finishes applying her mascara. Then her face brightens. "Why don't you look through my closet? You can wear whatever you want! What's mine is yours."

It's a sweet thought, but I can feel my palms get sweaty at the suggestion. I'd be lucky to be able to fit my leg in any of Amelia's dresses. Why can't she see that? She makes suggestions like this all the time, offering to let me borrow a sweater if I'm cold or a T-shirt and leggings if I'm staying over. Once she suggested I use her bathing suit when I forgot mine. All moments so kind and well intentioned. All moments that leave me feeling so ashamed of my size. Does she really not see how different our bodies are?

Maybe Old Me would let this well-meaning comment slide completely, not even acknowledging the difference in our sizes. But New Me doesn't feel like she should let this moment pass.

"You're the best, Amelia. Thank you," I say. "But you must know that nothing in your closet would fit me, right?"

She looks over at me with a frown. "Oh," she says. "Well…"

"Let's try my closet," I say. "I know you'll be able to help me find something in there. I mean, just look at you! You look amazing."

Amelia bites on her bottom lip. "Really? You think?"

"Really. I know."

"This is the first official party I'm going to with Kira as my girlfriend," Amelia says. "I want to look nice."

Aw. "Well, you nailed it."

Amelia smiles. "Thank you, Charlie. Now, let's head to your

house and get you something to wear!" She looks at her phone. "We have an hour. Go, go, go!"

We go—straight to my house and right to my closet, where Amelia starts rifling through everything I own. She starts to make a pile of maybes on my bed. When she's finished, we look through the heap. None of it goes together.

"Maybe the sweater and some leggings?" Amelia suggests. She grabs the sweater and tells me to try it on. I put it on over what I'm already wearing and look at her to see if it's any good. Her face tells me all I need to know.

"It's terrible, isn't it?" I ask.

"Not at all. Just not exactly the look we're going for, right? It's good for school and stuff, but for your birthday party, it's a little..."

"Boring," I finish. "Totally."

"No worries. I think one of these dresses could work!" She points at the few she's laid out on my bed: a floral empire-waist dress, a polka-dotted wrap dress, and a sweet (though young-looking) Peter Pan–collar dress. "They're all really pretty."

I groan. "But everyone's seen me in them before. Not exactly turning-seventeen material."

She sighs, looking around my room. "Well..." Her eyes land on something and she jumps to her feet. "Have you been holding out? Is that a bag of new clothes?" She snatches a torn-open bag from my closet floor, a leftover package from my Charlie-experiments-with-fatshion shopping spree that I haven't yet gotten around to returning.

"There's nothing good in there," I protest.

"I will fully be the judge of that," Amelia says, dumping the clothes out on my bed. She starts sifting through the items. "Oh! How about this?"

She holds up a wine-colored pleated miniskirt. I bought it

hoping it might offer a nice alternative to the body-hugging silhou-
ette I wasn't quite ready to dive into. The pro: it nipped at my waist
pretty nicely, actually. The con: I wasn't sure I'd have the guts to
wear it, so, in a huff, I decided I would just send it (and everything
else I'd ordered) back.

"With?" I demand.

Amelia goes to my closet and picks out a short-sleeve black
V-neck. "This," she says, handing them both to me. "Try it on. Now!"

I grab a bra and slip into the bathroom, where I wiggle out of
my pajamas and pull everything on, tucking the shirt into the skirt.
I squeeze my eyes shut before I take a look in the mirror, afraid to
disappoint myself.

Only, when I look up, I think I look...cute?

Amelia knocks. "Well?" she asks.

"I don't know," I say, opening the door.

She lets out a little gasp. "Charlie! Don't be silly! You look so
amazing!"

"Really?" I bite my lip, walking over to the bed and getting a
little excited.

"Yes!" She digs through my jewelry and hands me a long neck-
lace and huge hoop earrings, which I add to the outfit. Amelia
claps her hands together. "Yes! Charlie! I can't believe you've been
hiding this beautiful outfit this whole time. God, you make me so
mad sometimes."

"I wasn't sure it would work on me," I admit.

Amelia shakes her head. "Enough of that. Now, let me do your
hair and makeup, and you'll be even more of a knockout. Come on!
We're running out of time."

We listen to music as she starts curling my hair. The songs help
distract me from the butterflies in my stomach.

Amelia's putting a little highlighter on my cheekbones when
the doorbell rings.

My eyes widen. I thought I had more time. "Oh, God," I say.

"We're done here, anyway," she says, picking up my mirror and showing me my face. "Well?"

I'm a little surprised by my reflection. The makeup looks precise, just like Amelia's, and my hair is beautiful: the loose curls cascade around my face and down my shoulders. There's a reason I always insist that my hair is my best feature. And that highlighter? The blush? The sharp-as-glass eyeliner? Divine.

I smile at her. "You did a great job. Thank you."

"*Charlie!*" I hear my mom yell from down the hall.

"Ready?" Amelia asks.

I take a deep breath. "As I'll ever be."

Chapter Twenty-Eight

Mom is parading her date, Fernando, around my party, which is surprisingly bumping...with everyone Mom's invited. She's already a few drinks in; she was actually a few drinks in the moment she called out to me to come see who was at the door.

"Nerves," she'd whispered to me as she held up her wineglass. All I could smell was the alcohol on her breath.

She's had at least two glasses since then, and now she's got her both of her arms wrapped around one of Fernando's and she's giggly and gazing up at him with big eyes, even if he seems a little distant, even if his hands are shoved in his pockets. She's gushing to anyone who will listen. She's bragging about his job—he's a *professor*, don't you know?—and running her hands down his chest.

Amelia and I exchange a glance. She pretends to gag and I give her a small smile. I feel like I could *actually* gag. I want to be supportive of my mom's new relationship, but...the way she's acting is too much.

Mom is wearing a skintight dress and modeling it in front of her friends from her weight-loss group, who *ooh* and *ahh* over her body and beg her to share her secrets. It's nothing, she says, just diet and exercise!

I eye her in envy. Moms shouldn't be prettier than their daughters. It's not fair.

Then my mom is telling everyone that her daughter is so great, doesn't she have such a lovely face, and she's so smart in school— yet my mom doesn't even bother to look at me as she speaks because I'm not there, not really, not to her. Her friends reiterate what a smart girl I am, how impressive my academic achievements are, what a great job she did raising me, and how, because of her, I turned out to be something real special.

I'm doing my best to smile through it all. Let her parade me and Amelia around. Try to ignore the way she and everyone else fawn over Amelia's striking beauty ("Ooh, you're a tiny little thing!" one says) yet can only muster up compliments about my brain and my schoolwork, not my appearance.

I keep checking the time. It's dragging.

Amelia squeezes my hand. "They'll be here soon," she says to me, thinking I'm watching the clock because I'm worried that the people I've invited won't show. Really, I'm wondering how long I'll have to keep enduring this nightmare.

When I reach for another handful of chips, my mother, in front of everyone, *tsk*s me, and my hand recoils to my side.

I escape away from her and into the back room, where Fernando is looking through some of the family photos that are hanging on the wall. He must've needed a break, too. My mom can be a lot.

Fernando the Professor is a decent-looking dude—light-skinned, muscular, dark eyes, goatee. I make a mental note that he should totally grow the goatee out into a full beard because this isn't 1992, but then I chide myself for being so catty when he's done literally nothing wrong.

"Hey, it's the birthday girl. Feliz cumpleaños," he says with a smile. Well, whoops. "¿Hablas español?"

"Oh. No," I say.

"No?" Fernando asks, looking shocked. "But you're Puerto Rican, no? That's what your mother told me."

"Oh, yeah, I am—I just don't speak Spanish. My dad never

taught me," I reply, then feel like a jerk for throwing my poor dad under the bus. To my mom's new boyfriend. Sorry, Papi.

"That's a shame," Fernando says. "But there's still time to learn. You should!"

"Yeah, maybe," I say. "Sorry, excuse me."

I sneak off to the bathroom and I lock myself in. God, shamed for not speaking Spanish at my own birthday party? I wish I could say this is the first time that's happened, but it happens all the time. Many who speak Spanish—particularly fellow Puerto Ricans—are disappointed when they learn I don't, like I've committed some grave sin or maybe am even *lying* about being Puerto Rican. My cousins *still* make fun of me.

And then the thought of waiting around for my cousins and tías and tíos to make their appearance and devoting tons of attention to my mom makes me cringe. They'll gas her up, she'll bask in it, I'll have to try not to vomit. I take a deep breath and slowly exhale.

In the mirror, my cheeks are flushed and my eyeliner is already a little smudged. I dab at the corners of my eyes with my finger to clean it up a little. It helps me look better, but it certainly doesn't help me feel better.

"I can't do this," I say to my reflection.

And then I decide I won't.

I text Amelia from the bathroom.

New plan, I write. **Let's leave.**

Now? she writes back. Then there's a soft knock at the door.

"It's me," Amelia says, and I let her in. "I am also having a terrible time, but we can't just leave. Your cousins aren't even here yet!"

I shake my head. "They won't be, not for a few hours. They're always late. So we should just go. This is *awful*."

"But what about everyone who's still coming? What about Brian?"

"They can meet us somewhere else. It's my birthday, right? And this"—I motion toward the craziness unfurling in the living room and kitchen—"is not what I had in mind for my party."

"Where would you even want to go?" Amelia asks, watching me.

"Let's text everyone to meet us at Jake's," I say. "I just want to hang out. Away from all of this. What do you think?"

She's quiet for moment. "I think that sounds a hell of a lot better than sticking around for what has clearly turned into your *mom's* party."

The acknowledgment that this party has gone off the deep end sends a wave of relief through my body. Sometimes I worry I pick fights with my mom about things I should just let go, but when others around me see the same things—see that my mom is *wrong*—it helps me feel sane. I could hug Amelia just for saying that.

So I do. "You get me."

I ask her to text her friends. I text Brian and Benjamin. Then we sneak out of the bathroom, slip out the back door of the house, hop into my car, and drive away.

* * *

When we arrive at the coffee shop, Brian's already there, waiting outside.

"Happy birthday!" he says when he spots me. I watch as he takes in what I'm wearing, his lips spreading into a smile. "You look...amazing."

I grin. After that slow, lingering look from him, I *feel* pretty amazing. "Thank you, Brian. How'd you get here so fast?"

"I was already on my way to your house when you texted."

My eyes go big. "Were you texting while driving?!"

"I was at a stoplight!" he insists.

"Don't do that," I say, serious.

"You could die, you know," Amelia says. "And we wouldn't want that."

Brian puts his hands up in defeat. "Okay, okay. Got it. You're both right. So what's going on? Why the sudden location change?"

I shrug. "We wanted to keep things exciting."

"You just wanted a clever way to finally get me to Jake's. You could've asked me straight up, Charlie, although this is good, too," he teases.

We walk toward the entrance and he holds open the door for the two of us. Amelia immediately starts pushing tables together, enough for our group to sit. Brian offers to get some coffees for the table—I give him my order and try to put a few crumpled dollars in his hand, but he refuses to take them.

"The birthday girl doesn't pay," he says, and I relent.

Instead, I sit at the table, still trying to shake off the bad feelings from my mom's party when I see our friends walk into the coffee shop. When they spot me, I'm greeted with a round of cheerful "Happy birthdays." Kira tells me I look nice, Liz compliments my outfit, and I'm caught up in the flurry of hellos and the relief that everyone actually came. No one even mentions it's weird that my birthday party moved last-minute to the local coffee shop.

Instead, we sit around our tables and make fun of Khalil for how sweet he likes his coffee.

"It's basically milk and sugar with a dribble of actual coffee," Maddy says. She and Khalil have been dating for a while, and they seem pretty adorable together.

Khalil shrugs. "I'm weirdly fine with that. It tastes good."

Liz wrinkles her nose. "It's too sweet. I can tell just by looking! See how light it is?"

"I just don't like the taste of coffee! It's bitter!"

"To be fair, the taste of coffee does take some getting used to," Brian offers.

"Thank you, man! Someone who has my back."

It's then that Benjamin walks into Jake's, and I call out to him. "Benjamin! Over here!"

Amelia looks surprised, whispering, "He came!"

I grin, waving him over. "We're pals."

"Benjamin!" John shouts, and Amelia gives him a quizzical look. "Love that guy. Kid's hilarious. We're in AP calc together."

"*You're* in AP calc?" Jessica asks.

John just flips her off in response as I get up to give Benjamin a hug. We're not typically the hugging type of friends, but I'm suddenly in a really good mood, and I definitely want him to feel welcome.

"Come, sit." I grab an empty chair and squeeze it in beside mine. "Thanks for coming!"

Benjamin gives me a small smile, pushing his glasses up, looking a little embarrassed by the big greeting he received. "Thanks for inviting me."

"Do you know everyone?" When he shakes his head, I do a quick round of introductions. "Now you do."

"Can't promise I'll remember everyone's names, but I'll try. Kinda wishing I hadn't spent so much time memorizing the periodic table and left some room for things like that, but we all make choices," Benjamin says, and we laugh.

Out of nowhere, I feel a kick under the table and glance at Amelia, who nods toward Brian. He's gotten up from our table and is standing near the counter, half-heartedly looking at the display case of baked goods. I shoot her a confused look and she mouths, *Jealous?*

While the others continue to chat around me, I shoot her a text.

What?! I write.

Her reply reads **Brian looked real puppy dog when you gave lil Benny a hug** and includes a shrug emoji, hair-flip emoji, and nail polish emoji.

I bite my lip, trying to hide a smile. Jealous? Really?

I excuse myself from the table and join Brian at the counter. "That blueberry muffin might be calling my name."

He breaks into a grin when he sees me. "I was eyeing the apple pie bite myself. Can I get you that muffin? It is your birthday, after all."

"I'm going to order some stuff for the table. Help me out?" I ask.

We take turns picking out an assortment of baked goods, and as the barista is getting them ready on a tray, Brian turns to me. "So, Benjamin, huh?"

"What do you mean?"

"Nothing. Just that he's a good guy."

I shrug. "Sure. He's a good friend."

And Brian doesn't try to hide his smile. "Friend. Okay. Cool."

And I smile, looking down at my feet, biting my lip again. "Yeah. Cool."

Then the barista hands over the tray of goodies and we head back to the table. Brian walks. I can't help it; I float.

"Anyone hungry?" I ask.

"Fooooood!" Khalil shouts, and he digs in, and so does everyone else. We eat a bunch and talk about silly things between bites: drama from school (the latest is that Casey Stiles is dropping out), college and how we're not even ready to think about it (but it's *all* the teachers talk about), the hot new substitute teacher at school, Mr. Brown (the boys are unanimously unimpressed), TV shows everyone should have seen by now (like *Breaking Bad,* which John hasn't watched!).

Kira is incredulous over that last discovery. "How can you not have watched that show yet?"

"It's been out for *years*," Maddy says.

Benjamin is wide-eyed. "Even *I've* seen it, and I'm not normally a TV guy. But Bryan Cranston is incredible—and the show is also surprisingly great commentary on the need for universal health care."

"It's on my list, guys!" John insists.

We're laughing and being loud and for once in my life I feel like I'm not on the outside looking in. And then before I know it, Amelia is carrying a muffin to our table and we pretend there's a candle in it as they all sing "Happy Birthday" to me and I blow the fake flame out.

It's the first year where I don't waste my wish on being skinny; I wish for more happy moments like this.

I'm rewarded seconds later when everyone pulls out their gifts for me. I get a generous gift card from Amelia's friends, who are maybe now a little bit my friends. From Benjamin, I get a travel mug that says I GLITTERALLY CAN'T, which makes us all laugh. From Amelia, I get a beautiful jade-colored scarf I saw while shopping with her at Macy's. I'm beaming.

Brian mentions that there's an arcade across the street, and suddenly we're all excitedly talking about how we should go, yes, let's do it! Trying to get a group of ten across a busy street proves to be difficult. We act like jerks and run across without waiting for the walk signal or even bothering to go into the crosswalk, which makes some cars beep at us. If I were watching, I'd think *These kids are obnoxious,* but since I'm part of the fun, I'm laughing and being rowdy and thinking that yeah, I get it now.

We play games for a while, till I nearly run out of money; I prove to the group that I'm secretly really good at playing pool, and it turns out that Brian is obsessed with old-school arcade games. I feel like I laugh the whole night, and I'm sad when I realize it's nearly midnight and we decide we should all get home.

As we say our goodbyes, I make sure to hug Amelia tight. "Thank you for helping to make my birthday special," I whisper.

"I'm sorry it started out so terribly," she whispers back.

I shake my head. "Doesn't matter. It ended perfectly."

She touches my arm. "You deserved it. Do you want to come back to my house and stay the night so you don't have to go home?"

For a moment, I consider it, but I decide against it. It will be better for me to go home and deal with my mom's anger now rather than later. "No, that's all right. But thank you." I see Kira lingering by her car and I nod in that direction. "Looks like *someone* might be waiting for you, though."

Amelia grins, then hugs me again. "Happy birthday, Charlie. Text me, okay?" She hurries over to Kira and gets into her car.

I've started to head toward my own car when I hear a voice.

"Hey," it says.

I turn, see it's Brian, and break into a big smile. "Hey back."

"You got a second, birthday girl?" he asks. I nod and he motions for me to follow. We walk toward his car. "That was my kind of party."

"Weird and in a coffee shop?" I don't know why I say that, because it actually wasn't weird at all. I loved it. But I'm worried he didn't, that he's being sarcastic.

"No, not weird at all. I knew you and I would make it to Jake's sometime. And I had a lot of fun," Brian says, holding my gaze. "I liked that we were all just hanging out. I like your friends."

"They're barely my friends."

He gives me a look. "They seem like they're your friends. And why wouldn't they be? You're fun to be around! They gave you gifts and everything." He motions toward the gift bag I'm holding.

"Yeah," I say, glancing down at it. "It's amazing."

"It's too bad that jerk friend of yours, Brian, didn't remember to take his gift out of the car and give it to you alongside everyone else." He ducks into his car and surfaces with a perfectly wrapped rectangle, then hands it to me. "For you."

"Brian, you didn't have to—"

"I wanted to. I'm sorry I didn't give it to you earlier," he says, a bit shyly. "And you don't have to open it now. I know some people feel weird being watched when they open their gifts."

I answer him by sticking the gift bag on my wrist so both hands are free, then carefully removing the bow and wrapping paper from his present to reveal an exquisite leather-bound journal. I can't help it; I gasp a little.

"It's beautiful," I whisper.

"Yeah?" he asks, and by the way his voice goes up, I can tell he's pleased. "A good writer deserves a good notebook."

I look up at him, feeling a little like I could cry. "This is the most thoughtful gift anyone's ever given me, Brian."

"I'm glad you like it," he says.

"I love it," I say. "Thank you."

"I just wanted your birthday to be special."

I look at him. At that crooked smile that makes my knees feel a little weak. At the way his dark hair falls a little bit into his eyes. At his perfect nose. At those soft, kissable lips.

And he looks back at me, so intensely, like maybe...there's something. My heart is thumping; I can feel it beating in my ears. And there's a moment. Just one.

Then I break the silence.

"So...I should go," I say. Before I do something stupid. Like try to kiss him.

"Oh, yeah," Brian says. "Happy birthday." But he says it with meaning, like if I can infer something from the words *happy birthday*, I should.

"You too. I mean, thanks." I laugh as I'm walking away. "Drive safe! And no texting!"

And I rush to my car and I'm still laughing and I can't help but think that this has been my best birthday ever.

* * *

When I get home, I find Mom drunk, her friends and Fernando gone, the house a mess.

She's livid when I walk through the door, and she demands to know where I've been. Before I can explain—*Hi, Mom, I've just had the most magnificent birthday of my life, and I think, maybe, I might have some friends, and I think, possibly, somehow, a boy might actually like me*—she's sobbing and saying I don't appreciate her and that I ruined my birthday and I never do anything she wants me to do.

Amid her yelling, I help her to her room, get her into some pajamas, offer her some water, and put her to bed.

I clean the house a little so she'll be less angry tomorrow morning. Then I go to my room, where I can't stop thinking about Brian.

And I can't stop looking at the gorgeous leather-bound journal he picked out, just for me. I run my fingers over the smooth cover; I wrap and unwrap the leather strap; I flip through the ivory pages; I hug it to my chest. I try to imagine him at the store, poring over the journals, looking through them all until he finds one he thinks I'll like. It's the sweetest image I can conjure, and I fall asleep with a smile on my face.

Chapter Twenty-Nine

I wake up to a text from Brian.

Morning, kid.

The events of last night flood back to me and I swear my heart does a little flip.

Good morning. Thank you again for the thoughtful gift, I write back.

I stare at my phone until those three little gray dots show up.

You're welcome. It will be perfect for when you write the next Great American Novel. Or Hunger Games. Whichever.

If I write anything, it will be the next To All the Boys I've Loved Before, I write back.

When it takes Brian a minute to reply, I feel shaky. But he writes **Obviously.**

And a second, separate message says: **Have you ever seen the movie Ladybird?**

No, I write. **Should I have?**

Yes. They just added it to Netflix. It's so good.

Then: **Do you want to come over later and watch?**

My breath catches in my throat. I literally pinch myself. Yes, I'm awake. But somehow I'm living some romanticized version of my life. Because Brian is asking me to hang out and watch a movie. And this is how my life goes now, apparently.

I reply with a casual **Sure!** before I can freak myself out and say no, or before I overthink it and write what I actually feel in my heart, which is *YES!!!!!!!!!!!!!!!!!!!!!!!!!!!!!!!!!!!!!!*

He texts me back with his address and says we should meet up at seven, making it official:

Brian and I are watching a movie later.

I almost text Amelia, but something stops me. It will be my first time hanging out with a boy, alone—something Amelia did for the first time in the fifth grade. And for some reason, I feel embarrassed to admit that, even though she already knows my truth. I'm worried she might accidentally say something a little insensitive. Something like "It's about time" or "Welcome to the club!" without meaning it, not really. And all that'll do is reinforce how alone I usually feel, how inexperienced I am, how embarrassed I feel that I'm sixteen—ugh, *seventeen* now—and I've never been kissed.

So maybe it makes me a bad friend, but I don't text Amelia to let her know what I'll be doing later. Instead, I text her to thank her for a great birthday, and when she asks me to hang out today, I deflect and say my mom's mad at me (which she is, and will be) and try to convince myself lying to my best friend is totally normal.

I shower and get dressed. Not in the outfit I'll wear to visit with Brian later, but the outfit I'm going to sit in to think about visiting with Brian later, because a girl needs to plan.

I bring all my gifts from last night with me out into the kitchen and pour myself a bowl of cereal. As I eat, I marvel over the fact that last night was *real* and it *actually happened*. I even have the pictures on my phone to prove it!

My rustling must wake my mom, because I hear the door to her room open. I expect her to come into the kitchen and be really angry with me. I mean. You don't ditch your own party and make your mom look bad in front of her guests and live to tell the tale. I'm already planning all the ways I'll argue with her about how I can't be grounded tonight of all nights because something important is happening. I won't tell her what; I'll make something up. I'm working on a school project or something.

And I'll listen to her lecture me about how it's impolite to leave a party someone has thrown for you and how disappointed she is in me. I'll try not to emote (except to try to look like I regret sneaking out of the party last night). I'll tell her I had a really miserable time after I left and I should've stayed. I'll grovel and apologize a million times over and maybe everything will be fine.

Only, I don't end up needing to do any of these things because she walks into the kitchen and says a quiet hello to me like nothing happened. Then she starts making breakfast for herself. Like, actual breakfast, and not a shake.

"Would you like something to eat?" she asks as she cracks some eggs into a sizzling pan.

I hesitate before replying. "I already ate, but thank you."

"Suit yourself," she says, adding a little adobo and scrambling it up. "Did you have a nice birthday?"

I consider my answer carefully. "It was really nice."

She uses her spatula to point at the gifts on the table. "You made out well."

"Yeah," I say. "I did."

"Good." Mom scrapes her eggs out of the pan and onto a plate and a silence hangs in the air.

"Mom, about last night—"

She holds up her hand. "Let's just forget it."

I blink. "Really?"

"I'm tired." Mom plops at the kitchen table and I study her face. She does look exhausted.

"Oh?"

She nods. "Yeah, and I don't need you lecturing me about how I got out of control. I'm well aware, thanks to a string of angry texts from Fernando. I don't even remember getting into a fight with him, and now I've got to deal with that, so just save it, Charlie. Seriously."

"I wasn't going to say anything."

Mom gives me a look. "Right. I black out at your party and you have *nothing* to say?"

And suddenly it makes sense. My mom may not even realize that I wasn't at my own birthday party.

"Nope."

Her shoulders slump a little, relaxing. "Oh, okay. Well, I guess I overdid it. I was just so stressed out about everything. I mean, I spent so long picking out my dress and getting all the food just right and keeping everyone happy. I just wanted everything to be perfect, you know?"

"Right. Perfect. For me."

"Of course for you. I've been whirling around like a tornado for weeks trying to get everything ready for this party for you. I didn't even get a thank-you." She sighs, taking a bite of her eggs.

The audacity.

"Sorry," I say, not meaning it. "But thank you."

She waves her hand dismissively. "At least everyone seemed to enjoy themselves. The girls loved what I've done to the house. And Lynn said she nearly had a heart attack when she saw me! So aside from everything with Fernando, I'm happy. He'll forgive me. I hope." She looks over at me. "It was a good party, right?"

I nod. "Yeah, it was."

"Best birthday ever?"

Memories from last night flood back to me—Jake's, the arcade, Brian—and I smile. "Yes, actually. Best birthday ever."

Chapter Thirty

I pass the time between Not Being at Brian's and Being at Brian's by doing the following: thinking about every single interaction I've ever had with Brian; arguing with myself over whether he's invited me to watch a movie because he likes me or it's just because we're friends; and thinking about what I should wear (I settle on a deep-purple top with a scoop neckline tucked into a black skater skirt), say (I have a long list of topics I can touch on if there's an awkward silence, like Hey, *what are your thoughts on climate change?*), and do (still haven't figured that one out yet).

Somehow, eventually, it's time for me to leave and go to his house. I get there early. I wait in my car. Then, at *exactly* 7 p.m., I knock on the front door.

In the time it takes from when I knocked to when the door opens, I think about bolting approximately seventy times.

But then a woman is standing there, grinning at me.

"Well, hello!" Her voice is sweet and she basically looks like Brian if Brian were a girl. She's shorter than he is, but she has the same black hair and black eyes and sharp cheekbones.

"Hi!" I say back, trying to match her enthusiasm.

"You're Charlie, right?"

"I am. You must be Brian's mom?"

"One of!" She lets out a little laugh. "I'm Susan. Come in, come in." Susan opens the door wider so I can get inside. "I've heard so much about you."

"All good things, I hope," I say.

"Oh, yes. Very much so." Susan is practically beaming at me. "Can I get you anything to drink? Eat? Anything at all?"

"Mom, chill," Brian says as he walks into the foyer. I notice his cheeks look a little pink, probably from embarrassment. It's adorable.

"I just want to make your friend feel welcome," Susan says.

"And she's doing a great job," I say. "Thank you."

"But let's quit while we're ahead and go outside, okay?" Brian motions toward the back door of the house, which I start to walk toward. He follows me and calls over his shoulder, "Thanks, Mom!"

We step into his backyard. The sun is just starting to set on this beautiful day in April and the breeze feels good on my skin. Outside, we have a moment to breathe, just the two of us, and it's then that I can finally take in the sight of Brian: he's wearing a fitted black button-up and a nice pair of dark denim jeans over some crisp Converse shoes. I bite my lip and my insides feel like they're trembling with glee; this is *totally* a date!

"Now, did you actually want something to eat or drink?" Brian asks. "I'm happy to get you anything you want. It's just that if you had said yes to my mom, she'd have started talking and talking and talking, and before you know it, she's pulling out my baby photos and that's it. It's over. There's no coming back from that."

I laugh. "I highly doubt it would've gone like that."

"You don't know my mom."

"Is she like that with everyone?"

"No. She's been a little jealous that Ma has already met you and she hasn't stopped talking about it." Then his cheeks go pink again. And then *my* cheeks go pink.

I find myself wondering how often I've come up during conversation. Enough for Susan *and* Maura to have discussed me, enough for Susan to wish she'd met me. I'm pleased.

"Anyway," Brian says, "there's something I wanted to show you." He heads toward the garage. "I think you'll like this." He stoops down and grabs the garage door handle, then pulls it up and gives it a good shove so it opens all the way. With his hands over his head, his shirt rides up and part of his stomach is exposed, but only for a second, which feels a little scandalous. Like I saw something I'm not supposed to see. "Well?" he asks.

I realize I haven't even glanced at what's behind the garage door, so I quickly avert my gaze from him and look into the garage—and realize it's not really a garage at all.

It's an art studio. There's an easel with an unfinished painting on it, a table with scattered paints, a pile of sketchbooks and brushes, some shelving with various art supplies—rulers, scissors, charcoal, pencils.

"Wow!" I step inside and take it all in. There are a few finished paintings hanging on one of the walls—a trompe l'oeil of Brian's hands working on a still life of art supplies; a manga-inspired boy with the top of his head open to reveal the contents of his brain, including a dragon wearing a suit of armor, a pile of tattered textbooks, a road leading nowhere, and a blushing heart; and a poignant piece of a woman's face illuminated only by the light on her phone. "Did you paint these?" I can tell by the style that he probably did.

Brian's grinning. "Yeah, I did. Cool space, huh? We just made it."

"Oh, yeah?"

He nods. "My parents insisted I get an art space so I could have a place to work, but I think it also had a little bit to do with the fact that my supplies were taking over the house."

"They wouldn't give up this space unless they appreciated your talent, though," I say. "They seem pretty great. I mean, one of your moms literally fixed my car."

"Yeah. They are great, actually," Brian says, and I can tell he means it.

I walk around the garage a little and touch the pile of sketchbooks. "Can I look?" He nods and I start to flip through the book, which is filled mostly with cartoons that combine angular lines with big, swooping ones, but some print and lettering, too. I look up at Brian. "These are really good."

Brian's hands are in his pockets and he shrugs. "They're all right."

"No, you're good. I mean it."

He shrugs again. "Well, so are you."

I crinkle my nose and put the sketchbook back in its pile. "Not really. I'm...decent, we'll say."

"You appreciate art, Charlie, I know you do. You gave me that really thoughtful critique in art on my triptych way back when. You don't pull that out of nowhere."

"I do really enjoy art. But I've been working on the same painting in art class for weeks."

"Yeah, so? Art isn't a race."

"True, but it's not even a great painting. It's supposed to be a horse in Central Park, yet my 'horse' looks more like a dog. Honestly, I don't even really like horses! I only picked it because I saw a video of a horse nuzzling a rabbit on YouTube and it was adorable and I was inspired," I say with a laugh, which makes Brian laugh, too. "Anyway, I don't have to be good at art. I like it, but I know where my strengths are. I'm a lot better at writing. But you knew that. You got me that beautiful notebook."

He looks pleased when I say that. "Have you used it yet?" he asks.

"Not yet. Don't laugh, but in really nice notebooks, I sometimes take a while before I write anything. It just feels so permanent! Like, what if I change my mind? If it were a one-dollar scratch pad or something, no problem. But that beautiful leather-bound notebook feels important. I want what I write in it to be important, too."

"It will be because it'll be done by you," Brian says. "I'd actually love to read something sometime. If you'll let me."

"Really?" I ask.

"Yeah, really! It's your favorite thing to do, so of course I'm interested."

"I don't know...," I say. "Maybe."

"Hey!" Brian protests. "I let you look at my sketchbook!" He's grinning.

"And for that I'm grateful, but a girl's gotta keep a little mystery." I grin back at him. "Actually...someday I'm hoping to write a book about a girl who looks like me." What I mean is a book *specifically* about a fat Puerto Rican girl with glasses. I've never once read a story about one, and something about that has always made me feel devastatingly alone. But I leave that part out. "A brown, female protagonist. Female protagonists still aren't the majority, and a woman of color? Even harder to come by."

"That's wild to me. It's not like people of color make up nearly half of the United States population or anything," Brian says.

"Amelia and I talk about that all the time! It's so frustrating," I say. "I'm automatically less interested in media that doesn't include at least one person of color. They're not even trying."

Brian's emphatically nodding. "I know. Don't white people get tired of seeing all-white movies?"

"Right?! And don't get me started on how incredulous some get whenever people of color are added to already-established franchises! Like, okay, I guess living in outer space and cohabitating with a giant fuzzy dude named Chewbacca is realistic, but a Black lead character is somehow out of the realm of possibility?"

We're both laughing, and it feels good to talk about this stuff with Brian. He's so easy to talk to, and when I speak, I feel like he's really listening. It's enough to make me swoon. Maybe I am a little.

"What about you?" I ask. "What do you want to do?"

Brian groans. "Please, not the what-do-you-want-to-do-with-your-life question. I feel like that's all people ask me these days." He puts on a voice. " 'Oh, Brian, you're going to be a senior soon, and then it's off to college! Where will you go? What will you do?' Sorry, *Linda,* but I have no clue, and even if I did, I wouldn't want to share it with you. I haven't seen you since I was ten years old!"

"Yikes. I touched a nerve with that one, huh?" I ask.

"Maybe a little. It's just relentless. You must get that question all the time, too, don't you?"

"I do. But I just say I want to be a writer. That way I can dash all their hopes of me ever making money or having a solid career, you know? Just get it right out of the way."

We both laugh. Brian shakes his head. "I hate that. I tried to share with a few people that I was interested in a career in art and you'd have thought I'd said I wanted to run off and be in the circus."

I shrug. "It's all the same to some people unless you're going to become a doctor or go into business."

"Which I'm not." Brian sighs. "I think I want to be a graphic designer. It's a practical art career. That's the best I can do."

"I think you'd be great at that." I've seen some of his design work in class and I'm always impressed.

The back door of the house opens and Brian's mom Susan is there on the porch. "Sorry to bother you two, but I made some food. Just in case you were hungry."

At the mention of food, I realize I *am* hungry. I haven't eaten much because I was too nervous. But I'll take my cue from Brian.

Brian looks at me and quietly asks, "You hungry?"

"I could eat," I say.

"Okay, we're coming!" he shouts to Susan.

She looks pleased. "See you inside."

We close up the garage and Brian leads the way into the dining room, where the table is set. We sit just as Susan walks in with a roasted chicken and Maura follows with both hands full, one with a bowl of spinach salad, the other holding a casserole dish teeming with macaroni and cheese. She clearly didn't just make food; she made a feast, and for us. So sweet.

"Wow, this looks and smells amazing!" I say emphatically.

Brian shoots a sheepish glance at his mom. "You didn't have to do all this, Mom."

Susan sets the plate in the center of the table. "Oh, nonsense, Tig. It's just something I whipped up."

Maura puts the salad and the macaroni on either side of the chicken, then smiles at me. "Good to see you again, Charlie."

"Good to see you, too," I say. "But I've *got* to ask about this nickname. What is Tig?" While his parents settle at either end of the table, Brian looks a little like he wishes he could make a run for it, and for a second I wish I hadn't said a word. "You don't have to tell me," I say.

"No, it's fine. My darling mothers insist on calling me this mortifying nickname," Brian says, shooting them both looks.

"What's not to love about the nickname? It's so cute!" Susan gushes.

"And a really hard habit to break," Maura says. "We've been calling Brian Tig since he was a baby."

"*Apparently,* I was being *thoroughly* neglected one night," Brian says dramatically.

Susan gasps. "You were not!"

"Oh, I was! Because—get this—tiny two-year-old me managed to get the basement door open and fall all the way down the stairs. And apparently, I seemed to *bounce* from one step to the next. Sproing, sproing, sproing."

"We were devastated, but he was absolutely fine," Maura assures me. "Susan thought we'd killed him. It was only four steps, but still."

"Glad to know that my *near-death experience* was so 'cute' to you both!"

"I had to find a way to make your mother laugh," Maura insists.

"The horrid nickname has stuck," Brian says, making a face, and I can't help but laugh.

"That's...pretty adorable," I say.

Susan nods. "We think so, too!"

"Can we move on, please?" Brian asks. "At this point, I'd rather talk about school."

"Fine, fine," Maura says.

We do talk a little about school, and Maura and Susan ask me about me, too, what I like to do for fun, my family, friends, the basics. Then they tell me all about Brian and his childhood: how he once got stuck in a tree and then cried until Maura came to his rescue; how he used to pretend to be sick on days when his favorite video games were released so he could play them at home the minute they were available; then back to the near-death-by-bouncing story again so Susan can tell it *properly*.

"I think that's enough for tonight," Brian says after they've shared that story for a second time, playfully arguing over the details of what really happened. He's rising from his chair and reaching for my dish when Maura waves him away.

"We got it," she says. "Go watch your movie."

"Thank you for the wonderful meal," I say, looking back and forth between them.

"Susan deserves all the credit," Maura says, gazing over at her.

"You're more than welcome, Charlie," Susan says. "So good to meet you."

I follow Brian out of the dining room and into the living room.

"Sorry about that," he says.

"Oh my gosh, don't be. I enjoyed every minute."

"You don't have to lie."

"I'm not lying. Your family is so...normal," I say. "I think they're sweet, Tig."

He shoots me a look. "Don't you dare!"

"I thought you calling me 'kid' was bad, but now I have something even better," I tease, taking a seat on the couch.

"You're evil, Charlie," Brian says, and we laugh as he grabs the remote and sits beside me.

As he turns on the television and navigates to Netflix, I'm suddenly acutely aware of how close we are. Our legs are almost touching. I can feel the warmth from his body on mine. I briefly worry that I've missed a spot shaving (it's so hard to get the knees!), but I tell myself to relax.

Only I can't. Because we're basically touching.

"So, *Ladybird*, yeah?" Brian asks.

I must not answer right away, because he turns to look at me. It's the closest we've ever been and he smells really good. I think about him intentionally putting on cologne for me and smile.

"Yes, great," I say, trying to ignore the fact that my skin feels like it's humming. Brian finds the movie on Netflix, puts the remote down, and settles back into the couch. And now our legs are definitely touching.

If he's nervous, I don't get that sense at all. *I'm* nervous. Oh my God. How am I here right now? With Brian? On his couch? Watching a movie? In the dark? He's looking straight ahead, but I can barely focus on the screen. My hands are resting on my legs and they're sweating a little. I coyly wipe them on my skirt, hoping Brian doesn't notice.

I try to focus.

Brian specifically asked if I'd seen this.

He must like it.

And I'm sure I would, too.

So I should really pay attention.

But we're sitting so close. Who cares about movies when you can sit this close to Brian?!

And then his pinky is touching mine. Is this intentional? I look at him, but he's looking at the TV. Probably an accident. Although he isn't moving his hand away.

Stay calm. I look back at the movie. I even pay attention for a little. I need to focus on something, and I'm hoping this film can distract me. It does for a bit.

Until his hand is on mine.

His *hand* is on my *hand*.

I jump at his touch, but I don't pull away. I look at him, and he looks at me, and we both smile.

This? This was definitely intentional.

And that helps put me at ease, even though I can't stop the thoughts from pinging around in my brain: *a cute (!) boy (!) is (!) touching (!) me (!!!)*.

As the film rolls on, I sneak glances toward him—at his face, his neck, his hand on mine. I take in how small my hand looks in his, the two small freckles on his wrist. His broad shoulders. The curve of his lips. I notice it all as if my senses have been heightened to the next level, laser-focused—on everything except for the movie. In fact, I barely register when the film ends and Brian asks if I want to watch another.

Anything to keep holding his hand.

So we do. We're quiet, just together, which I'm thankful for;

I'm not sure I'd be much of a conversationalist right now. Besides, it gives me time to savor this.

Before I know it, the credits on the second movie are rolling (What was it even about? What were we watching again?), and I feel my phone vibrate. It's my mom. She's texting to ask if I'll be out much longer. I check the time—it's after midnight. I'm usually home by now.

"Everything okay?" Brian asks.

"Oh, yeah. It's just my mom."

Brian checks the time on his phone and frowns. "Yeah. I guess it's getting late."

I frown, too. "Yeah."

He rises from the couch, and I quickly text my mom that I'll be home soon. When I look up, Brian is reaching out a hand to help me up, and I'm thrilled that the handholding isn't quite over yet.

By now, the house is dark and quiet; his parents went to bed hours ago. I tell him he doesn't have to walk me out (even though I want him to), but he insists. So it's just us walking out to my car.

Outside, the air is cool. The street is so quiet it feels a little like we're the only two people left awake in the entire world.

"That was fun," I say, keeping my voice soft.

Brian squeezes my hand but keeps his voice soft, too. "It was. I had an amazing time."

I smile. "Me too."

We get to my car and it's then that we're supposed to drop each other's hands. But Brian doesn't let go, so I turn to face him. Under the moonlight, he looks extra cute. Or maybe I'm just so into him that he's extra cute all the time now.

"I'd like to hang out again," he says.

I nod. "Yes. Soon."

"How soon?"

"Tomorrow?" I offer.

Brian breaks into a wide grin. "I was hoping you'd say that."

My heart is beating so fast, and I know this is the part of the night where we're supposed to kiss. But I've never done it before. I find myself nervously adjusting my glasses.

I'm terrified, and in my terror, I blurt out, "Are you going to kiss me now?"

I feel mortified as the words leave my mouth, but I can't stop them. I've blown it.

Only, Brian chuckles and surprises me by leaning in. There is a moment of hesitation on his end, but then his lips are on my cheek—sweet and soft and wonderful, and I feel light and warm and delicate.

"Thank you," I say.

He laughs and squeezes my hand once more before letting it go. "Good night."

Chapter Thirty-One

How is this my life?

Seriously. How. Is. This. My. Life?

I'm giddy, and *giddy* is not a word I use often. But that is the only word that perfectly describes how I feel.

I'm giddy when I get home. I'm giddy when I'm getting into my pajamas and Brian texts me **Home safe?** I'm giddy when I text him back to say yes and good night and see you tomorrow. I'm giddy when I realize I have a boy to see tomorrow. I'm giddy when I try to sleep (so much so that I let out a little squeal directly into my pillow, which I hope my mom doesn't hear). And I'm giddy when I wake up the next day.

It's exhausting to be giddy and I'm relieved by the distraction when a text from Amelia comes through.

Miss you! Let's hang out, she writes.

Miss you back. I can't. I'm hanging out today with . . . Brian, I write.

My phone immediately starts to ring. "Hello?" I say, keeping my tone casual.

"WHAT THE FUCK, BITCH?" (If you can't call your best friend a bitch, is she really even your best friend?) "Were you secretly with Brian yesterday when you said you couldn't hang out?" Her voice is full of excitement.

I start laughing and everything comes tumbling out of my mouth. The text inviting me over. The stressing. The art studio. The dinner. The movie. The other movie. I leave out the part about the handholding and the cheek-kissing, worried it will seem too immature.

"Ahhh! You like a boy! You like a boy!" Amelia chants.

I feel my cheeks flush, but I can't stop smiling. "I do *not*," I say, even though I very clearly do.

"Charlie, I'm so happy for you," she says, and I can tell she really is.

"Thanks, Amelia. I'm pretty happy, too."

"But I can't believe you didn't tell me." Her voice sounds a little wounded.

"I'm sorry," I say. "I wanted to, but I was just...nervous, I guess."

"Yeah, but that's what I'm here for! So you can tell me you're nervous and I can assure you it'll be fine."

"I know, I know. Sorry."

She sighs. "You better be." Then she pauses and asks, "So?"

"So?" I repeat.

"So, tell me about today! You're meeting him soon. Where?"

"At the Spring Festival downtown. He texted me to say his parents have a booth. So I'll meet him there."

Amelia squeals, and I feel both grateful to be sharing this with her and a bit remorseful that I boxed her out last night. "I want to meet you there. Not go with you, but just, like, casually bump into you. I'll bring Kira so it's not a big deal. I just...I want to see you two together. Like, together-together."

"Okay, but no ogling!"

"Promise," she says.

"Meet me there around two. Sound good?"

"Yes. Text you when I get there."

* * *

I'm with a boy at the Spring Festival.

That's a thing I can say now. If I run into anyone from school, who's like, *Hey, Charlie, how are you?* I get to say, *Oh, you know, good, but have you met this boy right here?*

And then I get to show off Brian, who manages to be hot and cute at the same time! Who has eyes you can get lost in! And bone structure celebrities would envy! And arm muscles that make you think he could maybe weight-lift a car just for fun! And a crooked smile that feels like it's just for me!

Sigh. I'm not swooning. *You're swooning.*

But he looks totally adorable standing there at his parents' booth, where they're selling birdhouses, and *I* get to help manage the table. You know. As *the girl he's here with.* We haven't had many customers, but lots have stopped to look. Behind the table, Brian has made a game of subtly using his pinky to reach out for mine, and each time they finally connect it feels like a jolt of electricity. It leaves me wondering over and over: When will we kiss?!

I don't even mind when Amelia and Kira drop by the table and ogle, making it painfully obvious they're here just to check out the two of us together. I make a show of shooing them away, but let's be real, I was into it.

Brian says we won't stay much longer, that we can walk around the festival soon. Truthfully, though, I wouldn't mind if we stayed at the table all day because that would mean I'd be sitting right here with him.

"So, how did you get into making birdhouses?" I ask Brian's parents.

"Oh, gosh." Susan looks at Maura. "It's been forever."

Maura nods. "We actually started making them together when we first started dating."

"Maybe on our third date?" Susan offers. "Either way, we started building them together. It just became a thing we did."

"If I'm honest, it was my suggestion. I was terrified our second date didn't go well and I wanted to have something concrete planned," Maura says, a wistful look taking over her face, as if remembering the beginnings of her and Susan.

Susan laughs. "You never told me that! Why birdhouses?"

Maura looks at her and smiles. "It was something I knew how to make, and I wanted to impress you."

"Well, it worked." To me, Susan says, "It brought us even closer together. Especially when I would get a splinter and need Maura's help getting it out."

"So many splinters," Maura teases.

Brian's rolling his eyes, but only so I can see. I think the story is cute, though, and I find myself smiling at it.

The giddy feeling from yesterday is still pinging around my insides, amplified by the fact that it's a gorgeous day. The festival is a quirky annual event that always brings good vibes, mostly because it's held on the first beautiful weekend of the season. After a long winter of slush and cold and misery, some time outside in the crisp air, looking up at the blue skies, knowing that the trees will soon be in full bloom, is exactly what we all need.

The festival is mostly meant to raise money for the town and some of its small-business owners; they ask for residents like Maura and Susan to set up tables and sell their wares. Residents pay a small fee to have a table, and whatever they earn is their money.

Most people at my school think the Spring Festival is passé; they show up at the end of the night, maybe sneak some booze, and make fun of everyone there. But I like it. The colors are soft and there are flowers everywhere and it always feels like it's ushering in a new season full of possibility. Plus, I like to go and look at all of the items that have been lovingly created by my neighbors—like these birdhouses.

"I love that story," I say to Brian's parents. "And I'd like to buy one."

Susan looks touched. "You would?"

"You don't have to buy one, Charlie. You can just have one," Maura says.

Brian chimes in. "Seriously, Charlie. Just take one."

I shake my head. "I want to pay. You've put your hard work into it." I take my time looking at each birdhouse before carefully selecting one that looks like a cute suburban home with a picket fence. "This one."

Susan smiles. "That's a good one."

It's thirty dollars, but I feel like it's the best thirty dollars I could've spent at this festival.

"Let's go for a walk," Brian says, nodding toward the main street.

"Okay," I say, waving at his parents, birdhouse in hand.

We walk along the street, taking everything in: the craft booths, food stands, organizations trying to solicit new members, volunteer groups trying to get the word out about their cause.

"You know...," I say to Brian, "one time, when I was a kid, my parents brought me here and I stumbled across a table that was selling personalized bookmarks made from popsicle sticks. The woman behind the table would ask your name and then she'd write it in calligraphy on the painted popsicle stick. It cost, like, ten dollars or something, but I begged and begged my dad until he relented. I still have that bookmark somewhere."

"Ten dollars for a popsicle stick? You got robbed, kid," Brian says.

"But it had my name and there was even a little sunflower embellishment glued to the end of it. I felt like that made up for the cost." I look at him for added effect when I ask, "Don't you, Tig?"

He wrinkles his nose at his nickname. Then he says, "If it meant a lot to you, I think it was worth the ten bucks."

I smile at that. I smile even bigger when Brian reaches out and grabs my hand. "Is this okay?" he asks.

After a whole afternoon of almost-but-not-really-holding-hands, it's the most welcome feeling in the world. "Of course."

We walk down Main Street hand in hand. It feels like something out of a fairy tale. Minus the birdhouse. I don't think I ever imagined holding hands with a boy while also holding a birdhouse. But it's perfect.

"So, yesterday was fun," Brian says.

"Yeah, it was. That was a great idea."

"Did you like the movie?"

I briefly consider lying and saying yes. But then I say, "It was good, but...I was struggling to focus."

A smirk from him. "Oh, yeah? Why's that?"

I laugh a little, embarrassed. "Well. You were holding my hand." I steal a glance over at him, and now he's smiling big.

"You liked that?" he asks.

"Don't," I tease. "Don't get all weird!"

"What? I can't be a little into the fact that you were a little into the handholding?" He's still grinning.

I hold up our interlocked hands. "I'm holding your hand now and behaving like a perfect lady. Not at all distracted."

I don't want to admit out loud that I like how natural our hands feel together. Our fingers twine and it's like they were meant to fit into each other.

He stops walking suddenly. Then he gets a look like he's up to something. "Follow me," he says. And he starts walking really fast, pulling me along behind him.

"Where are we going?" I ask as we leave Main Street.

"You'll see," he says. We take a left, then a right, and I'm following him excitedly, not really caring where we end up, caring only that he wants to be with me, and only me. "Here," he says finally.

We're behind the library, which is closed today to accommodate the festival, so it's completely deserted. I've never paid much attention to what it looks like, but today, I notice the intricate stonework that makes up the façade; the arched windows; and the steeple on the roof, which gives it a churchy feel. I realize that this building I've visited literally hundreds of times is actually really beautiful—especially where Brian and I are standing, in a grassy area beside the back entrance.

"What's here?" I ask, glancing around, noting only the weathered wooden bench, the budding trees that sway in the spring breeze.

"Us." And he says it so simply that it nearly sucks the breath out of me.

My eyes meet his. "Us," I whisper.

"Yes." He's facing me, looking right at me. I wish I could see what he sees. I know what I see: a beautiful boy, slightly taller than me so I have to look up at him, just so full of kindness and laughter, who is slowly starting to take up space inside my heart. He pushes a curly strand of hair out of my face, his fingers grazing against my skin, leaving goose bumps.

"Oh," I say, softly, barely audible.

Brian steps closer to me. "Oh," he whispers. We're standing closer than ever before. It feels like something.

And then—he leans toward me.

It's that moment. The moment. The moment before the kiss, the one I've been waiting for. My breath catches in my throat.

I feel my heart beating inside my chest. I feel the blood pumping through my veins. I feel the warmth of his breath before I feel his lips on mine. I feel, I feel, I feel—and then I feel our lips meet. And my heart bursts.

It's the sweetest, gentlest kiss. The softest.

I've been kissed. My first. It's just.

Oh.

It's everything, even if it's just a moment.

Brian pulls back the smallest bit, leaving our noses touching. My eyes are closed. I'm scared to open them for fear this will all be part of my imagination—that my dreams have gotten so good that they *feel* real, even when they're not.

I can't help it; I sigh.

Brian strokes my cheek. "I should have done that yesterday," he says softly.

"It was worth the wait," I whisper.

I want to live in this moment forever. Birdhouse in hand and all.

Chapter Thirty-Two

I've realized I was wrong.

The moment before the kiss isn't the best part of a kiss. Don't get me wrong: it's pretty goddamn amazing.

But after an evening of kissing with Brian at the Spring Festival, I now know that the *kissing* is the best part of a kiss.

I spend most of my time thinking about how badly I'd rather be kissing Brian than doing anything else, like going to school.

But that's okay. Because Brian is waiting for me at my locker on Monday morning when Amelia and I walk in. Like he and I are a couple or something. His face brightens when he sees me and I'm sure mine brightens when I see him, too. How could it not?

"Hi," I say.

"Hi," he says, leaning in to give me a quick kiss on the lips. Because we have different kinds of kisses now. Long kisses and short kisses, quick pecks on the lips. I am collecting all of these kisses. I could write a whole book on these kisses.

"*Hi,*" Amelia says, waving at us both and reminding us she's there, too.

"Hey, Amelia," Brian replies. To me, he asks, "How was the drive in?" Maybe an awkward question, but I kind of love that he doesn't always have the right thing to say. Like maybe I make him a little nervous, too.

"It was good," I reply, trying to open my locker. I mess up the combination, though, because I keep sneaking glances at him. When I finally get it open, I start to put my bag on the floor so I can unzip it and unload some of my books, but Brian offers to hold it. It's such a couple thing to do. I say yes.

"I'm going to head to class," Amelia says. "See you later?"

"Yes, definitely," I say, though I'm grateful to be left alone with Brian. Once she's gone, I look at him and give him my best coy smile. "Last night was good."

He pulls me a little closer to him and smiles. "Yes. Really good. You want to hang out again tonight?"

"Yes," I say, before remembering I've made plans. "Only I can't. I'm going to Amelia's."

Brian looks a little disappointed but doesn't say so. "Okay. Tomorrow?"

I nod enthusiastically. "Yes. Tomorrow!"

"Can I walk you to class?"

"Please," I say, holding out my hand for him to take. He does, interlocking his fingers with mine. We start to walk down the hall. "You know, people will think we're together now."

"Well, we are, aren't we?" Brian asks.

My heart flutters at that. I actually think that sentence in my head, too—*My heart flutters*—because I've only dealt with romance through writing for so long that I want to savor all these feelings I've only ever written about. I feel like I'm a character straight from a romance novel and I really, really like it.

I squeeze his hand. "I just wanted to hear you say it."

In English class, I can barely focus. It's giddiness. *Again*. But at least I get to let it all out during the free-write.

It's during the rest of the class that I sort of drift off, spending most of my time gazing out of the window. It's not like I'm at the level of doodling my name as Mrs. Brian Park or anything, but I am definitely thinking about Brian. I'm thinking about his lips. His eyes. His hair. The kissing.

It's only the voice of Ms. Williams that jolts me back to reality.

"How are you, Charlie?" she asks.

I glance around the classroom to realize I'm the last one left. I missed the bell.

"Good. Spacey, apparently." I let out an embarrassed laugh and start tucking my notebook into my bag. Ms. Williams smiles.

Please don't ask me about the writing contest. Please don't ask me about the writing contest. Please don't—

"So, have you had a chance to get started on your submission for that writing contest?"

Well. Shit.

Obviously I've gotten started on my submission. But my follow-through has been less than stellar, especially these past few weeks. I've been preoccupied. And procrastinating.

"I've definitely started," I say. "It's the finishing I'm having trouble with."

"Oh, yeah? Well, maybe I can help," Ms. Williams says. "Why don't you send me what you have and I can offer some notes?"

"Really?" I ask.

"Of course. You have my email address. Try to send it before Friday and I'll take a look this weekend."

"That would be amazing, Ms. Williams," I say, standing up and slinging my bag over my shoulder. "I will. Thank you!"

I make a mental note to get moving on my submission. During a really slow history class, I even pull up what I have on my phone and take a crack at it, but I really need some dedicated time and my writing nook, which unfortunately I won't get until later tonight after I'm home from Amelia's. She and I have promised each other some serious bonding time and that's a promise I don't want to break.

In between my next couple of classes, I find myself searching for Brian, who I haven't seen since before homeroom. But no such luck. I don't see him again until the afternoon in art class.

"Hey, you," he says when I walk into the classroom. He's sitting at his table, already set up with a palette of paints.

"Hi, stranger," I say. "Where were you at lunch?"

"Sometimes I come into the art room during my lunch period to work on some things," he says, and then a grin slowly spreads across his face. "Why?" He reaches out and tugs on my shirt sleeve. "Did you miss me?"

I playfully pull my sleeve away from him but wish he'd grab at it again. "No. I was just wondering."

"Well, Just Wondering, you should join me tomorrow. At lunch. It'll be nice."

"Yeah?" I pretend like I'm thinking it over, even though I've already made up my mind. "I guess I could probably use a little extra time to finish my horse painting, since I've been working on it for about a hundred years."

"Hey, you said that. Not me."

Mr. Reed walks into the classroom and I realize I should already have gathered my painting and supplies. Amelia's sitting at our table and she's already working on her piece.

"So?" Brian asks. "Lunch tomorrow?"

I grin. "Yes. Definitely."

After school, I'm a smidge disappointed that I don't have to work. It would have been nice to see Brian, maybe goof off in the back together. Kiss. Definitely kiss. But instead I'm with Amelia at her house, and I remind myself that that's a different kind of great.

We've got our homework spread out in front of us like we're going to do it. But we're obviously just going to talk instead.

"Did you and Kira have fun at the Spring Festival?" I ask.

Amelia's all smiles at the question. "We did." She reaches into her purse and pulls out a Polaroid photo, which she hands to me. It's her and Kira, both of them wearing flower crowns.

I can't help but smile as I study it. "You two look happy." I hand it back to her. "Really happy."

Amelia looks down at it, then says, "I mean, I can't speak for her, but...I am." She looks up at me. "Can I be honest? I think... I think maybe what I felt with Sid wasn't what I thought it was. I mean, I was infatuated with him, of course. But I don't think it was love. With Kira, though, I think I really could fall in love. The real kind. Actually, truly."

"Oh my *God*." I practically squeal as I scoot toward her and throw my arms around her. "I'm so happy for you, Amelia." I let her go, then squeeze her shoulders. "Does this mean you're in love now?"

She starts laughing and shaking her head. "Gosh, no. Not yet. But I feel like I'm getting there, faster than I ever thought I could, and it's scary and exhilarating all at the same time."

"Have you told her?"

"Yes and no. We talk about how much we like each other all the time. That feels like enough for now."

The ecstatic look on her face makes my heart feel full. "Update me the *second* something changes. The millisecond, actually. Like, you should probably just be writing out a text to me as you tell Kira you love her."

At that, Amelia laughs. "Of course. But tell me about you! How did *you* enjoy the Spring Festival? And *Bri*-an?" She emphasizes his name like a little song, and I like it.

"Oh, you know...it was fine."

"Don't even! You will not hold out on me! So spill it. Tell me everything. You guys seemed pretty cozy."

"We were, I think," I say. "We may have kissed a bunch."

And then it's Amelia's turn to squeal and grab me by the shoulders. She shakes me back and forth. "*OhmyGodohmyGod!* I knew it! That casual little peck at the locker this morning *sold you out!*"

"I know. I know!" I say. "I can't believe it! He's my first kiss."

Amelia clasps her hands together and looks at me wistfully, like she's equal parts proud and nostalgic. "Your first kiss," she repeats.

"I feel silly that it's taken so long..."

"Well, don't! It doesn't matter how long it takes. We all have our own timelines," Amelia says. "And can I please just have a moment to say something important?"

"Of course."

Amelia clears her throat. Then she's singing, "Charlie and Brian sittin' in a tree, K-I-S-S-I-N-G—"

"Oh my God!" I shout over her.

"First comes love, then comes marriage, then comes Charlie with a baby carriage!"

We both erupt into laughter until Tess comes stomping down the hallway toward Amelia's room. "Can you *please* be *quiet*? You're being rude!"

"Get out of here, Tess!"

"Not until you shut up!"

"If you don't get out of here, I'm going to call Mom!" Amelia shouts. "Go!"

Tess does, but not before sticking out her tongue at her sister and glaring at me. Amelia slams her bedroom door shut behind Tess. Then she sighs. "She ruins everything."

"You mean she ruined you teasing me about pushing Brian's baby carriage," I say. "And by the way, I never realized how sexist that rhyme is."

"Right? As I'm singing it, I'm thinking, jeez, why does Charlie have to be the one pushing the baby carriage?"

"And why are babies, like, an inevitability? What if I want to push a puppy carriage instead?" I ask.

"That's your right," Amelia says. Then she breaks into a huge grin. "Look at us! Just two best friends in relationships. Oh my God! Double date?!"

I laugh. "Are you being serious right now?"

"Of course I am!" She starts to chant: "Double date, double date, double date!"

"I'll think about it," I say, still laughing. "Now can we do some homework?"

I'm not sure about a double date. I kind of want to keep Brian all to myself while everything is still so new and exciting and full of possibility. But for Amelia, I'll consider it.

Chapter Thirty-Three

It's already late when I get home from Amelia's house. Mom's car is gone, so I have the house to myself. Perfect writing atmosphere.

I change into some pajamas, set myself up at my desk, and put on a coffeehouse playlist for a little inspiration. Maybe it's the darkness, or maybe it's the fact that it's raining a little and I can hear it just beneath the music, or maybe the stars are finally aligning...but whatever it is, something about tonight is good for my writing.

My story is taking shape. I've opted to go with the story about the complicated mother-daughter relationship. I take Ms. Williams's advice and use some of my own journal passages as inspiration (though I fictionalize them, obviously).

The story follows a mother-daughter duo who (shockingly!) don't see eye to eye on nearly anything, from the daughter's weight to the person she falls in love with to the career she chooses to, eventually, how she raises her own daughter. Over the years, they come together and they drift apart; this is chronicled through short scenes that take place at pivotal moments in their lives. The story ends with them spending Mother's Day together in the kitchen of the family home. It doesn't have a happy ending, only an ambiguous one, but it feels real, almost like glimpsing my future, where my relationship with my mom never morphs into the one I wish it were but is just the one I have and that's that. For me, it feels raw, and I hope it resonates.

Before I know it, I've poured hours into the story, hammering out a first draft. It's late now. In the morning, I'll read it over, then send it off to Ms. Williams.

Feeling accomplished, I climb into bed with my laptop, not ready for sleep yet. I switch gears and open up a not-appropriate-for-the-writing-contest story I've been working on. It's about a young brown girl who meets a cute Korean boy.

I know. I *know*. But I want to write about characters that remind me of me and Brian. They don't bear our names, but the resemblance is there. They're older than we are—college age—and the main character, Selena (named after Quintanilla, not Gomez), is Practically Perfect. She's super focused on school because she's working on becoming an astrophysicist—only she falls in love with Jae, and that's not part of the plan. I live for these kinds of romance plots.

I've sketched parts of this story out, but I'm ignoring all that plot stuff right now because it's late and I really just want to write a love scene.

To be clear: I have not even fully made out with Brian yet. But it's like kissing him has made it so that all I can think about is sex.

And if I'm not ready to have it yet, I can at least write about it.

I get into it. Serena and Jae are at the library late; they get caught in a rainstorm. They run back to her dorm and by the time they get there, her clothes are drenched and so are his and they're so into each other they can't help but kiss.

I'm typing a paragraph about how they barely make it into her dorm room before Jae is kissing the nape of Selena's neck, hands roaming her body, when my phone vibrates against my leg and I'm jolted out of the scene.

A text from Brian.

Heyyy.

Timing!

Hiii, I write back.

What are you up to? it reads.

Well, he's not getting an honest answer. Should I go with something coy?

I type **Wouldn't you like to know?** and then immediately delete it and send **Can't sleep. What about you?**

Can't sleep either.

I had fun today. Being a couple.

It felt good to hold your hand walking down the hall. I've been wanting to do that forever.

My heart feels like it skips a beat and I push my glasses up the bridge of my nose—habit. I had no idea Brian even liked me as a friend, let alone had given any thought to holding my hand. He kind of pined? For *me*?

Really?

Of course. I'm just glad you finally noticed me.

I write **I'm glad you noticed me, too.**

You're the only girl worth seeing, he writes.

I can't think of anything remotely cute or clever to say back, so I just text a blushing emoji three times in a row. Sometimes, words escape even writers.

* * *

Well, as it turns out, day two of holding hands with Brian at school is better than day one. Day three is even better than that. Day four is the best—but only because with each passing day, it feels a little more normal, a little more like it's *me* who's holding his hand and not some character I've dreamed up in one of my stories. This is real life.

At work, I find it hard to focus on my duties. I'm supposed to be writing some thank-you letters for Nancy, but I keep finding excuses to work in the back with Brian. We haven't shared with our coworkers that we're dating, which makes it feel even more exciting.

So, instead of writing those letters, I'm stacking boxes with Brian in the warehouse. Brian keeps bumping his hand against mine, and I don't stop him.

Then he doesn't stop me when I start stacking boxes high enough to construct a wall between Dave's cubicle and the stock room. And he doesn't stop me when the wall is tall enough to hide us both. And he doesn't stop me when I start to kiss him.

We come up for air for just a second and he grins so big at me I feel it in my chest. "We could get caught, you know," he says, taking both of my hands in his.

I interlock our fingers. "That's part of the fun," I say. "And who's going to catch us? Dave has never even set foot in this part of the building."

"You make an excellent point." He pulls me closer to him. He smells nice, like the cologne from our date. "So, I was thinking..."

"Yes?" I ask.

"We should go on a proper date."

"A proper date?" I repeat.

He nods. "Yeah, like, I could take you somewhere nice."

"I don't need to go anywhere nice."

"You *deserve* to go somewhere nice," he insists.

"Nice makes me nervous," I say. "Let's do something fun. Something we both like."

"We both like this," Brian says, leaning in to kiss me.

I laugh when we pull apart. "Definitely. Yes. But what else?"

"We both like music." Then Brian scrunches his nose. "But not the same music. I'm not about to listen to Beyoncé."

I pull my hands away from him like I'm hurt. (Maybe I am a little. It's BEYONCÉ. How can he not like her?!) "Don't you even say that! You'll listen to Beyoncé and you'll like it!"

Brian rolls his eyes. "We'll see." Then his face lights up. "I've got it."

"What? Were you just struck by the magnificence that is Queen Bey?"

"No. Our date. I've got it."

"Well?" I ask.

He shakes his head. "Nope. It's a secret. Are you free Saturday?"

It's cute that he asks, like I've *ever* had Saturday plans beyond hanging with Amelia.

"I'm definitely free on Saturday," I say.

"Great. I'll pick you up at two."

I grin. Okay. I like the sound of that.

Chapter Thirty-Four

I'm a feminist. Let's get that straight.

But I'm also the kind of girl who changes her outfit a zillion times before a date. You can be both, okay?

I don't know exactly where Brian and I are going, but I do text him to get a hint about how I should dress. While I wait for his reply, I finish editing the draft of the short story I wrote for the writing contest, then quickly email it to Ms. Williams and ask for her honest feedback. I'm a smidge late (she wanted this by last night—oops!), so I'm apologetic when I email her, hoping Saturday morning offers enough time for her to take a peek. Regardless, it feels really good to cross that one off my list.

Brian eventually texts me back to say casual dress is fine and I sigh. Boys. What *kind* of casual?

I decide to go with a simple T-shirt dress that I belt at the waist and some ballet flats. Something cute but also relaxed should carry me through either an outdoor or an indoor adventure. I grab a jacket, too, just in case.

Brian picks me up right on time.

"So...," I say after we've been in the car for a bit. "Where are we off to?"

"Uh-uh."

"Can I get a hint?"

"Nope."

I sigh dramatically, but I don't let up, not for the whole car ride, and I don't even care if I'm being annoying. I think Brian thinks it's cute that I'm curious because he's playing along and that feels good and right and like we're in a rhythm. It isn't long before we're pulling into the parking lot of an art museum. From the outside, it may not seem like very much—just two stories, though there are large picture windows all around that let in breathtaking amounts of natural light—but I know the inside houses a mix of awe-inspiring modern and classical art that's not admired nearly as often as it should be.

I look over at him and he seems pleased with his choice.

"Well? Is this good?" he asks.

"Yes! So good! I used to come here as a kid. I haven't been back in years!"

"You've been missing out, then. It's incredible."

We pull into a parking spot and start to walk into the building. We pay to enter the museum—Brian tries to pay for me, but I insist on paying for myself—and then we head into the first room.

Art museums are the best. They're quiet and allow for contemplation and reflection, which is perfect for an introvert like me. I really like to take my time and appreciate each piece of art—I even like reading the descriptions next to each painting. (I mean, I'm not super pretentious about it or anything. I just really love a good art museum.)

Brian seems to be the same way; we're mostly quiet throughout our tour, pointing out things we like or dislike about certain paintings, talking about artists we love and those who are overhyped. Turns out, Brian is not a big fan of Andy Warhol. When we reach one of his pieces, Brian actually scoffs. "Totally overrated."

I blink. "But it's *Andy Warhol*!"

"The Campbell's soup can? Marilyn Monroe? Gimme a break. It's easy art. *Boring* art."

"He's, like, one of the biggest artists of all time," I say.

"I will give the guy credit for his impact. It's massive. And I get that he was making a statement about consumerism and blah blah blah. But I can't get behind his talent. There's just no heart. When Warhol was at his peak, he wasn't even making the art himself! He had conveyor belts set up and workers doing the screen printing *for* him. I'd take a beautiful Bob Ross painting over one of Warhol's so-called masterpieces any day."

"You're really fired up about this!"

Brian nods emphatically. "I am! Guy's a loser."

I turn to the Warhol piece. "You hear that, Andy? Brian Park thinks you're a loser!"

We both stifle our laughs, and I loop my arm through his as we walk to the next painting. "You know, you do make some good points," I admit.

"Of course I do," he says with a grin.

"He's convinced me! Sorry, Andy!" I call over my shoulder.

"Andy'll get over it."

"Will he, though?" I tease. "Ooh, I think there's a Monet around here somewhere. Please tell me you're not going to roast him, too?"

"Nah," Brian replies. "Monet's my boy."

We talk a little about how they never have enough work by female artists displayed, and when Brian agrees and says there are female painters beyond Georgia O'Keeffe that deserve recognition, I could kiss him. I'm not one to think that men deserve a cookie every time they show some humanity, but I'd be lying if I said I didn't feel pleased that the guy I'm dating is at least a little woke.

I'm smiling to myself when I notice a painting by Peter Paul Rubens. I discovered him on a body-pos art Insta I follow, and since then, I've really appreciated his work.

"You a fan?" Brian asks.

I nod. "It's not typically my style—I like Impressionism—but I love that he paints women with bigger bodies. It's beautiful."

Brian inspects the painting, his lips spreading into a smile. "Yeah. It is."

It can be difficult for me to look at paintings like this, at bodies like this, and see that they are beautiful but still sometimes struggle to see myself in the same positive light. I think about my body, about all of its imperfections, and I don't necessarily see beauty. Yet. But I'm working on it.

"I wish my mom agreed that bodies like these can be beautiful," I say.

"She doesn't?" Brian asks.

I shake my head, not removing my gaze from the painting. "No. Ever since I was a kid, I've been taught that fat is bad. Even when my mom was fat, back before she lost a ton of weight. She's constantly trying to get me to lose weight."

"Mine, too," Brian says softly.

Without thinking, I say, "But you're perfect," and he laughs.

"Far from it. I mean. I struggle," he says, motioning toward his stomach. "This could use some work. At least according to my mom. Ma always tries to get her to chill out, but...Mom's got opinions."

I try to imagine Brian's mom Susan being anything other than pleasant, but I can't. Then again, if you asked anyone else about my mom, they'd probably tell you she was wonderful, too.

"I'm sorry," I say.

"I'm sorry for you, too." Then he holds out his hand to me. "But they're wrong about us."

I give him my hand, which he takes and uses to gingerly pull me close to him. I rest my head on his shoulder, look at the beautiful bodies in the painting before me, and think, *Yes. They're wrong about all of us.*

Chapter Thirty-Five

Just a day after our museum date, I seize the opportunity of an empty house to invite Brian over. I mean, we're not going to *do* anything but, like, maybe a little.

"Can't believe I get to come inside this time," Brian teases when I answer the door.

"My mom barely liked you being in the driveway working on the car. There was no way you were coming inside that day," I say with a laugh.

"Fair enough." He steps inside, closing the door on a beautiful mid-April morning.

I nod my head toward the hall. "This way."

He follows me to my room, his eyes flitting around and taking everything in—my vanity, overflowing with beauty products; my bookcase, stuffed with books; my closet, bursting with clothes; my reading nook. I cringe a little, seeing it through his eyes. Too much stuff. Messy. Maybe weird? Do I have a weird room?

But Brian doesn't say anything like that, just this: "Man, you really *do* love Beyoncé." He points at a framed photo of I have of her on my bookcase.

"Do you not have a framed photo of Beyoncé in your room?"

"I mean, yeah, but yours is bigger."

"I worship it every morning, obviously." We laugh. I walk toward the bay window, saying, "I want to show you something." Peeling the curtains back, I point outside. "There."

Brian walks over to the window and looks out, breaking into a smile when he sees what I'm pointing to. He turns back toward me. "The birdhouse."

"The birdhouse," I say, looking at him. "From the first time we kissed."

He keeps his voice soft when he responds. "Oh, I remember."

Brian leans down toward me and I close my eyes to savor the just-before-the-kiss moment. Then, of course, I savor the kiss when his lips meet mine.

When we part, I press my forehead to his. "The first time was good. But it's gotten even better since."

Brian starts to nod, but something catches his eye, and suddenly he's rushing away from me and toward my dresser. "Is that Mjölnir?!" He grabs the hammer that's sitting on the dresser and pretends to use it to smash my lamp. I can't help but laugh a little at how strongly Thor's weapon has grabbed his attention.

"Of course!" I say. "I love Thor."

"Iron Man's better, but I get it," Brian teases, sitting on my bed.

"Well, you're wrong, but okay." I take the hammer and set it back in its spot. "So Mjölnir is the reason we stopped kissing, then?"

Brian laughs. "I just got excited. We *will* be discussing fan theories at some point. But come here." He pats the space beside him on my bed, and I sit.

We're close, knees touching, facing each other. It feels like my skin tingles whenever I'm near him.

A silence falls between us and I break it by blurting out, "Who was your first crush?"

Brian gives me a look. "Not at all what I was expecting you to say." He thinks for a moment. "I had a crush on one of the girls in my neighborhood when I was five. We played video games together. It was great. What about you?"

"I was in kindergarten, and it was Aaron Cyr," I say.

Brian makes a face. *"Aaron Cyr?"*

I nod. "It was love at first sight. I even wrote him a love note, you know."

Brian scoffs, then says, "He gets a love note, but I don't?"

"You haven't written me a love note, either!"

"Yes, I absolutely have!" he protests. "That card I gave you on Valentine's Day?"

I think about the valentine that's sitting in my wallet. I moved it there when I started having feelings for Brian because…well, because I liked him. "Don't get me wrong. The valentine is beautiful and I *treasure* it, but I'm not sure it counts as a love note. We were just friends when you gave it to me."

"Sure, but I wanted to be more."

I feel my cheeks flush. Is it possible he was interested in me all the way back in February? And if so, what was I doing wasting my time not being interested right back?!

"But you gave a valentine to every girl in the class," I say.

"Yeah, I did, because we talked about how Valentine's Day makes people feel bad about themselves. I didn't want anyone to feel bad about themselves," Brian says. "But if I could only have given one valentine to someone in class, it would've been you. Yours was the only one that was even a little romantic."

"I don't know about that," I say. I reach over to grab my purse, which is hanging from my bedpost, and dig the valentine out.

Brian looks surprised. "You keep it on you?" he asks.

"Of course. It's the only valentine I've ever gotten," I say. "And it was from you."

He smiles at that, and I do, too.

"Here's what it says." I clear my throat dramatically before reading it aloud. " 'Just my type. To someone who makes my workday wonderful. Happy Valentine's Day, Charlie—Brian.' See?" I say. "There are no underlying romantic feelings in this."

"What are you *talking* about? The drawing is of a typewriter, which I *specifically* chose because you *love* writing and you'd done that charcoal drawing of one *earlier* in the semester, *and* it is telling you that you're just my type—*of person,* that I want to be with," Brian says, pretending to get worked up. "That's some of my best work, Charlie!"

I start to laugh, tucking the valentine back into my bag. "I didn't know! I just assumed everyone got something like this!"

"No! Everyone else's puns were much tamer and less personalized. In fact, I'm pretty sure I gave Layla a valentine that just said 'stay cool,' with a drawing of a penguin, because I didn't want her to infer any type of feeling whatsoever," he says with a laugh. (He probably made a solid choice there given that everyone in art class knows Layla is kind of in love with him.) Then his voice softens and he looks over at me. "I liked you then." He reaches out and touches my cheek.

"You did?" I ask.

"I did," Brian says. "And I *really* like you now."

My heartbeat quickens, and I lean closer to him and whisper, "I really like you, too."

Brian kisses me, soft at first, which I think might be my favorite way to kiss, until we start to deepen the kiss, and I think no, *this* is my favorite way to kiss.

When we part, we're both a little breathless, and I say, "You're good at that."

"So are you." Brian grabs hold of my hand and strokes it with his thumb.

"That's the kind of kissing I've dreamt about. The kind I write about."

He breaks into a devilish grin. "Oh, yeah? You write about us kissing?"

"Well, not us. But people."

"But people are us, right?"

"Sometimes, maybe," I say. "And I don't write about kissing *all* the time."

"Sure. Of course."

I playfully push at his arm. "I swear!"

"I believe you," Brian says, and I still feel like he's playing, but I don't mind. "I really would love to read one of your stories someday."

I feel shy at the thought. Like I've said, sharing my writing is a way of being vulnerable. It leaves me feeling exposed. But writing is such a big part of me that maybe I should share it with Brian.

"I think we can make that happen," I say finally.

"Really?" he asks. When I nod in response, Brian grins. "And the main character will be a handsome Korean, right?" (I don't dare mention that one of the main characters in my latest stories is already modeled after him.) "And there's this smart and wonderful Puerto Rican girl, right? And they're really into each other? And maybe there's a dog? A golden retriever?"

I roll my eyes. "Oh my God."

"Okay, fine, it doesn't have to be a golden retriever, but let's agree to some kind of dog."

"What can I do to shut you up?" I tease.

He gives me a look and says, "I think you know...."

So I kiss him again, stroking the back of his neck as I do.

He deepens the kiss, one hand on the side of my cheek, the other around my waist, pulling me to him. I feel myself trembling, but I don't stop him as he leans back onto my pillow and I follow, leaning with him. I'm losing myself in this, in the feeling of his mouth on mine, his fingers on my skin, his arms wrapped around me.

There's a noise. I push Brian away and quickly sit up, but it's too late: my mother is in the doorway of my room, looking livid.

"Mom, hi!"

Her eyes are narrowed, her hands are on her hips. "What do you think you're doing?" she demands.

"*Nothing,*" I say.

"That"—my mom motions back and forth between me and Brian—"didn't look like nothing!"

"We were just—"

"Just *what*?" Her voice is sharp. "Just making out with a boy on your *bed*? In my house? Under my roof? What's wrong with you?"

"It was just a kiss," I say.

Brian stands. "Mrs. Vega, I apologize."

"Who even are you?" Mom asks.

"That's Brian, Mom, you know that!" I snap.

"I don't care who he is. Not in my house!" she yells. "Your behavior sometimes, I swear, Charlie. It's embarrassing. You should be embarrassed!"

Now I'm mad. "Fine!" I yell back. "If I'm so embarrassing, then we'll just leave."

"Excuse me?"

I look at Brian and take his hand. "Let's go."

I stomp toward the front door, ignoring my mom calling after me, demanding I stay and fight it out. But I don't have to. And I won't.

Chapter Thirty-Six

In Brian's car, all I can do is apologize. "I'm so sorry about her," I say for what feels like the twentieth time.

"*Please* don't worry about it," he says, reassuring me for what's probably the twentieth time, too. "We weren't doing anything."

"I know!"

"I mean. Not technically anyway. But maybe it looked a little bad," he admits.

I bite at one of my nails. "Yeah," I say. "Maybe. But freaking out like that? Pretending not to even know who you are? She takes it too far."

"I'm sorry," Brian says.

"No, it's fine, and not your fault."

We're quiet for a minute before Brian asks, "Will you be okay when you get home later? I mean, will she calm down?"

"Yeah," I say. "I'll be all right. She'll probably be over it and everything will be fine." It's a little white lie, but I don't want to freak Brian out. The last thing I need is for my family drama to push him away.

And honestly, maybe I did cross a line. It's not like there's a playbook for how to behave under your mom's roof when you've got your very first boyfriend. Are you really not allowed to kiss your boyfriend a little?

I don't know. I'm seventeen and things will happen. But if she doesn't want anything happening under her roof, fine. We can find other places.

"Does she always talk to you that way?" Brian asks.

"Oh," I say. "I mean, not always."

"Well, she shouldn't. Yelling should not be someone's preferred way of communication, even when they're mad," he says. "It was like she was trying to humiliate you."

"Are you saying your parents don't try to humiliate you on the regular?" I joke.

"Don't do that, Charlie," Brian says. "I'm being serious. It's not cool."

I nod. "I appreciate that. But that's just how she is."

He shakes his head. "Doesn't make it right."

"Amelia says the same thing, but it's like, what am I supposed to do about it? That's my mom."

Brian gnaws on his lip, deep in thought. After a moment, he says, "I honestly don't know. I don't have a good answer. I just—I need you to know you deserve better. Okay?"

I give him a small smile. Because hearing that is equal parts wonderful and painful. It's something I occasionally need to hear, while also serving as a reminder that this relationship with my mom is...a challenge.

"Thanks," I say. We drive for a bit in silence and then suddenly Brian pulls the car over, startling me. "What's going on?"

"I just realized it's finally nice enough out to do this." He loosens the handles on the roof of his convertible, then presses a button, and the top slowly starts to fold itself into the backseat. I can't help but smile as a breeze rustles around us. "A long time ago, I said I thought you'd enjoy the feeling of the wind in your hair. So. You ready to go for a drive?"

"Yes!"

"Where to?"

"Someplace far. Someplace like..." Then an idea strikes me. "You know how you took me on that amazing date to the art museum?" I ask. Brian nods. "Well, if that was one of your favorite places, I think we should go to one of *my* favorite places." I plug the address into my phone. "Let's go!"

We do, and the combination of the sunshine on my skin and the wind whipping through my hair (just like Brian once said) feels great. I look up at the sky and let out a laugh. "This is amazing!" I yell.

"I knew you'd like it!" he yells back.

We bask in the sun and turn up the music and sing along to the Smiths as we cruise. It's a joyful ride and I feel lighter because of it, savoring how sweet and simple this is.

As we reach our destination—the quaint center of a perfect New England town—Brian turns down the music and finds us a spot. I fix my windswept hair by tucking it back into a quick braid while he perfects his parallel-parking job.

"Ready?" I ask, and Brian nods.

I hop out of the car, holding out my hand for him to take. The town is, admittedly, a little earthy-crunchy, with stores that sell kombucha and tie-dye shirts, vegan eateries as the norm, and a lingering smell of patchouli oil. But I'm not mad about it, not when there's a rainbow flag proudly displayed in the center of town and posters affixed on storefronts proclaiming FEMINISM IS FOR EVERYONE. Plus, they have the best thrift stores here, as evidenced while we walk along the sidewalk, passing several—as well as a record store and a pot shop—until we get to a used-book store, Page Against the Machine.

I look over at Brian, who grins and touches my cheek, a gesture I have come to anticipate and love, and says, "This is *perfectly* you."

"Isn't it?" I ask. "Come on."

The moment we push open the door, the smell of the used books greets me like an old friend. I've spent many mornings, afternoons, and evenings here after fights with my mom, licking my wounds by treating myself to a bunch of new additions (as if my collection needs more).

"The best books have inscriptions in the front or notes in the margins," I say as we meander through one of the aisles. "Some people think writing in books is like an act of desecration, but I think it's kind of sweet. You get to see what other people think. For that moment, you get to share the story—just the two of you."

"That is pretty sweet." He reaches for a book. "What are the odds this one has an inscription in it?"

"Pretty cocky of you to assume the first book you select is going to have an inscription. They're like the four-leaf clovers of the used-book store."

Brian waves the book in front of me dramatically before opening the first page. Then the second. Then the third. And then he pouts. "No inscription." He puts it back on the shelf. "You try."

I look at the shelf and run my fingers along some of the spines of the books before settling on a copy of *Little Women*. I pull it off the shelf and open it up. Then I clear my throat and say, " 'To my darling Marilyn—You are my Jo. I love you always.' "

Brian's eyes go wide. "Really? You found a four-leaf clover, just like that?"

I turn the book around to him and show him the empty page. "No. But I made you *think* I was lucky, huh?"

He grabs the book from my hand and snaps it shut, putting it back on the shelf. "You!" he says, grabbing at my waist and pulling me close to him. We both laugh, and he gives me a kiss. "I'm really the lucky one."

"No, me," I say, meaning it, and giving him another kiss. "Hey, did I mention there's a whole comic book section upstairs?"

His face brightens. "Really?"

"Yes!"

Brian gives me a quick peck on the cheek. "Adore you, but the comics section calls. But you do your thing. Be whimsical. Wander." Brian disappears upstairs and I go back for the copy of *Little Women,* which I'm totally going to buy.

My purse buzzes and I dig out my phone to see a text from Amelia.

Hey, it says. **What are you up to?**

I take a photo of the book in my hand and text her back with it. **In my happy place.**

I would have gone with you! she writes.

Next time! I type. **I'm with Brian.**

Enjoy, she writes, and then I tuck away my phone in my bag.

I spend some time meandering up and down the aisles, adding more and more books to my pile: *Lotería, Alex & Eliza, The Book of Unknown Americans, The House of the Spirits, The Poet X,* another notebook (this one with a holographic cover) to add to my collection. Already, I feel much calmer after the fight with my mom. Eventually, I make my way to the second floor and find Brian, who's sitting on the floor with a pile of comic books beside him and one open on his lap. I smile to myself, pleased that he's enjoying himself in a place that I love, too.

I walk over to him and sit down. "Hi."

He looks at me, wide-eyed. "This. Place. Is. Awesome!" He holds up two comic books, one in each hand. "You have no idea the treasure I've unearthed here."

"Told you!"

"You *undersold* how great it was. There's even a cat in here! Did you see the cat?!"

I nod. "His name is Chap."

"Chap?"

"Short for Chapter."

"Short for Chapter. Of course." Then he asks, "How'd you even find this place?"

"Gem from my dad. He used to take me here back in the day," I say. "Want to show me what you found?"

"Absolutely," Brian says, patting the spot next to him. I scoot closer to him, our legs touching. "But just so you know, we're going to be here awhile."

At that, I grin. An afternoon of books and Brian? Yeah. I don't mind.

Chapter Thirty-Seven

It's a good thing Brian and I have a great time out because when I get home, my mom is pissed. Obvi.

She's sitting on the couch holding her phone, but she puts it down when I walk in and looks directly at me. "It's about time," she says before I can even sit down. "You can't just leave whenever you feel like it."

"I didn't want to subject Brian to whatever was about to happen."

Mom rolls her eyes. "Don't be so dramatic."

"I'm being dramatic? You stormed into my room and started yelling at me."

"You were practically having sex with some boy I don't even know in my own home!"

"Now who's being dramatic? We were fully clothed!" I retort. "And technically, you do know him because you've met him already!" (I am not making things better.)

"You know what I mean, Charlie!"

"I don't really! We were just kissing, Mom, and that isn't just 'some boy.' That's my b—" I almost say it—*boyfriend*—but I catch myself and stop. Still, I'm surprised when my mother's face seems to drain of color.

"That's your boyfriend?" she asks in a voice that's infinitely softer than I expect.

"I mean, we haven't really hashed that part out yet, but we're kind of, you know, dating. Or whatever."

"For how long?"

"A bit," I say.

"Oh." She looks away from me.

I'll admit it; I'm perplexed. I really don't know where this conversation is going. I mean, that's often my mom's tactic when we're fighting, but this feels genuine.

"Mom, I'm sure it was pretty mortifying to see that when you weren't expecting it. But I am seventeen now. I mean..."

"Why didn't you tell me about him?"

"I was going to...," I say, but it's a lie. I wasn't.

"But...?"

"But you weren't exactly warm to Brian when you met him that time he helped me with my car. Or when we ran into him at the mall a few weeks ago. And you seemed upset that I'd invited him to my birthday party, which I'm not even sure I understand, by the way. Why were you freaked out by that?"

"He's..." Mom starts to speak but stops herself.

"He's what?" I ask. "Because if this is about him being Korean, Mom, I *swear.*"

"No! It's not that. Not at all," she says. "He's just not someone I imagined you spending time with, that's all."

"Who, exactly, were you imagining me spending time with?" I ask. She doesn't offer up an answer. "Mom?"

"Someone...different, I guess. Less...nerdy." Then, in a small voice, she adds: "Maybe someone thinner."

"*What?*"

"Now, don't freak out on me, Charlie," she says. "You can't fault me for imagining the best for you."

"What are you even talking about, Mom? How would Brian being *thinner* be better for me?"

"I just thought it would serve you well to find someone who could help put you on the right path."

I feel like I've been slapped in the face. "Oh my God!"

"Don't do this, Charlie," she says.

"Don't do this? Don't *do* this?! You're unbelievable! You just told me you were being outright rude to a guy I like because you think he's fat. But guess what? I'm fat, too!"

"Oh, stop it." As she speaks, she's rubbing her temples as if somehow I'm exhausting her. "I'm sorry I care about you, Charlie. Sooo sorry!"

"God, you are impossible! You want to know why I didn't tell you about Brian, Mom? *This* is why I didn't tell you! Because you don't give a shit about me and what makes me happy—the *real* me, not the fake me you make up in your head, not the me you wish I'd turned out to be, not the me you hope will someday exist, but *me*. The actual person standing in front of you. You don't give a shit about anyone but yourself!"

"Charlie—"

But I'm not listening. I hurry toward my room, slam the door behind me, and pray she won't come after me.

She doesn't. It's the nicest thing she's done for me in weeks.

Chapter Thirty-Eight

After a night of angry-crying and barely sleeping, I know I must look like hell the next day at school, but Brian doesn't say anything when I get to my locker except for "You good?" When I say yes, he doesn't press the issue.

My mom and I haven't spoken, so I'm not grounded or anything (yet), but things aren't great. Last night, I strongly considered calling Amelia to tell her everything that had happened, but I was too tired even for that.

So instead, I texted her to say I missed her and she texted back that she missed me, too, and I left it at that.

This morning, I did everything I could to avoid seeing my mom, even waiting until the very last possible second to get ready for school. She was gone by the time I left, but I barely had enough time to brush my teeth, let alone make sure my hair was tamed.

So, yeah, I'm feeling rough when I get to school, and not especially talkative.

"We still on for lunch today?" Brian asks as we walk down the hall together.

"What?"

"We had plans for you to join me for lunch in the art room again today, right? Or did I imagine that?"

We stop in front of the door to homeroom. I know we talked about this, and yet I feel too tired to remember. "Oh, yeah."

Brian shrugs. "We don't have to. No big deal."

"No, we're still on." Then I force a smile.

He smiles back. "Okay. See you later?"

"Yes. See you later," I say.

I keep to myself for most of the day, but I do join Brian in the art room at lunch. I forgot to pack anything this morning, so I show up empty-handed and he offers to split his food with me.

I nibble on a little here and there, but I don't really feel hungry, so instead I slowly take out my art project and supplies and set up my spot beside him. I work on my horse painting—it's, like, a day or so away from being done and it still looks pretty terrible—but I don't say much.

Brian chooses some music for us and then does all of the heavy lifting with the talking. He tells me all about a marathon video game livestream he and his friends will be doing soon, and I listen closely, thankful for the distraction.

In last period, Amelia asks if I want to grab dinner with her after work, but I don't feel like it, so I ask for a rain check. She asks what's wrong. I say that I've gotten into another fight with my mom, and she gives me a sympathetic look but says nothing.

On the way out of school, Brian catches up with me and we start to walk toward the parking lot.

"Hey," he says. "You working tonight?"

"I am. You?"

"Yeah, I'll be there." We head toward my car, and as I put my key into the door, Brian touches my arm. "Is everything okay, Charlie? You seem out of it."

I look up at him and see that his eyes are big and his eyebrows are furrowed.

"Yeah, I'm sorry. I got into a fight with my mom when I got home last night. It was bad. It was really bad." I tell him a condensed version of what happened, omitting certain parts—there's no way in hell I'm going to make Brian feel bad about himself because of my mom's own body issues—and he listens.

"I'm so sorry, Charlie," he says, pulling me into a hug. I hug him back, hard, and realize this is exactly what I needed.

"I wish we could skip work today," I groan.

Brian pulls back from me and smiles. "Why can't we?" He puts the back of his hand on my forehead. "You're a little warm. Are you sure you're feeling well?"

I smile. "Hmm…I guess I am feeling a little overheated, now that you mention it. And you sound a little raspy, don't you?"

Brian touches his throat. "It hurts to talk, actually."

"I guess we have no choice but to call out of work."

"I guess so," Brian says. "See you at my house in ten?"

Suddenly, I feel much better.

Chapter Thirty-Nine

The next time my mom speaks to me, it's just to let me know I'm grounded, of course. But it's just for the week, which passes quickly and (let's be real) quietly with my mom and I not exactly on speaking terms. I spend all my copious free time working on my story for the contest, the fight with my mom adding fire and feeling to my words.

Before I know it, it's Friday. Unfortunately, Brian texts me to tell me he'll be out sick (he thinks he has the flu, **Karma for faking**, he says), and I find myself at my locker alone.

It's then that I realize I've barely seen Amelia recently.

I feel awful about it. (The awfulness comes over me in a flood, actually.) I don't want to be the girl who forgets her friends because of a boy, I swear. It's just that I'm so happy around Brian that it's hard not to want to feel that good all the time.

I scold myself and swear I'll be a better friend. Starting now.

I try to catch Amelia at her locker, but she's not there. (Our morning routine is all messed up because I've been walking to homeroom with Brian instead.) It's not until third period that I even *see* her, but she's late to class and we have a test that takes up the entire period, so we don't get to talk.

At lunch, I'm grateful when I spot Amelia, Kira, and the group eating outside at a picnic table.

"Hey, guys!" I say once I'm within earshot.

Liz and Maddy smile and wave. "Hey, Charlie!" Liz says.

"Long time no see," John says.

"Joining us for lunch today?" Jessica asks.

I eye the spot beside Amelia and look at her. "If that's cool with you, I'd love to. I miss you guys. Can I?"

Amelia answers without looking up at me. "You don't have to ask."

"Thanks," I reply, taking a seat.

Amelia's friends resume their conversation about how excited they are for summer break, which is rapidly approaching. (Liz will be working as a lifeguard. Maddy will be traveling with family for most of the summer and she's worried about being apart from Khalil. Jessica will be attending volleyball camp. Tyler remarks that he just wants to party.)

I smile, nod, and join in when I can, but don't offer much. Instead, I keep trying to talk to Amelia, but her responses to my questions—*How are you? What have you been up to lately? Intense test we just took, huh?*—are as close to one-word answers as possible. In fact, at one point I swear I see her angle her body away from me and toward Kira.

When the lunch bell rings and Amelia stands, I reach out and put my hand on her arm. "Is everything okay?"

Amelia exchanges a look with Kira, who nods her head and motions for the group to leave.

When they do, Amelia says, "No. It's not, actually."

"What's wrong?" I ask. Amelia looks down, but she says nothing. "Seriously, Amelia. What's going on?"

"I don't know, Charlie. You tell me."

"What do you mean?"

"Kind of seems like you've been avoiding me lately. I've barely seen you at all," she says. "Seems like you're *always* with Brian."

"I'm not," I insist, even though she's right.

Amelia shoots me a look. "Really?"

With a sigh, I say, "Okay, I'll admit that I have been spending a lot of time with Brian. But I'm free tonight! Do you want to hang out?"

"I'm already having Liz, Jess, and Maddy sleep over."

"Oh."

"Yeah," Amelia says, and there's a long pause. Finally, she asks, "Do you want to come?"

I put my hand to my heart. "Oh my God—I really thought you were going to freeze me out."

She smirks. "Good. I wanted you to sweat a little."

"So, meet you at your house after school?" I ask.

"It's a date," Amelia says.

The rest of the day crawls by, but only because I'm actually pretty excited about this sleepover. It will be nice to have some girl time and it's been forever since I've stayed the night at Amelia's. After the final bell, I rush to my car and head home to pack a bag with the essentials: some pj's, an outfit for tomorrow, beauty products, my phone charger. Then I shoot a text to Brian to let him know I'm thinking of him and hope he feels better and I head to Amelia's.

Mrs. Jones answers the door after two knocks. "So good to see you, Charlie!" She gives me a hug. "It's been a bit, hasn't it?"

"It has," I agree, feeling guilty. Even Mrs. Jones has noticed my absence.

"The girls are downstairs in the basement," she says. "Dinner will be ready shortly. Can I take your bag up for you?"

"Sure! Thanks so much." I hand it to her and then head downstairs, where I'm greeted by Amelia, Liz, Maddy, and Jessica.

"Hi, Charlie!" Maddy says.

"Charlie in the house!" Liz yells, and Amelia and Jessica both laugh and say hello. Amelia gives me a hug and I take it as a good sign.

"Okay, okay, so Liz was just starting to tell us about how Wren Bellamy ate total shit today in gym," Jessica says. "Keep going!"

"Right! Yeah, so, we *all* know how much Wren loves to show off her gymnastics skills whenever she can," Liz says.

Jessica rolls her eyes. "It drives me nuts. Like, we get it, Wren. You're rich and you've taken gymnastics classes since you were three and you think you're better than the rest of us. Cool."

"The girl has no chill," Amelia says. "Also, she once called me the poop emoji, so there's that."

"*What?*" Maddy asks. "What's that supposed to mean?"

"I have no idea!" Amelia laughs. "But Charlie was there—you remember, Charlie, right?"

"I will never forget," I say. "It was literally one of the weirdest conversations ever. Amelia and I were talking about our most-used emojis or something stupid like that, and for some reason, Wren just butts right in."

"Out of nowhere!" Amelia says. "And she goes, 'Well, Amelia, if you were an emoji, you'd be the poop emoji.'" We all start laughing. "Like, what do you even *say* to that?"

Jessica shakes her head. "Nothing, because Wren is so rude she isn't even worth responding to! In econ class, Wren once turned to me, unprompted, and said she won't eat from the cafeteria because that food is for poor people. 'It's all corn and bread and tacos.'"

I'm appalled. "Ex-*cuse* me?"

"That is a *seriously* insensitive thing to say," Maddy adds. I've noticed that Maddy tends to stay quiet when it comes to gossip, so when even she chimes in, you know it's bad. "Like, even if that were true, why would it be *bad*?"

"Fuck *all* of that," Liz says. "You guys will love this."

"Yes, we are fully ready!" Amelia rubs her hands together eagerly.

There is a delighted look on Liz's face, knowing we're hooked before she's even begun the story. "Okay, so, I'm in gym class and we have a sub so it's kind of a free gym period. Some people are walking the track, some people are playing HORSE, whatever. It's mostly super chill. But *Wren* decides she wants to pull out the balance beam from the storage room. And she somehow convinces a few of the people in class to help her set it up."

"What's the sub doing while this is all happening?" Amelia asks.

"I don't know, messing around on his phone, maybe watching the class descend into chaos—clearly checked out, though. So it takes Wren and them forever to get the balance beam out, but once it is, Wren decides 'fuck the rules.' She's supposed to be using a spotter and she doesn't, and she's supposed to lay down mats, but she doesn't do that, either."

"Oh, no," Maddy breathes.

"Oh, yes," Liz says.

Jessica looks over at Amelia. "God, I wish I had some popcorn right now."

Liz grins and leans forward to dramatically continue with the story. "So Wren gets up there, starts talking about how she won regionals last year with this routine, and she's a champion, and we should all pay attention to a champion's routine—and then she launches into some intense cartwheels and, like, *midtwirl,* her foot misses the beam! She absolutely eats shit and falls all the way to the ground!" Liz slaps her hands, together mimicking the sound. "THUNK."

We all cringe at the idea of falling on that wooden gym floor from a few feet up.

"God, that must've sucked!" I say.

"It looked like it hurt," Liz admits.

"How mortifying," Maddy says, and we're all nodding.

"But...it was kinda funny, too, wasn't it?" Jessica asks, a playful smile on her lips.

Liz can't help it and smiles, too, before insisting, "Only because she ended up being totally fine!"

"Yeah, of course," Amelia says.

Maddy nods. "Absolutely."

Then we all exchange glances and start laughing. "God, we're horrible!" I say.

"The worst," Maddy agrees. Her phone chimes and she glances at it, a huge smile spreading across her face as she reads whatever has popped up on her screen.

"Oh. *That* must be Khalil," Liz says knowingly.

Maddy turns her phone over shyly, leaving it screen side down. "How can you tell?"

"Girl, that grin," Amelia teases. "No shame. We all smile goofy like that when our person texts."

"He was just checking in before he heads out with the boys. I can't help it; I still get excited to hear from him," Maddy says.

"I get it," I say, excited that I really do.

Jessica nods. "Oh, yeah. You and Brian! You two are *super* cute."

I beam. "Thank you! Yeah, he's really, really great."

"Is he out with friends tonight, too?" Maddy asks.

"No, not tonight," I say. "Unfortunately, he's home sick with the flu."

"Oh, that's too bad," Liz says.

"Home with the flu?" Amelia asks sharply. "Guess that explains why you were suddenly free."

"Hey, no," I say, caught off guard. "Not true at all."

But maybe it is—at least a little?

"Of course," Amelia says, crossing her arms.

I see Jessica raise her eyebrows and exchange a glance with Maddy and Liz.

"I'm really excited to be here," I insist. "And I'm so happy you invited me."

"Well, we're happy you're here, too, Charlie," Maddy says with a smile.

Mrs. Jones rescues me by calling downstairs. "Girls—dinner!"

Amelia starts to go upstairs, but I grab her arm. "Wait," I say, and Maddy, Liz, and Jessica head up without us, leaving us to it.

"What?" Amelia asks.

"Don't be like this."

She huffs. "I'm just annoyed because I thought you actually wanted to hang out tonight."

"I do want to hang out tonight!" I say. "I'm here, aren't I?"

"But only because Brian is unavailable." Amelia puts her hands on her hips. "I mean, it's whatever, Charlie, but that kind of sucks."

"I don't want you to feel like this is my last resort or anything. It's not. I'm genuinely happy to be here. And I'm super excited to get to know the girls a little better."

"Yeah?" Amelia asks, thawing slightly.

"Yeah! Let's not let this ruin the night, please," I plead. When she doesn't look convinced, I add, "Please, please, please, please!"

She finally caves—and even smiles. "Okay, fine. Let's just have a good time, then."

I loop my arm through hers, relieved. "Let's."

Chapter Forty

I don't want to catch the flu, but I miss Brian. The next morning, after leaving the sleepover at Amelia's, I pick up some chicken noodle soup and drop it off with his mom, Susan. Brian waves pathetically at me from the window of his room.

He and I spend the whole weekend Snapping and texting. Thankfully, he's back to school on Monday, so I attack him in the parking lot like it's been years since I've seen him.

"I missed you," I say, and Brian pulls me into a giant bear hug. The warmth of his body on mine was sorely missed. I nuzzle my face into the crook of his neck and don't even care if we've become *that* couple.

He kisses the top of my head. "I missed *you*. Thanks again for keeping me sane while I was cooped up inside."

"Of course." I pull back and look at him. "I was so bored without you."

"Me too." Then he snaps his fingers. "Oh! Shoot, I forgot something in there." He points to his car. "Can you help me look?"

He unlocks the car and we both climb inside, closing the doors behind us. I put my backpack on the floor in front of me. "What are we looking for?" I ask.

Brian breaks into a grin as he hits the lock button on his doors. "This," he says, pulling me to him and kissing me hard, like it's been days since we've done this, *which it has*. I don't know how long we're kissing, but I don't care because this is so much better than literally everything else. When we finally break apart, all I say is "I'm glad you're feeling better," and Brian kisses me again before the parking lot guard knocks on the window and tells us we need to get going because we've missed the bell.

Worth it.

School is fine, lunch is fine, everything is fine, but all I want to do is go to Brian's house and hang out. So imagine my disappointment when my mom texts me midday to say we need to talk when I get home.

I go from riding high to pretty much feeling like I've suddenly come down with the flu myself. But I tell her yes and postpone my afternoon plans with Brian.

Once I'm home, I change into some comfortable clothes, walk over to my mom's room, and knock. Might as well get this over with.

"Come in," she says.

I push open the door. Behind it, the room looks nothing like when my dad was around. It's like his memory has been scrubbed clean away, which I both understand (I'm sure it's hard to constantly be reminded of the man you loved, who's gone) and resent (I miss him so much sometimes). There is one thing that's the same— from one of the bedposts hangs my dad's favorite hat.

I *always* used to be in this room when my dad was around. We would hang out and watch movies, or spend time reading books, or sometimes, when I was home sick from school and he had to take care of me, we'd play board games all day (if I promised not to tell Mom). I don't come in here much anymore.

"You wanted to talk?" I ask.

"Yes," she says. Then she pats the bed. "Come; sit."

I join her and settle into a cross-legged position.

"So," she says.

"So," I say back.

"I've been doing a lot of thinking."

"Yeah?" I ask.

"I realized that maybe what I said was...harsh."

"Harsh," I repeat.

"Yes. I do want what's best for you, Charlie, but you know. You're seventeen."

I take this as her acknowledging that I'm growing up and can make my own choices. Progress! "Yeah! Exactly! I'm sort of figuring things out."

"Or you're just going to do what you're going to do and I can't stop you." Bubble burst. "And if that's Brian, well...yeah. It is what it is."

A spark of rage swells up in my chest, but I know there's no use letting it burn. I imagine dousing it with some water, and I can almost hear the *tss* sound as I let it go out. My mom doesn't get it; she doesn't get *me*. And...she won't.

"Yeah, it is what it is," I echo coolly.

"But, I mean, it would've been nice if you had at least told me you were dating someone. Daughters typically tell their moms things like that, you know."

Part of me wants to scream: *But this is exactly why I didn't! And you kind of I-told-you-so'd me after Cal! And you continually judge me about my weight! And you couldn't say anything kind about Brian! And you never ask how I'm doing, and you never take an interest in my hobbies, and, and, and!*

But I don't. Because the main reason I didn't tell my mom about Brian is that I'm so used to *not* sharing things with her that the thought didn't even cross my mind. And maybe that's worse.

"Well, at least you know about him now, even if you found out about him in an awkward way. And I'm sorry about that."

"It's all right," Mom says. "But you know. Be cool."

This is her way of saying *Don't have sex here.* "Yeah, of course. We'll 'be cool.' "

"Well, good."

I nod. "Yes. Good."

She looks over at a text that's lit up her phone, signaling unceremoniously that the conversation is done, so I slink out of the room. I know now that we may never be okay, and we'll never have that mother-daughter relationship I so desperately yearn for...but we aren't fighting, and maybe that's all I can really ask for.

Chapter Forty-One

If you'd told me a few months ago that I'd soon find myself standing in front of the mirror admiring a new lacy bra I bought to show off to a boy I'm dating, I would have called you a liar. Maybe even shoved you a little. Yet here I am.

After the intense make-out session in Brian's car the other day, I picked up a few nice bras. I just feel like we can only make out for so long. Pretty soon, he's probably going to see my bra, and I'd rather it not be a geriatric bra from hell (AKA the only kind I own right now).

I'm not saying we're going to do anything—not yet, anyway. We've only been together a month (today!). But given that we've casually started calling each other boyfriend and girlfriend, I can only assume that yeah, things are bound to happen. I've even added a trip to Planned Parenthood to my list of things to do in hopes I can get on the pill, because this girl is *not* trying to get pregnant.

My phone vibrates and I look down to see a text from Brian that says **Be there in 10.**

That leaves me scrambling to finish getting dressed to prepare for our date tonight. We're going to a fancy dinner—like on a real, grown-up date at a nice restaurant—in celebration of our one-month anniversary. Which I can hardly believe. One official month of hanging out and handholding and kissing and being there for each other. It's been pretty incredible.

Finally, there's someone interested in me and *only* me—not just talking to me because they want to get closer to Amelia.

For clothes, I opt for an off-the-shoulder red dress that flares at the waist. It makes me feel much older and sophisticated than I actually am, and with a new bra that pushes up my boobs a little, I feel kind of hot. I hope Brian thinks so, too.

Tonight, I'll celebrate one month with my first boyfriend, and that feels like a night worth remembering.

Another vibration on my phone lets me know that Brian is here, so I take one last look at myself in the mirror before I run out to the car to greet him. I haven't seen him in two days—he had to travel to a family wedding—so I'm extra excited.

Brian is walking up my front walk to greet me, but I meet him halfway and throw my arms around him. I take him by surprise, but he hugs me back tightly and I think to myself I could probably stay like this forever.

But we do have dinner reservations to get to.

"Hi," I say, pulling back from the hug to look at him.

"Hi," he says, his eyes wandering over my body. "Damn, Charlie."

I push my glasses up shyly. "What?" I ask.

"You look hot," Brian says, leaning in for a kiss. When he pulls back, he keeps his head close to mine. "Really hot."

"You too," I say, eyeing him back. He's wearing a long-sleeved fitted Henley over black jeans. I can fully see the outline of his strong arms in it, and I am not complaining. Why do boys look *so good* wearing the simplest things?

He shakes whatever thoughts he's having away. "Okay. Okay. We ready?"

I nod, secretly so, so, pleased, and we're off.

On the drive to the restaurant, I fill him in on what I've been up to the last few days, which is a whole lot of nothing. But I did finally submit my story to the contest, and Brian is all smiles when we're seated at our table and I tell him that.

"You did, really?" he asks.

"I did, *finally,* is what you mean."

"No. You did it, and that's what matters," he says.

Despite writing what I thought was a compelling, emotionally raw short story, I really struggled to hit that Submit button. I found myself consumed with worry that it wouldn't be good enough, even though Ms. Williams had walked me through several rounds of edits and given me excellent suggestions. But I kept reading it back and thinking it was far too emotional. When I shared those feelings with Brian, he offered to read it for me, so I emailed him a copy. His response was a simple text: **Wow.**

Between that and some tough love from Ms. Williams ("Charlie, send it or don't"), I finally worked up the courage and submitted it.

I smile at him. "I'm glad, too. Thank you for looking it over for me."

"Of course. I'd been trying to get you to let me read something of yours forever!" He laughs. "But it was well worth the wait. You are an incredible writer, Charlie."

"You're an incredible artist," I say.

"What does one have to do with the other?"

"I don't know. Just seems like we're a good fit."

At that, Brian smiles.

"So," I say, a little flushed. "Tell me about the wedding!"

"Way too many Ed Sheeran songs."

"Oh, no!"

"It was even their wedding song."

"No!" I say in a hushed voice.

"Yes!" he whispers back, and we both start laughing. Sorry, Ed Sheeran.

The waiter comes back to ask if we're ready to order, so we do, and then Brian continues. "It would have been better if you were there."

"I wish I'd been there, too," I say, smiling. My phone vibrates on the table and I see it's Amelia. "Do you mind?"

"Go for it."

I can see in the text preview that she's asking if I can hang out tonight, and I feel a little stab of guilt. Despite my vow to be a better friend, I still haven't spent much time with her lately. I've been really busy with Brian and writing my story and work and everything, and every time Amelia and I do hang out, she's been hot and cold. It's frustrating, so I've pulled back, maybe intentionally, maybe not. I don't think I even told her it was our one-month anniversary tonight.

Hey, sorry! I'm actually out with Brian tonight, I write. **It's our anniversary!**

The three gray dots show up and I watch them for a while before they disappear. They come back, then disappear again. Then they come back and a text comes through that reads **Happy anniversary** but without any punctuation or emojis or anything.

Why can't she just be happy for me?

"Everything good?" Brian asks.

I lock my phone and push it away from me. "No." I sigh. "Amelia's been acting really weird lately."

Brian frowns. "What's going on?"

"I think she's kind of upset that we've been hanging out so much," I say carefully. "But it seems really unfair. She always has somebody, and I've never said anything to her about it, not even when she's ditched me or made me feel like a third wheel!"

"That sounds a little hypocritical."

"Right? Why is it so bad if I hang out with my boyfriend sometimes? Plus, she's been after me to have us all go out on a double date and I don't want to do that. I just want to spend time with you, Bri."

"A double date doesn't sound so bad," he offers.

"That's sweet of you. But I feel like I'd just be obsessively comparing myself to Amelia the whole night or comparing our relationship to hers and Kira's, and I don't want that. I think maybe she's mad I keep putting it off."

Brian reaches across the table and gives my hand a little squeeze.

"Anyway, I'm absolutely not going to let her ruin our celebration." I give him a smile. "It's our anniversary!"

"One whole month. How have you put up with me for so long?"

"Seemed pretty easy to me."

"Yeah," he says. "It's been pretty easy for me, too. I really feel like—I don't know about you, but I just feel like we *work*. You just get me. And I just love being around you."

My stomach does a little flip. "I love being around you, too. I mean, I thought a lot about what it would be like to be with someone, but this is so much better than I ever even imagined. I know that sounds super cheesy, but it's true."

Brian is beaming at me and I can't help but smile back. "Happy anniversary, kid," he says.

"Happy anniversary, Tig," I say, holding up my water glass. He clinks his to mine just as our meals arrive.

Brian and I politely thank our waiter, then make conversation about how good the food looks, but all I can think about is how happy I am and how happy this night is making me. So I feel a little bold and I lean forward toward him.

"I have a secret," I say.

"Oh, yeah?" Brian asks.

"I bought a new bra," I whisper.

Brian is midbite and starts to cough. He takes a big sip of water before saying, "Excuse me?"

"You heard me," I say. I don't know where I've suddenly gotten all this confidence from, but I like it. I want to hold on to it and keep it and channel it whenever I can.

"Damn, Charlie," Brian says, his eyes glancing to my chest and back up at me. Then back down again and then back up at me. *"Damn."*

"Maybe we can hang out after dinner?"

Brian holds up his finger like he's signaling for the waiter. "Check, please," he says, which makes me laugh.

"No, no! Let's finish our food. Take our time. It's better this way, isn't it?"

"Says you."

I eat my meal deliberately slowly, delighting in the number of times I catch Brian eyeing my cleavage. When the waiter asks if we want dessert, I even pretend to mull it over, and Brian lets out a small sigh of relief when I say I'm all set. He pays for dinner, then takes my hand and leads me outside to the car, walking fast.

When we get to his car, instead of letting go of my hand and climbing inside, he uses my hand to pull me closer to him and he kisses me—urgently, passionately, with need.

The kiss leaves me tingling. "We should get in the car," I whisper. "Maybe find somewhere a little more private?"

My heart is pounding as I say this, and Brian nods. We get into the car and go. He drives for a bit till we're back in town, then turns into a park and pulls over in a deserted lot. When he cuts the engine, he turns to look at me.

"Hi," I say.

"Hi," he says, a smile tugging at his lips. He stares at me for a moment, putting one hand on my cheek. Then he says, "God, you're beautiful."

"Yeah?" I ask, biting my bottom lip.

Brian leans over and he kisses me. This one is sweeter than the last, more delicate, like he's trying to show me, not tell me, that I'm beautiful. And I *feel* it.

They say you can't really be with someone until you can love yourself, but I'm learning that it can also sometimes take the admiration and support of someone else to help you get there. I was already on the path to seeing my own self-worth, but Brian took my hand and made the route less lonely. Whether that's right or wrong, I can't say; all I know is I feel beautiful and wanted at Brian's touch.

Which makes me deepen the kiss. I stroke the back of his hair, pulling him to me, closing the gap between us. One of his hands is cupping the back of my neck, while the other is on my knee.

I am able to forget how I'm supposed to feel *about* my body and instead I enjoy what my body *actually* feels. I don't worry what Brian will think as he's touching me; I just let him touch me. My hands, my back, my neck, my chest.

Up until this point, our touching has been entirely over our clothes. But when I feel Brian's hand gently tugging at the strap of my dress, slowly pulling it down my shoulder, I don't push him away; I let him.

Because I like him, and I trust him, and he makes me feel like I don't need to be ashamed of myself or my body.

And because I didn't buy this bra for nothing.

Chapter Forty-Two

After an incredible night with Brian, I know I need to tell Amelia, so I ask if she wants to grab some lunch the next day and she agrees.

We go to our spot, Jake's, but don't speak about anything too meaningful—small talk, mostly, and some gossip from school, but not much else. I can never find the right moment to tell her about Brian, so I just...don't. Thankfully, she invites me back to her house, and I hope the familiar setting will help restore some of the normalcy between us.

At her house, we sit on her bed and she immediately pulls out her phone. Sometimes we do that together, go on our phones and share funny, dumb things from the internet, but I'd rather talk. I ask her how things with her and Kira are going and she says they're fine but doesn't offer anything else. So I figure now's as good a time as any and I start to tell her about last night.

"Brian and I celebrated our anniversary last night. It was amazing," I say. "He told me he loves spending time with me and that I just get him. I don't know, Amelia, but this really feels like something, you know?"

She doesn't glance up. "That's nice."

"Yeah, it is," I say, trying to press through how much her lack of response is bothering me. "It feels so big and wonderful and scary all at the same time. After dinner, we—uh, did some stuff. Like...*stuff*-stuff."

"Cool," Amelia says.

"Cool?"

She looks up from her phone at me. "Yeah. Cool." Then she returns to whatever she was doing.

"That's all you have to say to that?"

"Yeah, I mean, we all do stuff with our partners, Charlie," Amelia says. "It's not exactly notable."

I feel my cheeks flush. I know she's just being hurtful on purpose, but still. *This* is why I sometimes get extra insecure. "I know that, Amelia. Sorry for trying to share something with my best friend."

"I don't know why you're getting so upset."

I scoff. "I'm getting upset because I'm trying to talk to you about important things and you don't even want to look up from your phone!"

She dramatically puts her phone down on the bed and stares right at me, crossing her arms. "There. Better?"

"No, it's not better. What's your problem lately? You barely talk to me!"

"*I* barely talk to *you*? That's real nice coming from you."

"What's that supposed to mean?"

Amelia gets up from her bed. "Only that you're never around anymore. You're *always* with Brian. I'm shocked you're even at my house right now."

"I was just at a sleepover with you and the girls!"

"Right, but only because Brian was sick so you couldn't hang out with him."

"Oh, God, that again? Seriously, Amelia?"

She crosses her arms. "You know I'm right! You never make time for me anymore."

"Ugh, that's so dramatic, Amelia. God forbid I want to spend some time with Brian, my *boyfriend*," I say. "You spend a ton of time with Kira, too! Don't act like you don't."

"I still make time for you, which is more than you can say," she retorts, and then she starts angry-cleaning her bookshelf, a weird habit she has when she's upset. Her mom does the same thing.

"I make time for you! But things change when you're dating someone. You know that," I say. "I've always been so understanding of that with your past boyfriends—especially Sid!"

"Oh, so I've just always put other people before you? That's a nice thing to say about your best friend."

"I *didn't* say that, Amelia. I'm just saying that when it happens—and it does!—that I've always been really patient about it, never complaining about being a third wheel, and just trying to let you do your thing!"

"Sure, turn this whole thing on me!" she yells.

"I'm not turning this on you. I just think you're being really unfair right now. Admit it: you kind of hate that I finally have a boyfriend!"

Amelia slams some of her books into a pile on her desk and turns to me. "That's absurd! I'm *happy* you have a boyfriend."

"Yeah, right! I'm trying to tell you about our anniversary and you don't even care!"

"Because when you're not with Brian, all you do is talk about Brian! God, Charlie, who even are you anymore?" she asks. "I feel like I don't even know you!"

"Well, *sorry* that I went out and got a life and you can't handle that! Even Brian agrees. He says you're being a real hypocrite!"

Her shoulders go up and she scowls at me. "You're talking shit about me with Brian?"

"Oh, give me a break. Like you don't talk about me to Kira," I say, rolling my eyes.

She sniffs. "I *don't*."

"Well, whatever." But I feel my cheeks getting a little hot in embarrassment.

"I can't believe I've literally spent weeks being upset that I barely see my best friend and she's off with her boyfriend just talking about me like no big deal," Amelia says. "And he called me a hypocrite? That's really shitty, Charlie."

"Well, he didn't actually call you a hypocrite," I say, but she cuts me off.

"I don't even care. Go ahead; talk shit about me. He's probably just pissed because I turned him down when he asked me out!"

That hits me like a punch in my gut.

"What are you talking about?" I ask.

"Oh, chatty Brian must not have shared that with you? Brian asked *me* out before he ever asked you out," she says, glaring at me. "I guess he preferred me. And *that's* why you're not ever supposed to choose a boy over your best friend, Charlie. Whatever. I'm over this."

Amelia storms out of her room to go God knows where and leaves me standing there, my eyes aching with the sting of tears.

I take in a shallow, unsteady breath, feeling faint.

I'm...stunned.

And all I can think is that I need to get out of here. I fumble around for my bag and keys and rush to my car. My heart is pounding as I drive away from Amelia's house.

I don't think Amelia and I have ever fought like this—saying hurtful things, things we can't take back.

But could it be true? That Brian asked her out? When? How? Why did I not know?

My brain can't help but jump to the worst conclusions—that none of Brian's feelings toward me are real, that this has all been a big ploy to get closer to Amelia, that I've slowly been giving parts of myself to a boy who doesn't care about me at all.

Chapter Forty-Three

My world feels like it's spinning so fast I could puke.

I don't know what to make of my fight with Amelia, and I *definitely* don't know what to think about what she said about Brian. I start to drive home but know I'm not guaranteed a place to cry in peace there, so I take myself to the sad, deserted mall instead and cry in the parking lot.

I thought the way I felt after Cal was bad, but this is so much worse. This feels like losing my best friend and my boyfriend in the same instant. Like I blinked wrong and—*poof*—everyone meaningful to me was gone. I'm sick at the thought. It's as if the hurt burning inside of my chest seeps into my veins and pumps all over my body.

She *knows* that my relationship with Brian has meant so much to me. She *knows* that I've been in a lovesick stupor experiencing all of these firsts. She *knows* how happy this has all made me. She knows, and yet she still set off a grenade and dropped it in my lap, not caring about the aftermath.

That she'd been holding on to the secret that Brian had asked her out first, that she chose a particularly vulnerable moment to share it with me, that she said it deliberately to hurt me—none of that feels fair.

And Brian. *My* Brian? Well, he was clearly not really ever my Brian at all, not if what Amelia says is true, not if he liked her first. Angry as Amelia was with me, she would never lie to me.

Yet how am I supposed to go back to a life where Brian is Just

Brian, some kid in art class, and not My Brian, the guy I'm head over heels for? Am I just supposed to forget how my hand fits into his? How we can laugh until we're crying, certain that our lungs can't take any more, and then erupt into laughter all over again? How we can easily settle into comfortable silences together? How it feels like we're always on an adventure, in on a secret? The way he can easily wrap me in his arms and pull me into a hug, like that's where I belong? The way his eyes crinkle when he smiles so big? The way he touches my cheek just so? That crooked grin? The smell of his cologne? I let out a sob thinking of having to say goodbye to all that.

It's not fair. It's not right. I finally had a person in my corner who delighted in me, someone to call my own. I had something *good*. I think about our relationship, how it grew like the heat from a fire—slowly at first, but then enveloping you, warming up your fingers and the tip of your nose until your whole body is cocooned in it, warm and safe and happy in ways you never thought you could be.

Brian was my person. *My* person. Mine. And I was his. And now.

Now I'll have to go back to my life, the way it was before, living in everyone else's shadow, trying not to be washed out entirely by their light. I'll have to let go of the comfort, give it back, like I was just borrowing it and it was never really mine at all.

Because Brian liked Amelia before he liked me. It confirms all my worst fears. It digs deep inside the trenches of my body, yanks out a searing insecurity, and places it outside me for all to see.

The shame sets me on fire, and my brain keeps returning to one thought: *We're done. We have to be.*

Brian and I are over.

And for the time being, so are Amelia and I.

My face crumples. *This* is how it feels to lose everyone you care about in one fell swoop.

Brian tries reaching out to me. He sends me cute pictures of a dog, a link to a funny Reddit post, and some texts about how he misses me.

I ignore them all and put his messages on Do Not Disturb so I stop getting notified every time he texts.

If I keep him in limbo, I don't have to admit to myself that I have to say goodbye.

I do the same with Amelia's text chain, though she hasn't yet reached out. Maybe she doesn't even care that she's hurt me.

Even with notifications off, I know I'll spend a good part of the night obsessively checking my phone just to see, so eventually I turn it off completely to rid myself of the temptation. I try to read, but I can't focus. I try to sleep, knowing the next day is a school day, but I barely rest. Instead, I toss, I turn, I cry, I stare at the ceiling.

In the morning, I purposely drag my feet getting ready for school, arrive late so that I can avoid both Brian and Amelia at my locker, and don't acknowledge Amelia in class. I stare at my notes and at the board and at my phone but don't even look in Amelia's direction.

In between classes, I do check my messages. I see the little blue dot, indicating unread texts, beside both Brian's and Amelia's names.

I can't look at Brian's—not at school.

But I do peek at Amelia's. There are two.

I feel like things got really out of hand tonight, one reads. **I'm so sorry.**

The other: **Can we please talk?**

But I'm not ready to. Not yet. So I tuck my phone away, spend the rest of the day avoiding both her and Brian, skip art class entirely, and go straight home.

I don't quite know what to do with myself. I've fallen into such a comfortable routine with Brian that suddenly doing nothing—a thing I've perfected over years—feels weird to me.

I can't help it; eventually, I give in and look at the texts from him. There are a *lot*. And though they started out funny and charming and lovely—the kind of things two people with lots of gushy, happy feelings toward each other might send—they get increasingly concerned, alarmed.

Missed you at lunch. See you in art?

Haven't seen or heard from you all day, kid.

Hmm...now you're not in art. I'm getting worried. Are you out sick today?

Maybe you've been abducted by aliens??? Do they come in peace or nah? Note to self: steal spaceship, rescue girlfriend.

Not trying to annoy you, but getting a little concerned. Text me back when you can!

I feel a pang of guilt reading through the messages.

Part of me feels like I could just reply and act like I don't know what I know. We could go on being together like it doesn't matter. I don't have to acknowledge that he likes Amelia more. We can just pretend.

But the other part of me could scream. This feels like a betrayal. With every fiber in me, I hate, hate, *hate* that Brian asked Amelia out before me. That he prefers her over me, just like everyone else. It makes my stomach churn. I feel vile and used and foolish.

I would give anything to extricate that knowledge from my brain and to forget it ever existed. For the first time in my whole life, I liked someone and he liked me back, and we were happy.

But I wasn't his first choice. I was his silver medal.

Is this bound to be my life forever?

The thing that kills me is that Brian never, ever made me feel like I was inferior to Amelia. He always made me feel heard and seen, like I could really be me—the best version of me—when I was around him. He listened to me; he fought for me; he cared for me.

In the way he pursued me, proudly and publicly; in the way he supported me during fights with my mom; in the way he believed in me and in my writing; in all these little and big ways, I thought Brian showed me again and again that he really cared. For me. Only me.

Yet now when I think of him, there is a pain in my chest that's so deep that I can only describe it as *guttural*.

I admit that I pictured a future with Brian. He was my first boyfriend, my first kiss, my first everything, and now I have to live with the fact that the first and only boy I've ever cared for in this way preferred Amelia, like everyone else who has ever disappointed me.

I think I might have loved him. And now I'm not sure I ever want to think about loving someone ever again.

Chapter Forty-Four

I pretend to go to school the next morning by leaving right on time so my mom doesn't suspect a thing—then turning back around and going home.

Outside, it's raining, which feels right. It frustrates me when the weather outside doesn't match how I'm feeling. Today, I welcome the rain.

I check on the texts from Brian again, but there's only one.

Are you okay, Charlie? Please text me back. I'm really, really worried.

I cave and write **I'm fine, just busy**, which only makes him call me. He must've had to sneak out of class to do so. I don't answer.

I check the texts from Amelia. There's a long one.

I understand that you don't want to talk. I really do. I've been thinking a lot and feeling really, really ashamed of how I behaved the other day. I know I hurt you and I'm so sorry. I hope that we can talk and you can find it in your heart to forgive me for the things I said. But I also understand if you never want to speak to me again. Know that I'm here and ready and willing to talk if/when you are.

I start to type out a reply, mulling over what I might say...but then stop. Put my phone away. Pull out my diary.

I haven't written in it in ages, so I start by spending some time reading old entries. They're so profoundly sad: the thoughts of a girl who doesn't love herself enough. Reading her deepest feelings makes me realize how much I've relied on others to build that girl up, on how much of her validation came from the world around her rather than from inside her. I thought I'd gotten out of that headspace, but is that how I've been with Brian all along? Only flying because he was holding a fan that blew air under my wings? I pick up a pen and write.

I decide that, in spite of everything happening now, I don't want this new entry to be as sad and lonely as the others. I want it to be hopeful and forward-looking and give Future Charlie something to look back on and feel proud of.

So I write about how I will find the strength to respect myself. I will find the courage to be kind in the face of hurt.

I write that I will put myself first.

I write that I won't succumb to—or believe—my mother's feelings about me.

I write that I will muster the strength to say goodbye to those who don't deserve me.

I write that in the face of my sadness I will find the sunlight.

I write about how I don't know how, but one way or another, I'll be fine.

* * *

That evening, I decide I need to get out of the house; I need something, anything to distract me. It's Tuesday night and staying home is suddenly the very last thing I want to do.

But I can't exactly text Brian or Amelia.

I consider reaching out to Maddy or even Jess or Liz—but I worry they might be with Amelia, and I don't want to risk it.

So I do something I haven't done in a while. I text my cousin Ana.

Hey! I write. **How have you been?**

She writes back: **Charlie!!! I've been good. What about you?**

I'm good! Miss you! Are you free tonight? I ask.

I'm with Carmen at Crazy Skates. You should come by! Ana says.

Another text rolls in and I see it's from Carmen. **COME NOOOOW!** There's a picture of her and Ana—both perfectly made up—on the roller-skating rink.

A quick wardrobe change, a little makeup, and a giant hair scrunchie later, I'm on my way. Tonight, I will fake it until I make it.

Here, I text Ana and Carmen once I'm inside. **Going to the rental line!**

I grab a pair of skates and a locker for my shoes and bag. As I'm changing out of my shoes, Ana and Carmen flank me on either side with a hug.

"You're here!" Carmen squeals while I finish lacing my skates.

"I'm here!" I say, trying to match her excitement. I rise to my feet, a little unsteady.

"You look cute," Ana says.

I smile. "You both look cute, too!"

Carmen pretends to do a model walk in her skates and we laugh. "I *always* look cute."

"Accurate," I say, taking in Carmen's outfit, one I'd immediately save if I saw it on Insta: a tight vintage tee with an oversized, open button-up on top, paired with some cuffed jeans. Her dark, thick hair is pulled back in a ponytail, and her blunt bangs accent the dramatic eyeliner she always wears. Ana, meanwhile, has her long, wavy black hair parted down the middle, and she's wearing the hell out of a crop top over some high-waisted jeans. "Now, I have to warn you, I'm a little rusty on these. I haven't been here since we were kids."

"Oh my God! Really?!" Ana asks.

"Really!"

"Okay, we'll go slow," Carmen says, linking her arm through

mine as we start to skate toward the darkened rink, where the music is playing.

"And we won't laugh if you fall," Ana adds.

Carmen throws her head back and lets out a dramatic cackle. "Speak for yourself."

It takes me some time to feel comfortable on skates again, but after a few songs, I'm feeling more confident—even dancing a little!—as the three of us circle the rink with the rest of the crowd and sing along to the music. I don't normally dance, but hey, I have nothing to lose, right? It feels good to be moving and getting some of my pent-up energy out.

"Do you remember when we were here for Carmen's eighth birthday party?" Ana has to shout over the music.

"The one with the piñata?" I shout back.

"Oh my gosh, yes! My kitty piñata!" Carmen grins. "Mateo was teasing me so bad, telling me a girl could never be the one to break it and get all the candy out. But I showed him!"

Ana laughs. "You sure did! Candy everywhere and then a few extra hits to poor Tío Armando, who was holding it!"

I burst out laughing, too. "Oh my gosh! I totally forgot about that!"

"All us kids dove for the candy immediately. Meanwhile, Carmen is beating the crap out of Tío Armando and none of the adults even cared!"

"In the end I barely got any candy!" Carmen fake-pouts. "Still salty about that."

I continue. "Oh! Oh! What about the time when we were here and that one guy was trying to show off for the crowd by doing a trick, but he tripped over his own feet and his hair went flying?!"

"*The toupee!*" we shriek in unison, then start howling. Soon enough, we're just reminiscing about being kids—the dinners and barbecues and holidays and backyard baseball games—and I realize how long it's been since we've really connected.

When we skate off the rink to take a break in the food court, I look over at the two of them earnestly. "I've *missed* you guys."

Ana smiles. "We've missed you, too."

"Yeah, but *we* haven't gone anywhere." Carmen sniffs and looks down at her manicured nails. "We still do stuff together. You're just not there."

"Carmen—" Ana starts, but Carmen cuts her off, locking eyes with me.

"I'm just saying. *You* stopped hanging out with *us*. I mean, not to be a bitch, but it was pretty shocking to even hear from you tonight."

I've always loved Carmen's blunt nature, but it is tough to have it directed at you. Still…

"You're absolutely right." I frown a little. "After my dad, I don't know. I just retreated inward, I guess. And things with my mom have never been good, so it's like it was just easier to be by myself. It's no excuse, though."

But Carmen's expression has softened and Ana is nodding.

"I can only imagine," Carmen says.

"After we lost your dad, it was hard to lose you, too." I feel a small pang in my chest, hearing that from Ana. She gives me a soft smile, though. "I don't know what made you reach out tonight, but I'm really glad you did. And honestly, that's what matters. That you're back."

Carmen arches an eyebrow. "Like, back-back, right?"

I grin. "*Back*-back. Like, good-luck-getting-rid-of-me back. Like, you're-going-to-be-so sick-of-my-shit back."

We laugh at that and Carmen offers to get us drinks, while I use this as a moment to take a bathroom break—and okay, fine, to swing by the lockers and check my phone.

There's a text from Brian that just says, **Charlie?**

Ana catches me lingering by the locker. "You okay, Mama?" she asks. "If it's about what we said, I hope you know we're all good."

"Oh, yeah, it's nothing," I say, shoving my phone back into the locker.

"Not sure I buy that. You just shoved that phone into your locker like it's poison."

I sigh. "Yeah. It's a boy."

Ana sighs, too. "Isn't that always the way?" She holds out her hand to me. "Come on." We skate toward the food court, where Carmen is hunkered down at a table with our drinks. "It's a boy," Ana says, as if continuing a conversation she'd already been having with Carmen.

"Ohhhh," Carmen says knowingly. She looks at me and pats the seat next to her. "Sit!"

"Tell us," Ana urges.

I shake my head. "I did not come all the way out to Crazy Skates to burden you with my problems. Not after you guys so generously let me crash your night!"

"Is that not what family is for?" Carmen asks. "Plus, you said you're going to make us sick of your shit. You've gotta live up to your promise. A little boy drama is the perfect way."

I look from Carmen to Ana. "You sure?" I ask.

They nod. And so it comes out.

Not all of it—there'd be so much to explain—but the important parts of it. Brian and our relationship. The fight with Amelia. What she said to me. How I haven't been speaking to either of them.

Ana sucks in air through her teeth once I explain that I've been kind of ghosting Brian. "You can't do that," she says. "You have to be up-front with him—even if it's going to hurt."

"I don't know. Guys ghost all the time," Carmen says. "Maybe they should get a taste of their own medicine! Let's just throw them all away, honestly."

"Yeah, but Brian would never ghost me," I say. "He's not like that."

"Then just cut him loose," Ana urges. "Don't keep him on the hook. That's the fairest thing to do, I think, if you've already made up your mind."

What she says makes sense—and suddenly, the bumping music and the skates and the disco lights on the rink feel so silly. I can't pretend my way out of this no matter how much I wish I could.

"Why do you always have to be so rational, Ana?" Carmen looks at me, defeated. "She's probably right."

I nod. "I think so, too."

Ana looks over at the clock on the wall, then at Carmen. She makes a face. "It's getting late, so we should head home." To me, she says, "You good?"

"I will be."

Carmen pats my arm and we rise from the booth and skate over to the lockers. "Thank you so much for letting me join you," I say. "And for your advice. I really, really needed it."

Ana gives me a smile. "That's why we're here."

"And we could be there for you more if you were just, you know, around more!" Carmen teases. "So text us! Okay?"

"Okay, I will," I promise. Then we take off our skates, return our rentals, exchange hugs, and head our separate ways.

When I get home, it's nearly eleven, but I text Brian anyway.

Can we talk? I write.

He responds almost instantly. **There you are! I've been going out of my mind. Are you okay? Can I call?**

I'm okay. Don't call, I write.

It's been DAYS since I've seen or really heard from you, Charlie.

I type, **I know. I'm sorry.**

Seriously, what's going on??? Is everything all right??? he asks.

I feel such a swell of hurt in my heart. Regardless of what's happened, Brian is tender and kind. He is thoughtful and caring. He is a good person. And part of me doesn't want to admit that what we had is over. But I also can't do this. I just can't be someone's next-best thing. I need to be the one and only, at least once in my life. So I have to let him go.

I type out my reply and stare at it until the words blur with tears. It's simple. It's clear. And I hate it.

I push send before I lose my nerve:

I think we should break up. I'm sorry.

There are those three gray dots and I brace myself for his reply. It doesn't come, and I think it's better this way.

Chapter Forty-Five

When it's time for school the next day, I relent and decide to go. Before homeroom, I run into Amelia at her locker. I miss her, and with the breakup text to Brian out of the way, I know it's time for me to face whatever difficult conversation lies ahead.

I give her a soft smile. "Hey."

"Charlie," she breathes, a remorseful smile on her lips. "How are you?"

I shrug. "I've been better."

"Yeah," she says. "I bet." A pause. "Have you seen my texts?"

I pull some books from my bag and stack them in my locker, not looking at her. "I have."

Out of the corner of my eye, I see her nod. "Well. I meant them. I'm so sorry, Charlie." She keeps her voice quiet. "And selfishly, I hope we can talk soon. Singing the *Hamilton* soundtrack is getting real lonely without Hamilton."

At that, I smile a little as I shut my locker. "I imagine it would be."

"I won't push. Just, think about it, okay? It would be good to talk," she says. "Anyway, I hope you have a good day today."

"Thanks," I reply. "You too."

We don't speak again during the day and I opt to eat lunch by myself, sitting at Benjamin's table (because at least there's one person in this world things are uncomplicated with). But at the end of the day, I bump into Amelia in the parking lot.

"We can't keep meeting like this," I say.

She laughs, toying with the keys in her hand. "At least we're seeing each other."

"Yeah. We should probably go back to talking to each other, too," I say.

"I would really like that," she says. "I'm so sorry for what I said."

"I'm sorry, too." I let out a sigh, releasing some of the jumbled feelings I've been carrying around with me. Then I ask, "Coffee?"

"Meet you there." I beat her to Jake's and snag our table by the window once I've got our drinks. She joins me shortly after and we both sit quietly. She breaks the silence.

"Is it okay if I talk first?"

"Please," I say.

"I've been rehearsing this in my head, but it might still come out all messed up. I'm just so, so sorry, Charlie. I said some really unthinkably cruel things. I *did* some really unthinkably cruel things—and at a really special moment in your life." Amelia's eyes are already glistening with tears. I feel myself getting emotional, too, thinking back to our fight.

"Yeah, it was...rough. I really wanted to share the excitement of my first anniversary with you, Amelia," I say. "And it hurt that you weren't interested, like, at all."

"I know! I know. You've *always* listened to me gush and you've been so supportive and I just totally blew it," she says. "I'm super embarrassed to admit this, but I think I was just used to being the one who got all of your attention. When that changed, I just...I guess I lashed out. I know that's stupid and it's not right and I'm heartbroken that we can't get that moment back."

"I'm sad about it, too," I say, frowning. "And it wasn't all you. It really wasn't. I've been kind of a crappy friend—no, scratch that, I *have* been a crappy friend—and you were right to feel like I'd been ditching you. I had been! I've been putting Brian first and just being the kind of person I've never wanted to be. I didn't mean to take you or our friendship for granted. And I never should have complained about you to Brian. That wasn't cool at all, and I don't want you to think that's who I am."

"I already know that's not who you are. So don't worry about that. And now that I've had some time to think, I realize what a massive jerk I was being. Yeah, you were kind of MIA, but I'd been icing you out for weeks because I felt like you weren't making time for me and that only made things worse." Amelia sighs. "I'm sorry. And I *get* the thrill of being in a new relationship."

"It was pretty thrilling," I say.

Amelia gives me a small smile. "Especially because this is your first! Of course those feelings are amplified times a million."

"They just kind of took over," I admit.

"As they do—but it's no excuse for how I behaved." She casts her gaze down. "I'm just so full of regret. I never should have said—well, you know."

I swallow and look away. "Yeah. I know." We're both quiet, and when I speak again, my voice is small. "But...it's true, right?"

By the way Amelia's fiddling with her coffee cup rather than answering the question, I know that it is. She just doesn't want to say it.

"Amelia, it's true, right?" I ask again.

She meets my eyes. "Yeah, it's true," she says, sighing. "I wish I'd never said anything. He asked me out last year and it was so not a big deal. Like, I'd *forgotten* he asked me out, even, but then I found myself in an angry-spiral one night and remembered and I...I used it as ammunition to hurt you. Which is the worst thing I could've done."

I can tell she's ashamed to say that out loud. "It's okay, Amelia. It's better that I know."

"It's not, though. On either count."

"It is. After Cal, I decided I was never going to mix our friendship with boys again. I need to protect myself and my heart. So I made a choice. I broke up with Brian." I say it very matter-of-factly, like of course this is what I've decided to do.

Amelia blinks. "What?! You're joking!"

I shake my head. "I'm not."

"But *why?*"

I bite my lip. How do I put into words that this one seemingly small thing is actually an indicator of something much larger? That it's another moment in years' worth of moments where Amelia came first—to friends, to boys, to my own mother?

How do I explain to her that sometimes being near her feels like I'm standing in the darkness of an eclipse? And that it's in no way her fault?

I pick my words carefully. "I want to be chosen first. I need to be somebody's unequivocal first choice."

"But you are his first choice!" Amelia insists. "He picked you!"

I shake my head. She's not getting it. "It's bigger than that. I've been coming in second place to you *my whole life,* Amelia. And it's not your fault, it's just how it is. You're you. I'm me. And the world has told me more than once that I'm inferior to you. So being with someone who liked you first . . . it just feels like all those fears are confirmed. Like I can't have anything just for me. Like I don't deserve it."

Amelia looks horrified—betrayed, maybe, confused. "What? Where is this coming from?"

"I'm sorry if that sounds terrible," I say. "But it's hard not to feel that way around you sometimes!"

There are tears rimming her eyes again. "I seriously can't believe you feel that way—that you've felt that way. This whole time. And never said anything. And now I'm the reason you're depriving yourself of someone you liked—maybe loved."

"You don't understand."

"No, I don't." She quickly swipes at her eyes. "Can we just stop talking about this, please?"

"Amelia...," I start, but I actually don't have anything to follow up with.

"I'll be fine. We good?"

There is so much more I should say. I don't. "We're good."

Chapter Forty-Six

I have Amelia back, so I should be happy.

But things are still a little weird between us since I told her about the breakup.

Oh, and there's that big, empty void where Brian used to be.

At school, I've gotten pretty good at avoiding him and I imagine he's avoiding me, too, which I get—but I admit that I take it personally. It hurts. It hurts even more when I find a note in my locker from him.

Charlie—

I know you prefer writing when it comes to things like this. I just want to talk. I don't want to push or overstep, but I'm just really confused. I thought we had something really, really good, and I don't know what happened. I don't know what I did. Please.

—Brian

It's just enough to hit a nerve by being too kind, too gentle, too... Brian. I can't stop the tears and I rush to the bathroom, locking myself in a stall.

The door creaks open moments later, and then, "Charlie?" It's Amelia.

"In here," I say shakily.

"You okay?" she asks, voice soft.

"No."

"What happened?"

Over the top of the stall, I hand her the note, which she takes. After a minute, I open the door to see her reading it. She glances up at me, concern all over her face.

"This is really sad. He's clearly upset. And look at you—so are you. I know you've been trying to hide it, but... you're not yourself."

"I'm not myself because it hurts," I say. "This *sucks*."

"Does it have to?"

"What do you mean?"

"Maybe you should talk to him," she says, like that's the simplest suggestion in the world.

"I can't."

"Why not?"

I don't have a good answer to that. "Because."

Amelia hands me back the note. "He seems really bewildered right now. Have you even talked to him, like, at all?"

"Aside from breaking up with him? No."

"I feel like he deserves at least a conversation."

I rub at one of my eyes. "I don't know if I have it in me."

"But what about him? If it seems like the breakup came out of nowhere to *me*, I just... can you imagine how he feels?" Amelia asks. "You guys were so happy together, Charlie. You were so, so happy. The way he looked at you..."

It's this that makes me start crying again.

"You were good together," she presses, gently.

"I *know* we were, but it was a lie," I say.

Amelia tenses, and I can feel that what I shared with her, those feelings of jealousy and insecurity, they're unresolved. Still bubbling. Lingering.

"Your relationship wasn't a lie," she says. "And it all seems unfair—to yourself, to Brian." There is a weighty silence at the end of her sentence.

"To you?" I ask.

Her voice is quiet. "A little." She looks up at me. "But it's not about that. Not right now, anyway. I really don't think that him asking me out meant anything. Last year is a lifetime ago. He and I have hardly even talked since. But you two—well, he's been dropping hints that he's into you since at least the beginning of the semester."

"I just don't know," I say. And I don't. Because I hear her and I think part of me thinks she's right. "Anyway, I'm going to be late to class."

Amelia looks like she wants to say more, but she doesn't, opting instead to give me a hug. "I love you, Charlie. And I say this with as much kindness and affection as I can muster, but I think you're making a mistake."

I look down at the note, crumpling it in my hand with a sniffle. "It's my mistake to make."

* * *

They say that nothing good happens after midnight. And they, whoever they are, are probably right. But I text Brian that night anyway.

Did you ask Amelia out? I write.

And suddenly my phone is ringing.

"Hey," I answer, like we're about to start the most casual conversation ever.

"I have no idea what you're talking about, Charlie. No, I didn't ask Amelia out." His voice sounds wild, desperate. "Is that what this is about? A rumor? I didn't; I swear I didn't."

"She told me you did."

"I don't know why she would say that, but I *didn't,* Charlie."

I know I probably sound obsessive, but here it goes. "It was last year," I say. "In English class?"

There is a silence. I can't tell if it's because he's thinking or because he's been caught. Then there's a soft "Oh."

"Yeah," I say.

"But that was so long ago! And I'm not at all interested in her now. I like *you,* Charlie. I really, really like you."

It hurts to hear him say that because it feels like it's not true. Or maybe it hurts because I can tell that it's true and it doesn't matter.

"I just can't," I whisper.

"You can't what?" Brian asks. "Be with me?"

"Yes."

"Because of *that*?"

"Yeah."

"So that's it?" Brian asks.

"That's it," I say. "I'm sorry."

Chapter Forty-Seven

The thought of having to work with Brian the next day fills me with dread. I don't want to see him; I'm certain he doesn't want to see me.

But Nancy asks me to take care of a big bulk mailing project for the company's upcoming summer giving campaign. There are a bunch of boxes I need to drop off at the post office, each filled with dozens and dozens of letters, and they're time-sensitive.

After I agree to go, she tells me to take Brian with me and gives me a little wink. I try to protest, but she insists, and I know she thinks she's doing me a favor. I can't even spend time fretting over how she figured out Brian and I were a thing because now I'm faced with two options: tell Nancy the truth—that Brian and I are over before we even really began—or pretend nothing's wrong and go get him.

I try to go with a third option of saying nothing, not getting Brian from the warehouse, and taking care of the project alone.

Except when I head outside to the big white company van that I'm supposed to take to the post office, Brian is already out there, loading up boxes. She must have told Dave to send Brian along, so here he is. Of course he would still help me, even though I just broke up with him. Brian's that wholesome.

"Thanks," I say, walking up to the van.

"Yep," he says.

"Need help loading?" I ask.

"Nope."

"Okay. I'll drive." I walk to the driver's seat and climb in. I spend way too much time adjusting the seat and mirrors while I wait for him to get into the passenger seat. When he does, I clear my throat and ask, "Ready?"

Brian nods in response but doesn't look at me. We drive. It's quiet, and I keep sneaking glances at him. I say nothing. It feels like the longest drive ever to the post office, and I'm thankful for the transactional conversations that fill the silence as we complete our task. The drop-off doesn't take very long, and before I know it, we're back in the van and heading to the office.

"It's been really warm these past few days, huh?" I say.

"Yeah. Warm," Brian says, looking out the window.

"I like warm weather, but I also like to have serene, spring weather. I don't like jumping straight from winter to summer, you know?"

"Yeah."

"But I guess I'd rather it be hot than freezing," I say with an awkward laugh.

Brian looks over at me. "Charlie, what are you doing?"

I quickly look at him, then back at the road. "What do you mean?"

"You know what I mean," he says. "You're acting like nothing happened."

"Well, how am I supposed to act?"

"I don't know, but not like this. I can't handle you acting like everything is fine. It's not fine. Fuck, I'm really upset." I look over at him. His face looks pinched, like maybe he's fighting back the urge to cry. Which makes *me* want to cry. I put the blinker on and pull off to the side of the road because I know I can't focus on the road and on this conversation at the same time.

I put the van in park. "I'm sorry."

"It doesn't make sense. I know it's not up to me, that it doesn't have to make sense, and that I need to just accept this. But I can't stop thinking about why I'm being treated this way for something I did a year ago—well before we were ever a thing. Why does it matter that I had some weird, stupid crush on someone else?"

It's clear he's been holding this in, and I don't blame him.

"It's not just that you had a crush on someone else. That I get. That I totally get. I know your life didn't start the moment I entered it." I swallow, then finish in a rush: "It's that the crush was on *Amelia,* my best friend, the one person I feel like I can never live up to. This feels like the ultimate proof of that."

"*What* is this obsession with Amelia?!"

His outburst catches me by surprise, and I immediately protest. "It's not an obsession—"

"Obsession, fixation, call it whatever you want, Charlie, but you can't stop comparing yourself to her. That's clouding your vision right now. You can't even see past it!" Brian's nostrils flare. He takes a breath and, more softly, he asks, "After all we've built together?"

Despite my desperate attempts to remain unfazed, I start to cry. "I'm sorry," I say again, my voice cracking.

Brian swipes at his cheeks to hastily wipe back a few tears. "I'm not sure you are. You're asking me to move mountains here, knowing full well I can't. I can't fix your feelings about Amelia, Charlie, and I sure as hell can't go back and un-ask Amelia out. But I guess we'll just say 'fuck it' because who cares, right?"

"*I* care."

"Then why are you doing this?"

My lip quivers. "Because my whole life, it's felt like I've never been as good as Amelia. My whole life, Brian. I was never as pretty or as charismatic or as *any*thing. I've had boys chase after her time and time again—or use me to get closer to her. Or pretend to like me just to be near her. She's always been better than me."

"Don't even say that."

"But it's true!" I insist, wiping at my eyes, feeling myself start to get flustered. "And now it's part of my relationship with you, too? I can't handle that. I'm just always coming in second to her. With my mom. With Cal. Now with you!"

"Not with me," Brian says. "*Never* with me, Charlie."

"Great, now you're invalidating my feelings on top of everything! You don't know what I've experienced. You *can't* know; you're not a girl. The way we're compared and how fat girls are treated and how there's all this impossible, suffocating pressure. Can you imagine what it's like for your own mother to *prefer your best friend*? No, because you actually have two parents who care about you. So you have no idea. You haven't lived this!" I struggle to catch my breath. The van feels small and hot, and I *inhale, exhale* until I'm ready to speak again. When I do, my voice is quieter than before. "Whether it makes sense to you or not, I just don't think I can move past this."

"Are you sure?" Brian asks after a minute.

"Yes," I say. "I'm sure."

Brian looks at me for a long moment, brows furrowed, searching my face as if trying to understand. He breathes in deep. Then he swallows hard, settles into his seat, and looks forward.

"Okay, then," he says.

I nod and look straight ahead, too. "Okay, then," I repeat.

But I know it's not.

* * *

After the car ride with Brian, I almost can't bring myself to return to work. But I have no right to bail out, not after Nancy tried to be so kind, so I walk in and go over to my filing to work this painful afternoon away. I'm grateful to chip away at some of it in the quiet, but then I look up and see Dora heading my way.

I find myself hoping she won't talk to me, that she'll move on and get back to work, but then...

"Hey, *you*," Dora says with a little waggle of her eyebrows. "How was the drive to the *post office*?"

Great. So everyone in the office must know about me and Brian now.

My throat tightens and I refocus my gaze on the stack of papers in front of me that need to be properly filed. "It was fine."

"Just fine?"

"Yes, fine." I try to read the file in front of me.

"Oh, come on! You've been holding out on me, Charlie," Dora says with a laugh. "You didn't tell me about you and Brian! I had to hear about it from *Sheryl*." I don't say anything. "Aww, don't get shy, sweetheart." She walks over to me and puts a hand on my shoulder. "I just think it's cute. Brian's a really good kid, Charlie. You've done good. You deserve it."

I look up at Dora, at the sincerity in her face, her words ringing in my ears, and I feel my face betray me.

"Oh, honey, I'm sorry! I didn't mean to embarrass you," she says, rubbing my back.

"It's not that," I manage to say through tears, and before I can say more, Dora is ushering me to the restroom. She closes and locks the door behind us.

"What's going on?" It's her mom voice—kind, full of concern, with a hint of *I will hurt anyone who has hurt you* in it—and that comforts me, even though I've done a lot of the hurting myself.

"Brian and I broke up," I say, and then I'm fully crying. "It's been awful and really, really hard. But obviously I don't want anyone to know and neither does he. It's all just, I don't know...a lot."

"Oh, honey." Dora wraps her arms around me without another word. "I'm sorry. Do I need to go have a talk with him?"

"No, no! I broke up with him."

She pulls back from the hug. "I'm sure you had your reasons.

You don't have to say another word, and I'll make sure no one else does, either."

"Does everyone know?" I ask. When Dora hesitates to answer, I know that they do. "How did people find out?"

There's a pause and then a small chuckle before she quietly offers this: "Two young people in love are not exactly the most discreet. Plus, Dave and his big mouth." I groan. "Why don't you get out of here? Seems like it's been a long day."

I nod, sniffling. "It has been."

She motions with her chin toward the door. "Go on, then. I'll take care of everything."

"Are you sure?" I ask, even though I sincerely just want to bolt for the exit and never look back.

"Of course. Go on, sweetheart," she says with a gentle smile.

"Thank you. I appreciate it." I wipe at my eyes, take a deep breath, and reach for the door handle. Then I look back at her. "Dora—you won't tell anyone about the breakup just yet, will you? It's still fresh." She uses her fingers to zip her lips and I smile with relief. "Thank you."

In the comfort of my car, I let myself sob. I'm ashamed of being overcome with emotion at work, and embarrassed at the idea that Brian and I thought we were being so secretive when we clearly weren't.

But what really, really hurts is that I can't even text him so we can laugh about how mortifying it all is, and the only person I can blame for that is me.

Chapter Forty-Eight

When I get home, I text Amelia. **Want to watch some bad movies?**

I mean, yeah, always, but you okay? she writes back.

Just come over?

On my way, she writes.

Amelia lets herself into the house and marches straight to my room. When she sees my undoubtedly puffy eyes and blotchy face, she holds her arms out for a hug.

"This is all such a mess," I sob, letting her hold me for a second.

"What happened?" she asks.

We sit on the bed and I recount the afternoon's events. It brings a whole rush of emotions right to the surface, leaving me feeling soft and vulnerable, like the tiniest pinprick could elicit another tsunami of tears.

Amelia listens intently, rubbing my back here and there.

"It's just been a really, really long day," I say, sniffling. "Week, really."

"I can only imagine."

"And on top of everything, I can't lie, Amelia. Things *still* don't feel right between you and me."

She meets my gaze and offers me a little shrug. "Yeah, well, because they're not."

"We said we were good."

"Yeah, that's what we said. We wanted that to be true. I mean, we don't really fight. Not like this. But honestly, you kind of dropped a huge bomb on me. I've been doing my best to just handle it, but I'm not Olivia Pope. You straight-up said you felt inferior to me. I was totally and completely blindsided. I mean. *Shit,* you know?"

"Yeah," I say. "Shit."

"It's sort of like you resent me."

"I *don't.*"

She presses. "But maybe a little, right?"

I say nothing, which says everything.

"Yeah. I never meant to make you feel that way, Charlie. Know that."

"It's hard, Amelia," I begin tentatively. "Being around you sometimes. You're just so...you. Beautiful and skinny and loving and confident, and sorry, but perfect. That's been reiterated to me a million times by every person around us in so many painful ways."

I see her fists ball up. "I'm *not* perfect. I'm not." Then she softens a bit. "When you said some of that stuff the other day, my gut reaction was—is, maybe—to pretty much say how dare you. But I've spent a lot of time thinking about it. I have. And as much as I hate to admit this, maybe it's true that I sometimes take some weird validation in being coveted. I am not proud of that."

I give her a half smile. "As someone who's rarely coveted, I can see the appeal."

Amelia puts up a hand to me. "Nope, we're not doing that. We're not going to be self-deprecating right now. We're going to be honest and real." Her voice is firm in a way I maybe need at this moment.

"You're right. No deflecting."

She nods. "Like, look, I know that the world can be really fucking shitty to girls, and even shittier to girls of color, and shittier still to, you know—"

"Fat girls like me," I interject. "You can say it."

"Okay, yeah, to fat girls like you," Amelia repeats. "But I think I relate to you more than you realize. I'm not saying I understand your struggles perfectly. I don't know what it's like to exist in a world as a fat brown woman. But I do know what it's like to exist in the world as a queer Black woman, and it's fucked in different ways and super hard sometimes. It's *impossible* not to be insecure, you know?"

"I guess I hadn't really thought of that." I bite my lip, considering. "I know this sounds silly, but I rarely ever imagine you as someone who struggles or has doubts."

"Right! You see me as superhuman! That's some serious pressure." Amelia laughs a little. "Sometimes it feels good, yeah, that people like how I look and act. But sometimes it's just so much. I already have a ton of pressure on me from my parents and from myself, so it's extra hard coming from you. Because we're *equals,* me and you. Imperfect equals. And you've *seen* my struggles and you've been there right alongside me for the ride. I mean, I was a hot mess when I was trying to figure out if I wanted to have sex with Sid. I couldn't face my parents over a dinner with my new girlfriend. I sometimes don't have the courage to stick up to people or for myself."

"But those are just normal human things."

"Yeah, *exactly!* This is my point! You look at me and you see me struggle through things and you root for me regardless, thinking I'm, like, killing it out there in the world, but when it's you, you don't cut yourself any slack and you beat yourself up. But I'm a regular person, and so are you," she says. "And a pretty badass one, too. You're so good at *everything.* You get amazing grades and you're an incredible writer and you're so smart—sometimes so smart that teachers assume I am, too, just because I'm around you. When I nearly failed my bio test earlier this semester, Mr. O'Donnell told me I should try to be more like you. And you know what?

Maybe that's a shitty thing to say to a student, but I *do* find myself wishing I could be more like you all the time. Not because I'm inadequate as a person but because humans yearn! Humans want to be better than they are! Humans feel jealous! And I think it's okay if sometimes I want to be more like you. Who wouldn't? You're smart and hilarious and fashionable and fierce and you would do anything for the ones you love. You put up with a lot of shit and you let it light a fire in you and I admire the hell out of that, babe."

Hearing these things chokes me up a little, because who wouldn't get emotional over their best friend gassing them up like that? I've never really considered that Amelia might look at me in any kind of aspirational way, and knowing that she has blows me away.

"Wow...That is maybe the nicest thing you've ever said to me, Amelia. And you've said tons of nice things to me. But this really means so much."

"Well, it's all true."

"And I never intended to make you feel like I was just one more person pressuring you to, I don't know, be flawless or whatever. The world is hard enough. You don't need me adding to it." I look over at her. "I'm sorry."

"I'm sorry, too. But you know. Sisters fight. They mess up sometimes. They're jealous. They want to be more like each other. They just can't let that become all-consuming."

I take her hand and give it a squeeze. "You're absolutely right."

"And...*as* your sister, I need to be frank with you. I think you just need to cut yourself some slack," Amelia explains. "For your own sake. All this Brian shit aside, you have to chill with yourself. Be kinder to you. Let yourself be human. And maybe stop chasing perfection. Because what the fuck is perfection anyway?"

"Wait, can we go back to the part where you're just complimenting me?"

Amelia smiles. "We can circle back to that, but I'm not off my soapbox yet. I'm just saying that sometimes, maybe, you try so hard to achieve perfection that the bigger picture escapes you. Like, yeah, maybe if you had it your way, Brian never would've looked my way. Maybe if you were the author of this story, you'd have written it differently. But this is life and you shouldn't just throw something away because it didn't go exactly as you'd hoped it would. I understand why you think him asking me out said something—I promise I get it now. I do. But I need you to know that it doesn't inherently mean something, because he loves *you*, not me—*you're* the one he pursued, Charlie." She puts a hand on my shoulder. "But hey, you know what? Forget Brian. You need to believe in your value for *you*, even if you're not some flawless ethereal being, even if not everyone will see what makes you special, even if your story is a little chaotic. We're *all* messy, Charlie. So when everything's a mess, it seems to me like you just need to give yourself room to breathe."

I'm quiet. Amelia has just said so much that my brain is buzzing and I don't know if I can process everything.

"Can you do that?" Amelia asks. "Can you try being kinder to you?"

She looks so sincere and hopeful.

With a deep breath, I say, "Okay. I can try."

Amelia scoots closer to me, draping an arm around my shoulders. "That's all I ask."

Chapter Forty-Nine

So okay, what do you do when your best friend has totally and completely rattled your mindcage and you're, like, goddamn it, I can't even trust my own brain anymore?

That's where I'm at.

I wrote out a really long thank-you text to Amelia, which I sent when I woke up the next morning, but now I'm supposed to just get up and go to school? Like I don't have a ton of things to think about? Come on.

My mom doesn't seem to get that, though, and she opens the door to my room and asks if I plan on getting up and getting dressed.

"I don't feel well," I say, meaning it and pulling my blanket over my head.

"Again?" she asks.

"Yeah. My brain has stopped working."

I hear her footsteps come closer to my bed and then I feel the weight of her body on the corner of my bed. She pulls the blanket off my head and peers at me. "You've been sick an awful lot lately," she says, ignoring my dramatic comment. "Should we take you to the doctor?"

"I think I just need to sleep it off." I'm trying to look as pathetic as possible, which is not very hard.

"Well, *I* think we need to go to the doctor," she says. "You can't keep missing school."

"But it's nothing a doctor can fix." I roll away from her. "Like I said. Brain. Not working."

"Hmm," she says. A pause, then an offer: "You can talk to me, you know."

I consider this. I could really use someone else's opinion, and...before I know it, I've told her what happened. "I broke up with Brian."

Her face softens. "Oh. Well, that'll do it."

"And I got into a big fight with Amelia. But then we made up. I don't know; it's been a lot to process, and now I'm all confused."

My mom frowns. "What happened?"

"You'll think it's stupid."

"I won't," she says. "Tell me."

I look down at my comforter and twirl it around my fingers so I don't have to watch her face as I share. "It's just been...I don't know. A lot's been happening. Amelia and I got into a huge fight because I was ignoring her and spending a lot of time with Brian. Which is true. I was. And during that fight, she told me that Brian had asked her out sometime last year. She kind of said it just to hurt me. But I still broke up with him. It just felt like the biggest deal ever that he had liked her first."

"That wasn't very nice of Amelia to do," Mom says.

"No, it wasn't," I admit, a little surprised that my mom feels the same way. "But she apologized profusely. And we talked. And it was hard, but I told her that I was hurt and it was really difficult to be around her knowing that everyone, including Brian, prefers her over me."

My mom furrows her brows. "How do you figure?"

"Oh, come on. Even you prefer Amelia."

The look on my mom's face is like I just slapped her.

"Why would you say that?" she asks.

There is an emotion in her voice I can't quite detect, but it makes me wish I'd never vocalized this, one of my deepest, darkest fears—and certainly not in such a flippant way.

"I shouldn't have said it like that, Mom. Sorry. But it's how I feel...more often than I'd care to admit. It's not just you, but yeah. I do think you prefer her sometimes. For a lot of reasons, I guess. You always encourage her to call you Mom, for one. And I see how you look at her compared to how you look at me, like she's just everything you wish I could be. It's like, you always compliment her beauty but keep your compliments for me focused on my smarts or whatever—even at my own birthday party! And you've always made sure she was invited to every single thing we did, so that it was never just you and me, but you, me, and Amelia. It always made me feel like you didn't want to spend time with just me." A lump in my throat is rising as I talk, but it feels good to get this out. "It sometimes feels like she was the daughter you wished you had. But instead you ended up with me."

Mom is quiet. When I look up, I see that she's a little teary, too.

"That is not true, Charlie," she says. "You are my daughter, my one and only." One tear escapes and rolls down her cheek. "I have always tried to be welcoming and loving to Amelia because I *do* love her—she's my daughter's best friend. Of course I care about her. And I went out of my way to invite her to things because I thought it would be nice for you to have a companion...especially after your dad..." Her voice catches when she mentions Dad, but she takes a moment to regain her composure. "Maybe I've gone a little overboard at times, and maybe I can be a little hard on you. I do see a lot of great qualities in Amelia, but I see *wonderful* qualities in you. I would never prefer someone else over you. Never. Do you hear me?"

I nod, wiping away some of my own tears.

"And if there is one thing I can tell you, one thing you should learn from me, it's that you can't spend your life comparing yourself to other people. Okay?"

"Okay," I say, realizing that what she's just said to me is a simpler version of what Amelia said yesterday.

"Okay," she repeats. Then she pats my leg and says, "Now, go to school."

Mom leaves my room and I sit there on my bed.

Maybe the biggest problem in my life wasn't that the world thought I came in second to Amelia. Maybe it was just that *I* thought that.

Chapter Fifty

It takes time to process everything.

But I find myself realizing I need to just let it go. All of it. I've got to shake these feelings of inferiority. I can't be Amelia, nor do I want to, at least not anymore. I want to be Charlie—unapologetically Charlie.

Shoulders back. Head held up high. Fat, beautiful body and all.

Shedding those thoughts leaves me feeling lighter than I have ever felt before.

Finally.

The talk Amelia and I had helps restore us to who we were, only better and more honest. It makes it delightfully easy to fall back into the rhythm of our friendship, back to our old ways, and I'm thankful for the normalcy.

Later that week, I invite Amelia over after school and she asks to bring Kira. The three of us settle in the kitchen to work on some homework, which I've seriously fallen behind on. We're steadily working—me on my history homework, Amelia and Kira on math—when my mom walks through the front door. It's a little earlier than her normal return from work, so I'm surprised to see her.

"Hi, Mom," I say.

"Hi, girls," she says.

"This is Kira." I motion toward her. "Kira, that's my mom."

"Oh, so *this* is Kira," Mom says with a little grin.

Kira, the most polite person Amelia and I know, rises and extends her hand. "It's so nice to meet you."

Mom keeps smiling as they shake hands. "Wonderful to meet you," she says, and I feel a little twinge of jealousy that she's so welcoming to Kira but hadn't been to Brian. I let that go, too.

"What are you doing home so early?" I ask, wishing the three of us had had a little more solo time.

"Oh," Mom says, looking a little sheepish. "I was going to prepare you some dinner. Rice and beans?"

She meets my eye and I realize she's trying to do something kind. I soften.

"That would be great, Mom. Thank you." I give her a smile, and she nods back.

"You girls sticking around for dinner, too?" she asks.

Amelia and Kira exchange a glance before Amelia says, "We'd love to."

"Great. I'll get started. Don't let me interrupt you." Mom starts to pull ingredients from the cupboard as we get back to our homework.

"I'm struggling with this history question. Amelia, have you worked on number three yet?"

She goes back into her notes and hands her notebook over to me, pointing halfway down the paper. "There you go."

"We're not copying homework, are we?" Mom asks.

"No. I'm simply glancing at what Amelia wrote and forming my own opinions based on that," I say innocently.

"Yeah, exactly," Amelia says. As I'm reading through her answer about the real Alexander Hamilton, not our dreamy Lin-Manuel Miranda version of Alexander Hamilton, I notice Kira elbow Amelia and they start to whisper, but not loud enough for me to hear.

"It's not nice to talk about me," I tease, looking up from Amelia's notebook.

"Okay, fine," Amelia says. "Don't be mad, but I ran into Brian."

I tense. "What?"

"I've been telling her she needed to tell you," Kira says.

I glare at Amelia. "I can't believe you *weren't* going to tell me."

"I *was* going to, just not yet!" She shoots Kira a look. "It was a complete accident. But we both ended up in the art supply closet at the same time. It was nothing, just a simple hello. And I asked him if things were going all right. He said they were okay, but he looked...sad. I don't know."

"Amelia," I groan.

"Well, what was I going to do—not acknowledge him at all?"

I sigh. "No, of *course* you should acknowledge him. He deserves that. It's just hard to hear about it."

"We had a chemistry class together," Kira offers. "Such a sweet guy."

I nod, too. "Yeah, he is. Like, the sweetest guy ever. That's what sucks about having to run into him. Or hear about him. Or think about him."

Mom sighs from across the room. "Oh, Charlie."

"What?" I ask.

"Stubborn girl," she says.

"I am not," I say.

She smiles as she adds spices to the caldero on the stove. "Okay. Sure. But it sounds to me like you still like the guy."

Amelia looks at me, trying to gauge my reaction. She knows I still do but would never say it unless I did first.

Kira says tentatively, "It does sort of sound that way, Charlie."

"Of *course* I still like him," I say defensively. "But I broke up with him. There's no going back."

"That's not true," Amelia says.

"You didn't hear him that day," I insist. "He was really, really hurt."

"But you can't know anything for sure unless you try," Mom says.

"We're not talking about this," I say. "Can we get back to our homework, please?"

Amelia and Kira look at each other with a smile. "Fine," they say.

"Fine," my mom agrees.

It's not fine, though, because I can't stop thinking about how they're right: I just want to be with Brian.

* * *

I have been trying not to think about Brian.

I have been failing.

The truth is, life is just a lot lonelier without him in it. I see him sometimes—how can I not?—but it's not the same, and that's what hurts the very most.

I'd developed a habit of texting Brian throughout the day and now that's a habit I have to fight. I hate driving by all of the places where we've had dates. I dread going to work and having to avoid him. I loathe going to art class. I don't even like looking at the stupid bras I bought.

Mostly because there is a nagging thought in the back of New Charlie's brain. It says that if I'm in the business of letting things go…shouldn't I let go of my feelings of betrayal, too? Forgive Brian? Say I'm sorry?

But I don't know.

I prefer to pretend that isn't an option and instead do my best to smile through everything for New Charlie's sake. I remind myself of the good things: Amelia and I are not fighting. My mom has been surprisingly kind. I get an email that informs me that my story is one of the finalists in the writing contest I entered. (Ms. Williams nearly flips.) I've finally finished my horse painting in art class. I have friends for the first time ever. I'm seeing my cousins again.

But the loneliness really hits me on the weekend when my mom is out, Amelia is with Kira, I fail to make alternative plans, and I find myself home alone.

I fill my night with research on dogs that are up for adoption, because dogs don't judge you. They just love you, and that's what I need right now.

By the time my mom gets home, I've got at least three dogs picked out, so I bombard her the moment she walks inside.

"Don't you think we should get a dog?" I ask. I'm holding up my phone and shoving it in her face. "Isn't this mini-dachshund cute? His name is Tiny! We should adopt him!"

"Give me a second to get inside, will you?" She closes the door behind her and kicks off her shoes. I follow her into the kitchen as she pours herself a glass of water. She takes a long sip. "Okay. What?"

"A dog. We need one! If you don't like this one, we can get another, but I think Tiny is perfect and exactly what we need."

My mom waves her hand at me in dismissal. "We're not getting a dog, Charlie."

"Please? Pretty please?" I ask. "I'll walk him. And train him. This site says he was abandoned on the side of the road! How can you say no?"

"Don't read that to me! It's a no. No dog."

I let out a long sigh, and my mom rolls her eyes.

"I guess you just don't care about my happiness....," I say.

"Oh my God, Charlie." She's smiling as she shakes her head and starts to walk out of the kitchen toward her bedroom. "I swear...."

I walk behind her down the hall. "If we can't get a dog, maybe a bunny?"

"Absolutely not. No rodents in this house," she says. She starts to pull her pajamas out of the drawer and lay them on the bed.

"It's not a rodent!"

"Why don't you go hang out with Amelia?" She cups her hand around her ear. "Oh, yes, I think I hear her calling now."

I scowl at her. "Ha *ha*. Amelia is on a date with Kira." I fidget with my phone as she lets her hair down and begins taking off her makeup.

"Well, you need to do something," she says. "You're bored."

"I know. I miss Brian," I say. She looks over at me and her face says *Oh, honey* without her actually needing to say *Oh, honey*. "Don't look at me like that."

"Remember that conversation we were having with Amelia and Kira the other day?"

"Can't recall."

"Oh, really?" she asks. "I remember it perfectly...."

I start to back out of her room. "Suddenly I'm feeling very tired."

"You know what I think!"

I run down the hall. "I'm not listening!" I yell.

"Text your boyfriend!" she calls after me.

I close my bedroom door and pretend I don't hear. But only because I want to text him so bad that the last thing I need is for someone else to encourage me. I just might do it.

Chapter Fifty-One

My days are full with writing and friends and family and chores and regular life things. I'm working on that whole be-kinder-to-myself thing. I'm active on social media in the #fat-fashion circles. I'm helping more around the house. Things are *good*—and yet I know they could be even better. If only...

No.

Let it go, Charlie.

So I take on a grocery shopping trip. Though Mom is still on her diet, she has agreed that I can prepare some of my own meals. Little victories. And little things to keep me busy.

I drive to the grocery store in the next town over—it's a nicer store, it will take me more time to get there, and there's zero chance of running into Brian. Plus, I love their baked goods section and I want to treat myself to a cookie. Because #Saturday.

Outside the store, I grab a cart and push it toward the entrance, where I notice a table set up. Probably Girl Scout cookies. They've been selling them everywhere lately and so far, I've resisted buying any boxes, but given that I decided I would get a cookie, it only seems fair to grab myself a box of Thin Mints.

When I get up to the table, I'm startled to see that it's not Girl Scout cookies at all; it's a table with birdhouses on it—and Brian's moms, Susan and Maura, are seated behind it.

"Charlie!" Susan exclaims. She runs out from behind the table and gives me a hug. "We haven't seen you in a while. How are you?"

"I'm doing all right," I say, anxious. "How are you?"

"Maura and I are doing well, thank you. We do miss seeing you around," she says. "Don't we, Maura?"

Maura gives me a smile. "We do."

"We don't know what happened with you and Brian—"

"Sue, please!" Maura interjects.

Susan waves her hand at Maura. "I'm just going to say this one thing." She turns to me. "Like I said, we don't know what happened, but I hope we'll see you at the opening of the art show next week. Brian's got a whole section featuring his work."

"Sue!" Maura says, a bit more sternly this time.

"I know, I know," Susan says, then turns back to me. "I probably shouldn't get in the middle, but I just think it would mean so much to Brian if you came. Consider it, all right? The info is on the school's Facebook page!"

"I'll think about it. Thank you," I say, my stomach tight. "I should get going. It was good seeing you both." I wave at the two of them and head inside the store, feeling very jittery.

I text Amelia. **I just ran into Brian's moms. They were so nice to me. I'm horrible.**

She writes back immediately: **You're NOT horrible!**

Susan gave me a hug, I write.

She likes you, Amelia writes. **And you know what that means, right?**

No. What? I ask.

Brian didn't badmouth you to them. Like, at all.

Oh. I hadn't thought of that.

He still likes you, Charlie, Amelia writes.

You really think so? I ask.

She writes back, **I think the ball's in your court, lady. You've just gotta make a move.**

But what if I'm really bad at basketball? I write.

Amelia just texts me back a flood of eye-roll emojis and I know what I have to do.

New Charlie has got to channel that girl at dinner who told him I bought new bras. Be bold. Be confident. Say yes.

Chapter Fifty-Two

There's a beautiful bouquet of lilies, my favorite flower, on the dining room table. I'm nosy, so I check out the card that's with them, wanting to see which one of my mom's suitors has sent them (and to read what the message says).

I'm surprised when the card has my name on it, and the message reads:

Congratulations, Charlie! — Mom

P.S. Don't be mad that I opened your mail.

An open envelope lies beside the flowers. The return address is Charter Oak Publishing—the writing contest! I rip the letter out of its envelope, hands shaking, and skim what it says.

Dear Charlie,

We are pleased to announce that you have been selected as the winner of the Charter Oak Publishing Young Authors' Writing Competition....

And I stop reading and start jumping up and down.

I won. I won! *I won!!!*

I text my mom to thank her for the beautiful flowers and she sends me back a string of firework emojis, and then I call Amelia and we're both squealing.

I'm so happy that I decide to text Brian, too.

It's the first intentional communication we'll have had since that day at work in the van. But...be bold, right?

I send him a picture of the letter: **Bri! I won the writing contest!**

I hold my breath waiting for a reply that I fully realize may never come.

Only...it does.

He writes back, **Shit, Charlie! Congratulations! I knew you would.** He adds, **They still send letters?**

I laugh and write, **You know how obsessed writers are with the printed word.** I add a shrug emoji and hit send. Then I write, **I don't think I ever properly thanked you for your support. But it meant the world. Thank you. I owe you.**

He writes, **Nah, you don't owe me a thing. You just needed to believe in yourself. And maybe to be reminded to stop and put the top down and let the wind in your hair, you know?**

I smile at the memory. Deep breath.

I write, **So I'm learning. Can we do that again sometime? Just you and me?**

A long, agonizing pause before the three dots show up. And then: **Only if we can listen to the Smiths.**

And my heart soars.

Hope.

* * *

There's nothing left to do *but* be bold. For real. In person.

As an aspiring writer, I am hyperaware of tropes, and one I love to hate is the grand gesture. I shared this with Brian one day in the form of a long-winded rant. Grand gestures always put too much pressure on the person on the receiving end of them, and they're totally unfair! They ask way too much! They often make the person feel embarrassed and totally put on the spot! They do more for the person doing the gesturing than for the person receiving the gesture! And on, and on, and on...

Then I confessed that even with all that knowledge, I had a hard time not swooning over them. Like the promposals at school. And Brian sheepishly admitted the same, saying he loved watching YouTube videos of couples who had planned to propose to each other at the same time.

It was one of those conversations that was seemingly small but made me feel so understood.

As I try to figure out how, exactly, I am to fix this situation with Brian, I find myself returning to that conversation, turning it over and over in my head until I realize *I* need a grand gesture. *I* need to go all in. *I* need to show Brian how I feel.

I decide to make a grand gesture and show up at the art show.

The town's annual art show honors the most talented students in each grade by showcasing their work at the local library—yep, *that* library, where Brian and I first kissed, because life is toying with me. Awards are given out for the most remarkable pieces, and only the most talented students have an entire display devoted to their work. It makes perfect sense that Brian's work is among the best.

I show up early. My hair is curled and I've changed my outfit about a hundred times but finally settled on a simple summer dress that Brian told me I looked pretty in. I have my notebook with me, the gift from Brian, and I'm thankful to have something to hold on to. It gives me purpose. Before I go inside, I sit in my car, hyping myself up. I ask Amelia for a brief pep talk where she tells me I've got this. (I don't feel like I've got this.)

I watch a bunch of families walk up to the library and tell myself I can watch three more families go in and then I have to, too. Two more...one more...go.

I do. I walk in and look around and don't immediately see Brian or his work. It's then that I realize I don't even know if Brian will be here. I've assumed he'd be here because it's opening night (so to speak—it's like five-thirty), but I can't know for certain.

I'm thinking this as I turn a corner, and there he is. He's looking down at his phone, but he glances up because I let out a small gasp when I see him.

Brian, surprised, smiles when he sees me, then makes his face neutral again. "Hey," he says.

"Hey," I say, biting my lip. He looks good. Like, really good. Of course. Because this is his night and I'm totally hijacking it for my own selfish reasons and oh my God, what am I *doing*?

"What are you doing here?" Brian asks, but not in an accusatory way or anything. In a soft way.

"I came to see you."

He raises his eyebrows. "You did?"

"Yeah. I mean, I ran into your moms the other day and they told me your work was going to be featured here, and I love the art show, and I love what you do, and I love your work." How many times can I say *love* in one breath? Jeez. "So yeah. I wanted to come see it."

"Oh," he says. "Thank you. They're around here somewhere."

"Great. Uh, and—and I'm also here because I wanted to see you." I pause. "I miss you." When Brian doesn't say anything right away, I decide I have nothing to lose.

Be bold.

All in.

Okay.

"And I'm sorry. I let my insecurities get the best of me and just completely take over. I wasn't able to get out of my own head or see what was so clearly right in front of me. Which sounds like a cliché. And, like, it is. But it's still the truth, and Brian, you were so good to me, in ways I never even imagined. We *worked* and what we had was just so beautiful and wonderful and magical. You made me so, so happy. I was...scared. Or jaded. I don't know. Both, maybe, but mostly I was wrong—unbelievably, embarrassingly wrong—and I will shout it from the rooftops if I have to. I'm sorry. I shouldn't have broken up with you the way I did, of course not, but also I shouldn't have broken up with you at all. I didn't want to; I just let my horrible self-doubt get the best of me and I let you go and I'm sorry. You mean so much to me."

It all comes out so fast, all the things I've been thinking but not saying, all the things I've been holding on to. I have no idea what Brian will say back, but I needed to tell him.

"Charlie, I've thought about it a lot, and I think I understand now," Brian says softly. "It wasn't right, no, and it really hurt me. But the place your feelings came from was so deep and dark and real, and I *get* that. I get that you've had experiences that made you suspicious of people, of the world. I get you. I do. I only wish I had understood that better then. So—yes, of course, apology accepted."

I give him a halfhearted smile. Still so good to me, even after everything.

"Thank you." I look at him, and then I see it: behind him, there's a painting. It's a boy with his arm around a girl and her head is leaning on his shoulder. They're watching the world, which is on fire. I point. "Wait. Is that...us?"

He turns to look at where my finger is pointing, and then he looks back at me and he shoves his hands in his pockets. His cheeks are flushed. "Yeah. It is."

"That's *us*," I say, stepping closer to the painting. And it is. The boy has jet-black hair, and he's wearing a hoodie (Brian's favorite one, actually), and the girl, she's got curly brown hair that's almost

334

black but not quite, and she's wearing a dress—*this* dress. The one that I'm wearing.

"It's us at the end of the world. I painted it the night after your birthday. Because I just knew," Brian says. "It's you and me, you know?"

I turn around to look at him.

"Oh my God," I whisper.

And then I remember what's in my hands.

I unwind the strap that's holding the delicate leather-bound notebook shut and flip to its first ivory page. There are four words on it, written in ink.

"Awhile ago, you asked me if I'd had a chance to use the notebook yet, and I told you it was hard for me to commit to any kind of writing in nice ones like this. The pressure, and all that. Do you remember that?"

Brian nods, looking at the notebook and then up at me. "Of course."

"I'd been putting it off and putting it off because I wanted whatever I wrote to be super important. And I realized something, and it made me want to do something big. Like, grand gesture big." I'm breathless trying to explain.

And Brian laughs a little. "Okay...?"

"So here." I shove the notebook toward him, trembling a little as he takes it. "It's not a stunning painting of the two of us at the end of the world or anything, but..."

He looks down at the page where I've scrawled the words— the ones that bare my soul, the ones that feel important—and then looks up at me. "It's better." His gaze falls to the page again and he smiles to himself, as if not believing what it says and needing to read it again, and then he closes the notebook and touches my cheek, the way he does, the way he always has. "I love you, too, Charlie."

My lip quivers, and I nestle my face against his hand and say it. "I love you, Brian."

He pulls me to him and kisses me, and the world really is on fire. It's the best kiss of my life. Better than the kisses I've written about. Better than the kisses I've dreamed of.

We keep our faces close after we part, foreheads touching. I feel the notebook pressed against my back, and I squeeze my eyes shut. This is real.

"So does this mean you forgive me?" I ask.

He laughs, and I open my eyes. "I'm getting there."

I laugh, too, and it's then that I see a red ribbon beneath the painting of us.

"What's that?" I ask, motioning toward the ribbon. His glances toward it.

"Oh." He grins. "Came in second."

I smile at him. "Not to me," I say.

And I kiss him.

And kiss him.

And kiss him.

And kiss him.

When I pull away slightly, Brian just looks at me. "Why'd you stop?"

"Because you said your parents are around here somewhere. And we're at a civic event."

He grabs my hand and wordlessly pulls me outside the library—the May sunshine hanging low in the blue sky, the flowered trees dancing in the gentle breeze, the green grass so lush you can almost feel it. "Better?"

I look around and then smile big.

"What?"

"*Brian,*" I say. "This is it."

"What's what?"

"This." I motion at the ground and the area around us. "It's where we had our first kiss."

Recognition washes over Brian's face and his lips spread into a wide smile.

"Us," he says.

I pull him to me. "Us."

Chapter Fifty-Three

There's a pile of golden retriever puppies on me.

I repeat: there's a pile of golden retriever puppies on me.

"Am I dead?" I ask, nuzzling one—*Cinnamon,* because the dogs are each named for different spices—into my neck. "I think I'm dead."

Brian reaches over to check my pulse with one hand while petting Thyme with his other. "You seem pretty alive to me."

I put Cinnamon in my lap and hold out a limp wrist toward Amelia. "Please. Am I alive?"

"You trust her assessment but not mine?" Brian teases.

Amelia sticks out her tongue. "*I'm* her best friend. And don't *you* forget it." She reaches over and presses two fingers on my vein. "Okay, yes, totally still alive. Unless I'm doing this wrong. In which case, maybe dead?"

"It doesn't even matter!" I shriek. "This is the best day ever!"

"Best *date* ever," Amelia corrects me. "Isn't that right, Paprika? Yes it is! Yes it is!"

Kira grins. "I'm so glad you guys are enjoying ourselves." Then she leans down to give Rosemary a kiss. She's let us all into the puppy playroom at the shelter for the best double date in the history of mankind. Bless Kira.

Brian rubs his face in Thyme's soft fur. "What's not to love about this?"

I sit up and look Kira in the eye, pointing right at her. "I would *die* for these dogs."

"But aren't you dead already?" Amelia asks.

"I'd die again, then!"

Brian hands Thyme to me, so now I've got two puppies in my hands and I've never been happier. "Please don't," he says. "I like you alive."

"Sorry, I don't make the rules." I give each dog a kiss.

"You know, we really should get going soon. It's already after hours," Kira reminds us.

Amelia looks at her skeptically. "But babe, I think we live here now."

"Do we really have to go?" I ask.

"Well, I *am* hungry," Brian says. "Especially being around all these delicious-sounding names."

I sigh, putting Cinnamon on the ground and watching as she runs over to her brothers and sisters and they start to wrestle. "I suppose our time's up, then."

"Where to?" Kira asks.

Amelia and I look at each other. "Jake's? *Jinx*. Double jinx! You owe me a coffee!" we both say at the same time.

Brian looks over at Kira. "What do you think? Should we leave them here? I'm not sure they should be out in public."

She grins at him. "I've got to get them out of here before I get in trouble, but after that, who knows?"

We rise to our feet and Brian and I go outside, leaving Kira and Amelia to lock up. The air is warm and thick—it's almost summer and I can already sense it.

The smell of the popcorn at Crazy Skates, Ana's signature perfume, Carmen's cherry ChapStick, as we skate around the rink a dizzying number of times. The sound of the giggles from the elementary-school-age athletes at the day camp where Kira will serve as a counselor. The photos of Benjamin suspended in the zero-gravity machine at Space Camp (weird and delightful and perfectly Benjamin). The feel of my hand wrapped around Brian's during the firework chasing, the mini-golf games, the long road trips to the beach, the late nights roasting marshmallows, and the dozens of other summertime adventures we'll have—including lunch dates at the museum where he'll be interning. The taste of the tart strawberry, the sweet vanilla, and the rich chocolate ice cream we'll sneak bites of in the shoppe (yes, with the extra *p* and *e*) where Amelia and I will be working as part-time ice cream scoopers, with flushed cheeks, sun-kissed skin, and hearts full of brand-new memories to relive again and again as only best friends can. I'm on the cusp of what I can only imagine will be one of the best summers I've ever had. I smile to myself just thinking of it.

Brian reaches for my hand, locking fingers with mine, as if reading my mind.

"Still fits perfectly, you know." Then he pulls me to him and gives me a kiss. Again, I can't help it; I sigh.

"I've missed you," I say quietly.

"I've missed you, too," he says.

"I need to ask you something, though."

Brian's face turns serious. "Of course."

I take a breath. "Do you think Amelia will really buy me a coffee?"

"Charlie!" He drops my hand and walks away, laughing.

"What? Those are the rules of jinx!"

The girls come out of the animal shelter at that moment and Amelia asks, "Are you talking about the rules of jinx? Because I'm pretty sure *you* now owe *me* a coffee!"

"It's a Coke, guys," Kira says as we walk toward her car.

I slide into the backseat and Brian follows, while Amelia goes for the passenger seat up front.

"All I'm hearing is that I'm getting something from Amelia!"

She puts her hands over her ears. "La la la, I can't hear you."

"Charlie, if *I* buy you a coffee, will you be quiet?" Brian asks.

"Maybe," I say. "Or you could kiss me instead."

"Guys, gross!" Amelia twists around to look in the backseat. "Don't make me come back there!"

I flip her off and lean into Brian for a kiss.

Because this kiss is mine.

Because this boy is mine.

Because this life is mine.

Because I deserve it.

Acknowledgments

How can you begin to acknowledge all of the people, places, and things that helped you get to where you are, with your very first published book, living a dream come true? Seems like an impossibly difficult task, but I will try. In no particular order (because I am NOT trying to get texts about hurt feelings!):

Thank you, Maya Papaya, for making the world better just by being you—and for napping during my final edits of this book. I hope you someday hold this book in your hands and know it is proof that you can do anything you've ever dreamed.

Thank you, Obi, for keeping my legs warm during early morning writing sessions.

Thank you, Grandma and Grandpa, for raising me and loving me the way I deserved, and for always encouraging me to try my best and follow my heart.

Thank you, Renz, for being a caring brother and for getting just as excited about my book as I did.

Thank you, Gigi, Auntie Patty, and Justin, for entertaining Maya so I could work on my book edits and for always being there for me.

Thank you to my family and in-laws for loving me and supporting me.

Thank you, Writer's Row (Cait, Jane, Judy, and Kerri), for being inspiring women who offer endless encouragement for all things writing, wine, and everything in between.

Thank you, Samm, Steph ("Duddie"), Laraine, Paige, Kelsey, the Nasties, and all of my wonderful friends for your love and kindness.

Thank you, Livejournal Fatshionista community, for teaching me as a teenager that I could be Fat and fierce.

Thank you, America Online, for giving preteen me access to the internet and boy band fanfiction and online friends who shared my passion for writing.

Thank you, Plainville Public Library, for inspiring a lifelong love of the written word. (Support your local library!)

Thank you, Beyoncé, just because.

Thank you to my agent, Tamar, for believing in me and in this book, and for not running for the hills when I asked tons of questions. Your phone call changed my life and I'm eternally grateful. You loved Charlie the same way I did and you understood this story so deeply, and there is nothing greater.

Thank you to my editor, Mora, for understanding everything about Charlie and me and helping to shape this book into what it is today. Charlie, Amelia, and Brian are all better because of your sharp eye and big heart. Also, thanks for letting me keep the name Clarence McConkey in the book so I could laugh for a million years over something so silly.

Thank you to illustrator and artist Ericka Lugo, who designed the breathtaking cover of this book and captured Charlie perfectly.

Thank you to the incredible teams at Context Literary Agency and Holiday House, with special thanks to Miriam Miller, for seeing the value in Charlie's story and working so hard to make it successful.

Lastly and most important of all, thank you to Bubby—for asking me out over AIM way back when; for laughing with me and loving me; for always encouraging me to follow my dreams; for reading and re-reading what I've written and never tiring of it; for making every day an adventure, whether we're nestled on our couch or watching the sun rise in Rome; and for our beautiful love story. This is one for the books.